LaRosa Chronicles

CANDY-
COLORED
CLOWN

K. Spirito

This book is a work of fiction. Persons, places, events and situations depicted in this book are the product of the author's imagination. Any resemblance to actual persons, places or events to actual events are purely coincidental.

First published by AuthorHouse; 04/30/04
ISBN: 1-4184-2357-2 (print)

Produced on CD by A Snowy Day Distribution & Publishing
ISBN: 978-0-9796513-9-7 (audio)

Second Publishing by A Snowy Day Distribution & Publishing; 06/07/10
ISBN: 978-0-9844681-3-3 (e-book)

Re-published in February 2011 by:
A Snowy Day Distribution & Publishing
P.O. Box 2014
Merrimack, NH 03054
(603) 493-2276

ISBN: 978-1-936615-04-9

Cover Design: A Snowy Day Distribution & Publishing

Printed in the United States of America

LaRosa Chronicles

Father Sandro's Money (available)

Kathleen (work in progress)

Roses Falling (work in progress)

Time Has A Way (available)

Everything Happens To Margi
(work in progress)

Yesterday, Tommy Gray Drowned (available)

Tomorrow Is Promised To No One
(work in progress)

CANDY-COLORED CLOWN (available)

Spiderling (available)

P I S C A T A G U A (available)

Summer And August (available)

Adriano Saves the Christmas Stroll
(work in progress)

Visit: www.kspirito.com

For Midoguespot

Forever in the window of my mind,

Curled up in his basket

CHAPTER ONE

Ken Waters knew all along that his second wife Julie wanted children. He thought he did, too. But now that it's a reality? Well, that's a different story.

"Baby," he said, his voice dull. His fingers tracked through his chestnut hair. What if he lost another child? That would just kill him. Never once had it ever entered his mind that he might lose his beloved four-year-old Katrina; and when he did, his mind railed.

Katrina skipped into his thoughts—*Know how much I love you, Daddy?*

"Too much, my little Katrina, too much."

There's no such thing as too much, Daddy.

Five years had come and gone; still, there was no accepting the loss that hibernated like a grizzly in winter within the vacuous cavern of his mind. Fatherhood a second time around aroused the hidden beast.

Pacing about the manse in Cohasset, Massachusetts, Ken mumbled, "If only I had known that night as I tucked you into bed that it was going to be for the last time. I'd've hugged you tighter, breathed in the essence of baby shampoo that lingers on those blond ringlets that flounce about your head. I'd've read one more story, kissed that button nose of yours a thousand times more, told you that I love you so much more than just a mere *too much.*"

No, there's just no way of getting over little Katrina's loss. So it was that with each passing day, Ken lost sight of new bride Julie and all the positive things she had brought to his life.

Her voice and complicated simplicity vanished quicker than the snap of fingers. No longer did he see the fairness of her face or her expressive cocoa eyes accentuated by lashes that picked up the golden hue of a summer's morn. Even her honeysuckle perfume failed to penetrate the defensive walls that he had built around himself. Eyes that gleamed in the sunlight and the engaging smile that outlined cheekbones that blushed like ripe peaches became lost in the darkness of tormented nights.

All the changes Julie had made to the manse failed to keep the ghost of Regina at bay. He fought off the ghost with denial, haphazard activity, and single malt Scotch—way too much Scotch. Nothing worked.

He tried to get away—on business trips, so he claimed. That was a lost cause, for everywhere he went, everything he saw reminded him of Katrina. He couldn't even pick up a book and read, for she wasn't there, snuggled up on his lap, listening to his every word. Worst of all, he dreaded the return to that manse, for Regina was there. She was always there. As a result, Ken stopped leaving the manse; therefore, he didn't have to return. Drowning in booze was so much easier.

Day after day, Ken sat alone in his office on the first floor of the manse. Rarely did he think to shower his five-foot-ten frame or to shave. More often than not, his mind conjured up one of the happiest days of his life, the day Katrina was born; and it seemed as though he was in the delivery room all over again. Cold, stainless steel scissors ringed his fingers as his hand contracted to sever the umbilical cord. Then the obstetrician picked up the newborn and offered her to Ken as though he were a great deity. Ken gawked at the tiny life. A grin wrinkled the obstetrician's green mask. "Go ahead. Take your daughter. She's not going to bite." A great belly laugh shook the delivery room and then he added, "Well, not until she gets you under her spell anyways."

Gingerly, Ken took the babe, so tiny in his computer wiz hands. His heart overflowed. He wanted his voice to soar high above the clouds and into the heavens beyond and proclaim that here was a miracle. But he was tongue-tied. The newborn had taken his breath away. He kissed the tiny nose and sputtered, "She's smiling at me."

Chuckles filled the delivery room. "Not quite yet, my friend," blustered the obstetrician.

Nobody's telling me that my baby girl didn't smile at her Daddy, thought Ken. He turned to Regina and cold reality slapped him down, for it was more than obvious that the entire event repulsed her. From day one, she resented the transformation that pregnancy had wrought upon her flawless body. She fought off stretch marks with every type of cream known to mankind and even went so far as to purge to stop all weight gain. Furious about being *knocked up*, she blamed Ken completely and threw him out of the master bedroom for good. "It'll be a cold day in hell before I ever go through this again," she had screeched over and over again. With each passing day, a host of new curses befell her mouth. That woman put four-letter words together in ways that even the devil couldn't conceive. And man, did she have a set of lungs! Worse than any predatory harpy in classical mythology! As it turned out the baby girl had to be taken by cesarean section. Regina was not at all happy about being cut. She had already scheduled a tubal ligation for the day after delivery, so now, not only was her world-famous Hollywood plastic surgeon going to have to do away with every scar and stretch mark, he also obliged to do something about that disgusting incision.

"Please hand the baby to her mother," the obstetrician had said.

Ken peered at all the eyes staring at him above green surgical masks. These people didn't know Regina like he did. Unsure what to do, he glanced at the obstetrician, whose eyes rolled from baby to mother. With a great deal of reluctance, Ken stretched out his arms and muttered, "Here you go, Regina."

She glared at the infant and then at Ken. "You've got to be kidding me," she scoffed. "Get that thing out of my face."

The obstetrician and nurses exchanged shocked looks. Suspicions about Regina wanting nothing to do with the baby confirmed, they never bothered Ken again.

The wee hours of the night found Ken preparing formula, changing diapers, and feeding Katrina, whom he had named after a character in a book that his mother had read to him as a child. He bathed Katrina, cradled her in his arms, and read to her. He slept in the nursery in the bed next to her crib, instead of the downstairs bedroom at the back corner of the manse where he had been sleeping ever since Regina had thrown him out of the master bedroom. During the day while he worked in his office, the bassinette was always within arm's reach. If obliged to go out on business, he bundled up Katrina and took her with him. She was a hit everywhere they went, plus her charming disposition landed several new clients. Ladies were attracted to this man who doted over his little girl, but he was never ever tempted, for he refused to do anything that might risk losing his Katrina.

Whenever a rare conflict in schedule arose, Ken's mother, Patty Waters, or Regina's mother, Gretchen Konstanze, came to the rescue. There also was Nanny Ellen whom Regina had hired long before Katrina came into the world. An inordinate amount of money—in advance—kept Nanny Ellen on standby twenty-four hours a day. No unexpected gaps—that was Regina's motto—which was in addition to the weekly maid service that had always been in place. She wanted nothing to do with children or housekeeping. To Regina, kids were no more than bloated ticks on a dog's back. The moment plastic surgery was possible she went under the knife. She concentrated on getting her figure back and nothing else. Her body, her manse, and her high-society lifestyle had to be absolutely perfect at all times.

Yet for Ken, being so involved in his child's life was no inconvenience. He relished every bit of it. Katrina was a blessing, the only good thing that came out of a loveless marriage.

In no time at all, he learned the language of babies, each tone, pitch, and cadence. One meant, "I'm hungry," another, "I have a dirty diaper," and still another, "I need a change of scenery." Then there was the one accompanied by a reddish-blue face when Regina held Katrina, "Mommy doesn't like me."

"The kid's colicky," insisted Regina. When nobody was looking, she chucked the little girl into the crib to languish in the dark, silent, and vacuous nursery until Daddy, Nanny Ellen, or one of the grandmothers discovered her plight.

After Katrina's birth ordinary conversation turned uglier, intensifying with the dawning of each new day. The moment Ken walked into the room, Regina griped, and it led to his wondering when the hostility had actually begun. There was the blowout on their wedding night when he found birth control pills on the wash basin. Then there was the face off in his Beacon Hill apartment. She wanted to move. He didn't.

"There's a manse in Cohasset," she suggested.

"We don't have that kind of money," he said flatly.

"Gretchen and Leopold are buying it for us," she claimed.

"No, they're not."

"Okay, you tell them that! Go ahead! Tell your brand new in-laws who adore you like their own son that you're snubbing their wedding present!"

The move into the manse came shortly thereafter.

Over time, Ken learned to ignore Regina. She never had a good word to say anyway. *You're late. Company's on the way. The manse is a mess. Your shoes are filthy. Look at your clothes—they're a disgrace! Would it kill you to buy new clothes? Clothes with style and flair? You need a haircut. Hurry! Go change. And for Christ sake, shave! Above all, do not disturb Katrina! She's already been fed and is playing quietly in her room. Nanny Ellen's been instructed to put her to bed.*

Ken never listened, for nothing kept him away from his little girl. Of course, Regina found out, and man, did the pooh hit the fan! She got so riled up during her high-falutin' get-togethers whenever he disappeared upstairs to cuddle his little Katrina and read her a goodnight story. Regina fumed quietly in front of her snooty friends—that is, at first. As months passed, however, she got mouthy, which cast suspicion that she wasn't the personage that friends thought her to be. She made up the most God-awful stories; everything from Ken was having an affair to his being a closet gay to his having unhealthy urges toward kids.

None of it mattered. Ken kept on doting over Katrina, holding her tiny hand from the first day when she could only clutch his pinkie finger through times when she dragged him off to see the latest get-up she had dressed Ralph the cat in or when they skipped all the way to the kitchen to dive into a batch of Gammy Getchen's latest baking delight. Regina went ballistic over the crumbs on the counter, crumbs that were visible to nobody but her.

When Katrina turned three, Regina had the crib taken down, so Katrina had to sleep in the bed that Ken had been using and he went back to the downstairs bedroom at the back corner of the manse. He couldn't hear if Katrina wanted a drink of water in the night or if she had a nightmare. Neither father nor daughter slept soundly, both missing each other terribly. Yet the bond they shared couldn't be broken.

One awful day, Regina stole Katrina from Ken and then the Cessna crashed deep within the Florida Everglades. Searches revealed an oil slick, traces of fuselage, and black silk snagged upon a saw-tooth palm. The silk was part of a dress, Regina's, the one with the plunging neckline and slit up the side. Since survival in the crock-infested swamp was impossible, no rescue was attempted. Ultimately, memorial services were conducted without the dead.

Five years later, impending fatherhood agitated Ken to the point that every time his eyes fell upon new bride Julie, his mind beheld Regina, long past crocodile bait. All the sorrow that Regina wreaked upon his soul lived again, worse than ever. Furthermore, the ghost of his beloved Katrina had made its presence known. The only thing that eased the pain was single malt Scotch, but getting through each new day required more and more. But on this June morning in 1989, Ken hadn't drunk so much as a drop, since the moment his eyes opened he believed Katrina was calling to him. He got out bed and went to the French doors. Pulling aside thick, olive-colored, brocade drapes, he saw Regina, not Julie, stretched out on the blue and white webbed chaise lounge at the edge of the patio. A tremor wracked his unshowered body. How could it be warm enough to bask in the sun like that, yet be so cold inside this damned shack? His hands raked up and down the arms of the gray plaid shirt he had worn for days. She had told him to change it and the faded denims that dragged the floor even when he wore shoes. But he didn't.

Ken turned and as he took a step, he kicked an empty liquor bottle. Clutching his shoulders, he watched it spin across the floor and when it disappeared under the bed, he muttered, "Scotch. Just what the doctor ordered."

Joints stiff from the long, sleepless night, he lumbered off to the great room, and stopped at the archway, because he forgot where he was going and why he was going there. He ran a hand through uncombed hair then leaned against the casing and itched the skin beneath a heavy growth of beard. His eyes fell upon the fireplace. He straightened. "Ah, yes. A fire."

He plodded across the great room and turned the dial beside the fireplace. Propane hissed within ceramic logs. Getting down on one knee, he held his hands to a heat that wasn't forthcoming. Somewhere within his disconnected mind, it occurred to him that the gas had to be ignited. Groping along the mantle, he groused, "Where's that box of matches?" His fingers bypassed the hand-painted apothecary jar. It never registered that matches were stored there.

A singsong voice called, "Daddy."

Ken froze. His eyes bulged as he mouthed, "Katrina?" He glanced over his shoulder and then got to his feet. His fingers grazed the apothecary jar, which tumbled onto the hearth and shattered. Matches scattered as he called in a tremulous voice, "Is that you, Katrina?"

When no reply came, his fingernails sliced across his scalp. He eyed the wet bar, catty-corner to the fireplace. She's hiding on me, he thought. Stepping over to the wet bar, he peeked behind it, cooing, "Come out now, baby." She wasn't there.

He searched behind chairs and hunted corners. Then he knelt on the sofa and leaned over the back to check behind it.

"Daddy," said a small voice.

His fingers burrowed into the upholstery as his head spun around. He zeroed in on the archway. Other than the infernal ticking of the grandfather clock, the manse was still as a graveyard at midnight. He sagged onto the sofa.

"Daddy!"

He bolted out of the great room and into the dining room, and when she wasn't there, he agonized, "Why can't I find her?" He crouched down and checked under the table.

"Daddy, Daddy!"

The frightened voice struck Ken like a cannonball to the gut. He lurched to his feet, knocking over the mahogany teacart. Silver pieces crashed to the floor as he dashed to the kitchen. A quick search yielded nothing, so he tore open each cabinet and then got down on hands and knees and yanked out pots, pans, vases, and canned goods. He slouched back on his heels, moaning, "Where can she be?"

Moments of silence passed. Gripping the edge of the counter, he pulled himself to his feet and dusted off his pant legs. The chaise outside the window caught his eye. His face contorted as he groused, high and mighty, Regina, lying there in all her glory. Rather get skin cancer than plaster on sunscreen. She should be keeping an eye on Katrina, but no, she only thinks about herself and that precious tan of hers. Gotta look your best for those snotty friends of yours."

"Daddy, Daddy!"

Ken spun around, eyes darting about the kitchen. Cabinet doors gaped open. Contents of the cabinets littered the floor. Chairs were askew to the table. He made a U-turn and stopped for a second to think. Maybe she's in the office. "Yeah, the office," he belched. "That's why I can't hear her too good."

Hurrying down the hall, he called, "Be right there!" He stopped at the threshold to the office and scoured the room. "Is my precious Katrina hiding in here?" He scanned the room then tiptoed in and checked all the nooks and crannies where she had hidden before. He yanked the chair away from the desk. "Found you," he gushed and poked his head into the cubbyhole. But there was only emptiness. "No," he wailed, clutching his head and sagging to the floor. Tears burned his face like battery acid. "Oh, my dear Katrina, where are you?"

"Here, Daddy."

"Where, for God's sake?" he pleaded, palms gesturing.

Getting no response, he hauled himself to his feet and tramped into the hallway. At the spiral staircase, he stopped dead. A great pain built in his breast, one that he couldn't account for, as his eyes climbed each riser all the way to the top landing. A voice in his brain shouted, *that kid's not roaming about my manse!*

"Regina," he seethed. "She says Katrina makes too much of a mess. What does she know?"

Again the voice, *Do not disturb Katrina! She's already been fed and is playing quietly in her room.*

"Yes, of course, my poor little Katrina," he murmured. "You're always in your room."

His eyes fixed on the bottom step. Go ahead, he thought. Take that first riser. Move feet. What are you so afraid of?

"Daddy, Daddy!"

The shrill cry penetrated his soul. Racing to the top landing, two steps at a time, he called, "Hold on! I'm coming!"

By the time he got to her bedroom door, he was choking for breath. He gripped the doorjamb. Heartbeats thumped as a vortex of angst swirled about his head.

Barely recovered, he swiped the perspiration from his brow with the back of his hand then stepped into the sky blue bedroom that had a red, yellow, and green rainbow arching between two corners. Katrina had always played beneath that rainbow, looking like a blond Dorothy from the Wizard of Oz. Instead of Toto, Ralph the cat was her playmate.

She's here, insisted his mind. She's going to jump out into your arms, just wait and see. Smell her sweetness. Feel her warmth and those silly golden curls that tickle your cheek.

He rushed to the closet and yanked open the door, but Katrina didn't jump out. He got down on hands and knees and ferreted through shoes, boxes, and toys and then backed out and collapsed against the door. His weight shoved the door into the wall. His head banged against the door and his neck crooked.

CANDY-COLORED CLOWN

Sweat slithered down his brow. Rolling into a kneel, he spotted the white canopy bed. The back of his hand swiped the sweat from his brow.

On hands and knees, he bobbled over to the bed. Lifting the pink coverlet, he planted the side of his face on the floor and squinted into the darkness beneath the bed. Only dust mice played there. He straightened up and flopped onto the bed, frustration overwhelming him. His eyes traversed the faded coverlet that smelled musty. The pillows were faded, too. He braced himself up on elbows and squinted. Those pillows weren't nearly as fluffy as he remembered them to be. He eyed the pastel stuffed animals propped against the pillows. In the middle was a mismatch—a candy-colored clown with scarlet lips drawn higher on one side than the other, smirking. Its eyes, its dilated pupils, the same as Regina's when she's pissed off, infiltrated his soul. A thickness built in his throat and his knuckles dug into his jaw. He swallowed hard.

Tugging his eyes away, he spotted the portrait of his blue-eyed cherub perched in the middle of the white bureau. Freckles powdered the ridge of her nose like gold dust and spilled onto her cheeks beneath the bluest of innocent eyes. Oh, how he loved those freckles—angel kisses—that's what Katrina called them.

He got to his feet and stepped over to the bureau. He picked up the portrait and held it in his right hand while fingers of his left hand caressed the image. Look at those pudgy arms. Why couldn't they be clamped around his neck, right now? If only he could grab a handful of those golden ringlets that swirled about her head and smell the baby shampoo that lingered there. He clasped the portrait to his breast. "Oh, my dear little Katrina, where are you?"

Just then, a reflection in the mirror startled him. Jerking to attention, he squinted past his image in the mirror and into the parallel room. "Who's there?" He listened. "Regina?" He rolled his eyes, thinking, don't tell me she's on one of her tirades again. Setting the portrait on the bureau, he yelled, "What do you want?"

10

He gave the portrait one last look then turned and went to the window. Shoving aside the Priscilla curtain, he was blinded by the June glare.

Hearing a noise behind him, he spun on his heals. "I heard you that time!"

He blinked away lingering floaters. Silence deadened the air. He ran a hand through his hair. Dread washed over him as his eyes traveled along the rainbow that arched high on the sky blue wall and down to the lavender doll carriage in which Katrina insisted that Ralph nap and then to the bed, all made up—pink coverlet, stuffed toys, and that foolish candy-colored clown.

"I don't belong in here," he whispered. His jaw clenched as resentment built within him. "Well, if I don't belong here, neither does all this stuff!" He grabbed the coverlet and gave one powerful yank. Pillows and pastel toys scattered and the candy-colored clown landed on the bed smack in front of him. He took a quick step back. His stomach knotted as bloated pupils and a sassy grin belittled him. The clown began to ripple, slowly at first, rhythmic, like a hula dancer, then quickened, faster, faster, turning into a multicolored torrent that sluiced like a nightmarish hurricane across a fragile windowpane. Sapphire eyes materialized then a twisted smile and Regina's face.

His gut soured. Teeth scraped together like fingernails across a chalkboard. Fists flexed, open, closed, again and again, tighter and tighter. The vein in the middle of his forehead reddened, throbbed. Resentment pulsed throughout his entire being. The power he had always lacked when dealing with Regina at long last came to him. Fury exploded. Snagging the thing's neck, he slowly, deliberately, squeezed. "Ah, yes, my dear Regina," he snarled. "It's your moment to pay for making life so miserable." Knuckles whitened. "Leave on your own. That'll make things so much better. But you cannot—you will not—take my Katrina! That'll just kill me, and you know it!" His face twisted up. "That's the only reason you want her in the first place. No! Katrina stays with me!"

"Daddy."

Ken spun around. "Katrina?" A chill swooshed over him, and he looked down to see from where it had come. The clown. He raised it to eyelevel.

"Daddy!" White eyelet fabric dotted with yellow-faced daisies slipped past the doorjamb. Ka-clump, ka-clump, ka-clump.

"Katrina's going downstairs," he belched and scrambled out the bedroom. Halfway down the stairs, he missed a step. His armpit hooked over the railing, and he slid the rest of the way down then rammed against the end-post. Air gushed out of him and then again when he flopped onto the bottom step.

Hacking, Ken went to get to his feet, but pain held him back. He rubbed his ribcage, trying to figure out what had happened. He took a deep breath, jammed his hand against his side, and labored to get to his feet. He steadied himself. "Katrina," he muttered. "Looking for Katrina."

He swaggered like a homeless drunk down the hall to the office doorway and held onto the doorframe to peer inside. All was silent. He pushed himself off the doorframe and hobbled to the guestroom, through the guest bathroom, and into his bedroom at the back corner of the manse—all dark and musty and lifeless.

"Oh, my dear little Katrina," he wailed. "Where in the world are you?"

His fist rapped against his temple, causing the candy-colored clown to bash into his nose. He drew the clown away and gawked at it. It leered back. "What the heck am I doing with this?"

In the great room where the air was thick and hard to breathe, Ken stomped on Ralph's tail. Rattled by a shrill yowl, Ken lost his balance and sprawled onto the floor, losing his grip on the candy-colored clown. It skittered across the room then became lodged between the sofa and floor. Its outlandish eyes burrowed into Ken as the same garbled taunts he had heard upstairs, spewed from its scarlet lips.

"That clown," snapped Ken. "It was that filthy clown all along!"

Ralph howled and clawed his way halfway up the screen door. He fell to the floor, squalled, and then clawed his way up the screen again.

Ken wriggled over to the clown like a soldier ducking gunfire, snagged onto it and doddered to his feet. At the French doors, he spotted the woman on the chaise and his veins iced, but then a thin sneer rippled one side of his upper lip. The wind was messing up her hair. "She's gonna be pissed," he snickered. His fists balled. "She cares more about that damned hair of hers than her own child. Time I told her a thing or two."

The second the door opened, Ralph barreled out and never looked back.

The door swung in the breeze as Ken stomped to the chaise, but by the time he got there, bravery had been cast to the rising wind. His stomach began to churn, *don't wake Regina. That infuriates her. Can't tolerate the way that woman hollers.*

He peered sideways at the great Atlantic where waves were crashing below the precipice. Minot's light signaled, *Katrina's down on the beach, building sandcastles.*

"Help me, Daddy."

As he started towards the precipice, the blue and white chaise griped. Dammit, he thought, I've gone and woken Regina. He stopped short. Don't look at her. His fingers tracked through his hair. Just don't look at her. But he did, and his head cocked to one side, because she had changed. Her hair barely reached her shoulders. It's a different shade of blond.

The scent of honeysuckle wafted up his nostrils. His brow fused. It's not like Regina to wear sweet perfumes, he thought. Good God, she's talking to me! His insides railed, and he stepped back. His head wavered side to side. She's not keeping me from Katrina any longer! Taking off toward the ocean, toward his beloved child, Ken ignored the screeching harpy.

She smacked him on the back.

He lost his footing.

Let go of my shirt, Regina! Let me go!

CANDY-COLORED CLOWN

CHAPTER TWO

Julie lay on her belly, her upper body hanging over the precipice. Blood was rushing to her head as honey-blond strands flogged her face, driven by the rising wind that also scattered spindrift off the angry surf until there was no more. The sight of Ken lying prostrate on the rock-strewn beach below, his chestnut hair bullied by that same wind, dulled her entire being. She had failed him. Now, it was too late. To protest would be futile. Unconsciousness closed in, graying the June sunshine and blurring the seaweed-draped boulder around which his left side crooked. Yet the almond-shaped, sapphire eyes of the candy-colored clown in his right hand glared up at her, brash and unforgiving.

Somewhere in the recesses of her mind, Julie sensed a hand snag her right ankle, and it tightened like a vice grip as an out-of-breath male voice wheezed, "Gotcha! I gotcha!" The voice was familiar, except her mind was too bogged down to place name or face to it. He latched onto her left ankle, fingernails dug in. "Here we go!" One solid, protracted tug brought her petite, twenty-year-old frame skipping up over the edge of the ragged precipice and skidding to a stop upon lush turf.

Sirens and shouts of firefighters and EMTs congested the air. Out of control conflagration hissed and snapped. Footsteps thumped the ground—many footsteps, running, closer and closer. Then a different male voice, deep, urgent, and foreign to her ear panted, "I'll take it from here."

"Julie…Julie Waters. Her name's Julie Waters," stammered the familiar voice. "And Ken…that's her husband…he's down there…on the beach."

"And you are…?" challenged the unfamiliar voice.

"Chuck. I live next door…over there. I was out for a jog when blam! The whole place went up! Never seen anything like it!"

Chuck, envisioned Julie. Rain or shine Chuck. Jogs the neighborhood same time every day like clockwork. Chuck. Navy running sweats—always navy. Shorts in the summer. Longs in the winter. No hat. Never a hat.

Just then, a blast jarred the neighborhood and the ground beneath Julie cracked as though it were made of glass. Bystanders hit the dirt; one fell upon her, head butting hers as a cyclone of dirt, ash, and debris blocked out the sun. His breath came in spurts against her ear.

Another blast, inferior to the first, united with echoes to pulsate along the coastline like native drummers hacking out an exotic beat. Somewhere within the deluge of debris, Chuck shrieked, "What the hell was that?"

"Propane tanks," spewed the stranger who was straddling Julie. "Cars in the garage."

As the deluge subsided, the stranger slipped off Julie and next thing she knew, worried brown eyes appeared within inches of hers. "Don't try 'n move, Jul'. I'm Lou. Let's gitcha checked out so's we can move on outta here, 'kay?"

She didn't have the will to answer. *Do as you wish* moved through her mind like lava flow. *I failed the man I love more than life itself. I have no reason to go on.*

Lou nudged her shoulder and asked, "Okay, Jul'?"

Her eyes slowly closed then opened. Taking that as a yes, Lou disappeared. His hands sculpted her feet and then the pads of his fingers explored her shredded toes and bruises on her ankles.

"Didn't mean to hurt her like that," whined Chuck. "I…"

"Booboos don't matter," cut in Lou. "She's safe, so forget about it." His fingers drifted up her legs and thighs, searching out injury and blood, and coursed up her back and into her scalp. "Appears hunky-dory to me." His voice had lost its urgency. "How 'bout it, Jul'…okay ta roll ya onto your back?" When he got no response, his face flattened on the ground again next to hers. "Whaddaya think?"

"Yeah…" she heaved. Mustering all her strength, she braced a hand against the ground.

"Hold it," scolded Lou, his hand pressing against her back. "Don'cha dare move one itty-bitty muscle. Me and all these good-lookin' EMTs here will gitcha flipped over, so veg', 'kay?"

Julie gave a weak nod.

Lou disappeared. "Come on, folks," he said. "Let's get it done."

Scores of hands took hold of Julie and rolled her onto her back. Despite the sea of concerned faces peering down at her, it felt good to be off her stomach, so it was only natural to take a deep breath; except the acrid, chowder-thick smoke that blistered the turbulent air and choked out the sun invaded her lungs. She struggled to breathe.

An oxygen mask swathed her mouth and nose. "Easy there, Jul'," said Lou.

When she regained control, she squinted over the mask. Lou wasn't at all the clean-cut, burly man in his thirties that she expected to see. He was about her age, unshaven with scraggly hair that billowed out from beneath his orange hard hat like scarecrow straw. He couldn't have weighed more than a hundred and fifty pounds, if that much. Masking tape with cylindered corners and smudged black scrawl that spelled out his name stuck to the breast pocket of his ill-fitting and faded blue uniform.

"Got it together?" he asked.

She closed and opened her eyes.

"Cool," he said with a jerk of the head. Once again his fingers hunted her body for injury.

Overhead a towering blue flame sheathed in yellow was devouring the manse. Julie covered her eyes with her forearm. How could a thing like this happen? Was it an accident? Was Ken falling off the cliff also an accident? That explosion that knocked her to the ground as she raced after him…was that only a dreadful accident, too? Or did Ken have a hand in that? She bit the inside of her cheek. No, he'd never do such a thing. Although…lately… She took a trembling breath. Geez, Ken's been so out of it—just like a couple of minutes ago when he… I've never seen him looking that bad. He ignored me so…so blatantly.

"Scraped and bloodied toes, knees, thighs, elbows, and fingers," Lou reported to the note-taker off to his left. Then his right hand flew up into the air as he called, "Gauze and tape, please." Somebody slapped a plastic bag of medical supplies into his hand. "Thanks."

"These offshore winds sure are stoking those flames," blustered Chuck. "Worse than a bonfire in February. Listen to it sizzle!"

Lou lifted Julie's arm off her face and made eye contact. "This'll sting a bit," he warned. He swabbed liquid onto her wounds.

Julie sucked in air and clenched her teeth against the pain. Her eyelids squeezed so tight that a tear budded in the corner of her eye.

"Gonna grow one mean bruise on that right shin, Jul'," said Lou. As he bandaged her knee, her eyes suddenly widened and the back of her left hand jammed against her mouth. Her right hand flattened on her stomach, and she turned away. Lou never missed a beat. "Hold it, folks," he spouted. "Jul's in the motherly way. Fetal 'scope! Monitor! Pronto!" He gazed down at her and calmly asked, "Any contractions? Cramps?"

Tears brimmed her eyes as Julie shook her head no. She'd lost Ken. What if she lost the baby, too? A shudder wracked her frame.

"White stretch shorts clean," said Lou, his tone matter-of-fact. "No sign of fluids, but Jul's hitchin' a fast ride."

"Here you go," said another EMT, tapping a plastic bag that contained a stethoscope on Lou's arm.

Lou snagged the bag, ripped it open, and yanked out the stethoscope. He shook it out then used the end piece to push up her halter top. Positioning the end piece on her naked belly, he listened, an absorbed expression on his face.

Please find a heartbeat, thought Julie. Her eyes skittered his face. His eyes met hers, and for an eternal moment, they shared mutual anxiety. Everybody held their breath. Plumes of smoke billowed off the flaming serpent that mocked from aloft. Lou moved the earpiece. He listened. He moved it again. He listened. Suddenly, his eyes rounded. "Ah-ha! There's the little shaver. Can't play hide and seek with big Lou!"

A toothy grin plastered his face as applause erupted and relief sheeted over Julie. A giggle sparked within her as Lou once again wallowed in the miracle of a tiny heart at work. The impish gleam in his eyes looked so much like…

Lou didn't hear Julie gasp, but he saw her face when she did. Yanking the stethoscope out of his ear, he belched, "Jul'?"

"Ken…" she whimpered.

Lou frowned and squinted toward the precipice. When he looked back at her, the expression on his face seemed to ask, you don't really want to know, do you? But her eyes insisted an answer, so he sucked in a lungful of air and turned toward the precipice. "Hey, Johnson," he hollered. "Gimme a status."

A woman's voice came back. "Situation contained."

Lou glanced at Julie. His brows came together. "Fill me in, Jul'," he said.

Her eyes skipped back and forth across his face as *fill me in…fill me in…* echoed in her brain. Lou wanted answers to how all this *had come about—answers Julie just didn't have. She knew full well that she was about to cry. Still, there was no way of stopping it.*

CANDY-COLORED CLOWN

CHAPTER THREE

"The last thing I remember, I was looking out over the ocean," said Julie, flat on her back on an emergency room gurney at Ste. Anne's Regional Hospital in Brighton. A pink and blue striped Johnny was pushed up to below her breasts, and a white warming blanket covered the lower half of her body. While a fetal stethoscope roamed across her exposed belly, her hands dawdled upon her upper chest. At times her fingers twisted her wedding and engagement rings.

A nurse who had introduced herself as Penny was taking vital signs. She smelled like jasmine, which made Julie self-conscious of her own body odor. A shower was definitely in order.

"And where was your husband?' asked Detective Gage Fleming, stepping out of the path of an orderly who scooted into the drape-walled cubical with an odd-looking gismo. Penciling details of the Cohasset case onto a spiral pad was nearly impossible. No matter where Fleming planted himself, he was always in the way. Plus the smell of disinfectant chafed his nasal passages so bad that he continually rubbed his nose with his knuckles. The tip of his nose felt hot. It's getting red, he thought. I must look like a circus clown. It's a total waste being here. Knew it from the outset. What happened on that cliff was an unfortunate accident, not at all criminal in nature, and that's that.

Be that as it may, the current trend in investigating cases on the domestic front dictated that the spouse of a victim was suspect from the outset so Fleming was required to read Mrs. Julie Waters her rights. He resented having to do so. This kid is no liar, he fumed internally. Seen plenty of liars during decades of pounding the beat. She's not even close. Don't matter anyways; reading rights always starts things out on the wrong foot.

Elizabeth Blair stroked her daughter's forearm and sized up the husky detective who was dressed like she expected plainclothes cops to dress—black loafers, gray pants (although a bit on the baggy side), and button-down white shirt. On the other hand, his blue paisley tie only marginally coordinated with his brown tweed sport coat and he wasn't sporting a crew cut. Might've been a good idea if he considered doing so, since his graying auburn hair of moderate length was thin and wiry and definitely overdue for a good trim as were his bushy brows that were deeper in color than his hair. Like caterpillars, his brows skulked above thick, outdated tortoise-shell glasses that hooked the red ball of his nose. The ridge bone of his nose had been broken a time or two. Not as tall as cops ought to be, thought Elizabeth, though not fat. On the other hand, he's not particularly lean, either. His hands are the size of a Vermont farmer's! His neck was thick like his face, clean-shaven and pallid with signs of acne as a teen. His demeanor was mechanical—she expected that.

"Ken was in the manse," heaved Julie while thinking of how blue the Atlantic was that morning, wrinkling at ebb beyond the broad precipice that terminated the emerald backyard. Whitecaps were brushing the surface. Minot's Light winked, flirting with her, so she had turned away.

Julie gnawed at the inside of her cheek and her head cocked to one side as if peering at the hundred-year-old brick manse that had loomed in the June sunshine like a righteous testament to the past, merely tolerating her presence. She had put her weight on one leg and imagined Ken and first wife Regina happily restoring the manse. The work was completed just before the plane crash. "Regina was so gorgeous," she had muttered then and nearly did again now. "And look at me. Running around a place like this in decrepit white sandals, unpolished toenails hanging out." Scrutinizing her pink halter-top and white stretch shorts, she had rocked back and forth. "An outsider—that's what

I am. Born to more modest means than this estate calls for." She had flexed her shoulders, sucked in sea air, and then exhaled, "I'm as out of place as those twittering sparrows flitting in and out of those shrubs. Look at those two over there, splashing about that marble birdbath. They're much too happy, much too carefree."

Fleming squinted through his glasses to read the time on the watch that he had picked up while investigating a student drowning at a diving school. Buttons lighted the face; one gave water depth, another temperature, all that great stuff that divers need to know. Someday, he was going to try scuba diving, just for the hell of it. He planted one foot upon the seat of a folding chair in the corner of the cubicle and huffed, "Continue."

Julie rubbed her arms, experiencing once again the gust of wind that had earlier set gooseflesh to spiking. The blue and white webbed chaises that lined the edge of the brick patio had looked so inviting. "Oh, if only to stretch out on one of those and close my eyes," she had murmured at the time. "If only to feel the sun's warmth on my face and body. If only to be rid of this confusion that clutters this dumb old head of mine. I need to bask in a little peace—if only for a couple of minutes." The thought that she had married Ken too soon made her swallow hard. She sucked in a breath and held it while considering the point. Her eyes rolled. "Shish," she exhaled. "What does dumb ol' Julie know about marriage, relationships, and all that stuff?"

"Sweetheart?" murmured Elizabeth, nudging her daughter's forearm. "You okay?"

"Huh?" mumbled Julie. Glazed eyes cleared as she spiraled back to the here and now.

Fleming gawked over the rims his glasses at the two women just as an orderly backed him into the corner. His foot came down on the floor with a thud as the folding chair it had been on slid out of reach. His forefinger resettled his glasses on his nose. Sick and tired of medical personnel jostling him around plus impatient with the lack of pertinent information he was getting, he spouted, "So tell me what happened next, Mrs. Waters."

23

Julie cleared her throat and said, "I kicked off my sandals then laid down on the chaise closest to me." She shook out her wrists, fighting the past that persisted in sucking her back. "I closed my eyes, but I didn't sleep." Her cocoa eyes squeezed shut just like they did when she had lain down on the chaise. It was a vain effort to shut out the world. It hadn't worked then, and it wasn't working now.

"Maybe Julie should rest a while," suggested Elizabeth.

Fleming frowned. With a fair amount of indignation, he flipped the page of his spiral pad and said, "You didn't sleep, Mrs. Waters."

Julie peered at her mother, lean, but well-muscled, tan, and wearing white jeans, a red and white polo shirt, and gold dolphin-shaped earrings that she had gotten while sailing with Dad. Her dirty blond hair was braided with a poof of bangs. She always looked good. "I was thinking about Mom," said Julie, "and didn't notice that a cloud was blocking the sun."

Elizabeth squirmed. Her face flushed as she asked, "Thinking about me?"

"The day you got shot," said Julie.

Elizabeth lifted her chin as her head filled with blam! Blam! Ping!

Confused, Fleming said, "Shot?"

Elizabeth peered into her daughter's eyes and smiled. Her fingers combed back honey-blond strands as she said, "There was a bank robbery on Washington Street, a year and a half ago. A bunch of us were in the wrong place at the wrong time."

"Just when I needed someone the most," said Julie, "Ken came out of nowhere and stuck by me without ever being asked." She envisioned his reassuring smile and sensed the gentle touch of his hand. For once in her life, she had felt she could face just about anything—as long as Ken was by her side. How unworldly she was back then, although she had to admit that she had grown with his wisdom since and learned to laugh at herself and breathe in each precious moment that life had to offer. Best of all, she had discovered that communicating didn't necessarily lead to a relationship blowing up in her face. But just the opposite had happened today. Lack of communication had blown her world to smithereens. "Ken asked me to marry him a year ago, a June day very much like today." Knowing what I know now, she thought, I wonder if I'd be so quick to make that kind of commitment. She looked up at the ceiling and pondered, yeah, that's good ol' Julie for ya. Quick to move out of Mom's. Quick to accept the suddenness of Dad's return and forget all those lonesome years without him. "Yeah," she muttered. "Ken was convincing all right."

"Convincing?" echoed Fleming.

Julie zeroed in on the detective. "Huh?"

Elizabeth spoke up. "You said that Ken was convincing."

Julie looked away. She inhaled deeply and slowly exhaled, "You know, the way his face lights up whenever he sees me coming."

Elizabeth chuckled. "Like a court jester pleased with his own antics."

"Not anymore," Julie said flatly.

Elizabeth looked down at her hands when Fleming asked, "Why not?"

Julie heaved. "Everything about Ken used to burn so openly for me." She sighed and then added, "Used to…"

"I don't understand," blustered Fleming as a great cavernous noise came from his stomach. The burger he had picked up at the hamburger joint near the station house was rubberizing on the front seat of his unmarked car. He had been waiting at the drive-thru when dispatch sent him here. By now, the chocolate shake had surely turned into hot chocolate.

"A kind of inner suffering always hangs over him," said Julie. "In all the time I've known him, it's never quite lifted."

"Any idea what's eating at him?" asked Fleming while thinking, my stomach's eating me.

Julie clasped her hands over her head. The butts of her palms rubbed the sides of her head. "Regina and little Katrina."

"Ken's first wife and their little girl," interjected Elizabeth. "They were on a plane that crashed in the Everglades, five years ago."

Fleming felt a jolt to his heart. First wife, kid—female, both deceased. That kind of information was hard to jot down.

Julie sighed. "The mere mention of them always wrecks his merry demeanor, and he rakes his hand through his hair every time, as if it happened only yesterday." Her stomach curdled. "How can anybody survive a catastrophe like that? I seriously doubt that I could've survived losing Mom, let alone a child."

Elizabeth squeezed her daughter's forearm, her gut knotting with the sorrow of her husband Peter turning up missing in action in Vietnam in the late 60s. Too bad he didn't find his way back during Julie's growing years. But at least he did come back. Miracles like that are more than rare.

Fleming plowed ahead. "Tell me about you and your husband, Mrs. Waters."

"He made last summer the best summer in my entire life," said Julie. "And our Christmas marriage six months ago started off so wonderfully. But now...now this..."

"This?" repeated Fleming.

A sledgehammer of disappointment came down upon Julie as her hand flattened on her stomach. "The news that we're having a baby should've made him happier than ever, but..." Every time she ran the scene over in her head her insides somersaulted. "His face lost all its color, and his fingers tracked through his hair. His voice was so dull. 'Baby...' he said—as if the possibility had never occurred to him—as if having children was something he hoped might never happen. Worst of all, gloom overtook him and bloated by the second, minute, hour, eating away at him, devouring all that I knew him to be, and he descended into a constant state of fretfulness, slugging Scotch down by the glassful. He paced about that manse that reeked of memory no matter what I did to mask it. I heard him babbling, and one time, I asked him what he said...and..."

Without looking up from his spiral pad, Fleming said, "And..." Now he was getting too much information, and it was a hassle to get it all down. His scribbles were becoming undecipherable. Later on, it's gonna "bite me in me arsh," as dear ol' Granny Fleming used to say, God rest her soul.

Julie bit the inside of her bottom lip. She shivered as horror sheeted her face. "Ken stopped in his tracks and gawked at me as if I were some sort of apparition!"

"You ask him about it?" asked Fleming with a cool air, but beneath the surface, this case was getting to him. He tapped the pencil on his bottom lip and chastised himself, ain't healthy, Fleming.

Julie shook her head. "I was afraid."

Fleming zeroed in on her. "Afraid of...?"

She shrugged. "I don't know," she said. "Many nights I woke up and Ken was gone. Most times, I found him passed out on his office sofa or on the one in the great room. A couple times, I found him on the floor, and I got scared."

Fleming chewed on the eraser end of the pencil, wondering, what the heck's going on with that guy?

Julie glanced at Elizabeth. "I'll never forget the night you and cousin Ruth, Emma and a bunch of her family came for supper."

Emma, thought Fleming. Name rings a bell.

Elizabeth rolled her eyes, "Dreadful evening, to say the least."

Julie nodded, visualizing the crooked fingers of lightning and the way they had zigzagged across the brutal sky and illuminated the backyard, cliffs, and turbulent sea beyond as though it were midday.

Elizabeth spoke up. "Ken looked awful. Haggard. Unkempt. Hair uncombed and beard scruffy. He sucked booze down like water."

"He hadn't showered or changed his clothes in days," added Julie. "No help whatsoever."

Elizabeth glanced at Fleming. "That is so uncharacteristic of Ken. Usually he has his fingers into everything, especially in the kitchen. He's quite the chef."

"All day long, his mind had been preoccupied," said Julie. "Worse than ever. I kept on glancing at my watch. Nothing was getting done. Then Emma called."

There's that name again, thought Fleming. "Who's this Emma?" he asked.

"Emma LaRosa," replied Elizabeth.

Fleming's caterpillar brows shot to his hairline. "Seth LaRosa's widow?"

"You knew him?" asked Elizabeth.

"Me and him go way back," said Fleming, concealing the fact that Seth LaRosa had ties to the Boston mob, albeit unwanted ties. Through the years, Seth had covertly kept law enforcement appraised of the mob's more serious activities.

"Julie and I never met Seth," said Elizabeth. "He passed away a couple of years ago, before either of us met Emma."

Time flies, thought Fleming. Why, it seems like only yesterday old man LaRosa was filling the precinct in on that shady construction contract involving the upcoming Big Dig. Talk about cost overruns. Oh well, nobody gets out of this life alive. "So, Mrs. Waters," he said. "Emma called you. Then what?"

"She offered to bring several of her specialties that she 'just happened to be putting the finishing touches on.'"

"That lady sure gets around the kitchen," said Fleming as thoughts of braciola stuffed with hard-boiled eggs made his mouth water. The LaRosa home always tickled the nostrils with pungent odors of garlic, oregano—you name it.

"I thank my lucky stars that Em was having one of her better days," said Julie.

His brow tightened. "Better days?"

"At times Emma retreats into another world," said Elizabeth, "as if she was with Seth."

"Well, after all," puffed Fleming, "those two were married over fifty-two years."

"As far as I'm concerned," said Julie, "Emma truly outdid herself that night."

"But it was plain as the nose on your face how uncomfortable Emma and the others were over Ken's inebriation," said Elizabeth. "Julie was a wreck. She had perched herself on the edge of the sofa, pressing the wrinkles that just weren't there out of her jeans. She picked lint off the sleeves of her blouse, but there wasn't any to pick." Elizabeth glanced at Julie. "You were wearing that green blouse I gave you for your birthday, remember?"

Julie nodded.

"You fidgeted something awful," continued Elizabeth. "Well, then, Ken started inserting curses into his slurred ramblings and embarrassment overwhelmed you and you bolted for the kitchen. I was going to go after…"

Fleming cut in, "What did you do in the kitchen, Mrs. Waters?"

Julie shrugged. "Leaned against the wall and tried to pull myself together." She shivered. "Bottles clinked and I knew without any doubt whatsoever that he was at the wet bar, pouring himself another drink." Her voice changed to a whimper. "Oh, come on. Don't do that." She wrung her hands as though it were happening again. "What am I supposed to do? Then I heard ice cubes tinkling in a glass. Well, now, I got mad." Her fists clenched. "I straightened right up and hollered, 'Ken!'"

"He joined you in the kitchen?" asked Fleming.

"It took a while," said Julie.

Elizabeth shook her head. "His gait was precarious."

"That's for sure," winced Julie. "His eyes were so glazed over, it was scary. He looked at me as though he were seeing some revolting nonentity." She hung her head. "I felt so guilty."

"Why's that?" asked Fleming while jotting, down, male vic'—boozer.

"I got on his case without thinking," said Julie, "and buttoned up his dirty blue polo shirt and straightened his collar. 'I don't know what on earth is going on inside your head tonight,' I said to him, 'but stop making a fool out of yourself in front of our guests! What's wrong with you anyways?' He shriveled like a whipped puppy, right before my eyes and his eyes fell upon me in a way they had never done before, real defeated like."

"He wasn't much help with the serving cart," said Elizabeth.

"He tried his best," heaved Julie. "He was still swaying pretty bad when everything was finally ready, so I figured that it might be best if he wheeled the cart into the dining room. That way, he wouldn't look quite so pickled, but the second we stepped into the dining room, he almost toppled right on top of the cart, but I snagged his arm."

"Just in the nick of time," added Elizabeth.

"Ken only picked at his food that night," continued Julie. "He's been doing a lot of that lately."

"And his body shows it," said Elizabeth.

"Before anyone else finished," said Julie, "Ken got up and wandered off. I pretended not to notice, though I did feel a bit ashamed, because I was relieved he was gone."

"After supper all of us gathered in the great room for coffee and goodies," said Elizabeth, "and cousin Ruth asked if Ken was looking forward to having another child."

"Boy, did I feel like crawling under a rock and dying," said Julie.

"But I came to the rescue," said Elizabeth as a look of amusement colored her face. "I said that I heard men get morning sickness, too."

"A bolt of lightning happened just then," said Julie, her hair standing on end, "and right on its heels, an ear-shattering thunderclap."

"Lights were still flickering when Ken came stumbling back," said Elizabeth.

"And he paced," said Julie. "Paced and paced, and all of a sudden, he stopped in front of the French doors, snapped off the patio lights, and yanked the drapes together. He spun around and raked his hand through his hair.

"I swear, he saw none of us," said Elizabeth, her head wavering side to side.

"His hands were running up and down his arms," said Julie, "and when he spotted the fireplace, he stopped. His eyes squinted and then he stalked right over and turned on the propane."

"Gas log fireplace," mumbled Fleming, writing it down.

Julie imitated Ken's slushy voice, "'Whar shah blue blashesh ish shah damn bocsh o' mashesh?' 'In the apothecary jar...,' I said.'" She paused then corrected herself, "*Were* in the apothecary jar. 'Wha' fwiggin' shar?' he says. 'That hand-painted one, right there!' I kept pointing to it." Her lips pursed as she looked at Elizabeth. Then she covered her eyes and sobbed, "We got it on our honeymoon."

Elizabeth grasped her daughter's arm. "It's going to be okay."

"How could he forget that quaint little gift shop down the street from the bed and breakfast we stayed at in the White Mountains?" wailed Julie. "Or that wonderful old couple who's been married forever and owns that shop?"

Fleming's eyes slammed shut, and his head jerked to one side as if a right hook had just caught his chin. He hated it when females started bawling. One would think that after all these years in this business he could take it. He coughed away emotion and then changed the subject. "Propane must've skunked up the air pretty bad."

"We were all very concerned," said Elizabeth with a firm nod. "Goodness! When he finally put a lit match to that ceramic log, flames swooshed—kind of like exploded."

"Exploded," repeated Fleming and jotted down, gas explosion? "Was your husband drinking this morning, Mrs. Waters?"

"I don't know," moaned Julie. "He sleeps late a lot, lately. Most days, I don't even see him before noon."

Fleming scratched his head with his pencil. Squinting at Elizabeth, he asked, "And after Mr. Waters lit the ceramic logs that night, what did he do?"

"He warmed his hands," said Elizabeth, "and swayed. Every so often, he looked over his shoulder and seemed surprised that there were others in the room."

"I wanted him to settle down," said Julie. "His restlessness drove me crazy. When he headed off to other parts of the manse, I was glad. Yet everybody was staring at me, like, maybe I should go after him or something."

"That's when the living room flashed white and off went the electricity," said Elizabeth. "The whole house shook with a deafening crack of thunder."

"Right after," said Julie, "light beams sliced the darkness like in Star Wars and Ken dumped flashlights and candles on my lap."

"When he retreated to the bar to pour himself another drink," said Elizabeth, "I grabbed the candles and said, 'Come on, Julie. I'll set up candles. You light them.'"

"I tried not to look at him," said Julie. "But when I did, it nearly scared me to death. The flickering light picked up his sunken eyes rolling around and around in their sockets something awful. Suddenly, his head jerked backward, and he belted down an entire glass of booze. He lost his grip on the glass. It shattered on the edge of wet bar, and shards flew everywhere!"

"Boy, did everybody jump," said Elizabeth.

"Not Ken," countered Julie, envisioning the mild surprise that had lifted his eyebrows as he squinted at the broken glass in the sink. "He just shrugged it off."

Julie left out the part about Ken snagging the neck of a half-empty bottle of Scotch and shuffling out of the room. She left off the part about her glancing at guests and their faces outlined in candlelight.

Wringing her hands, Julie said, "I just don't know what got into him that night. Emma said that he's jittery about the baby and having all us around, so excited and all…plus the terrible storm…well, that makes things so much worse than they ought to be. She patted my arm and said that he'll do just fine, 'cause time has a way of setting things right, but I'm not too sure about that."

Elizabeth and Fleming exchanged stares as if about to ask each other, how much time is it going to take for Ken to get over whatever it is that's eating at him? Julie needs him, especially now that she's pregnant. The baby needs him.

Elizabeth recalled being pregnant for Julie and Peter coming up missing in Vietnam. What a horror story. Poor Julie. She was all grown up by the time he finally turned up. How blown away we were when he took off the second time to help search for MIAs still missing over there. I don't know how I did it, but both times, I rose above it and managed to keep things going. Boy, did Peter get a stiff talking to when he got back that time! He's not about to go traipsing off without me again! I don't know whose problem is worse. At least mine is over with. I've just got to help Julie figure out what's bugging Ken and fix things.

"Anything else significant happen that night?" asked Fleming.

"No," said Julie thoughtfully. "By nine o'clock, everyone except Ruth and Mom had gone home." Her stomach somersaulted. "But I found Ken spread-eagled on his office floor. Honestly, I thought he was dead. His eyes were so glassy, staring at nothing."

Fleming stopped writing and glanced up at Julie. Bites the inside of her lip a lot, he thought. Mouth must be all chewed up. She's too young to be in a predicament like this. He got an unpleasant taste in his mouth. Wish I didn't have to make her relive all this. Fleming, you got no choice. It's your job. He caught himself biting the inside of his lip. He cleared his throat. "Continue, Mrs. Waters."

"I bent down and noticed drool oozing out his mouth. His breath was shallow and slushy. I was really relieved, but then I got mad and yanked an afghan off the back of the recliner and just let it fall on him." She paused. Color drained from her face. "You don't want this baby," she whispered, "Do you?"

"I missed that, Mrs. Waters," said Fleming, turning an ear to her. "Say again?"

"You don't want this baby, do you?"

Fleming shot a look at Julie. *I* don't want this baby? he was about to ask, but the past had overtaken her. He had seen things like this before.

In the midst of reliving the terror, Julie was running towards the great room, her eyes bugging out, and her hands clamped to her mouth. She collapsed on the sofa, crying, "What am I gonna do, Mom? What if…"

Arms wrapped around Julie as her mother said with an unconvincing chuckle, "Ken wants the baby. He's having a hard time, that's all. Hang in there."

This is going nowhere, thought Fleming, so he said, "Let's talk about how your husband ended up down on that rocky strand below that cliff."

A tremor raced through Julie. She swallowed hard and said, "I was lying on the chaise…"

"You said that already," snorted Fleming.

"Shush," scolded Elizabeth, eyes boring into him.

"The sun was gone," said Julie. "And the wind was coming in off the ocean. I got goose bumps and thought about going back into the manse, because whenever I shivered, the chaise I was lying on made awful noises—kind of like, you know, somebody screeching." She grabbed at hair strands just like she did back then when they had flogged her face. She wound them around her ear. "I was worried about Ken and his business."

Fleming shot a wary look at Elizabeth and ventured, "Business?"

"Computers," said Elizabeth, her gaze fixed on him.

He hesitated before writing, computers.

"He's not going out as often as he used to," said Julie.

"Runs the business out of the house?" asked Fleming.

Her face scrunched. "Used to. Clients need calling on once in a while, so I wondered if he was keeping up with all that. And bills, too." She shook her head. "I know so little about running a household. Ken always takes care of that end of things and gives me extra spending money."

"You don't work," said Fleming.

Julie inhaled audibly. "I work."

"Here at Ste. Anne's," added Nurse Penny. "In Patient Records."

"Ken thinks I don't make enough money," said Julie, scratching her head. "But I don't need much anyways. Come to think of it, he didn't give me any, this week."

"So you were lying on the chaise," said Fleming. "You was cold. Then what?"

34

"The sun came out—real sudden-like," said Julie, "And hot. Instantly, I felt how cold I had gotten, so I shielded my eyes with both hands, because now the sun was so bright that I couldn't see, and I looked for the cloudbank that had blocked the sun so long that I had turned into an ice cube. Must've been one big, dark one, that's for sure, I thought. My eyes burned and watered something awful, so at first, I thought I imagined somebody standing over me, but then the shadow moved."

Fright zinged through Julie, just like it did the moment it happened.

"Somebody was there! Backing away from me! 'Ken?' I asked, but the dark head just bobbed side to side. I began to see better and it was him. 'What's going on?' I asked, but he headed off towards the cliff. 'My God, Ken, where the heck are you going?' I hollered. But he didn't stop. He kept on trudging along as if somebody had hypnotized him, and it seemed to me that the ocean beyond the cliff was waiting for him, just waiting to gobble him up, like the ocean had all the time in the world. So I hollered, "Ken! You're going to walk right off that cliff!" And I jumped up so fast that everything spun like a madcap merry-go-round. I grabbed my head to stop it and took off after him. 'Somebody stop him!' I hollered and then came a horrendous blast and a bright light zinged past and I got this feeling of a giant hand slapping me on the back and it knocked me off my feet. I kept on hacking to get back my breath and braced my hands on the grass and lifted up my head. I didn't know where the heck I was or how I ended up on the ground. That's when I looked over my shoulder. I can still feel the heat of those flames eating up the manse."

Julie gagged, head wrenching side to side, denying the sight was still beyond any realm of possibility. Bile bubbled in her throat.

"Go on," said Fleming, almost in a whisper.

Julie glanced at Elizabeth. Neither woman wanted this interview to continue.

Fleming tried not to care, circling his pencil in the air, egging Julie on to finish. He wanted out of here ASAP.

Julie drew a breath and said, "I was sitting there with my legs tucked under me, thinking, this is going to devastate Ken. Then it all came rushing back. Where is he? I spun around and lost my balance and toppled onto my side. This has got to be a bad dream, I thought, but when I got to my knees, I spotted Ken only inches from the edge of that cliff!" In a voice, protracted and distorted, Julie vomited, "No…"

The hair on the back of Fleming's neck spiked. Penny grabbed one of Julie's wrists and Elizabeth grabbed the other, both pleading, "Calm down."

Locked in the slow motion of past horror, Julie was stumbling to her feet. Her legs were heavy as if weighted by lead as she loped towards Ken. Panic threatened to calcify every fiber in her body. "Stop!" she wailed, voice mutilated and coming from deep within her.

Elizabeth took hold of Julie by the shoulders and shook. "Julie, come back!"

"I'll see if Doctor Shirlington's here yet," said Penny, rushing out of the room.

Fleming felt helpless as Julie pushed aside Elizabeth and extended her hand toward an imaginary Ken. Suddenly Julie got up on her knees, stretching forward. Fleming jumped for her, overturning a tray of instruments, while Elizabeth and a couple of orderlies grappled to restrain Julie.

"Gotcha!" exclaimed Julie, latching onto Fleming's shirt as if it were Ken's. She flatted on her belly as if going down on the edge of the precipice once again. She cried out in pain as if muscles were lengthening beyond limits and bones were curving in ways bones don't allow. Pain tore up and down nerve endings. Blood rushed to her head. Hair billowed in all directions and flogged her face. Below her, Ken swayed to and fro. Suspended in an unnatural position, he bounced off the rocky outcrop, arms jouncing to the sides. The only string that kept this puppet from plummeting to the rocky strand below was one slender arm—hers. "Grab hold of my hand, Ken," she screeched.

"This interview has ended, detective," barked Doctor Curt Shirlington, rushing into the cubicle. Ken's physician and longtime friend was clad a white clinic jacket, a blue-striped button-down shirt open at the collar, navy pants and socks, and black loafers. His blue eyes and carrot top gave away a Scottish and English heritage, but not the soft spot he had in his heart for Julie. He vowed it would never escape his lips, yet time and time again, he feared he might come apart at the seams and scatter at her feet, confessing like a blathering idiot that he loved her. "Let go of Mrs. Waters."

Fleming looked at the doctor like he was nuts and yipped, "She's got me!"

In Julie's mind, she was teetering on the edge of the precipice. Ken's head lolled to the side and his eyes swiveled up to meet hers. No life remained within those mischievous eyes that she had fallen in love with last summer. The body circling below was not the man she had known while roller blading along the Charles or walking on the beach or lying in the long grass, gazing up at stars. Those lifeless arms were not the arms that held her in the secret of night. Those hands... Her brows came together. *What's in his hand?* Her eyes widened. *It's that clown!* The fuzzy pate blazed brighter than the flames that were consuming the manse.

Fleming pried at Julie's fingers.

Dr. Shirlington barked, "Penny, get a line into the patient."

"Yes, Doctor," said Penny who had dated Curt a couple of times. They had a nice time, but nothing ever came of it. Neither couldn't understand why.

Julie was aware of nothing but Ken's tee shirt twisting and stretching, becoming mere twine in her hand. "Ken!" she hollered. "You gotta listen to me! Grab hold of my hand!" But his eyes remained dull, so horribly unresponsive. "Don't you want to be with me anymore?" she whined. Nothing brought him back to the man she once knew. Then his left arm dropped out of the tee shirt. "Grab my hand," she howled. "Now!"

"Give me that needle," snapped Doctor Shirlington. "You're butchering her arm!"

Penny shot a pained look at Curt.

"No!" shrieked Julie as the moment that Ken started to slip out of his tee shirt flashed through her mind. "I won't let you go!"

Julie drilled her toes into soft turf and mustered all her strength to reach left arm over right and grapple for a second hold on his shirt. She got it, and his body stopped slipping...for the moment...but now what?

"Syringe, Penny!" exclaimed Doctor Shirlington.

Every muscle in Julie's body retracted as once again she became determined to be the victor in a standoff between life and death. She strained to tow Ken and herself back to safety, but his weight proved to be too much. She lost ground, her feet leaving tracks in rich dark soil that had been trucked in to give base for sod across the skull of the rocky precipice. Her toes hammered at rock beneath the soil and bent like deformed talons to grab at jagged edges. Toenails shredded. Her teeth gnashed against the stinging pain. She thrashed about, skidding closer and closer toward the edge of the precipice. As her upper body slipped over the edge, her eyes squeezed shut. This is one God-awful nightmare raced through her head. Any second now, I'll open my eyes and all will be right with the world.

The next thing Julie knew, she wasn't sliding any more. Her eyes slit open. In her hands, the tee shirt hung like a rag, and Ken was plummeting to the rock-strewn strand below.

"Medication's taking affect," said Doctor Shirlington.

Elizabeth sobbed.

Julie let go of Fleming's shirt—in her mind, Ken's—and grabbed a tuft of sea hay, which in reality was the top sheet of the hospital bed. Fleming, suddenly freed, tumbled into Elizabeth. Struggling to regain footing and dignity, he blathered, "Sorry, Mrs. Blair. So, so sorry!"

Chained to the past, Julie watched the tee shirt drift down like a deflated parachute and land near Ken. Her head drooped.

"Mrs. Waters is asleep, Doctor Shirlington," said Nurse Penny.

CHAPTER FOUR

Inside the coma that held Ken prisoner, life before the plane crash intermingled with the life he had led since. Regina's parents, Gretchen and Leopold Konstanze, played a big part, though it wasn't all that curious, given the fact that Julie claimed they were still a part of his life and always would be. She was the one who had insisted on inviting them to the wedding and to all family functions since. They were so grateful, since Ken had been and still was like a son to them. He had all but disappeared after the loss of Regina, their only child, plus Katrina, their only grandchild. Vast emptiness existed in their lives until Julie came along.

Ken twitched within the dark sleep. Regina had always looked down on her parents. In a snotty sort of way, she had claimed, "They look too much like immigrants and utter much too much East German verbiage within that nasty-accented English of theirs."

Regina was an absolute beauty—there's no denying that. She carried herself above everybody else as if she had come from royalty, but wishing didn't make it so. She should've been thankful for such loving parents. Leo, a tall, gray-haired man, worked hard all his life, stonecutting, making good money—money enough to give his daughter a lot more than she ever deserved. There was never any need for Gretchen to work outside their middle-class home in Weymouth. She kept an immaculate house—a person could eat off the floors. Both parents catered to the every whim of an only child, and that didn't end with adulthood. They did whatever had to be done to keep her happy—that included the day Ken had come home early from work and discovered them arguing.

Torrential rain and hail had accompanied a thunderstorm, which caused major power outages on the North Shore where Ken had been servicing computers. When the power failed to come back after a half an hour, he spewed, "That's it. I'm calling it quits."

Running for his car, he sheltered paperwork beneath his shirt and wondered if Katrina was up from her nap yet. He jammed the key into the lock then fumbled with the door handle. He hopped behind the wheel, yanked the paperwork out of his shirt and tossed it onto the passenger's seat. He checked his watch. "Fat chance, she's up."

By the time he got to the on ramp of 93 South the rain had let up, and at the entry to the lower deck beyond the Somerville Ave. Exit, he shut off the windshield wipers. "Probably should head over to Brighton and check out the computers at Ste. Anne's Hospital," he muttered. He twisted his wrist at eyelevel to read the time on his watch. "Really feel like goofing off with Katrina."

His eyes narrowed on the exit sign. Storrow Drive. Next Right.

Traffic ahead was light. Commuters hadn't begun to thicken up the expressway yet. "Could be home in no time."

He checked the rearview mirror. The sideview mirror. One hand beat a gentle rhythm on the steering wheel. In the same beat, he said, "I could put a call into Ste. Anne's when I get home."

At the last possible moment, he yanked the wheel and swerved into the passing lane. Shortly thereafter, he drove through the open wrought iron gate at the manse. Regina's parents' car was parked next to the front walkway.

He pressed the button on the remote clipped to the visor. The garage door gaped open, and he eased the car into the garage. He shifted into park, shut off the engine, and unlatched the door with one hand while grabbing a small white paper bag off the dashboard with the other. Embossed script on the bag revealed that it had come from a craft shop in Salem. Ken made it a point to bring Katrina some sort of trinket whenever he went out. He used to do the same for Regina, when first married, but his taste didn't coincide with hers—to put it mildly. Fishing through the contents of the bag, he settled on a card with two butterfly barrettes attached to it. He tossed the card on top of the stack of paperwork on the passenger seat then stuffed the bag under his seat. He gathered up the paperwork and shouldered open the door. While skirting Regina's latest acquisition, he glanced at his watch. "Made it home a whole lot earlier than usual. Hope Katrina's up."

In the foyer, Ken was about to call out that he was home when he heard angry voices filtering down from the second floor. He set the paperwork and card of barrettes on the antique altar table in the hallway then stepped over to the spiral staircase. Regina's hollering at her parents again, he mused. She rakes those poor souls over the coals as often as she does me.

"I don't care a flying fuck about him!" screeched Regina. Then came a crash, and Ken instinctively ducked. It was Regina's style to throw things.

"You must not do such thing," shouted Leopold, his voice strained and harsh. Years of stone dust and cigarettes did that to the larynx. "What about Katrina?"

"That's none of your God damned business," bellowed Regina.

"What become *meine Enkelin*?" cried Gretchen.

Unable to make out the response, Ken guessed that Regina was going from one bureau to another or in and out of the closet, putting away laundry. She always had tantrums doing that.

"Leave granddaughter," pleaded Leo. "We help Ken raise."

Hysterical laughter echoed throughout the manse, chilling Ken to the marrow. "You and Mother?" yelped Regina. "And Ken?" Again laughter. "Over my dead body!"

Ken felt himself shrink inside. Regina's not putting away laundry. She's packing! She's leaving! He gripped the banister for support. It took him by surprise even though in his heart he had known for some time that the day was coming. Wait a minute…she's taking Katrina?

"You no safe, no matter you go," wailed Gretchen.

"Momma right," belched Leopold. "Do what they say or they hunt you down like dog."

"I've got the key that will get me away from them *and* this god-forsaken hellhole," shouted Regina. "Not until I'm positive that I'm safe will I give it up."

"You got all figure out, don't you?" snapped Leopold, his voice laced with scorn.

"I'm almost free of all you leeches," touted Regina. "*I* am going to lead *my* life the way *I* want, and *nobody's* going to stop me!"

"You no go that man," cried Gretchen.

Ken staggered backwards. "Man? What man?"

Regina laughed in that harpy-like way she always did.

"That man worse than devil," bellowed Leo. "He take all he want! Leave you nothing!"

"That man can't live without me," jeered Regina. "No man can. Look at that weak excuse of a husband I have. If I didn't have the hold on him that I do, he'd be long gone by now. You hear the disgusting things I say to him. Real men don't put up with that."

Ken spun around, unable to tolerate her tongue any longer. He wrung his hands wondering, how am I going to stop her from taking Katrina? He glanced over his shoulder up the stairs. "I'll figure out a way," he whispered. "I've got to." His fingers tracked through his hair. "Time. I need time." His eyes darted about the foyer and fell upon the door leading into the garage. "Regina mustn't find out that I overheard her plans." He hurried to the door, opened it, and purposefully slammed it. "I'm home," he called out. "Hello."

All fell silent upstairs. Then came whispers too low to make out.

"Where's my little Katrina?" he sang out while stepping over to the stairs.

There came a thud. Next, tiny footsteps.

"Daddy! Daddy," squealed the four-year-old darting out of her bedroom. She bounded down the stairs, ka-clump, ka-clump, ka-clump, dressed in pink napping pajamas embellished with miniature Noah's arks and animals by the pair. Golden ringlets fell loose and forward. She looked as though she had slept through all the commotion that had gone on up there.

All worry vanished as quickly as a thunderstorm on a July evening as Ken scooped his little girl and miniature arms wrapped about his neck. "My sweet princess is just like her Daddy," he said. "He sleeps through everything, too."

Katrina planted a kiss on his lips. Tiny hands cupped his cheeks as she peered into his eyes and asked, "Know how much I love you, Daddy?"

"Tell me," he said.

With a decisive hitch of the chin, she said, "Too much."

"There's no such thing as too much," said Ken, picking curls off her face. He lowered his voice. "Where's your mother?"

One little arm released his neck and a wee finger pointed up the stairs.

Ken dreaded summoning that harpy, but it had to be done. "Regina?"

"Just a minute!" Her voice was impatient. So were the undertones that followed.

He grinned a silly grin and shrugged. Katrina copied him. Then the two covered their mouths and giggled.

"Well, my dear Katrina," whispered Ken, "I could use some chocolate milk right about now. How 'bout you?"

"Uh-huh," she squeaked and nodded, "and may I have one of Gammy Getchen's Toll House cookies, too, please?"

Feigning ignorance, Ken asked, "Gammy Getchen is here?"

"Uh-huh," chirped Katrina. "Gampy Leo, too."

"Oh," he said in a singsong voice.

He put her down and took her hand, but as he started for the kitchen, Katrina yanked on his arm. "Wait, Daddy." Her finger pointed to the card of barrettes on the alter table. He allowed her to tow him there. Her eyes popped out of her head. Picking up the card, she murmured, "Oh, I do so love butterflies. Put them in my hair, Daddy, please?"

He heaved a chuckle and said, "After milk and cookies."

In the kitchen, Ken took hold of Katrina under the armpits and swung her onto a stool at the breakfast bar. He kissed the tip of her nose then backed away, snapped to attention, and saluted her. She saluted back and then covered her mouth to withhold a giggle. Her eyelids squeezed shut.

A high-kneed march brought Ken to the refrigerator where he took out a carton of chocolate milk and poured two half cups, all the while pretending not to see the cookies on the counter next to the stove. He set the cups on napkins, one in front of Katrina and the other in front of the empty barstool to her right. She took thirsty sips and showed great concern when milk dribbled out the side of her mouth. Quickly she set down the cup, picked up the napkin, and ever so delicately dabbed away seepage.

Ken squinted at the ceiling and stroked his chin. "Now where did Gammy Getchen stash those Toll House cookies?"

A diminutive arm launched that infamous pointing finger. "There, Daddy."

He glanced at the finger and then bent to follow its trajectory. "Gosh," he squawked, "those cookies could've bitten me right on the nose!" He scratched his head. "Katrina, your Daddy's getting blind as a bat."

Again, she covered her mouth and giggled and her eyelids squeezed shut. When she opened her eyes, he winked.

He brought the cookies to the bar and sat down next to her. Lifting a section of plastic wrap, he reached underneath, took out a cookie, and started to munch on it.

"Daddy…" whined Katrina.

He looked at her, dumb-like. His brow scrunched. "Oh," he said. "You want one, too?"

She crossed her arms. Her little lips pursed, jutting out as she gave a mighty nod.

Ken was handing Katrina a cookie when Regina strutted into the kitchen. The child snatched the cookie in one hand and the card of butterfly barrettes in the other. Regina never caught wind of the card that Katrina secreted away in her pajamas. Then the little girl pulled into herself like a turtle pulls into a shell, swaying, head down, back and forth. The card of butterfly barrettes dropped to the floor

As usual, Regina was dressed to the hilt—spikes, red silk dress, gobs of gold and other jewels, and fully made up. "You're home early today," she said loftily.

"Power outage on the North Shore," he said in a matter-of-fact tone between chews, which he did on purpose just to rile Regina. And it worked. Her brows jammed together. Here it comes, he thought.

"Look at the mess you two are making," she barked. "Crumbs all over the place! And I let Nanny Ellen leave already. Who's going to clean it all up?"

There were no crumbs. Ken and Katrina knew better than to leave any. He winked, but the child was not about to show the slightest reaction in front of her mother. He scraped invisible crumbs together with the side of his hand and then gathered them up into his napkin. "Why'd you let Nanny Ellen go so early?" He knew the answer already, but he wanted to see Regina's expression when caught with her hand in the cookie jar. She had let it slip, she hadn't meant to, and he knew it.

"Oh, uhm," she said, "no reason."

Ken had all he could do to hold himself back. Oh, how he wanted to tell Regina that he knew exactly what she was up to, but first, he had to come up with a way of stopping her. He peered at Katrina. Nobody's taking my little girl away from me, he thought. If Regina wants to go, good riddance, but she can't have Katrina!

Gretchen slunk into the kitchen and headed towards the table. It appeared as though she intended to stay a while, but Regina put the kibosh to that plan. "Mother and Father have things they really must get to. Still they want to say hello before leaving. Isn't that right, Mother?"

Clearly, Katrina wanted her grandparents to stay, but she didn't make a peep.

Gretchen cowered and glanced at Leopold leaning against the doorjamb. A disgruntled expression lined his puss. They had learned a long time ago that if they wanted to maintain any kind of a relationship with their daughter, grandchild, and son-in-law, they better do whatever it took not to provoke Regina. Leo itched the back of his ankle with the front of the other one. "Yah. Yah," he spat. "We go."

Little Katrina let out a whimper.

A year after the plane crash, Leopold retired from stonecutting. Not long after that, he and Gretchen moved into an over-fifty-five townhouse complex in Brighton. Ken suspected that Regina's memory drove them to the change.

All said and done, the Kostanzes were ordinary folks in every way, respected by many. Julie thought they were just the greatest. "Gretchen reminds me of Mrs. Claus," she once told Ken. "She makes me want to crawl up on her lap where it's nice and warm and watch her knit mittens."

Ken had tossed his head back and howled with laugher. When he finally got a grip on himself, he asked, "What about Leo?"

"Why, he's the tin man from Oz," she had replied, "only heavier set."

Ken's parents, Richard and Patty Waters were also immigrants from East Germany, but they had become Americanized in every way. They spoke with no accent. They owned a beautiful home in Brookline. Richard ran his own investment company, which was listed on the New York Stock Exchange. They played golf and enjoyed driving to Atlantic City to gamble. He was a man of average build and height, passing on his looks to Ken, although he sported a closely cropped mustache. His son didn't. The first time Julie heard Richard laugh, she giggled, "You and Ken are so much alike. Both of you wrinkle your nose and toss your head back exactly the same way whenever you laugh."

Patty was trim and fair, quiet yet candid, kind of like an 80's version of Donna Reed. The stay-at-home wife and mother designed luxurious quilts that told stories and fetched high bids at charity auctions for local and national charities.

Regina had never hidden the fact that she had no use for Patty and Richard and avoided them like the plague, especially when they came to the manse to help care for Katrina. She took their suggestions as insults and took it out on Ken. "Tell your parents to keep their mouths shut in my manse! I'm not about to listen to them—or anybody else for that matter. Tell me how to raise a kid…humph. Who do they think they are?"

Patty and Richard knew full well that they weren't welcome and so visited only when it was absolutely necessary or when Regina wasn't home. Ken didn't force the issue. Instead, he made it a point to bring Katrina to his parent's home as well as to other places where Regina wouldn't lower herself to go.

Julie, on the other hand, adored Patty and Richard and had them over for dinner quite often, as was the case with Gretchen and Leopold. The in-laws got along famously.

With Julie, entertaining took on new meaning. Company was family and friends, down-to-earth people, not at all like the social elites that had strutted around the manse when Regina ruled the roost. No more miniature forks spearing hors d'hoevres that must be eaten with raised pinkies. No more fizzy drinks that made the sinuses swell and tear ducts water. No more stuffy sit-down dinners, one hand on the lap, small bites that had to be chewed forever before swallowing. Now folks brought their own specialties, which made meals adventures, and beer and wine, brewed in the Konstanzes' cellar, satisfied the thirst.

Cookie crumbs, children, and dust mice became commonplace. In the great room, adults tossed stuffed animals over the heads of kids in games of keep-away. Hockey, played with peanut pucks and yardsticks, created chaos in the kitchen until Julie shooed players out to the backyard. Dodge ball, touch football, and bocce matted down the lush emerald lawn.

The abysmal darkness of Ken's coma shifted like a gathering storm and out of it surfaced eyes—wide, almond-shaped, sapphire with exaggerated black pupils. He turned his head to the right. The eyes followed his. He looked up. They were there. His head went to the left and then to the right. There was just no getting away from those eyes. Facial features materialized, first ruby lips—one side higher than the other while in the middle a well-defined cupid's bow puckered. Next came ball-like hands and feet no bigger than wads of Bazooka bubblegum, punching and kicking Ken as his brother Jake's laughter arose from the shadows. Ken strained to see the illusive playboy. Infernal teasing about Ken remarrying grew louder and clearer. "Thought by now you'd've learned, ol' bro' of mine. Life's too short to be shackled to one bitch."

"Shut up, shut up, shut up," howled Ken, but his voice dissolved into the dark abyss. He wanted to cover his ears, but his hands refused to respond.

Then a swell of female humiliation beat on Ken and tore at his gut. A scowl seized his soul.

"Get out of my face, Regina!" he howled.

The apparition put her back to him and stomped away, dragging Katrina by the hand, kicking and screaming. They were getting smaller and smaller, fading away. "No…wait, Regina. Please," he cried as he willed an unresponsive hand to make them stop. "Don't take Katrina!"

Regina's neck twisted and stretched and her distorted face loomed up against his, seething, "You can't have her."

Ken fell backward into the darkness, moaning, "You don't want Katrina. You never wanted her."

"Wanting is irrelevant," bellowed Regina. "It gives me endless satisfaction just knowing that you two must live without each other."

Ken clutched the sides of his head and groaned. "Oh, why do you hate us so?"

"Daddy," wailed Katrina. Terror filled her eyes as fingers on her tiny hand spread wide, grappling for him. "I want to stay with my Daddy!"

"No, don't take her! Please," begged Ken. His voice rippled in the blackness and then was lost. He ran after them—

except his feet weren't beneath him. "Please, don't keep Katrina from me!"

Regina fell in beside a silhouette that came out of nowhere. She had Katrina's hand, tugging her towards the dark, fog-shrouded horizon. They were getting farther and farther away.

"Daddy! Daddy!"

Ken willed his eyes to see clearer. The silhouette was that of a man.

As the three dissolved into the horizon, a tiny voice echoed, "Daddy! Daddy!" And it gave Ken no peace.

He shriveled into a solitary figure, arms and legs flaccid, heart sickened. He had nobody now—nobody to wake up to in the morning, nobody to tell triumphs and sorrows to, nobody to understand. No little arms about his neck. No Katrina.

In the sterile Intensive Care Unit of Ste. Anne's Regional Hospital, a nurse dabbed away a tear that trickled from the corner of the comatose man's eye.

CANDY-COLORED CLOWN

CHAPTER FIVE

Living up to New England's schizophrenic weather patterns, the day after the fire brought a significant drop in temperature and mackerel skies that doomed man and beast to unsettled conditions. Gulls flocking to the safety of offshore nesting islands complained. The wind, which yesterday had spawned spindrifts off whitecaps beyond the precipice, revved up to a bone-chilling gale at times, whipping the ocean into a churning caldron and carrying off the stink of burnt wood and plastic from the smoldering cinders that once was the manse. The scene looked like a battlefield. Deep within, Julie sensed that the war was just beginning.

Overexerted muscles ached, but not nearly as much as her heart. Tomorrow looked bleaker than ever. "Twenty-four hours ago I had a home, a husband, a life."

Elizabeth felt so helpless. She put an arm around her daughter and squeezed. "I shouldn't've brought you here," she mumbled. "Looking at this makes the pain worse, and there's absolutely nothing that'll take any of it away."

Julie gazed at the metal remains of a blue and white chaise beneath charred, crisscrossed timbers. Gusts tussled honey-blond strands that fell loose from the purple alligator clip that earlier, she had halfheartedly secured against her head. She heaved a sigh and said, "Had to find Ralph."

Elizabeth combed her dirty blond hair around her ears, thinking the real reason Julie wanted to come here was to see the devastation that's so hard to accept. It would've been better to go shopping for clothes, shampoo, whatever, only Julie had insisted on finding that darn cat. "Your father came out here I don't know how many times yesterday afternoon and evening. That little imp is nowhere to be found."

Julie gnawed on the inside of her bottom lip. The lavender sweat suit she was wearing was her mother's. It was the only thing that fit, since Elizabeth was a couple of inches taller than her daughter. Elastic cuffs kept the sleeves off the hands and pant legs off the ground. In a lame effort to connect and ease the suffering, Elizabeth had also donned a sweat suit, mint-colored, and tan sandals. The white shorts and pink-and-white-checked halter-top that Julie had worn yesterday were beyond repair. Underwear had been hurriedly washed and dried. The white sandals, which she had kicked off before lying down on the chaise, were in worse shape than ever, pockmarked from embers landing on them. Bandaged toes and ankles that bore blue handprints were more than obvious.

"Yesterday, a cardinal sat at the top of that white pine," said Julie, pointing to a towering spike. "Singing like there's no tomorrow." The bird's crooning filled her head and the sea beyond the precipice kept time. "How right he was." Her mind wondered back to the chaise that had screeched and the wind that had whipped her hair as she teetered over the precipice. And Ken lying on the rocky strand below.

Elizabeth leaned her head against her daughter's, emotion knotting her stomach. "Come on, now," she murmured.

Julie pulled away. "Hear that?"

For a moment, they listened. Then Elizabeth ventured, "That a cardinal?"

"S'pose it's the same one I saw yesterday?" asked Julie. Wayward locks of honey blond pestered her vision as she searched out the bird.

"There," gushed Elizabeth, index finger aiming at Chuck's backyard. "Perched on the highest branch of that oak!"

Moisture filled Julie's eyes. "Glad you're safe, bird," she whimpered. "Ken's in a coma. Everything we own is gone." Tears overflowed. "I'm living with Mom and Dad." She hid her face in her hands and sobbed, "Oh, God, I'm so ashamed."

Elizabeth tugged on her daughter's hands. Uncovering eyes a shade lighter than her own, she said, "You have absolutely nothing to be ashamed of."

Julie broke away. "Oh, yes, I do, Mom."

"What, for heaven's sakes?" demanded Elizabeth, hands on hips.

"I contributed so little," cried Julie. "I don't have a clue about finances or where insurance policies are. Nothing." Her right sandal mashed ashes as through they were cigarette butts. Numb to the fact that the bandages on her toes were becoming soiled, she hung her head. "Ken always took care of those things. What am I going to do if he doesn't pull through?"

"You mustn't think that way," said Elizabeth as shivers raced up and down her spine. "Ken's going to be okay. Curt and the other doctors assured us of that."

Julie believed it. Still, life was never going to be the same.

"Ken broke his left arm and leg," said Elizabeth. "They'll mend in time. So will the hairline fractures in his ribcage. It could've been a lot worse. What if he had broken a rib and it had punctured his spleen? He might've bled to death before paramedics ever got to him."

"Or be crippled for life," winced Julie, rolling her eyes with the memory of his left side crooked around the outer edge of a seaweed-draped boulder.

"He's very lucky," said Elizabeth.

"If luck's involved in it at all," said Julie.

"Curt's quite adamant about a full recovery," said Elizabeth.

"Yeah, whenever he wakes up," murmured Julie.

Just then, the wind caught a puff of smoke rising from the middle of the rubble and scattered it aloft. Julie's head filled with the first time Ken had bought her to this place, the purr of the car engine, and the soft jolt as his foot hit the brake in front of the wrought iron gate. When he had pressed the button on the remote clipped to the visor, the gate had opened and her jaw had dropped. Perched upon the crest of an emerald knoll at ocean's edge stood the most magnificent hundred-year-old brick manse she'd ever seen. She had no idea that he was so well off. He dressed nice enough, sure, and drove a real cool car, but he acted like any ordinary, down-to earth guy.

Shutting off the motor in front of the garage, Ken had noticed her sitting there aghast, as if she had just awoken in a fairytale wonderland. His mirth filled the air and echoed in her head to this very day. Then he had gotten out of the car, came around, and opened her door. He took hold of her hands and hauled her out into air full of the sea; and it struck her like the tang of lemonade on a scorching Fourth of July. Her ears filled with chirps and wings taking flight as hoards of sparrows flitted in and out of foundation shrubs. Overhead, seagulls and terns wheeled about thermals and screeched for attention.

When a plaintive meow drew her attention, Ken had said, "That's Ralph." Sadness laced his voice.

The gray, longhaired cat scampered around the corner of the manse then weaved in and out of her legs, back arching high. When he looked up at her, he didn't meow; he sort of clicked.

"You get awful lonesome being here all by yourself, don't you, ol' Ralph," said Ken, scooping up the cat and rubbing his chin back and forth across the furry head. "You and Katrina used to play together for hours on end." He let out a burdensome sigh and handed the cat to Julie. She still remembered the lonesome, fervent clicking.

"Katrina used to dress Ralph in doll clothes and make him nap in her doll carriage covered with pink and yellow baby blankets," said Ken as he led the way around the manse. "He never openly objected, although you couldn't help but notice his tail twitch beneath the blank…ets…" He stopped in his tracks and stared at the swing of a child's gym set as it swayed back and forth in the breeze.

Julie had stepped around Ken and noticed that a terrible sadness had taken over him. Ralph was also staring at the swing, clicking. Her heart broke in two. At a loss as to what do, she wrapped a wayward strand around her ear and held it there. Unable to bear seeing them like this any longer, she hooked her arm in Ken's and gave a gentle tug.

As they neared the edge of the broad precipice, he warned, "Watch your step. Sometimes, rock loosens up near the edge."

On the rocky strand below, sandpipers chased receding surf and dodged incoming waves in a never-ending search of miniscule tidbits of food. Ken ran his hand through his hair and murmured, "Katrina and I used to build sandcastles down there."

"You did?" asked Julie as her eyes traced the edge of the precipice. "How on earth do you get down there?"

"Those stairs over there," said Ken, pointing to the property line. "My neighbor Chuck and I chipped in and hired a contractor to build them."

"You have good neighbors," said Julie.

"Nice bunch of folks," he said. His lips pursed momentarily and then under his breath, he added, "Put up with the likes of Regina."

"What did you say?" she had asked.

"Uhm, nothin'," he had stammered. "Come on. I'll show you the old dungeon."

She looked at him in a weird sort of way and repeated, "Dungeon?"

It seemed as though Ken hadn't heard. He bent over and picked a blade of grass, lining it up between his lips and blowing. A scream that sounded like a child in terrible agony made Ralph wail and jump out of her arms. He dashed towards a fieldstone patio and the French doors on the other side.

Ken flung the blade of grass away as if it were a match searing his fingers. His hands raked across his pant legs as if ridding them of a heinous crime. Then he hurried to the patio and flung open the French doors.

Ralph dashed inside the manse as Julie hurried to catch up. She stepped onto the polished oak floor of the great room endowed with antique furniture and dated nautical prints. The brick hearth was cold, and the room smelled that sour smell of a fireplace that hadn't been cleaned or used in quite some time. A wet bar was catty-corner to the left of the fireplace and a spinning wheel occupied the corner to the right. "I simply adore spinning wheels," said Julie, clasping her hands against her breast.

"Regina wasn't one to use such things," said Ken. Bitterness laced his voice. "Nor did she appreciate nautical prints, for that matter." He stopped short of saying that the only time Regina had ever set foot on a boat was for booze cruises in Boston Harbor. Julie found out about that later, plus so many other things—much, much later.

Sunlight, magnified by the ocean, flooded the elegant dining room where a mahogany teacart had caught Julie's eye, but it was the spacious kitchen equipped with every gadget imaginable that overwhelmed her. She felt as though she were in Julia Child's very own kitchen.

On the other hand, the two bedrooms on the main floor left something to be desired. Thick, olive-colored brocade bedspreads and drapes made them dark and lifeless. When Ken switched on the light in the back bedroom, Julie crossed the room and made a peephole in the drapes. On the other side, French doors opened to a private patio. "Wow," she breathed and glanced over her shoulder. Her eyes asked if he minded her opening the drapes.

A hint of levity crossed his face. "Go ahead," trickled from his lips.

Julie drew back the drapes; and the sunlight that was shimmering off the ocean flooded into the bedroom and cavorted across walls, the ceiling, and their faces.

Brilliant, wind-filled spinnakers accentuated the blueness of the ocean and cloudless sky. Sailboats without spinnakers heeled, motor craft left foamy wakes, and a silver cruise ship rode the horizon. "Oh, to be out there on one of those," she wished aloud. "Wind blowing in my hair…"

Ken stepped up behind her and murmured, "Yeah."

His hand came over her shoulder and pointed out the lighthouse a hundred yards or so off jagged ledges that shielded the entrance to sandy Cohasset Harbor where sailboat keels had been known to scrape bottom at low tide. "That's Minot's Light—the I Love You Light."

Her brow lifted. "I Love You Light?"

"Watch the flashing sequence," he whispered. "There's one flash—I. There's four—l, o, v, e. And three—y, o, u."

"Bodacious," she puffed. "Imagine something so romantic warning of danger?"

When Ken didn't comment, Julie glanced at him. He was staring at the scene as if seeing it for the first time. Hadn't he ever noticed all the color and the continuity of the sea? She studied his profile and the way the light played upon it. That's when she made a startling discovery. She loved this man named Ken Waters, yes, loved him in a way she'd never loved before—pure, simple, and virtually to the depths of her soul. She felt as if she had just taken the first breath of life. As his eyes locked on hers, seeming say the very same thing, happy embarrassment washed over her. She looked away, jabbering, "The water churns like a blender out there at times. Of course, that depends upon which way the wind and tide are headed. See those boulders surrounding the light? High tide's hiding a whole lot more of them out there."

Ken chuckled. "And how do you know that, pray tell?"

"Dad told me so," she bragged. "He and Mom sail all the time, and he says there's treacherous ledge that goes out quite a ways."

"He's absolutely right," said Ken. "Come on, I'll show you the rest of the place."

He guided her into a walnut-paneled office equipped with the latest computer technology. Stacks of papers and folders were everywhere, and hi-tech manuals, ancient reference books, and full collections of literature cluttered built-in, floor-to-ceiling bookshelves that spanned the length of two walls.

"Where'd you get all these?" asked Julie, running her fingers over the bindings of the Tom Swift series.

"My mother squirreled those away for me and also the Hardy Boys series," said Ken with more than just a little pride. "She saw me reading to Katrina and told me she had them."

"And here they are," said Julie.

He nodded. "I had many a pipe dream about becoming a dashing Tom Swift inventing amazing machines and driving roadsters, wearing a duster coat and flat cap."

Julie thought Ken was a dashing Tom Swift, but was too timid to say it. Instead, she pointed to books with blue covers and asked, "What about those?"

"I found these, rummaging through old bookstores," he said and pulled out one. "Several of these individual titles are the original. You can tell by the artwork and covers."

"Where do you find time to rummage bookstores?" she asked.

"Well, I..." he stammered. "I haven't done any lately...not since...since Katrina..." His fingers glided over some children's classics that the little girl had adored. He cleared his throat. "The two of us spent hours in bookstores...so many hours, reading..." His hand raked through his hair. "...together..."

Feeling her insides knot, Julie said, "Show me the rest of the house?"

"Yeah," he said.

In the foyer, she had admired an antique altar table. It was stacked with paperwork. While Ralph nonchalantly rubbed against the lower spindle of the spiral staircase, her eyes ran up the stairs to the top landing.

"Nobody's set foot up there in over four years," said Ken in a low tremulous voice. "Not even a maid." His mouth touched her earlobe. "You go ahead up. I just can't."

"No. Uhm, no," she stammered, skin spiking. "I don't need to go up there." She turned and searched his face. "It's okay...uh...really."

His hands clamped her arms, forcing her to look into his eyes. "I want you to."

"But I..." Something inside prevented Julie from finishing what she wanted to say. She pulled away from him and wrung her hands. Why did she have to go up there all by herself? What did he want her to see? Her head wavered side to side as she scoured his face for answers. None came. Yet the need in his eyes, one that only she could fulfill, was overwhelming. Their relationship depended upon her going up those stairs.

Nodding ever so slightly, Julie slowly turned towards the stairs. On the bottom step, Ralph sat on his haunches, expectant. She felt Ken's hands on her shoulders and had the urge to turn and demand for him to tell her of the terrible things that awaited her up there. What pained him so? Her hand gripped the handrail. She took one uncertain step then another. His hands fell away. She hesitated. She glanced at the landing above then back at Ken. He was sitting on the bottom step, his back towards her. She gazed at the cat, and they studied each other for a long moment. She took another step and nearly had a heart attack when Ralph zoomed past. He stopped, several risers above, and gave an urgent meow-like click. She looked back at Ken still sitting on the bottom step, elbows braced upon knees, fingers digging into the sides of his head.

Ralph made a clicking sound.

She squinted at him. What's going on? Was she supposed to somehow save both cat and master from some unknown, never-ending nightmare? She took another step. So did the cat. Wait! He's leading me. Why?

Upstairs, Ralph pawed at a closed door, but Julie couldn't bring herself to open it. Down the hall, a door was open, so she tiptoed to it and peeked inside. It was the master bedroom, walls, off-white, and a skylight with sunlight streaming down onto a sleigh bed. Dust moats drifted above the burgundy comforter, faded and laden with dust. Images of Regina and Ken in that bed stabbed Julie.

The entire room seemed dominated by the bridle portrait of Regina centered on one of the oak bureaus. Flawless make-up brought out her sapphire eyes and gold tresses that washed over one shoulder and looped into a casual curl across a tanned arm. Pearl earrings complemented a single pearl droplet attached to the silver chain about Regina's neck. Subtle curves of breasts filled out a low-cut bodice of beaded ivory satin. An opulent train meandered the floor. Tall, elegant, and incredibly beautiful,

Regina held in her hands a cascading bouquet of white lilies and stephanotis.

Julie bit the inside of her bottom lip and wondered, how can Ken ever be satisfied with a plain Jane like me? After being married to a gorgeous creature like Regina? Her hands balled and squeezed. The back of her hand covered her mouth as she spun around and fled the bedroom. She skidded to a stop at the closed door and Ralph. Her hand ran along the doorframe. The prospects of entering that bedroom frightened Julie to no end. Her heart pounded. Surely her soul could never cope with the anguish that Ken was bearing. She wanted to run, run as fast as she could, out of this manse, hide, hide from his past—hide from her future.

Just then she felt his warm breath upon her ear and heard him say, "Go ahead…" She spun around, but Ken was nowhere in sight. Yet, his eyes seemed to be burrowing into her soul.

Ralph rubbed against her leg. He clicked and arched his back.

Julie swallowed hard. She took a deep breath and reached for the doorknob. The brass chilled her through and through. Her hand tightened and rotated the knob.

Ralph head butted the door. It swung open and he scooted into the bedroom. He hopped into a lavender doll carriage and settled in to watch her.

Everything appeared to be the same as the day the four-year-old had forsaken this world. The white canopy bed was made up with stuffed animals propped against the pillows. Centered in their midst was a candy-colored clown with almond-shaped, sapphire eyes. Its smile seemed to invite fanciful amusement. A thickness built in her throat.

Her eyes coasted along the red, yellow, and green rainbow that arched from one corner across the sky blue wall and ended in the opposite corner behind a white bureau. Noticing a photograph perched on the bureau, she rubbed her palms on her thighs. The photograph beckoned. She went to it and picked it up. She used her sweater sleeve to wipe away the dust that defiled the image of a blue-eyed cherub. Freckles splattered the ridge of her nose, and golden ringlets swirled about her head like a halo. Wee arms lay across the hand-smocked white dress dotted with yellow-faced daisies.

Like a giant hand to the face, the reality that poor Katrina was no longer of this world smacked Julie. Tears stung her cheeks like acid. How awful this must be for Ken.

In the mirror, Julie's image stared back at her and made her feel as though she had just committed the most grievous sin. She set the photograph on the bureau and backed away. Her hands scraped together, ridding themselves of clamminess.

A small voice spun Julie on her heels. Gooseflesh spiked her skin. No, she thought, I must be dreaming. She blinked hard. The blue-eyed cherub in the photograph was hovering over the lavender doll carriage. Its wee finger pressed against tiny lips to admonish Ralph to be still, for it was naptime for all good little kitties. Without warning the image misted into nothingness. Ralph let out a soft click and then jumped out of the carriage and rubbed against a wheel. He sorely missed his young mistress.

Julie picked up the cat and held him close to her breast. Glancing at the doorway, she half expected to see Katrina skip into the room. "For Ken's happiness, I wish it were so," she choked and rubbed her cheek against soft gray fur. "And you know what, Ralphie? I'd even be willing to give him up, and you, too, if only to make it so…if only to take away the desolation that now I too possess."

A high-pitched meow shook Julie back to the present— back to standing amidst the ruins of the manse and the disaster she called her life. She heard the meow again and tried to zero in on it.

"Is that Ralph?" asked Elizabeth.

"Think so," said Julie, stepping out of the ashes. "Where are you, Ralphie?" Her lips came together to whistle the way Ken had taught her.

The cat meowed.

"He's hiding under that rhododendron bush beside the shed," said Elizabeth.

Julie headed towards the bush, softly urging, "Come on out, Ralph. Everything's going to be okay." She squatted and whistled again. When a furry gray head bobbed out from under the bush, her heart fluttered. "Poor Ralphie," she murmured and scooped him into her arms. She held him almost as close as the child within her.

"That cat certainly has had more than his share of catastrophes," said Elizabeth.

About to bury her nose into the long, gray fur, Julie noticed its matted and grimy condition. "Look at you, Ralph. You smell like cinders." She examined his paws. "Your fur's burnt off your toes. I can see your claws. Did you go back into the ashes?"

A rumble sounded deep within the cat.

"Our home isn't here anymore, Ralph," said Julie, thankful that she had found the cat. She prayed that neither of them ever had to return to this horrible place.

Elizabeth scratched the fuzzy pate. "Listen. He's purring." An uneasy smile lifted her lips. Her eyes met her daughter's.

"Oh, Mom…" cried Julie.

"We're going to put things back together again," said Elizabeth, wrapping a steadying arm around her daughter. "Better than ever before."

Julie scrutinized the burnt-out ruins. No feisty sparrows flitted among the foundation shrubs that were now charred nubs. A jagged shell of what used to be the garage guarded two burnt-out vehicles. The swing of a child's gym set in the middle of the backyard swerved to the dictates of the rising wind.

Ralph made a short clicking sound, and both women looked down at him. His ears were alert, and his eyes were fixed upon a small mound in the midst of the rubble. Without warning, his claws gored into Julie's forearms, and she had no choice than to let him go. He scurried into the ashes and stopped at the edge of the mound. He pawed at it as though detecting a rodent tunneling beneath.

"Don't do that, Ralph," shouted Julie, running into the ashes. "You're enough of a mess already!" As she squatted to pick him up, she felt her sandals absorb the heat of the ashes, and then she spotted the metal remnants of the doll carriage. "Is this what you're after?"

She scanned the area for the pink and yellow baby blankets that once swaddled the cat and his twitching tail. Sorrow overtook her, for they were gone, burnt to smithereens.

Holding the cat close with one hand, she used the thumb and forefinger of her other hand to dislodge a twisted wheel robbed of its lavender finish by intense heat. Under it was a mangled handlebar minus pink rubber grippers and streamers. Julie gasped.

"What's the matter?" cried Elizabeth.

"I must be standing in what's left of Katrina's bedroom," said Julie. She rubbed the back of her neck and squinted up at her mother. A stray raindrop landed on her lower lip as she asked, "What did you say?"

"I didn't say anything," said Elizabeth.

Julie tossed away the handlebar. "Then who…?" The same sensation of somebody speaking to her washed over her again.

Ralph made clicking sounds. This time, the pupils of his eyes went wide and focused upwards.

Julie followed his line of sight. Several feet away, blue-eyed Katrina hovered, wearing the same hand-smocked, flowered dress that she had worn in the portrait. The golden ringlets that swirled about the diminutive head were unmistakable. So was the pint-sized arm that extended—index finger pointing at Julie. The cherub levitated higher and higher and then, as if on solid surface, skipped off.

Julie's heart cried out, *Come back! Come back!*

As rain splattered her head and rubble sizzled, desolation swept over Julie. She fell to her knees, and a mangled handlebar penetrated her lavender sweatpants and gored her knee. She lifted her leg and picked up the handlebar. She stared at it. Her head cocked. What was she supposed to do with it? For some unknown reason, she drilled it into the mound and when she lifted it, the warped frame of Katrina's portrait was hooked over the end. Flames had eaten most of the image. Only a fragment of arm lay across a bit of hand-smocked flowered dress.

Elizabeth winced. "How awful losing his wife and child must've been."

Choking on heartache, Julie nodded and dropped the handlebar and frame. Metal clinked against metal.

"How awful for you," said Elizabeth as she knelt down on one knee and leaned her head against her daughter's.

Julie swiped away tears with her sleeve and drew a tremulous breath that distorted her voice. "How could I...have been so blind to Ken's troubles?"

Thunder rumbled in the west. Lightening arced. Sprinkles turned into rain.

Elizabeth got to her feet and said, "This isn't doing us one bit of good, especially you, in your condition." She brushed the ashes off the knees of her sweat pants. "I'll go get the cat carrier and we'll be off."

Dashing to her car, Elizabeth recalled the day several months ago when she had helped Julie to pick out maternity clothes, which certainly wasn't necessary at the time, but all reason had been lost with the excitement of the first grandchild. She had purchased the perfect crib, matching bureaus, and comforter outfit embellished with colorful teddy bears and butterflies. The next morning, Julie had gotten right down to setting up the first-floor nursery. It came out so cute. Not one to swear, Elizabeth huffed, "Crimminy. It's not fair!" She slapped the white canvas top of her red convertible. "All of it is dust in the frickin' wind!"

Back in the ashes, Ken's words echoed in Julie's head. *You go up. I just can't. You go. I can't.* She gazed at the ruins of the manse. "But what was up there?" She got to her feet. "What was I supposed to see that I didn't?"

"Here you go, Ralph," said Elizabeth, hustling back with the cat carrier that a neighbor had let her borrow. Seeing her daughter's face devoid of color, she set down the carrier and tugged on her sleeve. "Julie?" Their eyes met. Julie's were dull, defeated. "Come on," said Elizabeth, hiding concern. "Let's get the little rascal home. Poor thing must be starved." Taking her daughter's hand, she pulled her to her feet. "We've got to make an appointment to get Ralph cleaned up." She brushed ashes off the knees of the lavender sweat pants. "Julie! Your knee's bleeding!"

Julie drew a deep breath and squeezed her hands together. "The groomer will take him right away, I'm sure…once we explain the situation. Come on, Ralph."

The cat headed towards Julie, but just out of reach, he paused and looked over his shoulder at the dregs of the home he had once shared with his wee mistress. A distorted rumble issued from deep within him. Then, as if Katrina was there, giving reassurance, he turned and trotted willingly into the pet carrier.

As Elizabeth secured the carrier door, lightning flashed and reflected off something in the rubble. "Another picture," mumbled Julie, going to pick it up. She scraped off grime with the side of her hand.

"Don't tell me," said Elizabeth. "Regina."

"Yeah," mumbled Julie.

"Held up well in spite of the flames," said Elizabeth. "That woman sure was a looker."

Julie bit the inside of her bottom lip as again the echoes in her head, *You go up. I just can't. You go….* She looked up into the pouring rain and pleaded, "What in God's name was up there?"

"Up where, sweetheart?" asked Elizabeth. Noticing her daughter's soiled hands she took a tissue from her pocket and tapped Julie's hand with it.

Julie took the tissue and scraped the dirt off her hands as though it were blood. "I don't know, Mom." Rain sheeted her face. "I just don't know."

CANDY-COLORED CLOWN

CHAPTER SIX

Julie stopped short and steadied herself on the doorway. "Geez, Ken," she winced, "You look like a puppet-in-the-making with all those lines fixed to your arm and leg casts dangling from the ceiling. For crying out loud, you're a southpaw."

The bleating of the cardiac monitor afflicted the stillness. The blood pressure cuff sucked in air, constricted around an uncomplaining bicep, and exhaled. Her insides deflated along with it. Things could've been a whole lot worse, she told herself. The look of peace on his comatose face, the first she had seen since telling him about the baby, could've been that of a dead man. Her stomach flip-flopped. Rushing to his side, she moaned, "How on earth did a thing like this happen?" She grasped his hand. It felt cold against her cheek ablaze with the horror of it all. Tears fell upon the bed sheets like rain. "What's going on inside of your head?"

The very notion that her pregnancy brought this on repulsed her. "Our baby's a good thing. Why does it upset you so?" She gnawed the inside of her cheek. Maybe, he's scared to death about having another child. "That's it, isn't it?" she whispered. "If the shoe were on the other foot, I'd be scared, too." She cupped the palm of his hand against her mouth and kissed it. "I *am* scared."

Ken rarely spoke of Regina and Katrina, but there had been signs that their loss had devastated him. "And I ignored all of them," heaved Julie. "My white knight's been knocked off his steed and I did absolutely nothing to prevent it. I even added fuel to the fire along the way." She punched the mattress. "Oh, I hate myself! I should've done something, stop it before it got this far, but no, I didn't have guts enough to make you tell me what's been bothering you."

The blood pressure cuff expanded and then collapsed—so did Julie onto the bed next to Ken. "Why isn't the love you and I share big enough, deep enough to sweep away their memory?" she wailed. "Why can't you love me and our baby the way you love them?"

Moments passed. She raised her head and peered at him. Swiping away tears with the back of her hand, she muttered, "It's up to me to make things better, isn't it?" Her head wavered side to side. "Question is—how?" She got to her feet and wrung her hands. "There's got to be something I can do to fix all this."

She adjusted the bed linen then smoothed out wrinkles. Near the crook of his arm, her hand bumped into a mound. She lifted the top sheet. Her eyes widened. Her hand covered her mouth. "It's that candy-colored clown that was on Katrina's bed!"

Its costume, hand-painted with colors of candy canes, butterscotch, licorice, and cherry lollipops stuck out like a sore thumb against white the sheets. In all the times that she had dusted Katrina's bedroom, Julie had never once disturbed that bed. It seemed sacrilegious to do so. She never set one finger on that clown.

Unable to comprehend what her eyes were telling her, she gawked at Ken. "You…you went upstairs?"

She wanted to shake him, wake him out of this God-awful stupor he wallowed in and rid him of the trance that for weeks had made him into a walking zombie. Her fingertips rubbed back and forth across her forehead and then dropped to her sides. She took a step back. Hands flexed opened, closed. "It's time to get real, Ken," she cried, snatching up the clown that was heavier than expected. She shook it at him. "Time to explain what got you into this stupid hospital bed. Why, after all this time, did you go upstairs?"

His chest swelled then receded, like the rhythm of waves lapping upon a sandy shore, in and out, without care, heedless of the world around him.

She brought the clown to eye level. "What am I supposed to make of this thing?" Her grip tightened. Then she shook it at him again. "What's this all about, Ken? Tell me! Tell me right now!"

When he failed to respond, her hand and the clown in it sagged. Her eyes rolled around the hospital room, stark, silent, devoid of hope. She pulled a chair up to the bedrail, crumpled onto it, and gazed at the candy-colored clown on her lap. It gazed back. She kneaded the stuffing. It lacked softness. Where had it come from? India? Turkey? Some Middle Eastern country, that's for sure. She probed the torso. Grains of sand? Her fingertips pinched. Feels like sand. She squeezed the muslin feet and hands, each half the size of ping-pong balls, hard as rock, and lacking digit definition. They bobbed out of rolling, lace-lined cuffs, tied off with twine at the wrists and ankles. The head seemed less dense—or maybe it only appeared that way. It seemed to be made of papier-mâché. A high rolling collar trimmed with Chantilly lace hid the lower quarter of the face, which with its flaming, fuzzy mane that was prone to static, gave the head the appearance of a paintbrush flower about to go to seed. The nose was just a nub off the high-browed, oval face, the tip painted scarlet, as were the lips drawn higher on one side than on the other and puckering in the middle into a well-defined cupid's bow. Immense, almond-shaped eyes with sapphire irises and overstated pupils that glimmered in the center stared sideways, though Julie got the feeling that they never quite left her no matter how much she rotated the clown. Delight, innocence, or quite possibly the opposite—it was hard to tell—exuded from its face. If not for the eyebrows that curved high across the forehead, she might have listened to the terrible foreboding that jabbed her gut. Indeed, she would've hidden that candy-colored clown away into the deepest, darkest region of an attic closet and locked the door so that it might never escape.

"Your husband held a death grip on that merry-Andrew long after the paramedics brought him in."

Julie glanced up and gave Curt Shirlington a weak smile.

He removed the green cap of the surgical outfit he was wearing and stuffed it into his pocket. Cupping her face in his hands, he planted a kiss on her forehead. His eyes closed as he savored a moment of socially acceptable contact. He picked up the odor of smoke and ash—not the usual honeysuckle essence that drifted across dreams of her in the midst of long, solitary nights. He stepped back and said, "You went out to Cohasset."

She heaved a forlorn "Yeah."

Curt took a controlled breath. If only he could to take her in his arms and shield her from all this pain. Lord, what would he have done if she had gone over that cliff? And not survived? He looked away. He wanted her too much, but fighting it left him numb all the way down to the very tips of his toes. No, Curt, ol' man, it's just not in the cards for you to have her. How would it look if you shagged your best friend's wife? Still, having her so near, he couldn't control the excitement that built within him. At times, it got so bad he feared it was getting out of hand. What was he to do?

He stepped to the bottom of the bed and unhooked the medical chart. His eyes skimmed the handwriting, but none of it registered, for out of the corner of his eye, he studied her every move as she fiddled with the clown's baggy costume. Closing the cover of the chart, he said, "The ol' chap didn't loosen up on that even during surgery. ICU nurses couldn't bring themselves to take it away from him. Must be special."

Julie scrutinized the clown. "It was on Katrina's bed," she said, patting its chest. "It's been months..." Her brows knitted. She squinted at Curt. "Years...since Ken's gone up one single stair, let alone all the way up to her bedroom. Why did he go up there? After all this time?"

Caught in her eyes, Curt sensed his insides turning to mush. His lips parted, but words failed him. She's searching for answers that only the ol' chap can give. His right eyelid twitched and his head wavered to one side as his shoulder jounced.

"How's the bro' doin'?"

Neither Julie nor Curt looked at the newcomer. The voice was recognizable enough. It belonged to Jake, Ken's older brother. Whenever he came around, something about him persisted in rattling Julie and Curt. But that's Jake. He rattled everybody. Tall and sinewy, he was incredibly handsome, which aided in keeping his salacious libido satisfied. He was wearing white tennis shorts and sneakers, red Polo shirt with the top button undone, gold Figaro neck chain and bracelet, and Rolex watch. Pomade kept his wavy, raven locks just so, while a solid gold clasp that an L.A. jeweler designed for him kept the length contained at the nape. Like a black adder, it trailed down the center of his back.

Wild and free, Jake used up relationships like toilet paper not only with the opposite sex but also with practically everyone he met. Julie, as well as so many others, long suspected that at her and Ken's wedding, Jake had his way with virtually every unmarried woman—and for that matter, maybe even a few of the married ones, too. His parents, Patty and Richard Waters, had a heck of a time keeping tabs on him, though for some unknown reason, he kept himself within arm's reach of Ken at all times—as with Gretchen and Leopold Konstanze.

Julie squinted at Jake, so totally opposite of Ken. Something percolated behind his coal black eyes, darker than Ken's as were his arrogant eyebrows. What exactly that something was, it was hard to tell, but whatever it was, it wasn't on the up and up.

"The ol' chap's going to sail through this with flying colors," said Curt, careful not to violate patient privacy. Still, he wanted to rub Jake's face in the fact that his brother wasn't easily put down.

"Cool," puffed Jake, now roaming about the room, hand tapping his thigh and jiving to music that only he heard. He inspected every insignificant item, toyed with the intravenous apparatus, and eyeballed monitor numbers. As if recording every detail, he stopped and rotated the diamond adorning his left earlobe. Zeroing in on Julie and then the clown propped upon

71

her lap he stopped rotating the earring. His brows came together. "Whatcha got there, toots?"

There were times when Jake's behavior and speech put Julie off, and she guessed that this was one of them. Other times, it verged on the comical, which irritated Ken whose opinion was *there's nothing funny about Jake.*

He sauntered over to her.

Panic zinged through every fiber of her body.

"The ol' chap doesn't appreciate your speaking to m'lady in that manner," spat Curt while stepping between Jake and Julie. A hand kept Jake at bay. "On occasion, I witnessed him tearing into you something awful about disrespecting her, his parents, or the Konstanzes. Now that the ol' chap's unable to keep you in line, I feel obliged to fill in for him—especially when it concerns m'lady. Let me add that I also do not appreciate your abrasive manner. A bit of respect is in order here, wouldn't you say?"

Jake looked down at Curt's hand. Black eyes rose like the devil from hell and knifed Curt with white-hot malice. His broad shoulders inflated. Forearm muscles constricted. Clearly, Jake was spoiling for a showdown.

Curt postured, jaw muscle bulging at the hinge. If that is what the bloke wants...

A dreadful hush fell over the room. Julie held her breath. Neither man was about to back down. Jake had height on his side, but Curt had Scottish might on his. She had seen Curt with his shirt off, broad chested and all muscle. Be that as it may, this was no place for a confrontation. Seeking to diffuse the situation, she said, "Oh, this silly thing?" She tinkered with the clown's hands and feet. "Nothing really. Just a little something I picked up along the way. Isn't it a hoot?"

Curt flashed her a look. Why did she feel the need to lie?

"Bah," snickered Jake, brushing Curt aside with the wave of a hand.

Curt shook his head. "Jake, you're not worth the effort," he said in a terse, businesslike tone. He leaned over and kissed Julie's forehead. His voice softened. "I'll check in again in a bit. No more worrying, you hear?"

Jake made the most ungodly face and spewed, "Nauseating."

"Call me, Julie…anytime," said Curt.

She nodded, all the while keeping a wary eye on Jake pretending to read the monitor instructions tacked to the wall. She got the feeling that he was just biding his time, waiting for Curt to leave. She was right. When the coast was clear, Jake leered at her. What's going on in that slimy mind of his?

With a mixture of condensation and annoyance, he asked, "Has Gina's old man or old lady checked in?"

Julie shook her head, not only to the question but also to the demeaning lingo. It's just not right to speak of Gretchen and Leo in that manner. Imagine calling Mom the old lady? If she ever found out about it, she'd freak for sure! The image instigated a veiled giggle, but then Jake swaggered over to Ken, clutched his chin, and yanked this way and that, not once, but twice. "Stop!" she shrieked, jumping to her feet. Her cheekbones flushed with anger. "Of all the nerve!"

Her protestations meant nothing to Jake. He simply stepped away when Ken showed no signs of life, just as swiftly as he had gotten there. Arrogance laced his voice when he said, "When old man K and his old lady show up, tell 'em I'll catch up with 'em soon…real soon. Count on it." He spotted her fists clenching and was instantly put on the offensive, but then he found uncanny humor in seeing this puny twerp dressed in oversized purple sweats ready to stand up to him. A grin, wide and toothy, sheeted his face. Sucking air through his upper teeth, he strutted off towards the door. He stole one last look at her over his shoulder, black eyes flashing ill intent. Then his hand poked out of his armpit and pointed at her like a gun. His middle finger slowly, methodically squeezed an imaginary trigger. His hand jerked back. Raising the invisible gun to his lips, he blew away nonexistent smoke and snickered, "Back atcha, toots." His head lurched back, and he spewed bone-chilling mirth that rippled throughout the hospital.

***

Jake's discourse ruptured Ken's unconsciousness, causing great resentment that he had no ability to purge. He felt obliged to get along with his older brother, since that was his mother's wish, yet many times, he wanted to tell him off—just like that day in his office. "What the hell are you doing on my computer?"

Jake instantly pressed the exit key and puffed, "Research, bro. Research."

Ken had bristled at the sight of a 9-mm semiautomatic pistol lying next to the keyboard. "I don't appreciate you bringing a gun into my home. I got a kid running around here, you know."

"Yeah, yeah," scoffed Jake, grabbing the pistol and stuffing it into his belt. He snatched up a glass containing a half-inch of vodka, saluted Ken with it then swilled down the contents. The glass and vodka had come from the wet bar in the great room.

"I'm thoroughly put off by your blatant violation of my personal property," fumed Ken.

With a smirk, Jake planted the empty glass on top of the monitor and got to his feet. Shouldering past Ken, he pretended to scratch his upper lip with the middle finger of his right hand.

Ken bit his tongue. Mother hates it when her sons are at odds.

"Back atcha, bro'," said Jake, just before the front door slammed.

Leering at the empty glass, Ken had the urge to pick it up and hurl the damn thing. "Someday, Jake, so help me…" He snapped up the glass. His hand squeezed so tight that his knuckles lost all color. Then the idea to trace Jake's electronic trail hit him. Setting the glass down next to the keyboard, he dropped onto the chair. It didn't take long.

"FBI. CIA. The War Department. What the heck?" muttered Ken. "That bugger's breaking into secret sites of government agencies!" Other sites, such as those of small towns all over the world, Russia, Israel, Iran, and Iraq, added to the confusion. Squinting at the site of an out-of-the way town in Mississippi called Judgment he leaned back in his chair and huffed, "Incredible."

He eyed the empty glass next to the keyboard and then the printouts on the paper tray that Jake, in his haste to leave, had forgotten to take. Snatching them up, Ken squinted at the top sheet. "Sources for biological agents?" He rustled through the stack. "Chemical warehouses. Layouts of U. S. airports. Subway and train systems across America—and the world!" His veins iced. "Holy Screaming Yellow Zonkers! What the heck is Jake up to now?" After several moments of trying to piece it all together, Ken tossed the printouts onto the paper tray and squawked, "Well, whatever it is, I'm having no part of it!"

He rummaged around the clutter that Jake had made on his desk and found an unused disc. "No more taking chances," Ken grumbled. "Not with all the high tech bells and whistles I've got invested in the business…plus all my records. Nope. Not with that light-fingered Jake sneaking around." He shoved the disc into the computer and backed up all the data, which included Jake's electronic trail. Afterwards, he stowed the disc in the fireproof safe hidden below the bookcase and then installed his own brand of security system on his computer—one that he was sure nobody, not even Jake, could crack. He purposely left the printouts on the paper tray and made it a point to change the lock on his office door. Didn't matter. The next day, the printouts were gone.

To say that Jake was crude at times was an understatement. Too bad, too. He was extremely intelligent with looks to match. On the other hand, he was a loner, a loose cannon, always spouting off stuff that agitated people—some individuals got downright furious. He made it easy to wonder just how far he'd go to get the things he wanted—and he didn't want for much, that's a fact. On several occasions, Ken had asked him about his occupation, which had set Jake to cackling like a triumphant hyena. At length, he sneered, "I work alone." He paused then added, "For my own benefit and mankind's affliction."

"Mankind's affliction," ruminated Ken. His gut told him that Jake was mixed up in the Mafia or something as equally deadly. It made sense too, because every time Ken turned around, Jake was all decked out in the latest fashion and driving new wheels—expensive, sporty ones at that. He bought as many cars as Regina did. A great rivalry existed between the two as to who owned the better vehicle.

Ken chuckled at the vision of the '58 Saab he had owned when he met Regina. Egad, that woman hated that car! It wasn't long before she managed to talk him into getting rid of it. Still, he had come to love that broken-down rust bucket with the grill that resembled the entrance to a caved-in mine. The starter had to be pulled like a lawnmower rope, and to Regina's chagrin, the motor sounded like a lawnmower, too! He still missed the attention he got while gunning the engine to get over insignificant hills. The racket turned heads, set dogs to barking, and arched the backs of cats. Kids scampered into homes. Women chatting over fences shook their fists and hollered, "You're disturbing the peace!"

"Back atcha, toots," rumbled through Ken's comatose brain. His eyes flickered as he remembered the day that Jake had spouted that very same thing to Regina while leaving the manse. As high a class act as she tried to be, she didn't take it as an insult. Purely by chance, Ken had caught her coy smirk. He had never noticed her looking at Jake like that, though he thought nothing of it at the time. She was known to tantalize men in so many different ways. It was all a part of her charm. Yeah, right, charm. Obviously, she charmed somebody into running off with her, because it was only days after Ken had come home from work early and heard her upstairs, arguing with her parents about leaving with whomever that poor devil was. Like a beam of light slicing through the darkness that was restricting Ken to that hospital bed, the truth revealed itself. Regina ran off with Jake!

The whole ugly scene played in his mind as though it were just taking place. Anger mixed with humiliation.

Hey, come on, now. It didn't make sense. His own brother made off with his wife and only child? Wait a minute. That's what Regina and her parents were arguing about. It was bad enough that Regina was taking away their grandchild, but running off with Jake? He was the man they labeled worse than the devil—and he was.

Ken recalled that night. He hadn't slept. He had paced the floor in the corner bedroom. "What on earth am I going to do if Regina leaves and takes Katrina?"

The next morning, long before Regina stirred, he had grabbed the black pants that he had worn the day before off the floor beside the bed and pulled them on. Sockless feet slid into brown deck shoes as he zipped up his pants. He grabbed an old sweatshirt that hung off the hook on the back of the door and while opening the door, stuffed one arm into a sleeve. Outside the bedroom, he shoved his other arm into the other sleeve and pulled the sweatshirt down to his waist. At the bottom of the stairs, he stopped to listen. All was quiet.

He made his way to the garage, got into his car, and pressed the remote. The garage door slid up. Backing out of the garage, he didn't miss that noisy '58 Saab.

He left the headlights off as he drove off in the direction he always did when leaving for work, except, down the street, he steered onto a side street. He spun the wheel. The car arced around and glided up to the curb. He cut the engine.

In gray silence, Ken sat there, trying to figure out how to stop Regina from leaving with Katrina. His fingers ran through his uncombed hair. Time seemed at a standstill. Coastal fog made the sunrise murky and dank. "If it weren't for Katrina, I'd gladly let that harpy go. All she has to do is say the word." His stomach knotted. "How stupid I was to let Regina seduce me into marriage in first place." But then there was that night in the garage…

It was at a benefit for hospitalized children and their families where Ken first set eyes on Regina. She had carried herself like a well-paid model in that low-cut, black silk frock that showed off long, suntanned legs to mid thigh. She never wore nylons. No, she wasn't about to cover up legs more flawless and smoother than satin. It was obvious to everyone except Ken that Regina had her eyes on him. When she laughed, her sapphire eyes and shapely hips angled ever so discreetly towards him. He shied away at first, thinking himself undeserving of woman like that. On the other hand, he had met with quite a few successes of late, and his company was growing. He had a little money in the bank. The college graduate, MIT, was certainly no carouser. So why didn't he deserve her? All he had to do was to get past his nerves and show some interest.

It went easier than expected. Regina practically fell into his arms at the mere suggestion of a dance. Her ruby lips parted into a provocative assent as she tossed her dazzling blond hair over her ivory shoulders. Her forearms wrapped around his neck to hold him closer than any woman ever had. The smell of fine perfume numbed his senses as her thighs rubbed against him through that silk black dress that slithered up his leg. The roundness of her hips pressed against his pelvis. Abdominal muscles tightened into a fist. The blueness of her eyes infected him, and her tongue sliding across her half-opened mouth triggered a fever within him. Yes, Regina was more sickness than love.

Within six months, the biggest wedding the likes of which the South Shore hadn't seen in decades went off without a hitch. But when the parties were over and married life kicked in, Regina got bored. Come hell or high water, she wanted out of Ken's Beacon Hill apartment. Somehow she manipulated her parents into buying the manse in Cohasset—a belated wedding present, so she claimed. The area was one of old money where people wore seersucker suits in the summertime and wintered on southern golf courses. Most were too old to have children young enough to ride bicycles or draw chalk outlines of hopscotch on driveways.

Ken felt as out of place in Cohasset as a polar bear in Arabia, but what the heck, ordering contractors about kept Regina busy and off his case—for a short while. However, remodeling done, she was worse than ever. With little else to occupy her time, she got on him about every little thing. Then she took to joining her uppity friends on a night scene that he couldn't tolerate. One night, she went off with them on a booze cruise in Boston Harbor—well, that's what she said anyway.

Ken had waited up, as usual. The night ticked by. Darkness was lifting to the east when high beams of headlights lit up the street and the rumble of an engine told Ken that Regina was coming. Nobody else in the well-to-do neighborhood owned a sports car.

He pushed the button that opened the garage door then watched the low-slung vehicle buzz in and screech to a violent stop against the back wall. He went over and opened the car door. The odor of alcohol bowled him over. "You're drunker than the lord," he belched. "How in the world did you manage to get home?"

Regina hurdled out of the car and tore off her coat. She was naked. Like a boa, her arms snagged his neck and as she nailed him against his car, her legs constricted his thighs and her tongue slithered down his throat. When she came up for air, she squalled, "Let's fuck," and shoved him to the garage floor. As they went down, the corner of her car door, still ajar, gouged his scalp. She tore into him as if she had just run across the last surviving male on a nuked planet earth. At climax, her teeth sunk into his shoulder and her nails dug into him from shoulders to buttocks.

The next day, Ken limped around, scratched and bruised, while Regina suffered through the worst hangover he had ever seen. She spent most of the day behind the master bedroom door. Every so often, he heard her carp, "Sonova bitch! Sonova bitch!"

Well, Regina came up pregnant from that encounter, which, of course, infuriated her to no end. She wanted to abort the parasite right at the outset. Funny thing, Jake, of all people, had talked her out of it. Come to think of it, from the moment Ken introduced them, Regina and Jake had clicked. It seemed as though they had known each other long before Ken had come along. Puffball that he was, he had sloughed it off. Regina and Jake were two of a kind. They thought they were better than everybody else, what with their fancy duds and fast cars. That's how come they got along so well.

The rumble of a sports car had rousted Ken. Struggling with sunbeams that sliced through the morning haze, he had found himself seated at the wheel of his car. The screech of tires took his eye to a black sports car zooming through the open wrought iron gate of the manse. When a nearby evergreen obstructed vision, he bolted out of the car to the front quarter panel for a better view. The door of the sports car opened. Jake, dressed in black from head to toe, got out and lit up a cigarette. Flicking the lit match into the air, he scanned his surroundings.

Ken ducked. A second or two later, he came up.

Jake was halfway to the front door, the gold clasp that controlled his raven mane glistening in the sunlight. He slid the key into the lock and glanced over his shoulder.

This time, Ken merely slouched, for he was chewing over the way Regina had insisted on Jake having a key to the manse—just in case of an emergency. "Yeah, right," he grumbled. "In case of an emergency."

When Ken straightened, the front door of the manse was closed. He scanned the street. Nobody around. He sucked in a lungful of air and then sprinted to the wrought iron gate. Stopping to catch his breath, he scanned the neighborhood. Not a soul around. He stole up to the front door. It wasn't locked. He let himself in and forgot to close the door as voices filtered down from the second floor. He made his way to the stairway, took a step and then another. Voices evolved from indiscernible to well-defined. He froze in his tracks. Regina and Jake were having sex! Wild uninhibited sex!

Reality smacked Ken like a ton of bricks. His world began to whirl. Vomit bubbled in his throat, and he couldn't figure out why he didn't upchuck.

At the top landing, he heard a tiny voice, and it freshened him like a spring breeze. He put his ear to Katrina's bedroom door. She's playing house with Ralph, singing him asleep, Brahms Lullaby.

His hand went to the brass doorknob, but it refused to turn. He stepped back and gawked at it. Locked? His teeth clenched. How could Regina do such a thing? His hand ran through his hair. He leered at the master bedroom door. Regina actually had nerve enough to lock Katrina in her bedroom while doing the dirty deed with Jake? From the ruckus, they're certainly having one hell of a good time. He shook his head.

Putting an ear to Katrina's door, he listened to her sweet song. "Good God, she's gotten used to this," he whispered. "Regina must've threatened Katrina with her life if she told me!"

His fingers roamed the top of the doorjamb. No key. His eyes narrowed on Katrina's door. "That's it," he growled, "That door's coming down right now!" Just as his leg elevated for an all-out attack, an inner voice erupted, *No, wait! That'll terrorize Katrina!* He stopped short. His fists clenched as he cursed that infernal door.

He charged down the hall like a battering ram and bashed into the master bedroom door. The latch broke and the door splintered open and jammed into a mound of clothing on the floor.

Rancid odor of burnt marijuana gagged Ken as he spotted the key to Katrina's door teetering on the edge of the bureau. Next to the key were ZigZag papers, straws, and a stash of transparent plastic pouches, several unopened. Others were torn open surrounded by leavings of white powder, pot, and pills in a myriad of colors.

It was then that he did the unthinkable—he looked at the bed. His insides railed at the naked, thrashing fornication. Emotion clouded logic. No. This picture's all wrong! Regina and Jake? His own brother? His head cocked. He had a hunch that Regina had been carrying on with someone else, though his mind had pushed it aside for Katrina's sake. Even earlier when Jake had strutted up to the front door, Ken had reasoned there must be some other explanation.

"What the hell are you doing here?" screeched Regina, shoving Jake off her.

A stunned Jake squinted at her and then followed her leer to Ken. He snorted. "Chill out, sweet cakes. Bro's bound to find out sooner or later."

Her lips wrinkled in a grin that broadened as Regina straightened up and flaunted her nakedness. "Right, Jakey," she sneered, her hand drifting across his bare buttocks. "That moron would've found us gone when he got home from work."

"Gone?" puked Ken. His head swam so bad he thought he was going to pass out.

"Come on," jeered Regina. "You're really such a bore. Can't you see that a woman like me needs more than a simpleton like you can ever give?"

Katrina pounded on her bedroom door. "Daddy! Daddy!"

"Now, see what you've done," blasted Regina. She grabbed for a nearby black satin robe. "You've woken the little leech!"

Ken seized the key and raced out of the bedroom, yanking the door shut behind him. At Katrina's door, he jammed the key into the lock, but as the door opened, Jake body-checked Ken. Flying into the railing at the top of the stairs, Ken snagged a spindle to stop from falling down the stairs.

Katrina charged out of her bedroom, but Regina was right there to latch onto a tiny wrist. "Daddy!"

"Leave her alone," howled Ken.

Regina hauled Katrina down the hall and at the door to the master bedroom, turned to Ken and scowled, "She'll be better off where I'm taking her!"

CHAPTER SEVEN

After Jake left Ken's hospital room, Julie sagged onto the chair and leaned against the bed. Fingering Ken's hair, she whispered, "Please, come back to me." Her left hand rested on his chest that rose and fell in harmony with the monitor. At intervals, the blood pressure cuff sucked in air and then let it out. Lulled into a dejected stupor, she pillowed her head on her right hand near his shoulder. Throughout the afternoon, Penny and other nurses checked on the patient. So did the surgeon. All went about their business careful not to disturb the sleeping young woman.

A little past five, Penny was midway through medication and status rounds when she spotted Doctor Curt Shirlington entering Ken Waters' room. She hung back behind a doorway across the hall. Then looking businesslike, she closed in for a better look. The tenderness as Curt gazed upon Julie stunned Penny. Four minutes, maybe five, he stood there. Then he picked up the extra warming blanket slung over the bottom of the bed and draped it over Julie. Again, he stood there; and it seemed like he was drinking up everything about her. He didn't want to leave. When he finally turned towards the door, Penny scooted back to the nurse's station. It wasn't easy to forget how he accused her of butchering Julie's arm that day in the ER. It wasn't easy to forget the look on his face or the tenderness as he draped a warming blanket on the sleeping Julie. But Curt's in love with Julie? How was Penny to fight that?

Nigh onto seven that evening, the out-of-date telephone shattered the lilt, and Julie lurched to her feet. Fumbling for the fiend that threatened to wake the entire hospital, including the dearly departed stretched out in the basement morgue, she stubbed her toe on one of the bed tray rollers, which knocked off a metal, kidney-shaped pan and created an ungodly racket. "Shoot," she grumbled. Latching onto the receiver, she clunked it against her ear and mumbled, "Hullo?"

"Julie? It's me, Patty. How's Kenny doing?"

Julie readjusted the receiver and tried to come to life. "Huh?"

"This is Patty."

Julie cleared her throat. "Uh-huh."

"How's Ken doing?"

Julie filled her lungs and glanced at the comatose form. His chest went up and it went down. No other muscle stirred. Her brow knitted. After all that noise, he still sleeps?

"Shouldn't he be up by now?" asked Patty.

"I was just thinking that very same thing," exhaled Julie. Bile roiled in her stomach. She couldn't remember the last time she had eaten.

A moment passed then Patty fumed, "You're not telling me everything."

"Nothing else is wrong," sputtered Julie. "Nothing that I know of anyways. I wouldn't hold anything back from you. You know that." The line was silent. "Patty?"

A more controlled voice came back. "Yes. I-I'm terribly sorry," said Patty. "I shouldn't take my worries out on you. You've got enough to handle without a paranoid mother-in-law breathing down your neck. But listen, Richard and I can take the next flight out of Tampa. Just say the word."

"Yes, yes, I know that," said Julie, "but you'll be back the beginning of next week anyways. And you wouldn't want to miss seeing your friends or their daughter's wedding. My goodness, you haven't seen them in ages. Ken will be crushed if he finds out you missed out on all that because of him."

"Yes, I..." stammered Patty. "...I suppose you're right."

"Tell you what," said Julie. "Ken's gonna wake up real soon—I just know he will—and when he does, I'll call you right away—even if he's not up to talking."

"Oh, thank you," gushed Patty. "You're such a dear. Kenny sure is a lucky one this time."

The words, this time, stung Julie worse than a scorpion's bite. This time? Is what she was? A *this time*? What about, *Kenny's sure lucky to have found you. You're so good for him. Not like that woman...* Julie straightened. "Tell me about Regina," she spewed. "What was she like?"

"Oh. Well," stammered Patty. "I...I..."

Sensing her mother-in-law was avoiding the question, Julie prodded, "Maybe if I knew what she was like. Why hasn't Ken let her go after all this time?"

"Well, uhm," started Patty. She took a deep, audible breath. "I really don't wish to speak ill of the dead..."

"I know, I know," spouted Julie. "But I need to know."

Silence.

"How am I supposed to help him if I don't know what's eating at him?" exhorted Julie.

Patty cleared her throat. Her voice was acidic as she said, "Regina was a stunning woman, no doubt about that, but I am quite certain of one thing. That woman did not marry my son for love."

"She didn't," said Julie. "Then why...?"

"Who knows," grunted Patty.

"Money?"

"No," said Patty. "Although his computer business was doing fairly well at the time. Certainly not enough to pay for that house in Cohasset."

"I know that it was a belated wedding present from her parents," said Julie, "but Ken and Regina still must've had to pinch and scrape to refurbish a place like that."

Patty snickered. "Either that woman had a real knack for stretching pennies—which I seriously doubt—or money was coming in that nobody knew about."

"Even Ken?"

"That place was not a wedding present," spat Patty. Then she gasped. "Oh, I shouldn't have told you that!" Her voice turned into a whine. "Oh, please don't tell Kenny. He doesn't know."

"He doesn't know?"

"My son was a bull with a ring in his nose. If Regina said something black was white, it was all the same to him. All he cared about was…" Patty broke off and drew in a breath full of repugnance. "Gretchen and Leo did not have that kind of money."

"Ken told me things went downhill right after they got married," said Julie.

"Pretty darned fast, let me tell you." Patty winced. "But that woman got pregnant and that kept my Kenny reined in no matter what garbage she threw at him. After Katrina came along, he took to her so…well, that poor man put up with all kinds of…uhm…stuff from the likes of that woman. He loved that little darling too much to do or say anything that might risk losing her."

Julie dropped onto the chair. Her heart broke. Why can't Ken love the life she was carrying as much as he loved Katrina?

"Hello?" said Patty.

"Uhm…" faltered Julie. "Uh, Ken told me he detested Regina's social gatherings."

"Well," hooted Patty. "That woman had it all wrong if she married my Kenny for social stature, that's for sure! He's just not that way. Maybe that's why she did everything she could think of to kill the man in him. Punish him for not being whatever her misguided fantasy expected him to be."

"So why…" Julie paused to wave to Regina's parents coming into the room.

"It's such a shame, that's all," said Patty. "Ken had so much potential. It was plain as the nose on your face that she was out to destroy him. She and J..."

Julie butted in, "Excuse me, Patty?"

"Yes?"

"Gretchen and Leo just got here," said Julie. "I'll have to call you back." The silence on the line led Julie to believe that Patty must have been embarrassed. After all, she and Richard were good friends with Gretchen and Leo. Tearing down their dead daughter wasn't nice. She cleared her throat and asked, "Patty? Are you still there?"

"I'll be waiting for Kenny's call," said Patty, short and to the point. "Or yours."

The line suddenly went dead. Julie pulled the receiver away from her ear and squinted at it. Undecided whether to feel angry or hurt she lowered the receiver onto the cradle and turned around. Leopold was right there to give her a hearty embrace. She felt like a rag doll in his burly arms. She breathed in the aroma of spicy aftershave. Much too soon, he let go of her. She needed more time to wallow in his comfort and security.

"They really keep him doped up, huh?" he blustered in a grainy voice while his hand swept above Ken.

Julie heaved a sigh while nodding. She bit the inside of her lip. Should she tell Leo and Gretchen that Jake came looking for them?

Gretchen put an arm around Julie and gave a reassuring squeeze. "Ken a fighter, *meine liebe*. Always be."

Julie eyed Leopold now hovering over Ken just like Jake did. Was he going to rough up Ken the same way? Not on your life! She got ready to spring.

"He sail through this, too," said Leo, running the nail side of his fingers across Ken's brow.

Julie's eyes pierced Leopold. Had there been other times? Not just the plane crash? Perhaps it's time to find out more about Regina's family—and Ken's, too. Why did they lie about buying the manse as a belated wedding present? A weird notion struck her. Why was Jake so interested in Regina's parents?

***

Within the void that held Ken captive, the blare of the telephone combined with the crash of the metal pan, resonating. A familiar voice spoke his mother's name. Next came Gretchen's voice, "Ken a fighter."

Then Leo's, "He sail through this, too."

With every fiber in his body, Ken struggled to shake off the cruel darkness and lash out, "What kind of fighter finds himself down for the count on the first punch? Yeah, that's right. That's what happened when I got in Regina's way the day she ran off." He never told anybody what happened during his first marriage—not the Konstanzes, his parents, Curt. Nor did he tell them that she had run off with Jake—his own damned brother! Nobody knew—not even Julie.

How shocked Ken had been when Jake had gotten in his face and snarled, "Easy now, bro'." His breath stunk of pot and stale booze. "Back off."

"I'm leaving and there's nothing you're doing about it," taunted Regina, one hand jammed against her hip and the other hand restraining Katrina.

"Let me go," screeched the hysterical child. "Let me go!" She squirmed and tugged and then her little fingers pried at her mother's hand. "I want to stay with my Daddy!" She stamped her foot then tugged some more. "Help me, Daddy!"

Regina raised her hand about to strike the child, and Ken knew it. "Don't," he seethed. On several occasions, he had seen the handprints that discolored Katrina's cheek. He never witnessed Regina doing it, but he didn't doubt she had. The fear in his daughter's eyes whenever Regina came around cemented the issue.

Just then, Katrina broke loose and ran towards him, bawling, "Daddy! Daddy!"

His arms opened wide as he bent forward at the knees. Once he had his little girl in his arms, they'd be home free. Then nobody, but nobody would ever pry them apart. But then, Jake's hairy legs interrupted vision. Ken crawled to the left. The legs shifted left. Ken swerved to the right. The legs did, too. There was no getting around them. Then came a knee and one solid bump, and Ken was on the floor.

Meanwhile, Regina snagged Katrina and lifted her off her feet. She had all she could do to maintain hold.

"Let me go," screamed Katrina. "I want my Daddy!" Her tiny arms and legs thrashed wildly. "Daddy, help!"

Ken rolled backwards full circle and jumped to his feet. His hand raked through his hair. He couldn't bear to see his little girl so upset. His hands balled into fists. "Go if you want to, Regina," he barked, "but you will not take Katrina!"

"You can't stop me," taunted Regina, using Jake as a shield. "Nobody's stopping me from what I want."

"Daddy! Daddy!"

"Over my dead body you're taking her," hollered Ken.

Jake rolled his black eyes then zeroed in on Ken. His square jaw loosened, and a monotonic growl rolled out, "Sure that's how you want it, bro'?"

"Daddy! I want to stay with my Daddy!"

Ken got eyeball to eyeball with Jake. "Get out of my way!"

Jake spread his arms wide, took two steps back, and said in a singsong voice, "I tried to be nice." His eyes iced as his jaw set. Arm and leg muscles flexed. His fingers beckoned as his words came from behind clenched teeth. "Okay, come and get me, if you think you're man enough."

"Daddy!"

"Katrina's staying with me," howled Ken. Head down, he charged at Jake like a crazed bull.

A blur of movements, excruciating pain, and then a tiny voice faded away, "Dad-dy! D-a-d-d-y…"

When Ken came to, he could hardly breathe. Somebody was standing over him. He took a swing.

"Easy there, ol' chap," said Curt, rolling back on his heels. The listening ends of his stethoscope dropped as he raised his hands submissively. "Take it easy."

Ken coughed. "What…?" His nose screwed up with the rancid smell of burnt pot. The old sweatshirt he was wearing had been scissored up the front, exposing his chest.

"You took a crushing blow right to the heart," said Curt while sticking the ends of the stethoscope back into his ears. He placed the listening end over Ken's heart, concentrated for several moments, then took the stethoscope out of his ears and said, "You're lucky to be alive."

Ken braced himself up on one elbow and spat out bloody phlegm. Eyesight cleared as he squinted sideways at Curt. With great effort, he moved his mouth. "What're you doing here?"

Curt rolled up the stethoscope, placed it into his medical kit, and secured the lid. He stood up and brushed his hands together. "You didn't show up at the gym."

Ken gave him a blank expression.

"Racquetball?" said Curt. "Weekly mainstay since Henry was a pup?"

Ken hitched his chin. Things had to be pretty bad for either man to cancel. Something deep in his belly rumbled. He looked down. A fist-size welt was forming in the middle of his chest. He pulled the sides of his shirt together.

"Tried to call," said Curt. His hands clamped onto his hipbones. "Phone's dead." He glanced around the master bedroom. Dust moats drifted in the sunlight that streamed through the skylight. Sheets hung off the sleigh bed as if somebody's foot had gotten caught while scrambling out. A burgundy comforter lay on the floor halfway to the door. On one end table a snifter glass, another one on the other end table, accompanied by a crystal brandy decanter. His mouth pulled back into a grimace as he thought, *Miss Prissy's screwing around right under our noses.* "So," he said, "Who worked you over?"

Ken lolled his head to one side.

Curt eyed the open, empty drawers and then stepped over to the closet. "EMTs are on the way," he said. His right index finger nudged one of the partially opened doors. Inside the closet, odds and ends of clothing were strewn about, lots of empty hangers. He heaved a breath and turned around. On the bureau was a portrait of Regina, flawless make-up, sapphire eyes, and golden tresses that washed over a shoulder and curled on a bare arm. Perfect neck. Subtle curves of breast. Under it all: an incredibly ugly woman. "I take it Regina flew the coop."

Ken glanced up at the ceiling. His eyes closed. He felt dead inside.

Curt crossed the room and peered down at the plastic pouches on the bureau and the trails of white powder. Marijuana leavings. Plastic straws. Empty ZigZag envelopes. He picked up a pouch, spread it open, and sniffed the contents. His index finger wormed into it then came out with white powder stuck to it. He dabbed a bit on the end of his tongue to analyze the taste. His head jerked with disapproval. "Tsk, tsk, tsk." He tossed the pouch onto the bureau, wiped his finger into the palm of his other hand, and turned. His left cheek tightened. Ken looked terrible, round-shouldered and dull. "Front door was wide open," said Curt.

Ken grunted.

Curt pursed his lips and leaned back against the bureau. "You're too good for her."

Again, Ken grunted.

"Her car's in the garage," said Curt, crossing his arms and ankles. "Yours is gone."

"It's down the street," wheezed Ken.

Curt squinted at him. "You have been spying on her?"

"Them," said Ken flatly.

"Them," echoed Curt.

"Had a hunch," said Ken.

Curt glanced down at his watch then at the bedroom door. Where's that bloody ambulance? He didn't want to say it, but... "Katrina's gone."

Ken shuddered.

"Gendarmes won't issue missing person reports for seventy-two hours," said Curt, stepping over to Ken and squatting down. "Could hire a gumshoe to track them down..." He scratched his chin. "Better to wait it out. See what comes down the pike."

Ken attempted to get to his feet. His sweatshirt fell back and then so did he.

"Stay put, ol' chap," said Curt, his hand pressing down on his friend's shoulder. "Get checked out at the hospital before larking about."

Ken pushed Curt away and struggled to get up again. He fell back again.

Curt caved and offered his hand.

"Don't need anybody's help," grumbled Ken, pushing away the hand. He staggered to his feet and swayed back and forth a second or two. The sweatshirt slipped off a shoulder. He hurtled out into the hallway and collapsed against the wall. Sweat beaded on his forehead, his neck sticky from it, armpits, too, and it glued his shirt to the hollow of his back. He gazed down the length of hallway and listened. His body throbbed. The noise in his eardrums was excruciating. He sucked in a lungful of air then pulled himself along the wall and butted into the doorjamb of Katrina's bedroom. His insides burned like fire, and he squeezed his eyes shut against the pain. "Let my little girl be in there," he moaned.

Swinging into the bedroom, the first thing Ken saw was the carriage where Katrina made Ralph nap. In the far corner was the pink dollhouse. The bed was all made up, stuffed toys propped upon the pillows, but one stood out, grinning at him. He leered back. "Stupid clown," he belched. Then it hit him. "They've taken Katrina!" His hands clasped his head as he shriveled to the floor.

Curt's voice grew murky. "Hang in there, ol' chap. We'll get the wee one back." Everything faded to black.

The next day, the evening news headlined with "Cessna Crash in Everglades. All Lost." The eleven o'clock news reported that the passenger list included two New Englanders. The call came at dawn—Regina and Katrina had been on that plane. Ken's little girl was gone forever.

A week later, a memorial service was held. Jake showed up. Ken glared at him with a heart full of hatred, yet for the life of him, the reason for feeling that way escaped him. After the service, he rubbed a sore spot over his heart while watching Jake strut down the street to his car. There's something about that bugger's silhouette against the horizon.

In the weeks and months that followed, Ken buried himself in work. Any time off was spent with Curt at the Old

Watering Hole in Quincy where spirits and sports were on tap, or at the gym, working out or playing racquetball. He listened to sports talk on the car radio, avoiding music at all cost, especially love songs that spoke of love as it should be, not the destructive kind that he had shared with Regina. The sun went down and the moon rose, again and again. The manse was quiet…always so ungodly quiet…and empty. Dawns came and went like slow-moving, faceless druids across moors of desolation.

Four years later, Ken was focused on business as usual while barreling down a hallway in Ste. Anne's Regional Hospital in Brighton where he had designed and now serviced the computer system. At a corner, he smacked into Julie. His client folder and her patient reports scattered like leaves on an October day. They dropped to their knees and as they gathered up all of it, her cocoa eyes streaked with gold set his stomach to buzzing like a bee happening upon the first nectar-filled blossom of spring. He couldn't draw air, for her nervous smile and the way her eyelashes fluttered with embarrassment had taken away his breath. Honey-blond hair teased his face. Essence of honeysuckle filled his nostrils. Surely she heard his thundering heart.

In the lounge, they sorted through the paper work. Julie sat on the sofa with her legs tucked beneath her, chattering a mile a minute, but that was fine with Ken, for her voice was like that of the nightingale, softening the heart that had turned to stone four years prior. His soul was drawn to her like a ship to a beacon on the bay. People may have come and gone, asked a question or two. The telephone might have wrung; somebody may have answered it. Neither Ken nor Julie was aware of any of it. In his world from that day on, there was only her eyes gleaming like sunlight and lighting the darkness of his solitary existence.

After that first encounter, Julie seemed to avoid Ken like the plague. He couldn't understand it, so he had a long talk with Ellen who used to be Katrina's nanny. Losing her little ward had been unbearable, so, having no desire to become attached to another child, Ellen ended up at Ste. Anne's Hospital, working in Patient Records. She and Julie were coworkers. "I'll put in a good word for you," promised Ellen, "but be advised. Julie just ended an abusive relationship. Give it time."

Weeks dragged by. Ken fretted. On a frigid winter day, fate at long last lent a hand. He had just gotten to the hospital after calling on a potential client out in Chelsea and hadn't even gotten his coat off when Ellen rushed up to him, spewing, "Julie's in the emergency room! She came in with blood all over her! I couldn't get near her!"

He jammed his briefcase against her and raced towards the ER, not caring who heard as he cried, "How unfair can you be, God? First Katrina and now Julie! I haven't even gotten to know her yet."

Elbowing through the crowd gathered outside one of the emergency cubicles, he heard someone say there had been a bank robbery, and people had gotten shot. Panic zinged through him. He collided with a dazed young woman who had long, auburn hair. "Where's Julie?" he panted. Blank blue eyes stared into his. He grabbed the young woman by the arms and demanded, "Where is Julie?"

Her finger slowly came up and pointed. He looked in that direction and craned his neck. Julie was huddled outside swinging doors that led to the operating room, apart from the chaos, alone, stupefied. "Julie," he whispered and let go of the young woman. He raced to Julie.

"We got caught in the middle of a bank robbery," she mumbled. Her hair was matted with filth and blood. Tears tracked through dry blood splattered on her face. Grimy crimson smeared her camel-colored coat, shoes, and nylons that had gaping holes in the knees. The blood belonged to her mother, Elizabeth Blair, whom Ken didn't know at the time. Julie had only minor scrapes and bruises.

"Mom's real bad," said Julie. "Emma, too. Margi's okay."

Ken didn't know any of those people.

"Thank God for Janice," she said, smiling faintly at the young lady with the auburn hair whom Ken had bumped into. "She's into Karate or Tai Kwan Do—something like that."

Ken squinted at the young lady in a black suede jacket, blue corduroy pants, and knee-high black leather boots. She was twisting a blue knit scarf into twine. "She brought down the bank robber all by her self?" he asked.

Julie nodded. "A cop was there, but he got shot, too."

So Ken stood by Julie in her hour of need. She had no way of knowing the need that had been lying dormant in his soul. Hours turned into days, days into weeks, speeding by as she opened him up and led him out of abysmal sadness. So many times she would stop merely to listen to the songs of the breeze in the trees on spring afternoons...or water lapping against the shore on August nights...or hummingbird wings hovering over morning glories...or the blessed silence of snowflakes that danced around streetlights at midnight. It had been so long since levity filled his soul and when at last silliness and humor escaped him, he was surprised. He learned to breathe in life and trust enough to give his friendship to her. Where or when it was that he handed her his heart, Ken hadn't a clue. All he knew was that his love was pure and this time, so very, very real.

And Julie never let him down.

CANDY-COLORED CLOWN

CHAPTER EIGHT

The next day, despite the fact that Ken lay in a coma, visitors came and went. On one occasion the room got too congested, which prompted Penny and other nurses to march in and eject all but two visitors. Julie stayed, of course, and though it was nice to know that she and Ken had so many friends, at a time like this, she found their company exhausting. Every so often, she glanced at her watch and wondered how in the world Ken could go on sleeping with all the commotion. When visiting hours ended, she collapsed onto the chair closest to the bed and let out a sigh of relief. She rotated her head and flexed her shoulders. She stopped to peer at him. "Oh, Ken. Please wake up."

The monitor droned. The blood pressure cuff bloated and wheezed. His breath came and went.

"I'm so sick of those machines," she huffed. Her chin dropped onto her chest and she closed her eyes. A frown rippled her brow, and her eyes popped open. She raised her head. "Oh gosh," she cried. "I should thank the stars above I do hear those machines."

It was bad enough that the monitor and cuff were getting on her nerves, but the candy-colored clown in the crook of his arm was staring at her, making her skin crawl as though a million spiderlings were scattering upon her. Her entire body revolted. Out of all the precious things he could have saved from the fire, why that stupid thing? She leaned over and fingered its red mop. "I don't understand any of this." Her fingers kicked its feet. She heaved a sigh. "Wish Mom and Dad were here," she murmured. "They're out buying us clothes and stuff. Insurance agent dropped by. He's nice. He's taking care of preliminary details regarding the manse and cars and says you have to sign some papers when you wake up. Know what? He gave us some money in advance to buy clothes and other creature comforts." She straightened up and clutched the candy-colored clown to her breast. "Creature comforts…" She looked down at the lavender sweat suit her mother let her wear. "Geez, I look a fright," she puffed. "Haven't showered or done my hair since Mom took me out to…to…get Ralph." She set the clown on the bed and dusted herself off. "Somewhere along the way I smudged ashes on Mom's sweatshirt. Oh, no, the knees are singed." A shiver raced through her as she spotted the hole in one of the knees and the ring of blood that surrounded it. She rubbed her hands together. Not wanting to think about it, she rolled her eyes and said, "I used the toothbrush and toothpaste from your hospital pack this morning. Can't believe I forgot to ask Mom to pick us up a couple new ones." A muted giggle emerged from deep within her. "Knowing Mom, she's already got them in her shopping cart. I'm lucky to have a mother like that." She picked up the clown. "Anyhow, it's nice of her to call and say that she and Dad will be in to see us later. I was getting kind of worried." She glanced at Ken. "Hopefully, you'll be awake by the time they… All this is my fault. If only I didn't get pregnant…"

"How's it going, m'lady?" asked Curt as he breezed into the room. He was dressed in clinic garb, white jacket, blue-striped button-down shirt open at the collar, navy pants and socks, and black loafers.

"Why isn't Ken awake yet?" demanded Julie, springing to her feet and shaking the candy-colored clown at him.

About to kiss her on the forehead, Curt backed off, his insides quaking. He didn't like to see her upset—especially at him. Collecting himself, he avoided her eyes and pretended to take Ken's pulse. "Ol' chap'll come around soon enough," he said. "Best to keep him under for the time being."

Julie squinted at Curt then at Ken then back at Curt. "How come?"

"He hasn't got a wink of decent sleep in months," replied Curt. Sleep was just an excuse. There was no valid reason to keep Ken under, but waking him would obliterate any likelihood of Curt ever having for Julie for his own. He noted the level of fluid left in the intravenous bag then the morphine drip. Almost gone. Numbers on the monitors were at normal levels and stable—had been for quite some time. Now, that's odd—sleep tapes indicate episodes of agitation. Nothing to be concerned with though. Curt, ol' man, looks like you have no other choice than to bring the ol' chap around.

"You knew Ken was having problems?" asked Julie. Her hand, still gripping the candy-colored clown, sagged to her side.

Curt pressed the call button. "I'll have a nurse get rid of all these doodads." He appeared calm, but his insides bulged like a volcano ready to explode, hey, world, this man possesses an all-consuming infatuation for a woman who just happens to belong to his best mate.

"Why can't I get any decent answers?" said Julie, tossing the clown onto the bed and crumpling onto the chair. "Only thing I can see is he's worse off than you're telling me."

"We have no secrets, and therefore you and I...we..." Curt faltered. She mustn't know how he felt, but...maybe...if he told her...she'd dash into his arms? Perhaps those breathtaking eyes of hers would stare into his for all eternity? Those eyes...those... His insides tightened. Those eyes were staring at him. "We just don't keep...things from each other. You of all people should know that." His mind went blank. He swallowed hard. What in God's name were we talking about? Secrets. Yes. No secrets. "Ol' chap and I grew up together," he sputtered. "Remember?"

"Well, yah, but..." stammered Julie.

Curt scratched the back of his neck. How hard it was to mask feelings.

His silence led Julie to believe that he was mulling over patient confidentiality, simple as that, but unacceptable in her book. "I'm his wife, for heaven's sakes," she spewed. "Why is it I'm being kept in the dark about my husband's condition?"

"There's nothing to tell," insisted Curt.

Julie slouched onto the bed. Her fingers skated over Ken's hand—so strong, yet so unbearably lifeless. She picked it up and held it to her cheek. "Tell me," she said. "What was Ken like back then, back before…before…"

Curt winced. "Before Regina." Now there was a woman everybody loved to hate, he thought. "Hell-of-a great mate," he said. A smile lifted his face. "Smart as a whip. Tinkered at everything and tore apart whatever he got his greasy little paws on. Had to know inner workings of things. We were kind of alike in that respect; however, where ol' chap tinkered with hardware and electronics, I tinkered with biology. But let's not go there." The twinkle in his eye made Julie giggle and it caught him off guard. He glanced at her. He didn't mean to. He wished he hadn't. His insides knotted. Grabbing the earpieces of the stethoscope that clung to his neck, he embedded them into his ear canals and pretended to listen to Ken's heart at work. He didn't straighten up until he thought he was under control. Unplugging the earpieces, he let them fall. As they snagged on his neck, he wished he'd never straightened up, because she was waiting for him to speak, but he didn't a clue as to what to say. He stepped over to the window. "Yup," he heaved. "The ol' chap and I spent many a day together."

"But then he got tangled up with Regina," she said.

Curt stared out the window. "Things went down the pipes in one big hurry. The ol' chap got lost in that woman's beauty and charms."

"I think that was kind of easy to do," said Julie, noting for the first time how everyone referred to Regina as *that woman*.

If only m'lady knew that it was more than kind of easy for me to get lost in her, thought Curt.

"I saw her picture—the one of her as a bride?" Julie whistled softly. "Sure was gorgeous."

Not as gorgeous as you, he thought and shook his head. "Yeah, well," he said, "that woman knew it, too. The rest of us saw right through her. She knew that, too. But not the ol' chap. Love was her disguise, and he fell for it hook, line, and sinker."

Julie sighed. "So he was a slave to her."

"You might say that," said Curt, but it was on the tip of his tongue to say, m'lady, you don't know how much of a slave I am to you. But he just couldn't do it. Instead, he said, "You're good for him. Brought him back to the ol' chap I knew as a kid…until…"

"The baby," murmured Julie.

With a rueful hitch of the chin, Curt leaned against the corner of the windowsill and crisscrossed his arms across his broad chest. She was off limits, more so now that she's pregnant. He peered at his forearms peppered with freckles and the same carrot-colored hair as his head. He flexed the brachioradialis muscle of his right arm. Maybe if he got out, he'd feel better. Get a wench, ol' man, maybe then your mind will let go of m'lady. There's got to be one out there that can make you forget her.

"You buzzed, Doctor Shirlington?" asked Penny, stepping into the room. She clicked off the buzzer.

Curt uncrossed his arms and straightened. This was it, time to wake up the ol' chap. But… He took one last look at Julie, cleared his throat, and stammered, "Uhm, yes. Time to rid m'lady's slumbering white knight of those fancy doodads. Don't you agree?"

A cold, professional nod accompanied Penny's reply, "Yes, Doctor Shirlington."

He sensed resentment. Understandable. He had dated her, a couple of times. Had a nice time, it's true, though nothing came of it. He knew he was to blame. Penny's a fine wench. It's just that ridiculous infatuation for his best mate's wife had Curt full as a tick.

Julie watched with bated breath as Penny disconnected the IV line, the heart monitor, and then rest of the equipment. "Too bad you can't disconnect those lines that suspend Ken from the ceiling like a puppet."

"Wish I could," said Penny. "Anything else, Doctor?" She repositioned the clown in the crook of Ken's arm and turned. "Doctor Shirlington?"

"Huh?"

"Anything else?" repeated Penny.

"No, I...no," he sputtered. "Thank you." He noticed a trace of emotion in Penny's demeanor as she nodded. Deep down, he knew she cared about him. Maybe he should give her a call...maybe later...sometime. Out of the corner of his eye, he watched her leave. Lovely lady. Why can't he feel for her what he felt for Julie?

"You didn't tell me that Ken had spoken to you," said Julie.

Curt glanced at her. Puzzled eyes stared back. His eyes shot at the ceiling. Relax. Don't look back at her. In a strangled voice he said, "I suggested that he bring you next visit."

"You should've insisted," she lashed out. "Maybe I could've helped him. Together we could've put a stop to..." Her hand swept over her comatose husband. "...this. Before this ever happened."

"I did insist," he argued.

"You should've called me then," she countered.

Curt sagged onto the windowsill. "The ol' chap swore me to secrecy."

Julie gazed at Ken, angry tears brimming her eyes. "Yeah, well," she choked, "look what secrecy wrought."

Curt wanted to make all this disappear; take away all her pain. He wanted not to care, but he was powerless to do so and much too confused.

Silence. Only her sobs and Ken's breathing.

Julie squinted at Curt. He's trying not to look me, she thought. He's hiding something. Something to do with Regina? Or maybe Katrina? With the wristband of her sweatshirt, she dabbed the moisture that trickled down her cheeks and asked, "How come Ken won't let go of the past?"

Curt scratched his head. "Wish I knew," he said flatly and stared out the window again. "That woman had him wrapped around her pinkie from the start." How well Curt knew how that felt. Only difference was that Regina knew she had the ol' chap where she wanted him; Julie had no idea how much Curt was under her spell. In a nearly inaudible voice, he said, "I so much as

told him so." He cleared his throat. "But I was treading on thin
ice, so I didn't push it. Regina got wind of my opinion and that
made matters worse." He stepped away from the window and
braced his hands upon his hips. "That woman didn't like me
much right from the outset. And it went downhill from there on
out."

Julie shrugged. "Other people were in that boat, so I've
heard."

He skimmed hospital policy posted on the wall. "She
threw a glass at me once," he said.

"No," she puffed.

He nodded. "Got real pissed off one day when I came to
get the ol' chap for our weekly racquet ball game." His voice
reflected deepening anger. "That woman preferred uptown folks,
loaded with money. Driving fancy cars. Wearing New York
duds." The side of his face twisted up and his eyes became heavy.
"I thought he had put all that and the plane crash behind him,
but like many other people who face traumatic situations, some
little thing set him off."

Julie gazed down at her belly and cocked her head. "That
little thing is our child."

Curt wilted.

Outside the room, steel instruments crashed on the floor.
Julie and Curt exchanged startled glances then looked at Ken.
Not one muscle moved. A flurry of activity ensued and the
pungent odor of rubbing alcohol drifted into the room. Curt
opened the window, and as a soft breeze blew in—clean, like
after a spring shower, happy birds twittering and all—he filled his
lungs and let it out. He summoned the nerve to steal a glance at
Julie. She was taking the candy-colored clown out of the crook of
Ken's arm. Maybe it's best to tell her exactly what the ol' chap
was up to just before taking the header off that cliff. He watched
her fluff up the clown's fiery red hair, her index finger trek
around the nub of a nose then skirt the crests of the scarlet
Cupid's bow. Drawn to her like a magnet, he took a step toward
her.

She looked up at him and snapped, "This is nuts."

103

Curt stepped away.

"When did you find out?" she asked.

"Find out?" he asked.

"That Ken was freaking out?"

Curt inhaled deeply and then exhaled, "He called me out of the blue one day, guess it was right around the time you told him of your condition. His nerves were shot. Did a lot of pacing, clutching his hands and such. I haven't seen him that riled up since the plane crash."

Julie felt her insides lurch. Her eyes bore into Curt.

"I tried to give him something to settle him down," he said, knowing better than to get caught in her gaze.

"He refused to take it, didn't he?" she said.

Curt nodded. "Then he left…just like that." He snapped his fingers. "And I couldn't figure out what just happened."

Julie winced. "Then I call you up and ask you about obstetricians." She tossed the candy-colored clown onto the bed.

"Yeah," he said. "But I knew before you told me." He dropped down on his elbows onto the edge of the bed and picked up the clown. "Well, four or five days go by. He calls me up again. I had patients up the wazoo and told him that, so we agreed to meet later on at the Old Watering Hole in Quincy." Curt turned the clown this way and that, dissecting its features. "Wouldn't you know, ol' chap shows up at my office, totally off the wall, breath coming in spurts, eyes darting about and such, never fixing on a thing."

Julie gasped. "He must've scared the bageebees out of your patients."

"You can say that again," he said, pinching the clown's ping-pong sized hands and feet. "I hauled him into my office real quick like. Lucky I did, because he started ranting and raving about dreams, nightmares that filled his head with God-awful laughter, male, female, children."

"Regina?" Julie asked.

"At least that's how he described some sort of ghost with scraggly blond hair and menacing eyeballs. He never actually called her by name." Curt pursed his lips and tried several times

104

to brace the candy-colored clown into a seated position. It kept flopping over. "There was an explosion and a child screamed." Curt's brows came together, and he left the clown flopped over on the bed. "In my mind I think that child was Katrina."

Julie covered her mouth and shot a look at her comatose husband. "Geez, Ken."

The concern that riddled her face bothered Curt to no end. He chastised himself for being more interested in his own troubles, his own infatuation that made him blind to his best mate's plight. Bracing his hands on the bed, he stood up. The clown tumbled onto the floor. "At the end of the dream, a dark figure comes out of nowhere and stands eyeball to eyeball with the ol' chap. The figure's grinning—big, threatening teeth. Hilarity slaps him in the face like a giant hand. Suddenly the figure's got its back towards him, strutting away." Curt paused and shook his head. "Poor chap covered his ears right there in my office. There just wasn't any way for him to get away from it. His legs got shaky, so I sat him down and gave him something to settle him."

"He let you this time?" asked Julie, stooping to pick up the candy-colored clown.

"I wasn't about to give him a choice," said Curt.

She gazed at the clown's outlandish face for a moment and then laid the clown on Ken's chest. "You sent him home all doped up?" she asked.

"Called him a cab."

"You should've called me," she fired back.

"You weren't at home," he countered, getting to his feet. He plodded to the foot of the bed, grasped the footboard, and gave it a jolt. "I was too bloody busy to take him home myself."

Julie stared at his back. "Gosh, I'm so, so sorry." She faltered. "It's just that…geez… I don't know."

Curt came over and rested his hand on her shoulder. "It's okay. Many factors had a hand in the ol' chap's meltdown."

She hung her head. "I was the worst."

He lifted her chin and murmured, "I don't see it that way."

"What other way is there?" she argued.

"I never told anyone this..." Curt swallowed hard. "And I don't think the ol' chap has either...but I...I found him all beat up..."

Horror sheeted her face. "When?"

"Right after Regina ran off with Katrina."

"Regina beat up Ken?"

"No," said Curt. "She didn't have the muscle to do that kind of damage."

"That kind of damage?" she asked.

"A blow like that is rarely accidental," he said. "Bloody idiot knew the exact spot to hit. Good thing I showed up when I did."

"So who...?" started Julie.

Curt shrugged. "Must've been the bloke she ran off with."

"Regina ran off with another man?" she belched. "But I...I thought she died in a plane crash!"

"She did," he said. "The night she left the ol' chap."

"So all three went down on the plane?"

Again, Curt shrugged. "That's how I see it."

"Who's the guy?"

"I haven't a clue."

"Ken didn't tell you?"

"I didn't push the issue."

"Push the issue? I thought you two have no secrets."

"Look, if you had seen him beat up the way I did and how devastated he was over that woman taking off with his wee lass..." Curt paused to pull himself together. "He adored the wee one, you know. Lived and breathed for her. And then the plane crash..."

Suddenly Curt found Julie in his arms, sobbing. He slowly raised his hands, afraid to touch her. It would only be natural to hold her at a time like this, but his reason wasn't right—nor was the timing. Would there ever to be the right time? The right reason?

He took her by the shoulders and made her look into his eyes. Should he confess the dreams he couldn't control? His heart thundered. Yes! Do it now! His brain held him back; Mrs. Waters belonged to Ken Waters. His insides imploded, leaving only a shell of a man to smile pathetically.

Nudging Julie onto the chair next to Ken, Curt forced himself to continue. "I told my nurse, Jessey, that from then on, any time that the ol' chap shows up at the clinic, I want him brought directly into my office and she's to get me stat. I have to admit, though, from that point on, things really got bizarre."

Julie got to her feet and started to pace. "I could just kick myself for not knowing all this stuff!"

"Come on," said Curt, his palms gesturing. "None of us are mind readers." Embarrassment colored his face. Thank goodness, nobody could read his mind.

"I should've known," she insisted. She stopped and stamped her foot. "There's no excuse for me not to know."

"Looking back, I guess I sensed this coming," said Curt.

Her hands jammed into her hips. "What do you mean?"

"Jessey busted into my office, white as the uniform on her back, with the ol' chap right on her heels," said Curt. "He insisted he'd seen Regina, her parents, his parents, and Jake. And little Katrina, too. Stuffed animals. Toys. All whispering, all at the same time, but when they spotted him, they stopped. He tried to approach them, but for every step he took, they got farther away and more blurry."

As the scene played out in her head, Julie wrung her hands and tried to imagine the significance of each person or thing—the same game that she played as a kid envisioning the father missing from her life. That father had been just as indiscernible as Ken's visions. Maybe that's the way the mind works when one wants something so badly. She collapsed onto the chair and moaned, "Why is it that so many others are in his visions but not me?"

*   *   *

Edging out of medicated oblivion, Ken heard Julie. Like a gentle hand taking hold of his soul, her voice plucked him from the firmament and led the way back. He took comfort in her vigilance and called out, "I'm here, Julie. I'm coming. Wait for me." But his words went unheard, lodged within his breast.

He heard Curt describe their youth. Yes, my friend, days were carefree back then—sun-baked faces in the summertime and wind-blistered in the winter. We lived through good times and bad, and for some stupid reason nothing ever hurt and the bad never stuck, two boys shaking it all off like puppies shake off the rain, and life went on like nothing meant a good God damn. But then a terrible thing happened—we grew up. That's what kids do. New scars marked our hearts—everyday, so it seemed. For crying out loud, why doesn't fate just butt out?

Curt was right about Regina and he tried to warn me, but did I listen? From the outset she was clearly way out of my league—any man's league. Everything about her appearance and personality excelled beyond perfection, but that was all one big ruse. Out of the public eye, she had a mouth that put truck drivers to shame. And man, what an arm she had! The Red Sox should've picked her up. They would've gone all the way to the World Series! Curt dodged the ball—correction—glass that day when Regina got pissed at him; yet when it came to pegging me, she rarely missed her mark.

The darkness echoed with Julie's voice, "Why is it that so many others are in his visions and not me?"

Oh, but you are, my sweet Julie, cried Ken's soul. Damn this infernal darkness! She can't hear me! Julie! I'm here! Please! You must hear me!

His head filled with the memory of the way she had looked that winter night just after her mother was shot. He felt her leaning against his shoulder. They turned up collars to biting cold yet somehow, they were oblivious to it. Incredible how their voices floated upon the frozen air like the snowflakes that cavorted around the street lamps. Only the two of them were there that night, but their presence filled that deserted street more than a hundred, no a thousand could have. Oh, how surprised he was to hear his own laughter sparkle with hers in casualness known to those together for a very long time. In her cocoa eyes he discovered the sunshine of a summer's day. She made him feel like a man, a protector and confidant; something he hadn't felt in a very long time.

Even when you're not near, my dear Julie, your honeysuckle tresses flit across my face as if you were walking ahead of me at that very moment. You're my friend, my lover. There's times when I feel like I'm making love to you, but it's not so. It's ordinary words—your gift to me every day—that fulfill me. Oh, eyes open. Please. Open now!

His eyes flickered.

Casting off the accursed darkness was a grueling task, but this was it, Ken was determined to come back to the real world. His whole being needed to come back to Julie. And after he did that, he vowed to find a way to cast Regina to the ages. What he had with her was not love. Love is Julie!

His eyes blinked, filtering out the glare that swarmed with undulating shadows. Gradually, they opened. Curt was perched on the edge of the bed, facing Julie who was slouched on the chair next to the bed. There was no denying her tearstained face or the worry and lack of sleep that dragged her down. Thank goodness, she had Curt to lean on. Nice to see them getting along so well.

Ken's brows came together. That lavender sweat suit she's wearing…he'd seen it before. Elizabeth's. Why was Julie wearing her mother's clothes?

Filmy visions of falling, fire, and sirens rippled through his mind as he spotted the candy-colored clown lying on his chest. And it spotted him.

What have I done?

CANDY-COLORED CLOWN

CHAPTER NINE

"Ken," squealed Julie, her eyes riveting on the bed. "You're awake!" She leapt to her feet and lowered the bedrail. The candy-colored clown slipped off his chest and fell to the floor.

Parched lips mutilated his voice as he heaved, "J-J-Ju-lie?"

Tears of relief flooded down her cheeks as her hands cupped his face and she planted kisses on his forehead, cheeks, and lips. "I love, I love you," she blubbered.

He wanted to speak, but facial muscles balked and feeble coughs were inadequate in getting rid of ash, blood, and anesthesia that polluted his mouth. Medicated sleep tugged at him, threatening to draw him back into its ugly clutches.

"Good to have you back, ol' chap," said Curt with a fair degree of honesty. He wasn't about to add to the garbage heap his best mate faced. Stepping up to take Ken's pulse, Curt kicked the clown across the room like a football.

The pressure on Ken's wrist triggered the fight instinct, but his body refused to follow through. His lips twisted into a stutter, "Wh-where…?"

"I'll get the nurse to bring you a cup of ice chips," said Curt while pressing the call button. "That'll clear out your mouth."

Ken searched Julie's face. "Wh-where 'm I-I-I…?"

"Ste. Anne's Regional Hospital," she said.

He swallowed hard. "Wha..what happ…en…?"

The color drained from her face. "Accident," she stammered. "Just…an accident."

Curt cut in, "Talk about it later."

Julie glanced at Curt and nodded. "Right...uhm...right," she sputtered then looked back at Ken. "He's right. Talk later." She clutched Ken's hand against her cheek and added, "Nothing else matters right now. Only you."

Curt felt the side of his face twitch. Bringing the ol' chap back was the right thing to do, although...

The touch of her hand bolstered Ken. Yet his fingers felt powerless and cold against her burning skin. He gritted his teeth and tried to get up, but muscles were stiff and uncooperative. He glared at his left arm. What the heck? His eyes followed a line up to the ceiling then down to his left arm. Cast? Another one on his left leg? Alarm sheeted his face.

"Take it easy there, ol' chap," said Curt, grasping Ken's shoulder and looking into eyes wild and full of question. "You busted up your arm and leg. Looks like you got me and m'lady here keeping you in line for a while."

"But how..." started Ken.

Curt backed away as Penny picked up the call button and switched it off. "This is Nurse Penny," he said. "Anything you want, she'll get it, so don't be shy in asking." He winked at her and it surprised him just as much as her. Both faces colored.

"Uh, yes, uhm, just press this red button," said Penny, waving the call button in front of Ken. When she got a nod, she said, "It'll be right here on the bed near your right hand." She waited for another nod. "Okay, then." She studied Ken for a moment then patted his arm and gave Curt a fleeting glance. "Will that be all, Doctor Shirlington?"

His insides told Curt that he still had a chance with Penny. Take it. Don't let chances sluice down the hopper. But how to get Julie off his mind? It's just not fair to Penny. He cleared his throat. "Ice chips for the ol' chap?"

"I'm on it," she said.

Julie toyed with Ken's hair. "It's heaven to hear your voice." He looked so confused. She squeezed his hand and whispered, "Everything's going to be okay."

"What hap...?" started Ken, but then he began to hack.

She pulled a tissue out of the box and shielded his mouth with it until the coughing fit subsided.

"How…how did I get here?" he asked.

"Shshsh," she murmured, dabbing bloody mucous off his lips. "We have each other, that's all that counts."

Curt spun away, insides somersaulting. Happiness for them suddenly turned to devastation for him. How long could he go on like this?

"Curt…" sputtered Ken. "Thanks for being here for Julie."

"It's about time you woke up," gushed Elizabeth, knuckles rapping on the open door. Her other arm cradled a vase of yellow roses and baby's breath. Peter was right behind her. Both were dressed in blue jeans, cream-colored deck shoes, and flowery tee shirts that they had picked up while sailing in the Bahamas. Both had great tans.

Julie raced to Elizabeth, squealing, "He's awake! He's awake!"

Just before the two women clamped onto one another, Peter grabbed the vase of yellow roses. Setting it on the bed tray, he spouted, "Okay, you two, let's call a halt to all the giddiness." He was slender, five-foot-nine, born to Virginia money, but nobody could tell by looking at his clothes, sensible, not particularly expensive. Clean cut, he sported a boyish haircut. Julie inherited his honey-blond hair, although his had begun to gray. He was a skilled yachtsman, having sailed most of his life off Chesapeake Bay with his father who had died of a heart attack shortly after Peter returned from Vietnam. His mother was confined to a nursing home in Virginia, loosing the battle against Alzheimer's disease. Peter Blair rarely expressed an opinion, which came from years of residing in the Hanoi Hilton where he had learned to keep his mouth shut—a basic necessity for survival. Yet it would be off course for one to assume that he was uninformed or blasé. Heads of state sought him out for counsel. Only after conscientious scrutiny of their motives for requesting it, did Peter acquiesce. The child of the 60s was a dreamer, a romantic, an idealist, an ex POW.

Breaking from embrace, Julie shot a look skyward and issued up a silent prayer, thanking the Man Upstairs for not busting up what little family she had.

Elizabeth kissed Ken's forehead then gestured to the roses, her eye sparkling. "Here you go, my favorite son-in-law. Now, we're even for the ones you sent to me back when I was laid up."

Ken felt himself flush. At least he remembered that. As the smell of roses wafted up his nostrils, he glanced at Julie who smelled of ashes and soot, not the usual honeysuckle. Why was she wearing her mother's lavender sweat suit? For crying out loud, how did he end up in this hospital bed with his arm and leg in casts suspended by ropes from the ceiling?

"Good to see you rockin' and rollin' again," said Peter as he jabbed Ken's arm. "Nasty fall you took."

"Fall?" sputtered Ken, his brows knitting and his head wavering side to side.

Julie rubbed his hand. "Now, don't go getting yourself all upset."

"The ol' chap doesn't recall taking a header off the cliff," said Curt.

A distressed look blanketed Ken's face. "Cliff?"

Peter shuffled uneasily. He knew full well what it was like not to remember things. So much about Vietnam remained locked in his brain, but after going back there not so long ago, he learned that sometimes, it's best to remember to forget what's lies in the past.

"At least your safe made it through the fire," said Elizabeth.

"I dug it out of the ashes," said Peter.

Elizabeth chuckled. "And Ralph has made himself right at home at our place." She bent down and picked up the candy-colored clown face down on the floor.

"Ashes?" reiterated Ken, a blank look on his face.

The room fell silent. A moment or two passed then Peter spoke, "It's all a blank."

Julie took the clown from her mother and placed it in Ken's hand. "How about this?"

Dilated pupils locked Ken in its trance. His eyes widened. He remembered it—and yet—yet he didn't. His grip tightened. Powerless to stop the evil that was invading him, every last fiber within him railed. His thumb and forefinger squeezed an unyielding hand and then bore into the vibrant costume and the graininess beneath. His eyelids sagged and his grip loosened. The clown flopped onto his chest.

Julie nudged his shoulder. "Ken? You okay?" Her eyes shot alarm at Curt and then back at Ken. She nudged his shoulder again and cried, "Ken! What's the matter?"

Spiraling down into the dark abyss once again, Ken closed his eyes to the clown and savored the image of his beleaguered wife. It helped when her hand jostled his shoulder and he heard her call, "Ken! Ken!"

Curt's voice also rippled across Ken's brain. "Not to worry, m'lady. Medication's not entirely worn off. Ol' chap'll be back with us in two shakes of a lamb's tail."

Her lips touched his ear, her breath warm as she whispered, "I'll be waiting right here, my sweet love." Her voice gave him peace until moisture plopped on his forehead and he realized that she was crying—and he was powerless to give comfort.

***

Exactly when the candy-colored clown showed up, Ken couldn't recall. Rarely did Regina go out of her way to buy food or clothing for their only child, let alone a toy. Nanny Ellen took care of things, and what she didn't either he, his parents, or Regina's parents did. One thing he knew for sure, he wasn't the one who had brought that nasty thing into the manse. Katrina wouldn't've liked it at all. Yet there it was one day when he walked into her bedroom after work. That candy-colored clown stuck out like a sore thumb, propped up against the bed pillows in the midst of other stuffed toys of muted pastels. Though smaller in size, it seemed to tower above the rest, completely out of place—kind of like sticking a dead rose into the center of a fresh spring bouquet. Strange. It wasn't at all like Regina to tolerate the clashing of style and color.

Whether Katrina liked the candy-colored clown or not was hard to tell, since she wasn't allowed on the bed after it was made and the stuffed toys assembled there were never to be touched. Her mother slapped the child's little fingers if even tempted. "After all," Regina had insisted, "that brat has plenty of other playthings," which of course, included Ralph. She couldn't stand the fuzzy gray cat. She took a real hissy fit when Ken brought it home as a kitten. "That fleabag is *not* staying in *my* manse," she asserted, puffing up her chest and crossing her arms. "It's loaded with germs. Just look at it licking itself." Her face twisted up as she spat, "Disgusting."

Katrina and Ralph took to one another so well that Ken didn't have the heart to split them up, so for once, he put his foot down. "The cat stays."

Taken aback, Regina started, "But…"

He cut her off. "I will personally bring Ralph to be groomed every month."

Her hands dropped to her side.

"And," he emphasized, "I'll also see to it that the litter box gets changed every other day."

The muscles in her face sagged. "Litter box?"

His arms crossed and his chin elevated.

Regina turned ruddy. All at once, her jaws clenched and her eyes screwed into his, but he was determined not to be the one to break the stare-down. An eternity passed before she looked away. He felt himself droop with relief, but then noticed her scanning the room. She's going to throw something. The soft toys within her reach weren't good enough for her. Her fists tightened into balls and her entire frame bulged like a blowfish. She gave Ken a hard look that promised he's going to pay dearly for standing up to her. An unholy moment passed and then off she stormed.

Ralph seemed to understand the predicament and never made a fuss when it came to getting into the pet carrier. After several trips to the groomer, that cat knew without any doubt whatsoever where he was going and what was in store for him. Eventually, it became unnecessary to cage Ralph while in the car. He simply curled up either on the front passenger seat or in the back window if the sun wasn't too hot. Ken thought it neat, almost like having a dog in the car with him. "Holy mackerel, Ralph," he exclaimed once.

Ralph looked up with a pensive eye.

"Imagine if I brought home a dog?"

A feline click vibrated Ralph's upper lip.

"No dogs, bub, is that what you're trying to tell me?"

Ralph gave Ken a look.

"Oh, is that so? Forget about Regina and dogs, you rule the roost."

Ralph got up and arched his back against Ken's elbow. As laughter tumbled out of the car, pedestrians stopped to stare.

Quite a few meaningful conversations occurred while cruising back and forth to the groomer. Ken and Ralph often reveled about Regina's revulsion the day she had opened the front door for one of her uptown guests only to discover the latest gift that Ralph left to impress her. She went berserk and groused to Ken about it. He was unsympathetic. "You have no one else to blame but yourself. You're the one who insists on kicking Ralph outside—against my wishes."

Each time Ralph returned to Katrina from the groomer, well now, the reunion between child and feline was like finding one's long lost brother, sister, or child.

CANDY-COLORED CLOWN

CHAPTER TEN

A week later, Ken was released from the hospital. With him by her side, Julie found that living with Mom and Dad wasn't all that bad. The fifth-floor, three-bedroom condominium on 158 River Street in Brighton was spacious enough and constantly smelled of roses—Dad made sure of it. Right after he and Mom moved there, he had arranged weekly floral deliveries.

Lying with her head on Ken's chest, Julie listened to his heartbeat and his low, even breathing. She drank up his essence as she fought off sleep and waited for him to drift off. The only thing that mattered in life was that they were together, safe and sound. With a smile on her face, she fell asleep only to awaken to sun-streaked, pale yellow walls, cotton gingham sheets, and his chocolate eyes staring into hers. She vowed to do everything within her power to make him whole again, not only in body, but also in spirit. He had gotten awfully thin, and his tan wasn't as deep as it usually was at this time of year. She got great pleasure from seeing the peace that materialized on his face whenever he sat in the living room recliner near the sliding glass doors and gazed at the Boston skyline beyond the balcony windows. Boston at night glowed blue and gold.

The weather for the most part was characteristic of June in Boston with the occasional afternoon or evening shower. Even in the rain, a slew of day-sailors practiced maneuvers or raced around giant orange buoys on the Charles River. Ken wasn't a sailor, though it seemed just by watching, he got the same satisfaction out of it as the day-sailors.

Ralph settled in better than expected and never once sought escape from the condo. If anything, he made the balcony his domain, his personal window to the world. When pigeons, gulls, and the occasional peregrine falcon soared past the open screened window, the hunter instinct consumed him. Spluttering and back rippling continued long after the elusive prey disappeared. Rain coming in the often-overlooked window was the only thing that sent the feline hot footing to drier quarters.

Julie was reluctant to tell Ken about the explosion and fire of which he had no memory; but when she did, surprisingly enough, he took it all with a grain of salt. None of it seemed to have an impact on him. She figured that the medication he was taking caused that. Nevertheless, she got the impression that he was more than content to be living at Mom and Dad's than he ever was in Cohasset. Her parents had a grounding effect on him, which allowed the mention from time to time of her condition, and that pleased Julie to no end. It was so awesome to hear his boisterous laughter when Mom taunted, "I'm going to be the grandmother from hell. Just wait and see. That kid's gonna get spoiled rotten." Julie flushed with joy, unable to remember the last time Ken reacted so lightheartedly. It brought tears to her eyes.

Peter set a good example for Ken. The ex MIA, who had lost his right hand just above the wrist in Vietnam, related his war experience—what he remembered—and how he had thought he lost everything in his life. "Four and a half years MIA," he said, staring at his prosthetic hand. "I turned up in a village somewhere in Cambodia. No clue how I got there. Didn't know my name. I'm told I was tortured. Brainwashed. Had malaria and other maladies. Didn't come out of the mental funk for a long time. Doctors at the VA Hospital in Virginia were surprised when I did. Worse thing I did when I got my mind back was not coming back to Bethie. I was too convinced that she wouldn't want a sick cripple hanging 'round. Didn't have guts enough to come back to us."

"You're here now," said Ken.

"Yeah," mused Peter. "So are you."

Ken said a quiet, "Yeah."

"A newspaper article brought me back, you know," said Peter.

"Newspaper article," echoed Ken.

Peter nodded. "Yup. Report of a bank robbery in Brighton where bystanders got shot. Lo and behold, there was Bethie's name. Never once gave it a second thought. Just took off—flew to her side, just like that. Amazing thing, she still wanted me. And I discovered I had a nineteen-year-old daughter to boot! Life don't get better than that!"

"I'll say," said Ken, wishing that beloved Katrina was alive.

"Sadly, I made a second, almost fatal mistake," said Peter.

"What's that?" asked Ken.

"I went back to Nam," said Peter. "That's when it finally sunk into this fat head of mine that tomorrow is promised to no one. There were times when I was lost in the jungle—not only the real jungle, mind you, but also the one in my head. I swore that if I ever found my way out I'd return to my sweet, morning eyes and our darling daughter and live life to the fullest, one blessed day at a time."

Little did Peter or anyone else know that life was about to throw them another curve ball.

***

Julie avoided all talk about what she and Ken were going to do about a home. Yet she worried. Were they going to rebuild? Buy an existing house? Mom won't hear of them moving into an apartment temporarily. If she had her way, Julie and Ken would be stay with her and Dad indefinitely.

Whatever the case, Julie decided that another car would lighten the load, plus, she wanted her own vehicle before the baby was born. Long before the fire turned her car into a hunk of metal, she had her eye on a Lumina minivan. The only decision pertained to which color it should be. Ken told her to make up her mind and go get it. Then the fire. So much for a trade-in.

Emma had given Julie the car that burned the first Christmas they had known each other. It used to be Margi's.

Times were pretty rough back then. Julie had just ended an abusive relationship and didn't know how she was ever going to put her life back together again, but mother hen Emma didn't let Julie stay down in the dumps. That was before the robbery—and before Ken.

The day that Julie and Elizabeth set out to buy the minivan, they planned to stop at a car dealership in Brookline, down the street from Fenway Park. Afterwards they were to have lunch with Emma, who lived on the other side of Brighton. Julie had talked to the old woman on the phone several times since the fire, but they hadn't seen each other. The three women were looking forward to kicking back, catching up, and enjoying a meal of traditional Italian fare. Their mouths watered with thoughts of lasagna, eggplant, and sauce—to say nothing of delectable deserts that Emma concocted without benefit of recipe.

Margi usually showed up sooner or later, but that wasn't in the cards this day. She and her family were off on vacation somewhere in New Hampshire. Julie had made Emma promise not to tell Margi about the fire and all. Margi had her own ups and downs—most of her own making. For her, life was one catastrophe after another. She blew the simplest little thing out of proportion. Take, for instance, running out of mayonnaise for the kids' lunch at ten o'clock on a Sunday night. Nothing was right with the world until mild-mannered husband Evan got dressed and trekked out into the dark, wind-swept night to find an open convenience store. Well then, Evan got home and all was swell, right? Wrong. Margi fussed and fumed that he had paid much too much for the mayonnaise. Angst built to fever pitch until she was totally convinced that they were surely going to go to the poor farm—all over a crummy jar of mayonnaise. Yes, everything happens to Margi.

In the parking garage beneath the condominium high-rise, Julie skipped around the car and waited for her mother to come and unlock the passenger side door. She was wearing a seahorse print tunic, turquoise pull-on leggings, half socks, and white slip-on sneakers, all of which Elizabeth had purchased while Ken was hospitalized. Neither woman worried about leaving Peter and Ken behind, since the men had hunkered down for a rip-roaring game of chess long before their wives set one foot out the door.

"Your father's going to miss Ken when you two leave," chuckled Elizabeth while sliding the key in and out of the lock. She had on a green seersucker shorts outfit with white leather sandals. "Although it appears that Ken isn't in a big hurry to go back to Cohasset anyway."

"Funny, I got that same impression," said Julie, opening the door then jumping into the passenger seat. "I'm hoping against hope that we can start over some place different."

"Any idea where?" asked Elizabeth as she skirted the car.

"I don't care," said Julie. "Just some place without memories for Ken."

"Memories can certainly drag down a person," said Elizabeth, getting in the car. She pulled the door shut and started the engine. "Look what it did to you, me, and your father—not to mention Tommy Gray." As she backed out of the parking space and drove to the exit, she thought, *still seems like only yesterday, Tommy Gray drowned.*

Julie pondered a few things that she and her mother had been through, the years, just the two of them, the loneliness, the secrets. No matter the circumstance or how far away they were from each other, somehow, someway, they still had each other. Well, secrets were out, and loneliness was gone, now that Dad came back. Relationships budded and blossomed. And it was all because her mother was not one to give up. She glanced at her and said, "Wish I was as brave as you."

Elizabeth tossed back her head and laughed. "Take it from me, a person is as brave as he or she has to be whenever vital issues are at stake."

"Ain't that the truth," said Julie, recalling that she had thought of nothing but saving Ken while teetering over that precipice. Just then the sun hit her square in the face. She shoved down the visor and rolled down the window to suck in the southwest breeze freshened by a thundershower last evening. The day exuded possibility.

"Just listen to the birds," said Elizabeth. "Rhododendrons look pretty happy, too."

Julie squinted at the crimson, lavender, and white blossoms unable to decide which color she liked the best. She wondered if a cat was hiding under any of the bushes the way Ralph hid after the fire.

Traffic slowed to a crawl as they approached a construction site where two roads converged into one. A crane on the opposite corner was poised to knock down the shell of a brick structure defaced with spray-painted curlicue graffiti. "I'll be so glad when this project is done," fussed Elizabeth as a whirlwind of dust and trash came at them. "Roll up your window," she said as she did hers. She switched on the air-conditioning as a cop blew his whistle, pointed an orange-gloved finger at her, and directed her into single lane traffic. Hitching her chin, she muttered, "As if we had any other choice."

A short distance beyond, she inched around a yellow backhoe with a red and yellow triangle attached to the rear end that jutted out into the street. She smiled and waved at a short, foreman-looking man whose stomach rolled over his belt like a mass of rising bread dough. The sleeves of his grimy navy-blue tee shirt had been cut off to flaunt sun-baked biceps.

"Flirt," said Julie.

"What?" postured Elizabeth. "That guy doesn't turn you on?"

"Oh, come on, Mom," said Julie a singsong voice.

"Dear daughter of mine," jabbed Elizabeth. "You don't think that's a macho piece of flesh?"

Julie snickered. "I think he thinks so."

"No doubt about that," agreed Elizabeth while glancing into the rearview mirror. "The guy's checking out the chick in the car behind us."

Julie crooked her neck and squinted out the side mirror. The man was bent down a bit, butt crack quite evident, gawking into the window of the car behind them. She glanced at her mother and shielded half her mouth to whisper, "You're jealous. I can tell."

Merriment shook the car and lasted until Elizabeth pulled into the car dealership. She inched past rows of high-end vehicles, past moderately priced vehicles and trucks, and came to a stop in front of the minivans. "Don't look now, but here comes a salesman," she said as they got out of the car and pretended not to notice the smartly dressed man in a casual gray suit, pale yellow button-down shirt open at the collar and beige deck shoes.

"Mom, he's not wearing socks," whispered Julie. Her hand squelched a giggle.

"Shush," puffed Elizabeth. She turned, a toothy grin plastered on her face.

"But Mom," insisted Julie, flexing her spine, "his anklebones look so funny!"

"Good afternoon," driveled the salesman. His opal eyes sparked with deviltry as his hand extended far ahead of his body. "I'm Neil Ebreg. Can I be of any assistance to you lovely ladies today?"

"Elizabeth Blair," she said, taking hold of his hand while Julie sauntered down the row of minivans. Morning coffee thickened his breath. "My daughter over there, Julie Waters, is interested in a minivan."

"Well, let's see what we can do, shall we?" said Neil, trotting after Julie.

Elizabeth waved away his coffee breath and followed.

"Nice weather we're having," he said.

When Julie paid him no mind, Elizabeth said, "Absolutely."

Neil slowed to let Elizabeth catch up. "Better than Florida," he said.

"Why's that?" she asked.

"Just got back from sport fishing off Clearwater," he said. "Eighty-five degrees at eight in the morning plus humidity to match. It was blistering on the water!"

"Is that right," she said. "My husband and I sailed out of Clearwater to the Dry Tortugas this past May."

"How 'bout that," he said. "Small world."

The two went on and on until the subject was more than adequately dissected and were quite surprised to see Julie leaning back against a blue Lumina minivan, arms crossed, eyeballing them.

"Looks like you've weeded down your choices," said Elizabeth.

Julie uncrossed her arms and stood upright. "It's either this one or that white one over there," she said, pointing. "What do you think? I really like this color blue, but if I get it, it might seem as though I'm having a boy, but I'm positive I'm having a girl. It just isn't right to put a baby girl in blue."

Elizabeth elbowed Neil. "You wouldn't happen to have a pink minivan running around the lot, would you?"

"Well, I, er," stammered Neil, his thumb and forefinger gripping his chin as his eyes scanned the lot. Where the heck was he supposed to find a pink Lumina? For that matter, a pink anything? A custom paint job's the only alternative. Cursing pink, he turned to Elizabeth and picked up the twinkle in her eye. "Pulling my leg, now," he said. "Aren't you?"

When Elizabeth and Neil roared with laughter, Julie put them off with the wave of her hand. "Come on, you guys. Cut it out."

Elizabeth shrugged; and Neil—being the sharp-as-a-tack individual that he was—spotted her eyelashes flutter ever so slightly, which set off an electric charge that zipped through him all the way down to his toes. Adjusting his suit jacket, he tried to look cool.

"This one here," said Julie, stepping over to the white Lumina. She gave it sidelong scrutiny, lips jutting out into a tightly packed pucker. Her head cocked to one side. "Uh-huh," she said with a purposeful nod. "I'll take this one."

Neil's mouth dropped. "Just like that?"

"Julie Waters knows what she likes when she sees it," bragged Elizabeth.

Julie gave her mother a high five, spouting, "Like mother like daughter."

Neil gave them the once over. "Say, what're your names again?"

Julie squinted at him. "Uhm, she's Elizabeth Blair and I'm Julie Waters."

"Blair. Waters," pondered Neil aloud. "Waters." His thumb and forefinger pinched his bottom lip. He looked up. "Waters." He looked down. "That name sounds extremely familiar." His brows fused as his brain shifted into overdrive. "Ah, yes," he spewed as his hand whacked the side of his head. "I knew a Gina Waters a ways back."

Julie felt as if someone had punched her in the stomach. She exchanged a furtive glance with her mother, both having bad vibrations about what they were about to hear.

"Whew, what a looker," exclaimed Neil, his hand jiggling as if scalded on a hot stove. His eyes snagged onto a 747 climbing the sky over the Prudential Building as if Regina's picture were plastered across the side of it. "Came in here with a dark-haired lady's man...ponytail, diamond earring, the whole ball of wax." His aversion towards men sporting such things was more than a bit obvious. Neil wasn't anywhere near as gaudy as Jake—well, that's not taking into account his sockless feet. "Those two had eyes for each other—plain as the nose on your face," said Neil. He bit his tongue so as not to spout out, *that is, in a snobby sort of way.* "Come to think of it, the guy's name was Waters too. Jake Waters."

Julie thought she was going to explode. Damn you, Jake! Fooling around with your own brother's wife! She circled the white Lumina to hide her reaction. Curt had said that Regina ran off with another guy. Was that guy Jake? Was it Jake who had nearly killed Ken? And if it was Jake...well, what's to be done about it now? The truth might very well tear the little family she had always dreamed of having to bits. Best to keep this under wraps—a secret. "I thought you two have no secrets," she had said to Curt in the hospital.

"Look," Curt had said, "if you saw that poor chap all beat up the way I did and how devastated he was over Regina taking off with little Katrina... He adored the wee one, you know. He lived and breathed for her. And then the plane crash..."

Meanwhile, Neil was trying to shake off the image of that doll Gina in the sack with that horny gigolo. "Those two really ate up the snazzy sports jobs around here," he said. "Had to have all the bells and whistles, too." He ran his right deck shoe across the blacktop while thinking, cripes, money was no object to those two. Really made living large on a regular basis for ol' Neil baby. He tapped the toe of his shoe a couple of times then with a slight hitch to the chin, said, "Wonder whatever happened to those two?"

On the opposite side of white Lumina, Julie pretended not to hear, but felt relieved, for some unknown reason, that Neil didn't know the circumstances surrounding the plane crash. It's all in the past. Let it go.

Neil heaved a sigh and thought, oh, well. An easy sale today certainly fills the bill. "Come on, ladies, let me take you back to the office and get the paperwork over and done with. You can pick up that new minivan of yours before closing tomorrow."

Paperwork finished, the two women headed back to Elizabeth's car. "Seems like Regina and Jake were carrying on a bit, wouldn't you say?" asked Elizabeth.

"Yeah," muttered Julie as she plopped into the passenger seat. She wished her mother would let it rest. She rolled her eyes, thinking that Ken must've found out. Her stomach somersaulted. Maybe he didn't trust her. Did he think she was going to have an affair, too? No wonder he fell apart when she told him she was pregnant.

Elizabeth got into the car, started it, and steered out of the dealership. Heading towards Emma LaRosa's, she stopped for a red light. She glanced at her daughter then back at the road, saying, "Wouldn't surprise me none if Ken stumbled onto those two."

Julie squinted at her mother.

Elizabeth glanced at her daughter again and got caught in her stare. "What?"

"Great minds think alike," said Julie.

Elizabeth snorted. "We do think alike at times, don't we?"

Julie scrunched up her nose and said, "Weird, huh?"

Elizabeth shrugged it off. The light turned green and she stepped on the gas. Clearing the intersection, she said, "From the way Ken obviously cared about Regina, her having an affair with his own brother must've devastated him."

"And if they ran off and took Katrina with them…whew! Then the plane crash? That had to be the last straw," said Julie. "That little girl meant the world to Ken."

Elizabeth let that sink in for a moment and then said, "Wow."

"You can say that again," said Julie. She felt like throwing up. "Oh, my God!"

"What?" gasped Elizabeth. Her daughter looked like she had seen a ghost.

"The milk and cookies," cried Julie. "A day or so before the fire, I walked into the kitchen and on the bar were two glasses of milk and a cookie next to each one. There were two butterfly barrettes on one of the bar stools!"

***

When was the first time Ken suspected that Regina was having an affair? When she went off to a cousin's wedding down south with her parents? Perhaps. On that very day, after they supposedly had left, he witnessed Leo and Gretchen going into their favorite ice cream shop in Brighton. He felt like confronting them or at least calling the cousin to find out if a wedding was really going to take place. But he had let it go, reasoning that Regina needed time away from the manse.

There had been other times as well. He certainly should've caught on that time he caught her sneaking in at four in the morning with smudged make-up and disheveled clothes—not at all like the prim and proper Regina. Quizzed about her whereabouts at such an unseemly hour, she summarily rebuffed him. "None of you fucking business where I go, whom I'm with, or what I'm doing!" She hurled her shoes at him, one at a time, the ones she had taken off to sneak into the manse.

Whenever the dawning had come didn't matter. Ken knew—that's all there was to it—and that set him to pacing in the middle of endless nights beset with angry rain. The gale that raged outside existed, however, only in his head, howling, swirling, flogging him. Deluges scoured the patio and crooked fingers of lightning drilled into the backyard, the cliffs, and the turbulent sea. Thunder shook the manse, lights flickered, and the great room flashed white. He yanked the curtains together, switched off the patio lights, and paced.

Chill got into his bones, so he lit the fireplace. Flames swooshed across gas logs, setting his face aglow, accentuating his ghostly eyes that rolled round and around in their sockets.

He sought sanctuary at the bar, in glasses full of single malt Scotch. Consumption increased with each successive night. When at last the alcohol took affect, he gestured with drink in hand towards the ceiling. "I tried to be what you wanted me to be." His voice was slushy. "What more can I do?" His pleadings lost within the thickness of the walls, his eyes dissected the ceiling. A low voice within him rumbled, "There you are, asleep in that king size bed that only I'm supposed to be sharing with you." He shook a balled fist at the ceiling and bayed, "If only I knew what it is that you want!" He spun around and hurled his glass into flames that danced like demons. "What words can I say that will make you love me? What does it take for a man to have a loving wife, for a child to have a decent mother and family life?"

He guzzled down another drink or two and then staggered off to that dreary bedroom at the back corner of the manse. Rarely did he switch on a light and by no means did he ever open the heavy brocade drapes that covered the windows and hid French doors, for beyond was the black and blue sea and Minot's light, choking in the hands of low storm clouds. All of the chaos existed only in his mind.

A new day dawned and Katrina was there, arms about his neck, tiny whispers in his ear, there's no such thing as loving too much. Only that quelled the storm. Night came again. Again and again it came. And then the night of the plane crash. Drinking and pacing stopped, not because Regina was gone. No. Katrina was gone—that's why.

As days blurred into nocturnal years, Ken was as dead as if the cold hand of death had also taken him. Oh, how he wished it had.

Then Julie came along and once again, the sun rose in his heart. For a short while, he breathed in life, but then she got pregnant, and all the storms of yesterday rained down upon his being with a vengeance.

CANDY-COLORED CLOWN

CHAPTER ELEVEN

Jake and Regina's affair distracted Julie from the pungent odor of garlic, oregano, and fennel sausages that permeated Emma's kitchen. Plunked down at the table, elbows planted with balled fists propping her chin, she brooded, "How can Ken and Jake be so different? Brothers. The same blood!"

"Heaven's to Betsy, dear, it certainly is beyond me," puffed Emma as she placed a casserole of piping hot stuffed shells onto a white metal trivet in the center of the table. Her slate eyes, once ebony-rich, sparkled like the wintry night, and the aura of honeysuckle, characteristic of the five-foot woman, encircled her like a summer breeze. A green apron with pink and blue pansies and dark green rickrack protected her short sleeve navy dress with white cuffs and Peter Pan collar. She wore navy blue stockings and leather flats and silvery-blue bifocals that blended with her recently permed salt-and pepper hair. Silver jewelry included a crucifix that dangled from her neck when she leaned over to uncover the basket of warm rolls.

"Gee whiz," chirped Elizabeth while uncorking a bottle of merlot. "A horde of storming paratroopers could eat off this table and there'd still be plenty of leftovers to send the Pine Street Inn!"

Seeming not to hear, Emma stretched a kink out of her back. But she heard. At her advanced age, her hearing was still remarkably keen. Emma derived tremendous pleasure out of making a nice meal. Her four children were married with children of their own and with Seth gone, well, there's just no one left to cook for, so limiting the amount of food for company was not in the cards. She chucked two apple-shaped potholders into the pockets of her apron then out of habit picked up the skirt of the apron to wipe off her hands. "My Seth was the youngest of eight—six boys and two girls," she said. "Not one blessed brother, or sibling for that matter, was like another." She inspected the table. "Why, my Seth—he was the youngest, you know—he was a worker bee with his first step."

Elizabeth set up two glasses and began to pour wine into them. "None for me," said Julie, patting her belly.

"There's milk in the refrigerator," said Emma, though she rarely drank milk. Alcohol had never touched her lips. She stepped over to the gas range, picked up the percolator simmering on a back burner, and poured coffee into an ancient flowered teacup. The matching saucer had disappeared some time ago. Just after Seth died, the teacup had fallen off the counter and the handle had broken off. Emma continued to use the cup like that, refusing to part with it, until one day, Margi blustered, "For Pete's sake, Ma, why on God's green earth are you drinking from that decrepit thing?" When she received no answer, she blasted, "Evan!" Her husband hot-footed it into the house from the backyard where he was playing touch football with the kids and, to make a long story short, glued the handle back onto the cup.

Emma set the coffee cup down on the placemat between Julie and Elizabeth then lowered her creaky bones onto the chair. "My Seth had an older brother, Vincenzo," she said. She picked up the basket of rolls and passed it to Elizabeth. "That man never held a steady job in his entire life—not that he was a bad person, mind you. He just had other things on his mind. He almost became a priest. Well, then there was Rom, he was a cop—not at all like Armand." She leaned over, her eyes ping ponging between Elizabeth and Julie as she whispered, "All tied up in the Mafia and such." She straightened, pursed her lips, and nodded with certainty.

"Wow. Mafia," said Julie breathlessly as she dug into the casserole of stuffed shells. Setting down the serving spoon, she glanced at Emma who was floating off into some distant time and place. Such incidents came and went, depending on the subject matter. Judging from the look on the old woman's face, wherever she ended up had to be quite peaceful. The first time Julie had seen this happen was the day after Emma rescued her from that pervert, Jim Martin. Emma had been playing the Rhapsody on a Theme of Paganini by Rachmaninoff on the piano, staring at aged sheet music that she didn't need and drinking up the melodic essence as though it were fine wine. That's when Julie decided to let the music take her away as well, which, of course, allowed her to discover her own tranquil world—one in which she never before traveled. When the music stopped, her insides cried out for more. After several moments, she took a deep breath and sighed, "That's the most beautiful thing I've ever heard."

"What did you say?" asked Elizabeth as she picked up the salad bowl and handed it to Julie. Getting no answer, she squinted at her daughter whose face possessed absolute serenity. "Julie," she said and nudged her daughter's forearm with the bowl.

"Huh," murmured Julie, casting off the dream state. Glazed eyes slowly focused.

Elizabeth exchanged glances with Emma. She set down the bowl and said, "It was part of the times."

"What was?" asked Julie.

"The Mafia," said Elizabeth. "Emma said that Seth's brother Armand was tied up with the Mafia and then I said, 'it was part of the times.'"

Julie hitched her chin and noticed Emma wink. Her face reddened. The old woman knew that she had a secret place, too!

"Paolo and Angelo were politicians in their own right," said Emma, dishing salad into Julie's dish and then some into her own. "Paolo was a barber. Poor thing, he wasn't too quick, you know. Yet if a person wanted to know what people were thinking or how to deal with them or some other sort of thing, Paolo the barber was the man to see. He played a big part in getting Angelo elected to the U.S. Senate."

"The Senate, no less," said Elizabeth.

"Now don't go getting excited," spouted Emma. "Angelo got killed in a car wreck before he even left for Washington. That was before my time, but Seth told me that Angelo was slicker than a back alley cat on a rainy night."

Elizabeth reeled with laughter and had all she could do to keep from spitting out a mouthful of lentil soup. She grabbed the napkin off her lap and jammed it against her lips.

Julie giggled. "You certainly have a way of putting things, Em!"

"Auch, you two," said Emma, waving off the silly guests. "Used to think that the first half of the 1900s were times of extremes; but now that I think of it, that's just the way things go. Even now there's good times and bad, very good people and very bad ones at that. Then there's us ordinary folks caught up in the middle, trying to do what is right and more often than not, going about it in all the wrong way."

Julie put an elbow on the table and braced a closed fist against her jaw. The skin on her cheek wrinkled. "Yeah," she spewed. "Jake's one of the bad ones."

"Why do you say that, dear?" asked Emma.

After revealing suspicions about Jake running off with Regina, Julie said, "He's such a jerk. Know what else he did? He grabbed Ken's chin and jostled it around and…"

"What?" cut in Elizabeth. "When did he do that?"

"While Ken was in the coma," said Julie. "Can you believe anyone would do such a thing?"

"Jake isn't a very likeable person," said Emma.

"You don't know the half of it," puffed Julie. She turned to Elizabeth. "Let's not tell Ken about Jake and Regina or about Jake doing that to him, at least until after the casts are off and Ken's feeling better, okay?"

Elizabeth raised her eyebrows. "Gonna have to keep an eye on that Jake."

"I don't want him around Ken," said Julie. "Period!"

***

The afternoon flew by and it was almost five o'clock by the time Julie and Elizabeth walked into the condo. Curt was

136

there, which didn't surprise them none, although he was a bit earlier than usual. Running outfit, sneakers, and stubbly chin publicized that he had taken the day off.

Elizabeth and Peter rushed off to a sailing function in Charlestown while Julie set about making Ken comfortable and then cleaned up the remnants of a day that had seen two men left to their own devices. She was at the kitchen sink, scrubbing dishes, when Curt moseyed into the kitchen and said, "Ol' chap's drifted off."

"Good to see him doing that naturally again," said Julie while rinsing a crystal platter that had teemed with brownies when she had left to go car shopping, that morning. They both knew that naturally meant without passing out from single malt. "Help yourself to coffee," she said.

"Make sure he takes his medication a half an hour before bedtime," said Curt, stepping over to the shelf where a space-saver coffee maker hung below a cabinet. He unhooked a mug designed with a lighthouse from a wooden mug tree and slid the decanter off the hotplate. "As long as the ol' chap is laid up, I want him getting plenty of rest." He filled the mug and replaced the decanter. Gripping the mug with fingertips, he drew it to his lips and blew away steam. He took his coffee black and strong, the way the Blair's did. Following Julie's every move over the rim of the mug, he thought, m'lady's a breath of fresh air in my hollow existence. Why can't I find someone like her? He took a sip of coffee and burned his tongue. Should've called Penny.

"Jake's the man Regina ran off with," said Julie.

Curt sucked in a mouthful coffee and hacked as it burned all the way down his gut. Bloody Jake, he thought and shook his head. Was this Regina garbage ever going to end? His eyes rolled along the ceiling while his hand raked through daily stubble. Nothing good ever comes out of shagging a chained vixen— major reason to keep the lid on errant desires for m'lady. Can't do that to my best mate. History repeating itself and all that. A short cough cleared his windpipe and he took a shallow breath. "I had suspicions that Jake figured into the mix," he said.

"It was him," insisted Julie while drying the platter. She stepped over to the hutch and attempted to put the platter on the top shelf.

"Here, let me help you with that," said Curt, setting down his coffee mug. He took the platter, set it in place, then turned and wagged a finger at her. "You shouldn't be stretching like that in your condition."

Her face flushed as her hand dropped to her abdomen. "I'm beginning to show, huh?"

Curt smiled. "Won't be long before you feel the flutter of life."

"Can't wait," she said. "Who do you think the baby will look like?"

"Hopefully you," he said without thinking.

She gave him a look.

"Or Ken," he quickly added. "Or maybe the both of you. Could look like somebody of a previous generation. My own dear Mum reminds me every time she calls me from Florida that I look just like my great, great granpappy." He chuckled and peered at Julie now braced against the kitchen table, white as a sheet. "What's wrong?"

"What if the baby looks like Katrina?" she said. A shiver raced through her. Gooseflesh spiked.

"She looked more like Ken than Regina," said Curt.

"That's one good thing," she said then added, "I guess. But who's to say that my baby won't look just the same? You know as well as I do, Ken will freak out again if that happens."

"For sure," was all Curt could say. He put his hand on hers.

As Julie looked down at his hand, sorrow replaced trepidation. A deep seeded ache for the child she had never known grew within her. Yet, it seemed as if she knew all there was to know about Katrina. "How unfair for a young life to be cut so short," she murmured. "How heartless of Regina to carry on with another man…having a child so young."

Curt dropped her hand and quickly distanced himself from her. How heartless for me to carry on like this, he thought, what with ol' chap's wee one in the oven. He crumpled onto a chair at the kitchen table. "So, uhm…" He cleared his throat. "How did you find out that it was Jake?"

Julie lifted the plug out of the sink and watched the dishwater spiral down the drain. "He and Regina bought cars where I got my minivan." She picked up the dishtowel and wiped down the sink. "The salesman spilled the beans. He didn't know my connection to them."

Curt scratched the back of his neck and tried not to look at Julie, but her movements were as addictive as a Longfellow poem. "Didn't know about the fire in Cohasset?" he asked.

"He's been in Florida, sport fishing," she said while shaking out the dishtowel. She draped it over the hook below the sink then turned. She met his stare, and it struck her funny how he instantly uncrossed his arms and looked away. Her eyes sought his that remained focused on his coffee mug as he went to the coffee pot. While pouring, he kept his back to her. Why didn't he turn around? she wondered. Sloughing it off, she sagged onto the chair that he had been sitting on and braced her elbows on the table. Her hands cradled her chin as she said, "I need to know more about Jake."

Unsure if it was safe to turn around, Curt stared at the steam curling off his coffee and asked, "Like what?"

Her shoulders heaved. "Geez, I don't know." Her eyes fixed on his back. He's awfully preoccupied, she thought, but not with Jake. Something else. She sighed. "One thing I can't figure out."

Curt sucked in air and then exhaled, "What's that?"

"Somewhere along the line," she said, "I got the impression that Regina didn't want much to do with Katrina. If that's true why take Katrina? Jake definitely isn't into kids."

"That woman wanted nothing to do with that cherub," spewed Curt. "She took the wee one just to give ol' chap more pain. Leaving wasn't good enough for Regina; she had to stab him in the heart with something that would make him bleed till his final day."

"Why did she hate him so much?" asked Julie.

"She couldn't mold him into what she wanted, that's my guess," he said.

"And Jake was the kind of man she wanted?" asked Julie.

"My guess again," said Curt.

"What about Jake and Ken?" asked Julie. "Were they close as kids?"

"Jake wasn't on the scene back then."

"Not on the scene?" she cried. "What do you mean by that?"

His fingernails scraped back and forth across the mug's lighthouse pattern and said, "He just showed up one day."

In high-pitched voice, she echoed, "Just showed up?"

"Right out of the blue," he said, turning, about to return to the chair where he had been sitting. Seeing Julie on the chair, he set the coffee mug on the table, stretched big and wide then bent and touched his toes, bouncing several times to release pent-up emotion. He straightened and raked his fingers through chin stubble. He took three cleansing breaths. Then he said, "I knew about Patty and Richard's flight from East Germany in the late fifties, but there was no mention of Jake. Blew me away when he showed up eight or so years ago. Seems that during the escape, the East German police snatched Jake right out of Patty's arms. Much as it was news to me, it was even worse news to the ol' chap. He thought Jake was crude and disrespectful, especially to his parents, but whenever he got on Jake's case, Patty got all worked up, so ol' chap backed off. "

Julie's mind raced. A question festered, growing into boil that needed to be popped. Ignoring it, its pus might continue to infect Ken's already pitiful existence. The words, what if, formed on her lips. Her frightened eyes drilled into Curt. "It's eating at you, too, isn't it?"

His eyes bugged out. Holy cow! The wench has gone and put two and two together and discovered I'm head over heels in love with her.

"I know what you're thinking," charged Julie.

"I-I," stammered Curt, casting her a sidelong glance. Horror sheeted her face. Suddenly, he couldn't draw air.

"Neither one of us has nerve enough to say it out loud," she raved.

His face drooped and his palms began to sweat. Vomit bubbled in his gut.

Her hands flailed as she put forth the question, "What if Jake isn't Ken's brother?"

***

Ken awoke from his nap with a start, Jake on his mind. As he glanced about the living room to get his bearings, a day, more than eight years ago crossed his mind. His mother had telephoned. "Come for dinner tonight, will you, dear?" Her voice was urgent. She wasn't about to take no for an answer.

"What's going on?" Ken had asked.

"Nothing, nothing," she had twittered. "It's just that…that…well, your father and I…well, we don't get to see you much now that you have your own place."

"But I was over there day before yesterday," he protested.

"Well," she stammered, "Your father and I miss having you around."

Ken had glanced at his watch, saying, "Was planning to meet Curt for a game of racquetball…"

"You can't make it," she had cut in. "Curt won't mind." Her voice got whiny, "Please, Kenny."

His insides flip-flopped. His mother never whined and only called him Kenny when something had her riled up. "Be over after work."

She had met him at the door, hands clutching the way they did when something was eating at her. Her eyes darted from him to the kitchen, back and forth. She gave him a hurried peck on the cheek and then took off for the kitchen. Something was burning.

When Ken got to the kitchen, his mother was racing to the sink with a pot of scorched potatoes that made the air acrid and hard to breathe. She turned the water on full blast. Steam billowed and the window above the sink fogged. Ken couldn't recall the last time his mother burned food.

141

He turned off the stove burner and then squinted at his father sitting at the kitchen table, looking old, frail, and at wits end. Alarm raced through Ken. He'd never seen his father like that. Then a slick, pinhead of a stranger sitting across the table caught his eye.

An ominous foreboding washed over Ken as his father and the stranger got to their feet. He shook his father's hand, and they patted each other on the shoulder, a custom since his early teens. It had been a long time since they hugged, but at that moment Ken had a strong desire to do just that.

"This is Jake," said his father, a quick hand gesture toward the stranger, and then he sagged onto a chair.

Ken didn't expect the manner in which the stranger latched onto his hand, casual and too buddy-buddy, elevating hands in a way that seemed customary to a secret cult of some sort. "How's it shaking, man?" Jake had asked, much too artificially.

Giving a tentative nod, Ken had pulled away. "Good," he had said.

He frowned at his mother clumsily putting supper together. Usually she sailed around the kitchen, singing an old German tune. Usually everything was on the table the moment he arrived. Tonight, the table wasn't even set.

His stomach growled. All day long, Ken had had his nose to the grindstone. Breakfast, which consisted of a measly corn muffin and Styrofoam coffee on the run, was long gone. Lunch wasn't even in the picture. "Need some help, Mother?"

Patty grabbed a hand towel and swiped her hands across it. Her eyes darted about as she said, "No. No, thanks anyway, Kenny. Just sit. Talk with…Jake…and your father."

Again, Kenny, mused Ken. His brows knitted.

"Sit down, son," heaved his father, unsuccessfully hiding a good case of nerves.

Jake dropped onto a chair across the table and hooked his heels onto the side rungs of the chair. He didn't have a care in the world. He acted as if he belonged there. And Ken didn't like that smart aleck one bit.

Lowering himself onto a chair, Ken shot a look at his father who pretended to be studying his fingernails. "What's going on, Dad?"

Without looking up, his father began, "Ken…" A sidelong glance at Jake.

"Dad?" prodded Ken, but got no response. Lowering his head, he tried to worm into his father's line of sight, unsuccessfully.

"Your mother and I came to America from East Germany."

"I know," said Ken. "In the early 60s."

Drawing out the word, "Well," his father said, "You don't know the entire story." He gave Jake another sidelong glance then looked down at his hands again.

Ken eyed Jake who had a gotcha-by-the-balls smirk plastered on his face. What the hell did this idiot have to do with Mother and Dad escaping from Germany?

"We almost didn't make it," said his father.

"Yah, Dad, I know," said Ken impatiently. "The People's Police were hot on your trail, they nabbed Mother, but then some guy who was helping you to escape fought them off until you managed to drag her across the border."

Jake snorted.

Ken shot him a look. His fists tightened. He felt like smacking that smart-ass.

"What you don't know is…" stammered his father, "…is that they snatched…your…" And then he spat out, "brother," as if it were cobra venom.

His mother dropped a pot cover. Ken jumped. Chills ran up and down his spine. "Brother?" he belched.

Jake stuck out his chest. The grin of a Cheshire cat caked his face as with two thumbs up, he boasted, "Yo, bro, in the flesh!"

CANDY-COLORED CLOWN

CHAPTER TWELVE

It was 2:35 the next afternoon. Ken and Julie were alone in the condo, sitting side by side on the couch and wolfing down fresh-cut vegetables dunked in sour cream and onion dip, mesmerized by television soaps. The doorbell chimed. Chewing stopped as eyes exchanged surprise. "Can't be Mom and Dad," spluttered Julie, mouth half full.

Ken rapidly swallowed and said, "Your Mom did promise to be back from running errands in plenty of time for you to pick up the minivan."

"Yeah, but not this soon," she said and reluctantly got to her feet. Her eyes never left the television screen where the soap's hero and heroine were about to romp in the sack. Violins swelled.

"Probably a neighbor," he said. "Wants to borrow sugar or something."

The doorbell chimed again. "Okay, okay," she grumbled and tore herself away, but the romantic refrain got into her soul and she broke into a waltz. Out of the living room and down the hall, her hands modulated up and down. Nearing the front door, she pretended that Ken, all decked out in white tuxedo and top hat, twirled her around and then bowed to her in an old-fashioned sort of way. She was in the midst of returning the gesture when the doorbell chimed again. She stopped and glared at the door. This better be important. She braced her hands on the door, closed her left her eye, and squinted through the peephole with her right. Jake! Taking a quick step back, she covered her mouth.

"Who is it, Julie?" called Ken.

She glanced over her shoulder and down the hall, barely taking a breath as memories of Jake manhandling Ken at the hospital blasted into her head and mixed with Emma's voice, "Jake isn't a very likeable person." She wrung her hands and backed against the wall. How did he get through the security doors in the lobby? The doorknob jiggled. Her gut screamed, don't touch it! Her eyes slammed shut. Go away, Jake! The television went silent.

"Who's at the door, Julie?" hollered Ken.

She shot a look down the hall. Hands tightened together. What should she do? Her head spun and her own spit gagged her.

"Julie?"

She swallowed hard and managed a shaky, "It's...Jake."

"Come on, sweet cakes," oozed Jake in a syrupy voice. "Open the door."

Her heart raced. Don't trust that jerk.

"Open the door," cooed Jake.

"What's going on?" shouted Ken.

Julie reached for the doorknob. Brass iced her skin, chilled her hand, and raced up her arm. Little by little, she turned the knob. Suddenly, the door flew open, shoving her back against the wall. When Jake's manicured fingers hooked over the edge of the door near her face, her eyes squeezed shut. The door slammed, and her eyes opened like those of a deer caught in headlights. Jake stood there, his black eyes full of loathing, giving her the once over.

Julie felt like scum. She crisscrossed her bare feet as fingers of her right hand wrested a wayward lock and wrapped it around her ear. Clad in faded jeans and old tee shirt, she had never gotten around to taking care of herself that morning, only took a second to run a brush through her hair. Ken's needs had come first.

Jake snorted. Then, as if he owned the place, he strutted off towards the living room.

She pulled away from the wall and straightened her clothes. The side of her face screwed up and her tongue waggled at him as he disappeared into the living room. In a high-pitched nasally voice, she spat "Mr. Perfect, in your little white shorts, burgundy polo shirt, and…" She wiggled her butt. "…ponytail."

"How's it hanging, bro'?" taunted Jake.

Julie gnawed her bottom lip, full of dread about going into the living room; yet no way was she leaving Ken alone with Jake. She drew a deep breath and then marched down the hall. Rounding the archway, she stopped short. Aggravation ripped through her. Jake was tramping from one place to another, picking up objects he had no business picking up, checking them out—actually manhandling them! On the verge of exploding, hey, get your grubby paws off Mom and Dad's stuff, she heard the voice of reason—Jake does that everywhere. Why should he be any different here? She swallowed hard and glanced at Ken. He smiled at her and one chocolate eye winked. Her insides tingled. He hadn't looked at her that way in a long time. Passion took control, trepidation flew out the window, and she rushed to the sofa. She was barely settled on the arm next to him when he grasped her hand and kissed the back of it. She brushed her head against his and reveled in the scent of spicy aftershave that wafted up her nostrils.

"Insurance paid off on the digs or wheels?" ventured Jake, now at the bookcase, latching onto a model of the U. S. S. Constitution that Peter had built. He turned it over this way then that and then shook it as if expecting something inside to rattle. He held it against his ear.

"Come on, Jake," said Ken. "Put that down, will ya?"

Jake glared at Ken and then at Julie. She shifted uneasily, but her eyes let him know that such actions bordered on rude and if he didn't cut it out, she'd to show him the door. He seemed only slightly put off, and that was only for a brief moment, because next thing she knew, he picked up a music box from the mantle, fished through the matches inside and then lifted it and examined the bottom. She glanced at Ken. His eyes rolled as he huffed, "Signed off on the cars, yesterday. Julie's picking up our new minivan this afternoon."

"Minivan," sniggered Jake, winding the music box key. "How disgustingly domestic." Theme from Love Story tinkled. His face twisted up, and he slammed down the cover. The music ceased.

Ken and Julie tried to contain laughter, but then she squeezed his hand, her eyes signaling at Jake now mauling the candy-colored clown. "For crying out loud, Jake," snapped Ken. "Cut the crap!"

Jake tossed the clown back onto the television. "No problemo, bro'," he scoffed as his palms shot into the air and waved side-to-side. His coal black eyes scanned the room. He scratched his head then jammed his hands into his hipbones. "What about Cohasset?"

"Julie and I haven't gotten 'round to discussing that," said Ken.

Jake picked up a sextant that once belonged to Peter's great grandfather. "Contractors must be breathing down your neck about now, wanting to rebuild that joint."

"Like I said," puffed Ken. "Julie and I haven't gotten around to discussing that."

Jake leered at Ken as if he had just heard a blatant lie. "So what are you waiting for?" he charged.

Ken shrugged.

"Nothing made it through the fire?" prodded Jake.

Ken shook his head. Suddenly, his brows came together. What was Jake getting at?

Jake set the sextant back where he had gotten it and stepped over to the door to the balcony.

Ralph, perched on the windowsill outside, cowered. Ears flattened against his head. Pupils dilated. Mouth gaped, baring fangs as he clicked revulsion for the person looming at the door.

Jake hissed.

Ralph bristled and hissed back.

Jake snickered and then said, "Who knows. Maybe I'll take Cohasset off your hands as is. Settle down in my own digs."

"The devil, you say," hooted Ken and then tossed back his head and guffawed. "Now I've heard everything!"

Jake took a gunfighter's stance; a sly grin plastered his face. "Come on, bro'. Nothin' wrong with movin' out to the 'burbs. Raisin' one's stature in life."

Ken eyed Jake and puffed, "Phshaw! You?"

"Might even think about a kid or two," said Jake and then the concept nearly choked him.

Ken's good hand waved off Jake. "I should live so long to see the day!"

"Hey," chided Jake. "What's meant to be…"

Chill tore through Julie's veins.

***

Alone in the living room, Ken was still shaking his head in disbelief, paying little attention to Julie humming in the bathroom. "Imagine, Jake on his way out to Cohasset, in his words, *to take a gander at the place*. What a crock." He gazed at the casts on his left arm and leg. "What's he looking for? Buried treasure?"

Rubbing a spot over his chest, Ken recalled overhearing Leo say, "He's worse than the devil."

Ken ran his hand through his hair and mumbled, "How can that idiot even consider rebuilding that pile of rubble?"

Leo had warned Regina, "He will take what he wants and leave you with nothing."

"Nothing," huffed Ken. "Not even her life. Nor Katrina's. Neither of them came back. Jake did though. Now he wants to live on the land where they lived?" He studied the fingernails on his right hand. "Does seem sacrilegious though." He gnawed at the jagged thumbnail. After a while, he spat out a scrap of nail and huffed, "The guy's got no scruples at all." Scratching the side of his neck, he envisioned Jake roaming around in high-class duds, white tennis shoes poking about in the ashes. "Humph. Probably thinks he can get the land off me dirt cheap." His brows came together. "Wait one second. Regina. Katrina. *They* didn't come back… *Jake did!* Why wasn't *he* on that plane with them?"

A squawk drew his attention to the television that wasn't on. He looked at the candy-colored clown perched on top. He

149

swore its eyes with overstated pupils had just moved. He peered at it sideways then blinked hard. Nothing changed. "Imagination's getting the best of me," he mumbled.

Uneasiness stuck to Ken as he glanced at the model of the U. S. S. Constitution on the bookshelf and then the sextant lying beside it. Images of Jake manhandling the objects rattled his brain. His stomach churned. "Jake—jackass extraordinaire. Worse than ever. Doesn't miss a blessed thing. Leo warned you, Regina. Jake would hunt you down like a dog, but you laughed in your father's face. You had the key and not until you were safely away would you give it up."

"That son-of-a-bitch is looking for the key," swooshed through the room.

Ken stiffened. "What'd you say?" His eyes hunted for the source. "Humph. What's the matter with me?"

At the edge of his vision, Ken sensed a rippling. His eyes shot to the candy-colored clown. "Why, of all things, did I save that stupid thing? Why not something Katrina cherished? Why not her favorite doll?"

He envisioned her birthday and the doll he had given her. He had taken the day off, bought three pink balloons, a cake with a rainbow on it, and three pink candles. What a joy to watch his precious little girl struggle to blow out the candles. And how delighted she was upon unwrapping that doll—even more so when she discovered that it drank and wet!

Of course, that pissed off Regina. She accused him of male chauvinism, of trying to mold Katrina into *a whelp-bearing robot with tits.*

Ken took a trembling breath. "If only I had known that it was the last birthday I was destined to spend with Katrina." He ran his fingers through his hair. "She'd be eight years old now. What would she have looked like?"

He wished he could look upon her portrait that had sat on her white bureau. Few pictures of Katrina existed, because Regina detested such things, forbidding cameras in the manse— that is, except for that snooty bridal picture taken several days before the wedding to insure she looked perfect. Ken wasn't in the picture. Regina didn't want him in it. The day of the wedding, pictures were taken, but only by the photographer. She showed off the album, of course, but then it disappeared.

Katrina's picture came about one day when Gretchen secreted the little girl off to have it taken. When Regina saw the picture on the bureau, a couple of weeks later, she blew her stack. Everybody had seen it by then, so she left it alone. Maybe it was because she knew she would be blamed if it had come up missing. No, Regina relished blame. Somehow, it made her stronger. Why then…

Julie humming in the bathroom brought Ken back from the past. He listened in. Rhapsody on a Theme of Paganini. Rachmaninoff. Emma LaRosa had played the song at their wedding. The pain in his heart eased. He had someone who understood now, someone to tell triumphs and sorrows to—if only he had the guts to do so. Turning to Julie in the night, her face set aglow by fanciful nightlights, always lightened his load. Sometimes, she set up candles, because darkness bothered her. Her mother was the same way. They claimed it came from being alone for so many years without Peter. "Maybe if I had a nightlight, Katrina wouldn't have haunted me so." Ken ran his hand through his hair. "Maybe if I had looked at her portrait once in a while, it might've helped me get over losing her. Now, what little is left of her has gone up in smoke—even those pictures I had snapped of her when Regina wasn't looking. The ones I put in the metal safe are gone. So is the safe."

He glared at the candy-colored clown. "Why did I take that tacky piece of garbage and not the portrait? Not the safe? Damn it! Where did that clown come from? Wait a minute. Julie dusted upstairs every so often. No, I can't ask her about the clown. Upsets the applecart to bring up the past." Peering fitfully at the casts on his left arm and leg, Ken prodded memory. "Who gave that thing to Katrina?" He rubbed his forehead. "Certainly not Regina. My parents? Gretchen and Leo?" Ken rapped his good hand on the arm of the recliner. "Time I found out." He lowered the footrest and hollered, "Julie?"

"I'm in the bathroom."

"I have to make a couple of calls," he shouted.

A second or two passed. She peeked around the archway, towel drying her hair. "Now?"

Poised on the edge of the recliner, Ken said, "Good a time as any."

She shrugged and puffed, "Okay." She bent over and wrapped the towel around her head then straightened and crossed the room to the wheelchair folded up next to him. "We should keep this thing opened up from now on," she said while unfolding it. "That way you can wiggle into it any time you want."

"Yeah, can't unfold it alone," he belched. He waved her off and toiled to get into the wheelchair. "I can take it from here."

Tossing her hands into the air and stepping away, Julie said, "Okay."

Ken settled into the wheelchair. Manipulating the lever, he put the wheelchair in motion.

Her heart swelled with pride. That stubborn little imp's doing so well. She unwrapped the towel and shook out her hair. She was never going to let him slip away from her again. There's got to be a way of erasing all the bad things that happened. Most of all, she had to find a way to keep that stinker Jake out of their hair. Question was how? Heading off to the bathroom, she called, "Holler if you need anything else."

"I'll do just fine, thank you," said Ken without looking back. He'd been practicing moving about in the living room, the last day or so, but this was his first attempt at making it all the way to the kitchen. His only blunder came when the leg cast scraped against the kitchen doorjamb. When he picked up the phone, a feeling of accomplishment bolstered him. He laughed at himself. "The road to recovery is truly a slow, arduous one."

The blow dryer whirred in the bathroom as he dialed his parent's hotel in Florida. They were overjoyed to hear from him, but no, they had no memory of the candy-colored clown. He called the Konstanzes and picked up on the hesitancy in Gretchen's voice when she said she didn't know what he was talking about. Leo was out on an errand, but she was sure he had no idea either.

Ken hung up the phone. How about Jake? Nah, Jake never reached down in his pocket for anybody but himself—not even for Regina. That narrowed it down to two, either Regina or Nanny Ellen. He shook his head and huffed, "Regina was just as stingy as Jake, even when it came to her own flesh and blood. But Nanny Ellen? It doesn't make a lick of sense. She adored little Katrina. Why would she have done such a thing?"

Ken dug the phonebook out of the drawer and looked up Ellen's number. He dialed. She answered on the second ring. Boy, did he get an earful!

"Oh, yah, I remember that disgusting piece of crap," she carped. "Regina brought it home after one of those extended trips she took to—let me quote—'get away.' Saw her put it on the bed with my own eyes, a day or so before the accident. I'll never forget how put off our little Katrina was when she first set eyes on that clown. Regina forbade her from touching it, you know. You don't know how much I was beside myself when that woman threatened our little Katrina that a monster would slither out of that thing and eat her up in her sleep if she ever so much as laid one tiny finger on it. That woman sure was a piece of work, I tell ya."

Ken tightened his grip on the telephone as thickness built in his throat and gagged him. He detested himself for letting Regina get away with such relentless cruelty.

"You know as well as I do that while Regina was alive, I tried to control my tongue, for Katrina's sake and yours, though clearly, I was not on Regina's list of favorite persons. Well, let me tell you this! That woman was not on my list of favorite person's either! It's a different story now that she's met her maker—who I believe down to my very soul is Satan himself. Bet your bottom dollar that I'm not about to mince words when it comes to the manner in which that she-devil conducted herself."

When Ellen stopped to take in air, Ken muttered, "I don't blame you none."

"Poor little Katrina," whined Ellen. "That nasty old clown frightened her so."

His stomach churned. He had no right to have had a child like Katrina—any child. No, he had no to right even to the child that Julie was carrying.

"When it came to going to bed," Ellen went on, "Katrina insisted that I put that disgusting thing into the highest, darkest corner of the closet and shut the door tighter than tight. Sometimes, we even jammed her dollhouse up against it. Until our little Katrina was completely satisfied, she refused to even go near that bed." Ellen cleared her throat. "And God help me if I forgot to put it back on the bed in the morning! Holy mackerel, did Regina hit the ceiling!"

CHAPTER THIRTEEN

"Well, that's it," said Neil Ebreg, salesman at the Brookline car dealership after having familiarized Julie with all the bells and whistles of the white Lumina minivan. He was sitting in the front passenger seat and she was behind the wheel. Elizabeth was outside, leaning on the back bumper, legs crossed at the ankles and arms folded. She looked like a teenager in a loose-fitting, yellow sundress, white half socks, and tennis shoes. "All set to hit the road, Mrs. Waters," he said, extending his hand.

Grinning in her father's silly little way, Julie shook his hand. As Neil got out of the minivan, she hollered out the driver's side window, "Follow me home, Mom."

Elizabeth bolted into action as Julie rolled up the window.

"Oh, wait! Mom," she cried and found her nose pressed up against glass. "Shoot!" She rolled the window back down. "Mom! I have to stop at the market. Ralph's out of food."

Elizabeth laughed. "Our lifelong joke about feeding an invisible feline has gone awry now that Ralph's taken over the condo."

Neil stared at her, kind of queer-like.

"It's a long story," said Elizabeth, sloughing him off. "See you at home, Julie."

Since the day was expected to be hotter than usual, Julie had figured a pale yellow tank top, matching shorts, and tan sandals would do the trick, and it did until she got to the market. Frigid conditioned air, devoid of odor, particularly that of fresh-baked cinnamon buns that permeated the market, especially in the morning, hit her with a jolt. "This is going to be one fast trip," she huffed. Scurrying up and down the aisles, she tossed cat food, litter, and other last-minute items into a shopping cart. "Geez, my nose feels like an icicle. Should've had brains to bring a sweater." She avoided taking in a deep breath since that would only serve to make her colder, so by the time she got to the checkout line, she was light-headed. Blue-tinged gooseflesh peppered her arms and legs. Her teeth clattered when she opened her mouth to speak. Shivering uncontrollably, she had all she could do to dig out a twenty-dollar bill from her shoulder bag and plunk it down onto the counter. Coins went all over the place since holding her frozen hand still long enough for the clerk to count out the change was out of the question.

As Julie shoveled coins up with her thumbnail and index fingernail, she noticed the clerk gawking at her. I must look like a doofus, she thought. She pursed her lips and gave him a hard look. College punk. Out for the summer, I suppose. Probably has the metabolism of a hummingbird. Nothing keeps his hormonal body from running hot. Look at him in those black jeans and button-down white shirt. She could read the lettering on the tee shirt beneath, Marshal Arts Academy of Brighton. What's a kid like that know about being cold? Her eyes narrowed on him as if to say, take those dumb old eyes of yours off me, bonehead.

She scooped up the bags of groceries and waddled toward the automatic door, grumbling through clenched teeth, "Can't wait to feel the warmth of the great outdoors."

The door slid open and a blast of searing parking lot air smacked her. It burned all the way down to the bottom of her lungs. Then the glare of the setting sun blinded her. She stopped short. The guy behind her smacked into her. As she hurtled forward, a strong hand seized her arm and she heard Jake's voice. That jerk was the last person on earth she wanted to run into and conversing with him was definitely not on her list of priorities. She shook her arm loose. After an eternity of blinking away floaters, she made out the face looming before her. "You're not Jake."

Casting her a puzzled look, the stranger said with much hesitation, "No, ma'am. Name's Bob."

"Bob," repeated Julie in a dull voice. She leaned against the granite exterior of the market. "Jake's been on my mind much too much," she muttered. The change of temperature and solar glare had a hand in it, too. She thumped her head against the granite. "Ow," she blubbered.

"Shouldn't do that, ma'am," said Bob in a monotone voice. "Hurts."

Julie squinted at the stranger, rubbing her head. "I didn't know that," she said dryly, beating her gums about being called ma'am.

"You all right, ma'am?" he asked.

She pushed away from the wall and spat, "Sure…young man."

Bob gave her a look, head cocked to one side. "I'm hardly a young man, ma'am," he said and sauntered away.

Julie sucked in a lung full of hot air and adjusted the grocery bags. "Ma'am," she puffed. About to take a step, she heard Jake's voice explode. As it echoed throughout the parking lot, she plastered herself against granite wall. There were other voices—familiar ones. She held her breath and listened. Leopold. Gretchen. She inched over to the corner of the building and stole a glance. It was them!

Gretchen was wearing a hand knitted, ivory sweater, a navy-blue dress, nylons, and navy-blue walking shoes. Leopold had on a tan short-sleeve shirt, khaki pants, and brown deck shoes.

Yikes! Jake! Dressed like a sleek black cat and right in Leopold's face!

His jaw muscles bunched at the hinges and his left eye twitched. Looking neither right nor left, Jake didn't give a damn who saw him making a scene. "I want what belongs to me!" he bellowed as onlookers shrunk away. "Gina took it. Now, you're getting it back for me, you hear?"

Julie drew back and cowered against the wall. Should've warned Gretchen and Leo at the hospital that Jake was looking for them. But they managed to avoid him all this time. She trembled. Bags of groceries quivered. Cans of cat food clattered.

"Now wait one minute, Jake," protested Leopold.

There came sounds of a slap, a groan, and Gretchen crying out, "Leopold!"

"Don't go hard-ass on me, *alt mann*," barked Jake. "Just find it! Hey! Ruski! Do I got your attention? Need another smack or what? Should I work over your bitch?"

Gretchen squealed and Julie cringed.

"No, no," groveled Leo. "I gotcha. I gotcha."

Then footsteps, heavy, determined footsteps, came towards Julie. "Jake's going to see me," she whimpered. She turned her face in the opposite direction. Her eyes squeezed shut as her arms tightened around the bags of groceries.

Jake stormed past, grumbling, "Shuddah checked out that brat's room before rigging that plane. Damn you to hell, Gina!"

Julie opened one eye. Jake was getting into his sports car double-parked right behind her new minivan. Chills rippled up and down her spine. He didn't know that was her minivan. She looked for Leo's car. The Konstanzes must've walked. She pictured the over-50 development where Leo and Gretchen lived and the entrance to it, just down the street. Yeah, they walked.

Jake slammed his car door and the engine jolted awake. Tires screeched across hot top as the car fishtailed through the parking lot towards the exit, sucking along swirls of burnt rubber. Julie squelched a cough as Jake cut into traffic without stopping. Horns blared and brakes squealed. Rubber and exhaust of an overtaxed engine stunk up the air.

Sweat trickled down Julie's brow. Then she noticed Leo and Gretchen. "Oh no," she wheezed and slunk behind one of the granite supporting columns of the market's façade. They won't like the idea of me witnessing how Jake thrashed them, she thought. They might even tell Jake I was here. Panic sliced her like a white-hot sword as she crushed the grocery bags against her belly and the Konstanzes passed by.

"What that beast want of us?" sobbed Gretchen. "He take of us everything worth living for. What more he want?"

"We can only do what we can do, *meine liebe*," said Leopold.

Gretchen was not to be consoled. "Oh, what we to do?"

"Now, now," said Leo. "Put all of this worry away and let us go make the stop that Jake wishes us to make. We will find what he is looking for and give it to him and we will be done of him."

"How can we find what we do not know?" sniveled Gretchen.

Leo took in a profound breath. "We will find whatever it is," he said, but didn't sound very hopeful. His voice lightened. "After we do, I will take you down to the ice cream shop, for those cheeks of yours must always be round and rosy."

Julie remained stuck to the column, sweating, her heart thumping. A kid whizzed by on a skateboard. A while later, a five-year-old on the hand of his mother doddered past and squinted up at Julie. She felt foolish, yet no way was she going to move until her insides deemed it safe to do so. Dusk faded. People came and went, paying her no mind. She shifted the grocery bags. Muscles ached. She wiped her brow with the back of her hand while peering to her right then to her left and back again. "Can't stay here all night," she muttered and fumbled the key out of her shoulder bag. She made a mad dash for her new minivan, jammed the key into the lock, yanked open the door, and tossed the bags of groceries onto the passenger's seat. Somewhere in all that, the nail on her left middle finger got bent back. Her hand flailed away the pain as the bag containing cat food burst open and cans rolled onto the floor. She started the engine, and as uncooled air blasted from the vents, she caught a whiff of her own sweat.

"Where the heck is that headlight switch?" she fretted. "Oh, there you are." She flipped the switch and gripped the steering wheel with both hands. "Calm down, Julie, or you and your new minivan might not make it back to Mom's in one piece," she said and took several quick breaths. She took a deep one. New car odors filled her nostrils. "Okay, okay," she said, stroking her forehead. "Don't think about what happened. Just get home."

Her eyes ran along the dashboard to the passenger seat and then into the back seat where she pictured a miniature car seat and buckled into it, a baby with eyes like Ken's, wearing a wide-brimmed yellow bonnet. Her hand dropped away from her forehead as a smile rippled her lips. She closed her eyes and listened to the minivan purr. She filled her lungs with cool conditioned air. "Everything's going to be okay."

***

"We have company," announced Elizabeth when Julie hobbled into the condo. "Good heavens, give me those bags! I didn't know you were going to do that much shopping!"

"Don't worry about it," mumbled Julie as Yankee pot roast, blueberry pie, and fresh perked coffee bowled her over. "Boy, am I glad to be home."

Elizabeth didn't hear, since she was listening to boisterous male laughter coming from the living room. After years of good times and bad, Peter's laughter still thrilled her.

All Julie really wanted at that moment was to take a nice refreshing shower, but she first had to kiss Ken and say hello to Mom and Dad's company. To do otherwise would be rude and uncaring. Shaking out her arms and wrists, she ambled to the living room. At the archway, she stopped in her tracks. Gretchen was sitting on the love seat and Leopold was perched sidesaddle on the arm of it. Steadying herself on the doorframe, Julie eyed them. The Konstanzes were the last people on earth she expected to see this night—and of all places, here!

"You all right, Julie?" asked Ken. "You look like you've seen a ghost."

Two ghosts, thought Julie. And they look awfully relaxed considering the tongue-lashing that Jake just gave them.

Ken gestured with his good hand. "Come over here."

She stared at his hand, her brain mush. Her legs felt like rubber as she stepped over to him. He grabbed her hand and gasped, "You're cold as ice!" When she tried to break free, he

160

tightened his grip. "Did you have trouble with the minivan or something?"

"No," she stammered. "Everything's great. Just great."

"Come. Sit beside me," said Gretchen, patting the cushion beside her.

Julie tugged on her hand and Ken reluctantly released it. The idea of going to Gretchen didn't exactly thrill her. She rubbed her hands together. Why did Jake hassle the Konstanzes like that? And why are they here now? Suddenly aware of the silence, she discovered that she was the center of attention. Better go to Gretchen and look for answers later, she thought.

Gretchen put out her cheek and Julie bent to kiss it. The scent of Jean Nate flavored the air as Gretchen patted Julie's stomach and said, "Little one make presence know, I see." She latched onto Julie's wrists. "You let me hold baby?"

"Of course," gurgled Julie, feeling her face flush, "wouldn't have it any other way."

A tear rolled out of the corner of Gretchen's eye. She brushed it away, whispering, "You blessing of angels."

"Now, now, let us not start water works, *miene liebe*," admonished Leopold, rubbing his wife's shoulder.

"Here we go," gushed Elizabeth as she wobbled into the living room, bogged down by a tray of glasses that brimmed with iced tea and clinking ice cubes. Lemon wedges garnished the rims of the glasses.

Gretchen loosened her grip on Julie and took a glass. She handed it to Leo and then took one for herself.

Ken could tell that Julie was avoiding him. As she backed away from Gretchen, he managed to stretch out his hand enough to seize the hem of her tank top and drew her to him. His eyes never left her as she sagged onto the arm of his chair.

"You are looking well, Ken," said Leo.

"I am well," said Ken. "Thanks to my lovely wife here and her Mom and Dad. I can honestly say I feel better than I have in quite some time."

Leo took a sip of tea then smacked his lips. "Rebuild that fine house of yours," he said, "Better than before. Look at the sea again."

"Nah, I don't think so," said Ken as Elizabeth came over with the tray. They exchanged surprised looks when Julie latched onto a glass and chugged down half the contents. Ken took a glass and nodded a thank you at Elizabeth.

"You no build?" asked Gretchen.

"Thinking about selling off and building elsewhere," said Ken. Sell off to Jake, he thought. Let him deal with the ghosts—which more than likely mean nothing to him.

"Make a fresh start of it?" asked Julie.

Ken nodded and the smile that grew upon her lips tickled his insides.

She sighed contentedly, thankful about not having to go back to Cohasset. Why tempt the ghosts now that Ken had finally put the past behind him?

"I know very good contractor," said Leopold. "Just say word."

"All lost to fire?" injected Gretchen.

"Yep." Not a hint of sadness laced Ken's response. Let the past lay, he thought as he shifted his weight.

Julie set her glass on the coffee table, saying, "Here, let me fluff up those pillows."

"Ah, such a good wife," said Leopold, nodding with approval.

Peter gestured to the television and asked, "What about that clown?"

"I haven't the faintest idea why I took it," said Ken as Julie pulled up a chair next to him. Clutching his hand, she drew it to her lips, and kissed the back of it. His heart brimmed with love. "You are much too good for me," he whispered.

"Feels good to be warm again," she said. "The market was freezing." Panic raced through Julie. Her eyes darted to Gretchen. Thankfully, she hadn't heard. What's Gretchen doing? Her eyes are signaling Leo. They're both looking at the television. But it's not on!

Leo got to his feet and stood there, itching the back of his ankle with the front of the other one, trying to look casual. Then he headed to the television and picked up the clown. He checked it out just like Jake did yesterday. Leo glanced at Gretchen whose eyes told him to bring the clown to her. His lips formed a pucker as if shushing her. He set the clown back on the television, went back to the loveseat, and sat down. His hand patted her knee.

"Wait," yelped Elizabeth. "We rescued that portrait! Remember, Julie?"

Ken's insides flip-flopped, overjoyed that Katrina's picture had made it through the fire. His eyes, golf ball size and full of hope, bore into Julie. "You, you didn't tell me..."

Julie cringed. Of course, I didn't tell you about Regina's picture, she thought. It would've only brought up the past. Oh no. It can't be. Ken's still in love with Regina! No matter where we live, he'll always love her despite all the terrible things going around about her. How's a person supposed to compete with that?

"It's in the hall closet," said Elizabeth. "Let me go get it."

Ken ran his hand through his hair, feeling like jumping for joy. The picture of precious Katrina had made it through the fire! He could look upon her face once more!

Julie felt like vomiting, thinking that Ken still loved Regina.

"I thought you might like to have it," called Elizabeth from the hallway. She came around the archway, swooshing dust off the portrait. "I tried my best to clean it up," she said. And then she held it up.

"Regina," gasped Gretchen. She grabbed the portrait and for several electric moments, she and Leopold drank up the image. Tears brimmed their eyes. Clutching it to her breast, she rocked back and forth, whimpering, "This wonderful. Very, very wonderful."

But Ken took a blow straight to the heart, worse than the one Jake had given him the day Regina had left. His eyes swerved away from the portrait, unable to bear the sight of that pretentious face. His fingernails screeched back and forth across the rim of the ice tea glass. Leo and Gretchen deserve so much better than incredibly cruel Regina, he thought. Yet they went overboard to keep her in their life. They were so careful not to stand up for me that day when I came home early and Regina was mouthing off, "Look at that weak excuse I have for a husband. If I didn't have the hold on him that I do, he'd be long gone by now. You've heard the disgusting things I say to him. A real man wouldn't put up with that."

Leo and Gretchen cared about Ken. He knew they did. But their silence that day hurt. And it still did.

Julie glanced at Ken. Anguish enveloped his whole being. She felt like all this time she had been merely a substitute for Regina, an understudy for the star of the show.

Ken leaned over and whispered in her ear, "It makes my stomach turn to think that that harpy's picture survived but not Katrina's. Makes you want to question the existence of God, doesn't it?"

All this time he's been grieving over Katrina? thought Julie. Not Regina?

"She made an elegant bride," said Peter. "You must miss her terribly."

"With every breath we take," said Leo. His arm tightened around Gretchen. "And our little Katrina..." His whole body appeared to quake. "*Lieb, lieb klein* Katrina."

Gretchen hid her face against his chest and sobbed, "Everything important taken of us."

CHAPTER FOURTEEN

That night, sleep was out of the question for Julie. Ken, on the other hand, had taken sleep medication so he was totally dead to the world. She tossed and turned, aching all over from being plastered up against the market's granite exterior, but what bothered her more was the memory of Jake badgering the Konstanzes. Though she hadn't told a soul about it, her gut refused to let it rest, rumbling on and on like a broken record, something was terribly wrong; lives hung in the balance.

Ken twitched.

Julie shot a look at him. Anguish marked his face as if an animator was detailing it that moment. He began to jabber. His hand stretched out into the shadowed night. Fingers spread as if beckoning or grappling for something. "Ka…tri…n…a," he moaned. His hand hung in midair, frozen in time, and then plopped onto the bed, and he was quiet once more.

"I was so darned worried about you missing Regina," whispered Julie, "and all along you grieved for Katrina. Her absence pained you so, and I was so blind. Signs had been there—like the first time you brought me to the manse and the sadness written all over you as you told me about Katrina dressing Ralph in doll clothes and making him sleep in her doll carriage all covered up with baby blankets. And there was the way you stared at that swing, moving back and forth in the breeze. Ralph stared at it, too, and made those short, clicking sounds he does whenever something's bugging him. At the precipice, your hand ran through your hair when you said that you and Katrina built sandcastles on the beach below."

A chill ran through Julie as if she were standing once again at the bottom of the spiral staircase and feeling his breath on her ear. "You go ahead up. I just can't."

Ken was so insistent. What was she supposed to see up there? Regina's portrait? Katrina's? Their bedrooms—dusty and untouched since the plane crash? The rainbow arching across the sky blue wall? What? Julie dug her fingers into her pillow. Did Ken want her to see the portrait of the blue-eyed child, freckles splattering her button nose, golden ringlets, pudgy arms, hand-smocked white dress dotted with yellow-faced daisies? "God, how awful this must be for him," she whispered. Then it dawned on Julie that she had spoken those same words back then in Katrina's bedroom.

She stuffed her pillow against the headboard then propped herself up. Chewing the inside of her mouth, she wished she hadn't left Katrina's portrait in the ashes. But seeing the way the flames had eaten away that freckled nose and golden ringlets would've killed Ken. Only a fragment of an arm was left lying across the hand-smocked flowered dress.

Julie rubbed the back of her arm and hit a sore spot. Her veins iced as against her will, her mind flashed back to the market and pinned her against the granite wall once again. Jake, eyeball to eyeball with Leopold, was spewing, "She took it! Get it back!" The parking lot echoed with his voice and now, throughout her being as granite block grated her skin and bags of groceries weighed her down. Stomach acid curdled. No place to run! No place to hide!

Suddenly Julie was at the hospital and Jake was roughing up Ken lying comatose in his bed. "Lives are hanging in the balance," she whispered and glanced at Ken. "Is your life in danger? From you own brother?"

Jake's coal black eyes loomed in her face like that afternoon when he burst into the condo.

"Maybe my life's in peril," Julie whispered. She tossed off the blankets and dropped her legs over the side of the bed. "But I haven't done anything to Jake! Not that I know of…" Her brows came together. Were Mom and Dad in danger? Her head shook violently. "Certainly not! They've got even less to do with Ken and his past than I do." She squinted at him. "The past. Is that it? Your past?"

Leo's voice blasted into her head, "But Jake…" Then came a slap.

"*Alt Mann,*" blasted Jake. "Ruski. No buts. Just get it! Got your attention? Work over your bitch?" Heavy footsteps. "Shuddah checked out that brat's room. Rigged that plane. Damn Gina to hell!" A car door slammed, gears gnashed, tires squealed, and horns bayed. Silence—heart-stopping silence. No wind. No birds. Only choking fumes—engine oil—putrid burnt rubber.

Julie slid off the bed. Too shaky to stand, she dropped back and tried to pull herself together. Regina's parents came at her. Sweat trickled down her brow. Bags of groceries jammed against her belly and she feared detection. She hid behind the granite column. "What that beast want from us?" lamented Gretchen. "He take from us everything worth living for. What more he want?"

Julie covered her ears and gnashed her teeth. One more word and she'd scream! She concentrated on the ceiling, but her mind detailed a rainbow instead of arched plaster lines as Leo's voice seeped through her defenses, "We can only do what we can do, *meine liebe*. Let us go make the stop Jake wishes us to make."

"Why did they show up here?" muttered Julie. "Of all places. Here." She wrung her hands then stopped. "It's the Konstanzes," she exclaimed and bolted out of bed. "They're in harm's way!"

She covered her mouth and gawked at Ken. Still sleeping. Deep down she wished she'd wakened him. She needed to tell him about Jake. Tell him that Jake rigged the plane to crash with Regina and Katrina on it. Her heart hammered. "But why did Jake….no, why would anybody do a dreadful thing like that?"

She grabbed her pink flowered robe off the bottom of the bed and in the middle of sliding an arm into a sleeve, stopped short. "What on earth did that sweet old couple do to get Jake so riled up? Enough to slap them around? In broad daylight?"

She finished putting her arm into the sleeve then wormed the other arm into the other sleeve. As she tiptoed out of the bedroom, she pulled the door closed, careful not to latch it or make noise. Heading down the hall, she cinched the belt too tight around her growing belly and at the living room archway, paused to loosen it.

From the balcony, Ralph caught sight of Julie and let out a ragged meow. He stretched into an all-inclusive arc then settled back on his haunches to track her across the living room to the other side of the door.

She stood there, eying the beacon atop the Prudential Building that blinked on and off as if someone were signaling, "I am here."

Ralph clicked.

Julie slid open the glass door and went to the cat. Stroking his lush, gray mane soothed her. His purrs did, too, that is until she squinted at the weather lights atop the John Hancock Building, red and haloed by murkiness. Edginess crept upon her. She took an uneven breath then said, "A storm's coming, Ralphie, and I'm so powerless to stop it."

The cat clicked and a tremor shot through Julie. She rubbed her shoulders and retreated to the living room.

Ralph hopped off the windowsill and hit the floor with a thud. His tail cleared the door just as it closed. He waited, arching his back against the footstool as Julie got seated upon the Canadian rocker. Then he jumped up on her lap and butted her hand until she fiddled with his ear. He purred in appreciation. When she stopped, he hunkered down and curled into a ball. She began to rock, her fingers diddling with wisps of fur. He feigned sleep until dawn brightened the room and Julie stopped rocking.

A shaft of sunlight crossed the room and illuminated the recliner. Ken's form lingered in the fabric and throw pillows.

Julie nudged Ralph off her lap and got to her feet. She arched backwards into a stretch as the cat arched the way cats do.

She stepped over to the recliner, picked up a pillow and put her face to it. Ken's essence filled her. She thought about him in the bedroom, sleeping. Oh, if only to crawl up next to him and warm her cold body against his. She heaved a sigh. Better not. Curt says that Ken needs his rest.

She picked up the other pillow, stuffed it and the first pillow under her arm, and then smoothed out the fabric of the recliner. She fluffed one pillow and angled it into one of the corners then fluffed the other pillow and placed it on top of the first. She crossed the room and did the same to the loveseat and the pillows on it. She puttered around, careful not wake anybody. While dusting off the bookshelf, she didn't notice her left shoulder twitch, but then it happened once too often. She stopped short. "Ralph?" She turned.

The cat was on the Canadian rocker, engrossed in daily ablution. He cast a sleepy one-eyed glance at her. The tip of his tongue stuck out. He retracted his tongue and clicked.

A shiver raced through Julie. She turned to the eyes of the candy-colored clown. Unable to look away, she took a quick step back. Her heel rammed against the hassock. Her hands flailed and grabbed at the air that didn't stop her fall. She plopped onto the oriental carpet. Wind spewed out of her. Flat on her back, she sucked in breath. She tried to sit up, but pain that knifed her in the small of her back. She crumpled.

She inhaled, exhaled, again and again, while staring at trowel lines in the plastered ceiling—rainbows. Was anybody up there? Did the people downstairs hear the crash?

Since the condominium was constructed with living rooms stacked on top of each other and bedrooms were elsewhere, more than likely nobody heard.

The clock on the mantle ticked. "Beans, nobody heard a thing. Not Mom. Not Dad. Not even Ken."

Ralph head-butted her arm and clicked.

"You're always hanging in there, aren't you, Ralphie?"

He leaned his flank into her and meowed.

"The house is so ungodly still," she whispered.

Five, ten, fifteen minutes passed. Still no signs of life other than her own and the cat, head butting her arm and clicking. "Well, Ralph," she heaved. "Can't lie here forever."

Rocking side to side, Julie got up enough momentum to roll onto her belly. She braced her hands against the floor and little by little, got up on hands and knees. "Didn't hurt as much as I thought it was going to. Actually, Ralphie, it's loosened things up a bit."

The cat got between her and the floor, going in one side and out the other, his back sweeping against her belly.

"You're not helping, Ralph."

He sat back on his haunches and clicked.

She dug her fingers into the arm of the couch, braced her right foot under her, and doddered to her feet. She steadied herself for a moment then hands on hips, rotated her upper body. Her lower back snapped. She sucked in a breath and said, "That did the trick."

Ralph heavy-eyed Julie and then kneaded the oriental carpet. But then an unexpected silhouette glided along the walls and his eyes popped. He clicked furiously as he dashed to the door and pressed his nose against the glass. His tail lurched side to side and the fur along his spine prickled.

"That slippery falcon again," said Julie as she limped to the door.

The cat squeezed his nose into the opening until it was barely large enough to squeeze though and then streaked across the balcony and onto the windowsill.

Julie chuckled and closed the door.

An unexpected tug—one that was not at all physical—caused her to spin around. Immense, almond-shaped eyes with sapphire irises and overstated black pupils yanked at her insides. Scarlet lips, fixed higher on one side than on the other, puckered into a well-defined cupid's bow. They never moved, yet somehow urged her to pick up the candy-colored clown.

She stepped over to it. Her index finger skimmed the edges of the rolling Chantilly collar. Strange, its eyes weren't looking at her any more. They were gazing off to the side, the way they always had. She studied the vibrant costume. An awful lot of material had gone into making this—at least a yard.

She picked up the clown and kneaded the grainy stuffing. She squeezed its fuzzy, red head and got the feeling that in her hands was the crux of everything that had gone wrong in Ken's life. Come to think of it, Jake had looked at it very oddly; both at the hospital and here again the other day. This had to be what he wanted Gretchen and Leo to get for him. "Well, he's not getting it," she huffed. "From here on out I'm keeping this thing real close."

Julie tiptoed to the bedroom, nudged open the door, and listened to Ken's soft, even breath. The innocence that gilded his sleeping face made her smile. She unhooked her shoulder bag from the back of the door and stole back to the living room, stuffing the clown into the bottom of the bag. Later, she paid a visit to Doctor Curt Shirlington.

The instant Curt laid eyes on Julie, warmth streaked through him; and when she stood up on her tiptoes to kiss him lightly on the cheek, he battled the urge to latch onto her and steal her away to some distant shore to keep her for his own. He could make her love him—he knew he could—if only given the chance. She'd forget about the ol' chap in no time. He squinted at her. Guilt rippled through him. What the hell was he doing messing with his best mate's world?

"Geez," said Julie, "you look like you just saw a creature from Mars."

"What..." he spluttered.

"Aw, forget it," she said, waving him off. She hooked her hands on her hips. "Anyways, I fell over the hassock in Mom's living room and..."

Curt felt like someone had just slapped his face. All he could think of was that day she fell on the precipice while trying to rescue that husband of hers. She could've gone over with the ol' chap. Then what would Curt have done? "Fell?" he asked. "You fell? Again?"

She nodded. "Don't tell Ken, okay?"

"He doesn't know?"

She looked down at her hands.

He watched her diddle with her fingernails. Reaching hyperventilation, he spewed, "Not even your mother?"

Without raising her head, she peered at him. A silly little grin rippled.

"Come with me, m'lady," he snapped while grabbing her hand. He towed her out of his office and down the hall, hollering, "Jessey!" As the nurse came running, he said, "Fetal monitor and assistance, stat!"

One thing led to another and before Julie knew it she was lying on an examining table covered with crinkly white paper, belly laid bare to the elements and plastered with gunk. Gooseflesh spiked as the cold end of the fetal stethoscope skated across her skin. "Geez, Curt," she winced, "you get that out of the 'fridge?"

Ignoring her, he grilled, "Any bleeding? Pain? Contractions?" Her eyes consumed him and as honeysuckle perfume wafted up his nostrils, he almost let slip, *feelings for me?*

Julie shook her head no, time and time again. His eyes grew so intense, gazing into hers that she had to look away. Jessie looked terribly grim. The room got so quiet that Julie was afraid to swallow her own spit, fearful that the noise might go through the stethoscope as it roamed here, there, then over there.

Curt found it incredibly hard to believe that Julie had no idea whatsoever how he felt about her. Surely she heard the thundering of his heart…heartbeat… He caught his breath. Should've had the heartbeat by now. Cut the crap, Curt, and listen for heartbeats! He concentrated on one spot and then another. "Hold it!" His eyes widened. "Yes," he exclaimed. "I got the bugger!" His face blossomed into one big, toothy grin as he squinted at Julie. "That kid of yours sure knows how to take a fall!"

He gave Julie a high five, another to Jessey, then listened at the same spot again and reveled in the sound. Too bad the wee one isn't mine, he thought. His insides somersaulted as the smile vanished from his face as though somebody had snapped him out of a hypnotic trance. Only difference was, he could recall each and every thought about Julie. Shame washed over Curt. He straightened up and took a cleansing breath.

Handing the monitor to Jessey, he said, "Wipe the lotion off Mrs. Water's abdomen, will you, please?"

Jessey gave him an odd look. "Yes, Doctor Shirlington."

"This is the second nosedive you've taken," he said, his voice controlled. Putting on a happy face, he turned to Julie. "How many more you going to take before this kid sees daylight?"

Julie looked up from watching Jessey wiping off the goop. Her head tilted to one side as she grinned sheepishly.

Curt lost it. Belching out a hearty laugh, he offered his hand to her. "Let's get this silly girl on her feet."

Taking hold of his hand as well as Jessey's, Julie pulled herself into a seated position. Upon regaining equilibrium, she slipped off the examining table and onto the step. She paused to adjust her yellow, V-neck tunic over her tan stretch jeans and then stepped down to the floor and led the way back to his office.

It was nearly impossible for Curt to hide his errant feelings. He wanted Julie, all of her, not just the bite that friendship allowed, not just the scent of her from time to time. He swallowed hard. She's poison. One taste will bring an end to life as too many people know it to be at this moment.

"Thanks, Curt, you're a gem," said Julie. "I probably should've gone to my obstetrician, but you'd keep it all under your hat. Ken's got enough to handle already."

"Good ol' Curt," he winced and sagged onto his chair. She's leaving. It's time. But he didn't want her to go. Yet it's torture to have her so near and not be able to tell her how he felt, not take her into his arms, make love to her, and have her in his life for ever and ever. Oh, if only she were his.

Curt loosened his tie and unbuttoned the top button of his blue, oxford shirt. Rolling up the sleeves, he tried to ignore the paperwork on the desk before him. Foolish stuff never ends. Got no use for this part of the job. That's why it's habitually elbow deep, Curt, ol' boy. On the other hand, being buried in paperwork might take the mind off m'lady.

He picked up a report—Mrs. Pollock's gallbladder. Of course it keeps flaring up, Mrs. Pollock. It will more and more until you find the time in your precious schedule to have it tended to properly. One of these days, that thing's going to jump up and bite you in the butt, my dear Mrs. Pollock, and then, talk about pain—ooowee! My dear Mrs. Pollock? You ain't seen nothin' yet!

Curt tossed the report back on the desk and swiveled his chair around to look out the window. His feet braced on edge of the sill and he tipped back and closed his eyes. These feelings have got to be brought under control. They're getting beyond the distraction level. Curt ol' boy, you know full well that you cannot have her. Still, there's no wanting another, no way to ever stop loving her.

"Well, uhm, see you later," muttered Julie. "I guess."

Her voice brought his thoughts to a quick end. Realizing that she had been speaking to him, Curt dropped his feet to the floor and swiveled the chair to face her. The puzzled look on her face made him scratch his head. He didn't have a clue as to what she said. Suddenly none of that mattered, because she was turning, about to leave, and that didn't bode well with him. "I'm terribly sorry," he gushed. "I was just thinking about a patient."

"You seem terribly bothered," she said, peering sideways at him.

"Strange case," he said. "Very strange."

She hitched her chin and shifted her bag onto her shoulder. Noticing unusual weight, she faced him and said, "Oh, one more thing."

Good Lord, how much more can a man take, thought Curt. Glancing up, he spotted the candy-colored clown in her hand. Confusion sheeted his face.

"This is it," said Julie, handing the clown to Curt. "This is at the heart of what's gone wrong in Ken's life. And I'm pretty sure that Jake wants it."

Curt studied it. "Jake wants this?"

"Looks like it came from some Middle Eastern country," she said.

He pinched the clown here and there. Grains of sand? He squeezed the muslin feet and hands. No toe and finger definition—obviously unimportant to the creator. Half the size of ping-pong balls. Quite solid, more so than the torso. The head seems less dense but yet still more solid than the torso.

"Know what else?" asked Julie. "Jake went out to Cohasset, because he says he wants to buy the place as is. He says he wants to settle down."

"No way!" exclaimed Curt, his eyes bugging out. "That bloke's never going to nest! I've known him long enough to be absolutely, positively sure of it!"

"Well, I haven't known him long at all," she said, "but I kind of think the same way. I know Ken does."

"You may be right about this being at the crux of the ol' chap's misery," said Curt, rolling his shirtsleeves up to his elbow. "Stay a wee bit longer, and let's take a gander at it." His heart thundered: Oh yes, m'lady, please stay.

***

Ken was in a strange place. Air, thick and acrid, clogged his insides. Chill penetrated to the marrow. Salted spray assaulted his senses, eyes stinging with it and souring his tongue. It dripped off his face when he looked down. Naked! He was naked and teetering on the edge of a rocky crag! Angry sea hurtled up at him like lecherous fingers of Satan, wanting to snatch him away. He struggled to maintain balance, his heart thundering. His heels hooked the back edge of a boulder, the only thing that kept him from plummeting into an endless firmament. Fog closed in, obscuring even his feet. He lost his bearings. The boulder his heels clung to tilted, then a hard object smacked into his chest and his lungs closed in on themselves like a collapsed bellows. Whatever hit him then shattered like glass somewhere within the din.

The boulder broke away. His arms flailed as he hurtled after it. Terror issued from deep within, but there was no sound as down, he plummeted—down, ever downward. Regina's laughter surged like the angry sea and resonated throughout the tumult. A hoary cast hailed down and a thunderous clap echoed throughout the canyon. The boulder ruptured. Pieces flew at Ken. About to cover his face, he noticed them change into tiny arms, golden curls, a nose splattered with angel kisses. Katrina? Her name lodged in his throat as breath became lost and end over end, he spiraled downward.

"Hey there, big fella," said Peter, jabbing Ken with the hook of his prosthetic hand. "Wake up." He jabbed again and waited for a response. When none came, he gripped his son-in-law by the shoulders and shook. "Come on, now. Time to wake up!"

Ken bolted, eyes the size of cantaloupes, gasping for air. He took a blind swing.

Peter ducked as an arm cast came at him. "Hey," he yelped. "Come out of it, will ya?"

Ken grabbed the shadow that hovered over him and clung to it for dear life, as if it might stop the endless descent.

"Hey, snap out of it. It's me—Peter! Julie's father!"

Ken tightened his grip. Sweat poured off him as he hollered, "You're not taking her!" Blinking away the glare, he found himself eyeball to eyeball with his father-in-law, clutching the tee shirt that Elizabeth had bought for him the previous summer at the America concert on City Hall Plaza. "Peter," gasped Ken as life came flooding back. "Where...?"

Peter extricated Ken's hand off his shirt and then rubbed his chest. "Bad trip, 'ey man?" His heart palpitated the way it did whenever he flashed back to Nam, which with the passage of time was happening less and less. He eyeballed the finger tracks in his tee shirt.

"Real bad trip," puffed Ken. A tremor wracked his body. His tee shirt and shorts dripped with sweat, grasping his body like giant hands. He might've even peed his pants.

"I'll get you some water," said Peter.

"I have some right..." said Ken while reaching for the tray beside him. "Where is...?" The tray was upended at his feet.

Shards of glass were everywhere. Water spread across the floor like arthritic fingers.

Peter rotated his shoulders. "I'll get the water." On the way to the kitchen, he tried in vain to shake the bulge out of his tee shirt.

When Peter returned, Ken snatched the glass, but his hand shook so bad half the water spilled before ever getting to his lips and he choked on the first mouthful. "Simmer down there, big guy," said Peter whacking Ken on the back.

Things stabilized, Peter returned to the Canadian rocker chair where he had been reading the morning newspaper. Acidity festered deep within as if napalm had just exploded in a nearby jungle. His nerves were shot and his good hand trembled while manipulating reading glasses around his ears and then securing the newspaper in his prosthetic fingers. He crossed his ankles on the hassock and before beginning to read checked out his son-in-law over the rims of his glasses.

"Where's Julie and Mom?" asked Ken.

Both men squinted at the clock. It was almost noon.

Peter snapped open the newspaper and said, "Julie's been gone for quite some time now—over at Gretchen's."

"Oh yeah, now I remember," said Ken. "Got their heads together over baby stuff or something or other."

"Bethie left just after you dozed off," said Peter.

Ken ran his hand through his hair. "Time to back off medication, I think."

Peter jiggled his eyebrows. "Curt's not going to like that idea."

"Tough," postured Ken. "All I do is sleep, and have nightmares."

Peter glanced over his glasses and said dryly, "Sleep sure does bring out the fury." He tried to concentrate on the sports page, but the newsprint blurred as bombs exploded in his head. Imaginary white light made him flinch. Blood mixed with body parts and shrapnel and rained down within a hail of gunfire...endless gunfire. And napalm. Duck! Captains bellow over the deafening noise. Soldiers cry out in agony. Death all around in tattered uniforms from countries thousands of miles apart. Maimed women, children, homeless and abandoned. Agent Orange. Disgraceful shacks substitute for orphanages.

"How did you get rid of the demons?" asked Ken.

"Demons?" sputtered Peter.

"You being a Vietnam vet, MIA and all," said Ken. "You must've had demons along the way."

Newspaper crumpled onto his lap as Peter ripped off his glasses and belched, "They come and go."

Ken harrumphed.

Peter gnawed on the right earpiece of his glasses. "Half the battle is figuring out what sets them off," he said. "Getting up guts enough to face the trauma eyeball to eyeball gets a jump on demons. Good thing is, time has a way of putting distance between good times and bad. Bad thing is the bad's always coming at you."

Ken pondered his nightmare and the crag he had stood upon, the ocean bubbling up all around him, his nakedness, his lungs collapsing, and his heart thundering so hard that he thought his chest was going to explode. Up till now, nightmares consisted of Regina, Jake, and Katrina. Cripes, now he had to contend with falling off cliffs? Where the hell's that coming from? He shook his head and glanced at Peter. "It's all just too much."

"Look," said Peter, using his glasses for emphasis, "since Regina and Katrina's death, you've been running from nobody but yourself."

"Ain't that the truth," snorted Ken. "I've run so far that I can't find me anymore."

"I know what that's like," said Peter. "Sooner or later we have to stop running."

Ken shook his head and grumbled, "It's the stopping that'll kill ya."

"Hey listen, bub, you're not alone," protested Peter. "I refused to remember, to even speak about Nam, but then one day, something I looked at, something I smelled, something I heard, I don't know what it was, but it all came crashing down about me. It was all too much at first, but with time and lots of help, I sorted it out. Don't get me wrong—I don't think it'll ever get totally sorted out, and maybe…I don't want it to be, either. War is a hell and shouldn't be forgotten. Bottom line is I did remember and I remembered Bethie. Suddenly, nothing else mattered."

"I'm pretty sure I've got a handle on my relationship with Regina," said Ken. "She was no good, and that's that." He hesitated. "Wow. I never admitted that to anybody, not even myself." He ran his hand through his hair. "Problem is Katrina. I just can't get over that last look she gave me, that last terrorized look as that woman pulled my little girl away from me. And when I think of that plane with Katrina on it, plummeting into that swamp, how frightened she must've been…"

Peter swallowed hard. When he came back from Nam, Elizabeth was alive and waiting for him—even though it took quite a while to get up guts enough to go back to her. And then Julie was an added bonus. And now Julie was the key to Ken's well being. "Bethie opened my eyes to the real things in life. Any time I have a negative thought, I think about her and those real things. My Julie can and wants to do the same for you."

Ken stroked his chin with the back of his hand. "Yeah. If Julie were here, we'd talk this out. Sharing things with her is like breathing in morning freshness. I missed stuff like that with Regina. When Julie came along, I should've put an end to all the years of refusing to accept the tragedy, refusing to speak of Regina and Katrina, doing everything possible to put it all out of my mind. I should've trusted Julie with my pain. Opened up to her."

Julie had opened Ken's eyes to so many things, like cool sand between toes on a hot day, snowflakes on the face in December, and bugs, creepy-crawly bugs walking across one's back while lying in the tall grass in the dunes of the Cape on a starry night. She had a way of appreciating everything, the late night, the rain—even if it's freezing cold. Julie had an infinite capacity for romance.

"Yes," said Ken, "there's no denying it. Julie's good for me."

"As your esteemed father-in-law, I must admit," said Peter with a glint in his eye, "I'm quite certain that you're good for her, too. Whenever you're around, she's happy. Even in this sad state that you're in at the moment, she looks at you as if you just rode in on a white steed."

"Works both ways," said Ken. "When she's not around, like now, something's missing. She's missing. I need her more than the air I breathe. And you know what, Pete?"

"What's that?"

"Sometimes that scares me to death."

Peter laced his fingers behind his head and said, "As my Bethie pointed out to me not too long ago, 'Just remember one thing—love is the saddest thing when it goes away.'"

CHAPTER FIFTEEN

After leaving Curt's office, Julie headed to the Konstanze's. That's where she had told Ken and her parents she was going before taking off that morning. She didn't tell them about going to see Curt nor that she had fallen. Plus suspicions about Jake would've stressed them out, so she kept that under her hat. They had enough to deal with. She wasn't about to add to the heap. Besides, Curt knew Ken inside and out, so if her suspicions were even remotely justified, he'd know what to do and how to do it so Ken wouldn't get riled up.

Thunderheads were playing chicken with the sun, and though it was almost lunchtime, it got so dark that Julie was forced to turn on the headlights. Passing the market where she had shopped the day before, she tried not to look, but peripheral vision wasn't on her side, so curiosity took over. One itty-bitty slant sparked yesterday to explode in her head. Faces loomed: Jake's, Gretchen's, Leopold's, and the little kid clutching his mother's hand. Her heart raced. Sweat beaded on her forehead.

Just then, the sun streaked out of the clouds. Nearly blinded, she flipped down the visor just as she bore down on the entrance to the over-50 development where Gretchen and Leopold lived. Jamming on the brakes, she yanked the wheel and the white minivan with lights on swerved around the corner. A landscaper, who was loading a ride-on lawnmower onto a flatbed trailer hitched to the back of a black pickup truck, gave Julie a dirty look. Embarrassment surged through her. She slowed to a crawl and switched off the headlights.

CANDY-COLORED CLOWN

Unsure of the Konstanze's address, she rolled down her window and gawked at the numbers on the gray-shingled dwellings with white trim and federal blue shutters. The aroma of new-mown grass filled the Lumina as she muttered, "They live on the right-hand side, that much I remember. Twenty-five...I think."

The brass numbers stood out clear enough on the doors, four to each building, one on each end and two side by side in the center. She had been there only once, because Ken disliked visiting Regina's parents, even in this new place where they had recently moved. He said they had too many pictures of Regina and Katrina hanging about, but that wasn't true. They had only a couple pictures, and those were grainy and looked as though they had been snapped on the sly. Julie had never seen pictures of Regina as a child. Did any exist? she wondered. At any rate, Leopold and Gretchen usually came out to Cohasset and other times went to Ken's parents', Mom's, or wherever the occasion dictated.

"Better check the address," she mumbled and pulled alongside the curb. The image of sauntering up to a door, ringing the bell, and making a fool out of herself when some crotchety old dude opened the door, scratching his butt and licking toothless chops, did not set well.

She chucked the minivan into park then ferreted through her shoulder bag for her address book. "Where the heck is it?" she grunted. "Geez, one of these days I've got to sort out all this junk! Ah, there you are, you little bugger—as Curt might say."

As Julie snagged the address book, the roar of an engine sent chills tearing up and down her spine. A sports car hurtled, hell bent for leather, towards her. "Jake!" she belched.

Terror surged through her veins as Julie slumped down behind the wheel a mere second before the car swooshed past. The minivan still rocked when she straightened up and squinted into the rearview mirror.

At full bore the car careened out of the community, brake lights never flashing. Horns blared, tires screeched, and the landscaper, now finished with loading the ride-on lawnmower onto the flatbed trailer, took off his cap and scratched his head.

"One of these days, Jakey baby," said Julie, shaking her head, "there's going to be one God-awful crash. Then they'll take your sorry butt away in a body bag."

As a tremor shot through Julie, she realized that her hand was still in the shoulder bag, clamped onto the address book. She pulled it out. One eye kept vigil on the rearview mirror while she flipped through pages. "K... K...." she mumbled. Her index finger skimmed the K page and stopped at Konstanze. Her eyes narrowed. "Hmm, 52, not 25. Good thing I checked. Had the right numbers—only backwards."

Julie squinted at the number on the building she was parked in front of. "25." She bit the inside of her lip and looked down the street. "To think what might've happened if I was getting out my car to check out this place and Jake came bombing along." Her eyes rolled and peered into the rearview mirror. "Okay. Let's get outta here." She put the minivan in gear and inched away from the curb. Down the street a ways, she spotted Leo's car parked in front of one of the units. She stopped to verify the number then pulled up to the curb and shut off the engine. She double-checked her surroundings. The coast was clear, so she hooked her bag over her shoulder, sucked in a breath, and got out of the minivan. Skirting the front, she stuck close and before leaving its safety, stopped to scan the neighborhood. Not so much as a robin bounding over the postage stamp size lawns. She made a mad dash across the grass to the fieldstone walkway and up onto the cement landing. After catching her breath, she rang the doorbell.

Moments passed. Her eyes narrowed on the brass handle. Was imagination playing tricks on her? Had she heard a noise coming from the other side of the door? Nah, temperature change caused the house to creak. Although... She bit the inside of her cheek. ...that noise could've been a squeaky floorboard. In that case... Gooseflesh spiked as she squinted at the peephole. ...somebody's got an eye on her at that very moment! Another clunk. The floor's griping under somebody's weight!

Everything within Julie cried out that things weren't right inside that house. Gretchen's the person on the other side of that door. "Let me in, Gretchen," she said in a low voice, tapping on the door.

When no answer came, Julie put an ear to the door. No television. No radio. She stepped back and jiggled the door handle. "Please, Gretchen, open the door. If we work together, we can stop all this." There, she said it, though she had no clue as to what *all this* was or how to *stop all this*. Again, she flattened her ear against the door. Her stomach somersaulted. Gretchen's crying!

Julie stepped back and rapped urgently. "I can help—I know I can. Things are going to get a whole lot worse if we don't figure out something real quick."

Efforts seemed futile, but then the brass door handle little by little pivoted downward. When the door cracked open, she put a soft shoulder to it and watched it yawn open.

A brass security chain lay on the floor, worming around the leg of a high back chair. She leered at the doorjamb where the chain had been attached. Shredded wood surrounded gaping holes where screws had been. Geez, she thought, lot of good security chains are.

Julie heard a moan and scanned the room. "Gretchen?"

A sniffle.

Julie's eyes narrowed on the credenza. Next to it on the floor, the old woman cowered, wrinkled old hands shielding her eyes. Her floral print dress was torn at the waist seam and a white tricot slip was visible.

"Gretchen!" shrieked Julie as she dropped her shoulder bag and rushed to the old woman. "For God's sake, what happened?"

Gretchen began to wail.

Noticing hosiery riddled with runs with gaping holes in the knees, Julie gasped, "Your knees are all scraped up and bloody!"

The old woman recoiled, pulling herself into a fetal-like position.

Julie pried at Gretchen's hands. "How'd you get that bruise on your cheek?"

Gretchen bent her head into the crook of her arm.

"Talk to me," prodded Julie.

Getting no response, she scanned the room. "What a mess!" An alarm buzzed inside her. "Leopold!" She turned to Gretchen. "Where's Leo?"

The old woman yelped.

"Look at me," cried Julie and yanked on old wrists. "Where is he?"

Stricken German blue eyes battled against making contact as Julie insisted, "Tell me where Leo is!" She shook the old woman. Then she picked up on Gretchen's eyes darting back and forth from here to the overturned sofa. "Behind there?"

Gretchen gave a nearly inaudible squeak and then shuddered.

Julie dropped the old lady's wrists and dashed to the sofa. Behind it, Leopold lay in a heap, shirt torn and hanging off one shoulder like a rag, buttons missing.

"He's dead!" shrieked Julie as her hands covered her mouth.

"Nein, nein," moaned Gretchen as on all fours she crawled over to the sofa.

Julie bent at the knees and stretched out her arm, hand trembling. The old man's cheek wasn't warm, yet didn't have the chill of death. She applied pressure to the side of his neck. "P-pulse," she stuttered. "I-I got a p-pulse."

Gretchen cupped her cheeks with her hands. Hope lit up her eyes.

"Go call 911!" yelped Julie.

The old woman scrambled to her feet.

"Hurry, Gretchen! Hurry," hollered Julie.

"Schnell! Schnell," cried the old woman, hands fluttering in the air as she scurried to the kitchen.

Julie wrung her hands. "Don't move him," she wheezed, gawking at Leopold. "I know that much." She got to her feet. "But I have to do something!"

She eyed a Bible on the floor, torn apart at the binding. Every last fiber within her railed, "This is Jake's work!"

Julie glanced toward the kitchen where Gretchen screeched on the phone for help. Julie pursed her lips. What did this poor old couple do to make Jake so mad?

Gretchen scampered back and knelt down. Clutching his hand to her breast, she sobbed, "*Auch mein lieb* Leopold."

Julie rammed her hands into her hips and spat, "Jake did this, didn't he?"

The old woman's entire body assented.

"But why?"

"*Puppe,*" cried Gretchen.

"*Puppe?*" echoed Julie.

"*Puppe! Puppe,*" insisted Gretchen.

Julie fell to her knees and clutched the old woman's cheeks in her hands. Her eyes bore into Gretchen's. "What's *puppe?*"

The old woman screeched, "Doll!"

"Doll?" echoed Julie, falling back on her ankles, hands gesturing.

"Auch, auch," stammered the old woman. "Puppet, *nein,* uhm, clown!"

"Clown," said Julie.

Julie's brows came together. Then she scrambled to her shoulder bag lying on the floor next to the gaping front door. She whipped out the candy-colored clown and wielded it high, shrieking, "This?"

"*Ya! Ya!*" exclaimed Gretchen, nodding vehemently. "Jake. He go get it."

Terror ripped through Julie. "He's going to Mom's?"

"Ya, ya!"

Old lips quivered. Horrified eyes jounced.

"But…but I have it," howled Julie, brandishing the clown at the woman. "I have it right here!"

Julie paced. Curt had found Ken all beat up right after Regina ran off with Katrina, but Regina didn't have the muscle to do that kind of damage. *A blow like that is rarely accidental,* Curt had said. *Bloody idiot knew the exact spot to hit. Must've been the bloke she ran off with.*

As "oh, no," trickled from her lips, Julie froze.

Denying what she knew to be true, she jammed her hands against her temples and the clown bashed against the side of her face. She extended her arm, eyeballing the clown. "This is why Jake came over to Mom's yesterday." *A blow like that is rarely accidental. Must've been the bloke she ran off with.* Her eyes widened. "Ken," she gasped.

As she raced off to the kitchen, the clown fell to the floor. She snatched up the phone, punched in numbers, and jammed the handset to her ear. "Busy," she cried and glared at the mouthpiece. She hit the off key then the redial. "Get off the phone," she cried and slammed down the handset. She gnawed her bottom lip. There's got to be some way of cutting off Jake! She snatched up the handset and hit redial. Still busy. Her index finger jabbed the off key and then the operator key. It rang more than a dozen times. "Come on, come on!"

"Operator."

"Yes. Yes, operator," gushed Julie. "I can't reach 555-7419. It's busy. You gotta break in! It's an emergency!"

Eternal moments passed. Julie fidgeted.

"That line is out of service, ma'am," said the operator.

"Out of service?" screeched Julie. "No. No! It's not out of service! Don't tell me that! Absolutely not!"

"Ma'am, ma'am," cut in the operator. "Shall I contact the police?"

"Yes. Police. Call the police!"

"I'm dialing them as we speak, ma'am."

Julie choked for breath. "Make them go to 158 River Street, unit 503. Jake Waters is headed there. He'll stop at nothing to get the clown."

"Clown?" asked the operator.

"Just tell the cops that," cried Julie. "Get the cops to that address! Hurry!"

"Yes, ma'am."

Julie slammed down the phone. "Gotta get to Mom's," she puffed and tore out of the kitchen.

As she grappled for the clown and then her shoulder bag, law enforcement and paramedics rushed in through the open front door. She stuffed the clown into the bag and made a mad dash for the door.

"Hold on there, young lady," barked a husky man in a brown tweed sport coat, white shirt, tie, and baggy gray pants. His right hand held a service revolver just below shoulder level as he stepped in her path.

Size and gun meant nothing as Julie screamed, "Get out of my way!" She sidestepped him, first to the left then the right.

"Nobody's goin' anywhere until I get answers," stormed the plain-clothes cop. Snagging her around the waist, he lifted her off her feet while his right hand aimed the revolver at the ceiling and took it off cock.

"Let me go! Let me go," she howled, arms and legs flailing.

Having all he could to maintain hold on her, he shouted, "What's the hurry?"

"Gotta get to Mom's," she screeched, fingers digging into his arm. "Let me go!" The struggled zapped her energy. All in tears, she whined, "Please, let me go. Please. Jake'll do the same thing there that he did here."

"Who's Jake and where's Mom's?" he asked. Setting her down, he instantly recognized her, the young lady who freaked out in the ER and wouldn't let go of his shirt. Husband took a header off that cliff in Cohasset.

Julie choked on her own spit. "Jake…he's…he's on the way to Mom's… Dad's… My husband…can't walk…an'…he…he can't defend himself. Dad…he…Nam…"

"We're outta here," barked Detective Gage Fleming while holstering his weapon. Hauling her toward the front door, he bellowed over his shoulder, "White, take over here!" Outside, he whistled at two uniforms. "Lane! Edwards! Keep up!"

***

The intercom buzzed as Peter sauntered down the hall on his way to the kitchen to make lunch. Stepping up to the speaker panel, he pressed the talk button and sang out, "Hello?"

"Jake here."

Peter hit the button that released the lobby door lock and at the same time opened the front door of the condo. Heading to the kitchen, he called, "Your brother's here."

In the living room, Ken scowled. He'd had just about enough of Jake and his shenanigans to say nothing of the part he played in Regina squirreling off Katrina and… His insides knotted. …And Katrina's death. The fingernails of his right hand scored the tapestry that covered the recliner armrest. "How much longer am I supposed to put up with Jake's blatant disregard for my life and everything dear to me?" he said. His hand squeezed into a fist then rammed into the armrest. "This is it! I'm having it out with him the second he shows his ugly mug!"

The front door slammed. The building rattled. Ken was startled, and Peter, taking a carton of orange juice out of the refrigerator, was unnerved.

Jake stomped into the kitchen, snagged the telephone, and yanked the cord out of the wall. He hurled it at Peter who didn't think twice before ducking. Then Jake stormed off to the living room, and Peter warily got to his feet and flexed his neck.

"Where's that fucking clown?" bellowed Jake.

Instinct primed the ex MIA for battle—except, this wasn't Vietnam, this was his home—and that made matters worse. Everything became a blur. Advancing to the living room, Peter didn't see the hallway; he saw jungle.

"Watch your mouth," hollered Ken. "You're in someone else's house, not mine!"

Peter rounded the archway as Jake assumed a sidelong stance and leveled the four-inch barrel of a Glock 19 pistol on Ken. His forearm bulged as Jake sneered, "And that means…?"

Ken pressed himself into the recliner. His face had lost all color and looked like he was reliving a bad dream. He was a sitting duck.

Rage exploded like napalm within Peter. "What's going on?"

Jake, caught off guard, spun around and took aim. Within seconds, he sniggered, "Why, if it isn't the hero crip'." His finger let up on the trigger, but his face remained intent and sinister. He reset his shoulders square and rigid. "Where's that stinkin' clown?"

Peter sent Ken a confused look. At the same instant, it dawned on both of them that Jake was after the candy-colored clown that had been propped upon the television ever since Ken got out of the hospital. They zeroed in on the television. The clown wasn't there! "It was here this morning," said Peter while stepping over to the television. "At least I think it was."

The business end of the Glock ping-ponged between Peter and Ken, too much distance between targets as far as Jake was concerned. His left fist opened and closed, opened and closed.

Peter craned his neck to see if the clown had fallen behind the television. "Not back here." He glanced at Ken. "When did you see it last?"

Ken bristled. "Always knew you had a hair-trigger temper, Jake, but this time you've gone too far."

"Outta my way, crip'," snarled Jake, shoving Peter aside. As he tugged the television away from the wall, the front legs got caught on a crack between two hardwood slats, and the television tipped forward.

"Hey! Take it easy," yelped Peter and braced his hands against the television.

"Shut up, old man," seethed Jake, stepping towards the ex MIA, gun menacing.

Peter raised both hands to shoulder level. "Now, hold on a minute."

"Hand over that fuckin' clown," spat Jake as his left hand arced, poised to strike.

"Julie took it to the bedroom," shouted Ken.

Peter gave a tentative nod and feigned submission. He knew he had to convince Jake that the clown was in the bedroom and get Jake to send him for it. Then he planned to get at the gun out of the duffle bag in the master bedroom closet. Peter signaled Ken with his eyes.

Ken caught the signal that his father-in-law had a plan. Didn't know what it was, but Pete's well versed in warfare strategies. That's all Ken needed to know.

"Come to think of it," said Peter, masking his intentions, "I remember Julie had the clown this morning."

"It's in the middle of a bunch of other stuffed toys propped against the pillows," said Ken, joining the bluff.

"Want me to go get it?" asked Peter.

Jake chewed over the idea, focusing on the archway then at Peter then at Ken, both trying to look trustworthy. He focused at the archway again as if he might go get it himself.

"I'll get it," said Peter, lowering his hands.

Jake shot a look at ex MIA. His left eyelid flinched. "Nobody's going anywhere," he barked. "Get over there next to the wimp!" The barrel of the Glock motioned. "Don't move a muscle, if you know what's good for you."

He yanked a book off the shelf and held it by the cover to shake it out. Nothing fell out. He did the same to the rest of the books and then hunted the bookcase wall for a secret door.

Ken braced himself on the edge of the recliner, eyes cemented on Jake.

"Stay put," whispered Peter. His plan needed time to run its course.

Jake dumped the contents of a magazine rack on the floor and then kicked the magazines as if they were a pile of autumn leaves.

"Get out of this house!" blasted Ken. "Now!"

Jake got in Ken's face; but what he said, Ken didn't hear, because another time, long ago, took over. Ken and Jake were eyeball-to-eyeball, just like now. Ken stood his ground as Jake spread his arms wide, stepped back, and said that he had tried to be nice. His eyes iced, just like now. His jaw set the same way. Arm and leg muscles flexed. Fingers beckoned as through clenched teeth Jake dared Ken to come and get him, if he thought he's man enough.

Then the past shattered with a vicious backhand that catapulted Ken out of the recliner, across the TV tray that collapsed under his weight, and onto the floor hard. Breath whooshed out of him and then the recliner crashed down upon him.

Peter sought to help, but a pistol barrel crammed up one nostril stopped him in his tracks.

"I wouldn't if I were you," growled Jake.

Close to passing out, Ken struggled to catch his breath. He rubbed his chest as if feeling the crushing blow to the heart that Jake had given him that day when he and Regina took Katrina away. Pieces of the past swiftly revealed themselves.

"I want that clown," howled Jake as he backed away from Peter and stalked about the room. M & M's that had been in the candy dish on the TV tray crunched under his weight. He picked up the sextant and hurled it at Ken. He picked up the model of the U. S. S. Constitution and hurled it at Peter. The gun barrel knocked over other treasured knickknacks.

When Ken wriggled out from underneath the recliner, it thumped on the floor. Jake shot a look at the recliner then his eyes narrowed on Ken. He dropped the chess set in his hands and started for Ken, yelling, "Fork over the clown, bro'!" He kicked the plaster leg cast. "Now!"

"I don't know where it is," shouted Ken.

"Don't give me that," howled Jake, aiming the Glock, trigger finger tightening.

"Bethie will get it for you," yelled the ex-POW, holding back his fury.

Jake spun around.

"Bethie can find a needle in a haystack when she sets her mind to it," said Peter while telling himself to keep his wits about him. "She and Julie will be back shortly, so how about we all settle down and wait? Come on. Help me with the recliner. Let's get your brother up off the floor."

"Brother?" belched Jake, gawking at Ken and then at Peter.

Ken rubbed his chest and sensed little arms about his neck. He eyed Jake who was livid, no doubt about that, but something else clenched his jaw, something else that he wanted to release on the world.

Know how much I love you, Daddy?

Too much, my little Katrina, too much.

There's no such thing as too much, Daddy.

"Tell me where Katrina is!" shouted Ken.

Jake stopped short. His head tilted to one side as his finger let up on the trigger and the pistol sagged. He swung around and eye balled Ken. His voice grated like fingernails across a blackboard as he said, "Ah, the memory returns." A lecherous grin swept across his face. "I must admit..." He scratched the side of his head with the gun barrel. "It's about time." Laughter, rich with contempt, exploded.

Now that it was an undeniable fact that Katrina was alive, Ken wasn't about to wimp out on her again—no, not even if his had to die at Jake's hands in the process. The hinges of his jaw fused. Muscles down the side of his face and neck constricted as he summoned every last bit of strength and braced himself up on one elbow. "What did you do with my daughter?"

The jackal closed in for the kill, hovering, heckling, "I'll never tell."

"Where is she?" screeched Ken like a madman, "Tell me!"

"Ricky, I'm home," called Elizabeth.

Jake was taken by surprise, just the opportunity that Peter was anticipating. Using the full force of his weight, the ex MIA brought Jake down within inches of Ken. The Glock 19 flew into the air, skipped off the Canadian rocker, hit the wall, and fell into the corner. Then the wrath of a prosthetic finger sliced the side of Jake's face from temple to chin.

"Old man?" blasted Peter. "Crip? You spineless sack of pig dung. This old sea dog still has a few tricks left in him."

Not knowing what hit him, Jake got to his knees and struggled for air. Vision unclear, he fingered the side of his face where liquid spurted like a geyser then eyeballed his hand. His mouth dropped. "Blood?" His eyes fired hatred at Peter as he snarled, "You cut me. You fucking bastard." He struggled to get to his feet. "I'll kill you with my bare hands!" He fell back.

Ken knew that survival depended upon quick thinking, yet being unarmed and one armed limited options. He glanced around. Just out of his good arm's reach were a teaspoon and an empty yogurt container. An afghan hung off the overturned recliner. In his sorry condition, he'd never be quick enough to latch onto it, throw it over Jake's head, and then hold him down.

He looked behind him. The candy dish! He snatched it up, arced it high into the air, and then brought it down, bashing it into Jake's skull.

"Over my dead body," yelled Ken. Hammering again and again, he rid himself of pent-up resentment. "Over my dead body!"

Elizabeth rushed into the living room. "What in the world?"

Peter caught hold of Ken's arm and shoved him aside. Jumping on Jake, he hollered, "Bethie! Get my gun and bayonet out of my duffle bag in the bedroom!"

Gone and back in a flash, Elizabeth shoved the weapon at Peter, his left arm now restraining Jake against his chest and the hook of his prosthetic hand goring into the soft tissue beneath the villain's jaw. "Don't need it," huffed Peter. "This son of a bitch doesn't dare move a muscle. Ain't that right, Jake, m'boy?"

Jake's eyes rolled upwards. His head drilled into Peter's chest.

The expression that sheeted Peter's blood-caked face was one that Elizabeth had never seen. The fury of war glazed his eyes. His chin jutted out in unholy defiance. "Never thought I'd be thankful for this hook," he said with levity bitter as Asian gingerroot. "Amazing, ain't it, Bethie? I put my life—our life on hold—and my health in jeopardy in God-forsaken jungles. MIA for God knows how long." His grip on Jake tightened. "All for the American way and Mom's apple pie." Blood seeped around the tip of the hook as Jake's face turned from red to blue to gray. "All for the likes of slime-balls like this? So they can invade my home? Terrorize my family?"

"Peter, no," cried Elizabeth.

Only once had Peter ever heard her speak in that tone, and that was over twenty years ago. If only he had listened to her then and not let Vietnam tear them apart. Nam. His flesh crawled. All the suffering. All the wasted lives. Years without beloved Bethie. Ignorant of fathering a child.

"No, Peter." Her voice was softer, more tender. "Please. No more."

Peter squinted at blood bubbling around the tip of the hook and then at Jake. His lip twitched.

"Bah, you're not worth it," spewed Peter, easing up on the stranglehold. He peered up at Elizabeth and smiled that silly little grin of his. "Best get the cops here, my sweet morning eyes." He watched her take off like a bat out of hell. "Controlling this fickle finger of fate—souvenir of Nam—isn't easy, you know."

CANDY-COLORED CLOWN

CHAPTER SIXTEEN

"Detective Gage Fleming."

Julie gave the plain-clothes cop a blank stare.

He tossed her a look. "My name—Fleming. Detective Gage Fleming." He looked back at the road, darkened by a fast-moving storm front and chastised himself for not doing a very good job diverting the young lady's attention from whatever's going on at the Blair condo. "Don't remember me, do you?" he asked as the emergency strobe on the roof zinged across buildings, vehicles, and pedestrians scrambling out of the way.

Her eyes fixed on the husky man. She'd seen him before. Where? When? That brown tweed sport coat he's wearing was somehow familiar. Those baggy gray pants, too.

"I interviewed you at the hospital the day your place in Cohasset went up in smoke," he said.

She squinted at his graying, auburn hair. The crew cut—that's what threw her off. "You got your hair cut."

He grunted and squinted into the rearview mirror. Edwards' black and white was so close that Fleming couldn't see the front hood. Damn rookie's inches off my tail, and Lane looks like he's attached.

"You don't look like a cop," said Julie.

Refocusing on the road ahead, Fleming rumbled, "What are cops supposed to look like?"

She jounced her right shoulder and glanced out the passenger-side window. Even his voice wasn't as deep and authoritative as she expected a cop's to be. "You don't believe one word I told you," she said, "I can tell."

Just then, Fleming yanked the steering wheel. As the unmarked car swerved around a corner, Lane and Edwards followed suit and Julie grabbed hold of the handgrip and held on for dear life. Ahead, strobe lights of countless local and state law enforcement vehicles sliced the murkiness like fingers of lightning. She glared at Fleming. His facial cast had changed. She pursed her lips, thinking, Different ball of wax now, huh, buster?

"You got no idea whatsoever why this Jake fella wants that clown?" he asked while maneuvering into the maze of cars.

"None," she spat.

"Or why he's so interested in Cohasset?"

Rain plopped on the windshield, forming circular smudges of road grime. No time for wipers as Fleming skidded to a stop at the main entrance to the condominium.

"No clue," she said.

Edwards screeched to a stop in the nick of time, but Lane hit Edwards and Edwards lurched forward. Fleming felt the jolt and cursed, "Damn rookies."

Julie grabbed the door handle.

Fleming clamped onto her left wrist.

She looked down at his hand and then glared at him.

"Stick close," he said.

"Sure," she puffed then shook him off. Yanking the door handle, she put a shoulder to the door. As she bolted out of the car, rain splattered her face.

Fleming hauled himself out of the unmarked car and tried to maintain the distance from Julie who was racing toward the high-rise condominium. He had all he could do to wave his badge. Getting too old for this stuff, he brooded. Don't even have the breath to holler, slow down. More time at the gym, old boy. "Outta the way! Outta the way," he boomed as an inattentive flatfoot stepped in his path. Now Fleming had very little breath left to make any kind of headway and was obliged to concentrate on the physical end of things, nothing else. Waving off others who got in the way became impossible.

Just then, Edwards loped past as if keeping easy time to military cadence. Neck thick and forearms muscular, he was impeccably groomed—after all, he did graduate Parris Island. Ah, the ladies do love a man in uniform.

Then Lane sprinted past, grinning real funny-like. Fleming almost lost his footing on the steaming pavement. Lane was tall and bony and his uniform didn't hang right. Lane had a pipe dream of being a hero cop that Fleming didn't have the wherewithal to correct.

***

In Unit 503, paramedics lifted Ken off the living room floor and onto the couch. Embarrassment washing over him, he raged, "I'm so sick and tired of being a helpless invalid." His fist pounded the arm of the couch. "Sick of Jake. Sick of everything!" His fingers raked through his hair. Why couldn't things be like they used to be—not back to Regina, but back to the way it was before Julie got pregnant? His insides railed. Regina? She was on that Cessna with Katrina. If Katrina is alive, what about that harpy?

"You all right?" asked Elizabeth as she fingered his hair into place.

Feeling like a mama's boy, Ken pushed away her hand.

"I'll get a wet face cloth for your face," she said.

He waved her off. "Don't bother."

Lightning lit up the condo. Eyes focused on the balcony. Rain was spattering the windows, and Ralph was clawing at the screen door. Thunder rumbled.

Elizabeth stepped to the door. The cat's mouth gaped into a full-fledged meow, fangs glistening. The instant she opened the door, he barreled into the living room and disappeared down the hall.

Peter nudged Ken's arm and said, "Hey, how about that? Katrina's alive!"

"Alive?" belched Elizabeth while closing windows. "Did you say Katrina's alive?"

"I sure did," said Peter.

"I," stammered Ken, "I…" His fingers ran through his hair. "I don't know where on earth I got that."

Lightning flashed and smack on its heels came a thunderclap. Peter rubbed the sore muscle above his prosthetic hand.

"Don't touch that metal, sir," said a uniformed cop. "Blood on it is evidence. Crime scene techs are on the way."

"Yeah, yeah," said Peter.

His father-in-law's blood-streaked body riled Ken. Nobody deserved that kind of treatment. His fist tightened into a ball. The memory of Jake's backhand, crashing onto the floor, and air spewing out his nostrils and mouth brought back four years ago. Jake's scheming face had taunted Ken then just like moments ago while he denied Ken of his own flesh and blood. Then Jake had cold-conked him, and when Ken had come to, Jake and Regina had taken off with Katrina—gone forever—or so for the past four years Ken believed. Pent-up wrath drained into frustration. "Why didn't I have backbone enough to track them down?" he groaned.

"Your mind simply blocked it out," said Peter.

"Jake says I'll never find Katrina," moaned Ken.

"That can only mean she's alive!" exclaimed Elizabeth as the onslaught of law enforcement swallowed her up and cut her off from asking about Regina.

Ken squinted at Peter. "You shouldn't've stopped me from smearing that bastard's brains all over this room."

"Justifiable homicide, no doubt about it," said Peter. "On the other hand, Jake holds all the cards now and getting Katrina's location out of him is going to be one big headache."

"Katrina's alive…" stammered Ken. "After all this time… Where…" A trembling hand covered his eyes as emotion overflowed. "My little girl is alive…"

***

In the lobby, Julie hit the Up button on the elevator panel at a dead run. The lighted arrow above the door indicated that a car was already on the way down. She hopped about, panting. Lane and Edwards jogged up, cool, as if taking a leisurely stroll. She glanced over her shoulder. Fleming, huffing and puffing, got there just as the elevator door began to slide open. It wasn't completely open when Julie charged into the car. She screamed holy terror. Edwards and Lane drew service revolvers, tripping over each other's feet to assume spread-eagle stances. Julie toppled into Fleming. "What the…" he belched, hooking his forearms under her armpits to keep her upright.

"This ain't over, toots," seethed Jake, handcuffed with a half a dozen state troopers keeping him in check. "Not by a long shot!" His black eyes skewered Julie as the troopers hauled him out of the elevator.

Fleming sucked in a breath and spluttered, "He's in cuffs. You're safe."

Julie thrashed about, all reason lost. Jake's eyes ablaze with the fires of hell and bloodied gauze taped on his face branded her mind, rendering her bound and determined to get away, away from Jake, away from the nightmare of recent events, away from the horror that surely awaited her up there on the fifth floor. And then she went limp.

Edwards and Lane holstered their weapons. Eagerness grayed to disappointment.

Fleming shook Julie and blustered, "Hey, come on now. That two-bit piece of dog turd can't hurt you." He shook her again. "Listen to me! He can't hurt anybody anymore!"

"Give her to me," barked Edwards, now bare-chested and grappling for the unconscious young woman. As he laid her down on the floor, Lane raced back from the main entrance with a rain-soaked strappy tee shirt. "Come on, come on," shouted Edwards, his thick hand high in the air. He caught the tee shirt that Lane hurled and then slowly wrung it out over her forehead, cheeks, and lips. When her tongue began to search out the droplets, Fleming was beside himself. Those two rookies were handy guys to have around.

"Lend me a hand, Lane," said Edwards. "Let's get Mrs. Waters to her feet."

Next thing Julie knew, Fleming had her braced against the inside wall of the elevator, the door closed, and the car rocketed skyward. Imagination ran amuck. Mass destruction, blood, and death—all awaited her on the fifth floor. She felt like throwing up.

"Mrs. Waters is a bit green," said Edwards.

"Come on, young lady," said Fleming, tapping her cheek. "Snap out of it! You need your wits about you."

"Yeah," snorted Lane. "Who knows what's going on up there?"

Fleming scowled at Lane. Damn rookie.

The car slowed then stopped. The door slid open to a hallway clogged with paramedics, bluecoats, plainclothes, and staties.

Julie quaked. Last thing she wanted to do was to set foot outside of that elevator. Her legs were as rubbery as gummy bears, and fright obscured her vision. A hand, big, powerful, and protective, took hold of her arm.

"Come on," said Fleming, tugging her out of the elevator. "Edwards! Lane," he hollered. "Clear out non-essentials!"

"Julie!"

"Mom?" blubbered Julie.

"Over here, young lady," barked Fleming, yanking on her arm.

"Mom!" shrieked Julie as she sideswiped a state trooper. Her shoulder bag slipped off her arm. Suddenly, her mother's arms were about her. "Mom, you okay? Ken? Dad?"

"We're all okay," said Elizabeth. "Calm down." She rubbed her daughter's back. "It's over now."

"Julie?" bellowed Ken from inside the condo. "Julie!"

She pushed her mother out to arms length and gaped at her.

Elizabeth smiled and nodded.

Julie squeaked then fled into the condo.

Elizabeth was hot on her trail when Fleming picked up the shoulder bag. "Holy smoke," he groused. "This thing weighs a ton! How's a sweet young thing like that carry around this much weight?" He eyeballed it. "Women," he huffed and tossed it over his shoulder.

"Julie?" bellowed Ken, unable to see anything but a sea of people.

"Ken!" she shrieked.

"Where are you?" cried Ken, craning his neck.

"Get out of my way!" she spewed, elbowing her way through the crowd. "Look out!" It seemed as if she was never going to get to him and then there he was. "Thank God, you're all right!" Tears gushed as she held his face in her hands and kissed him.

Fleming passed the kitchen, catching a glimpse of a lab technician rewiring the telephone. He was nearing the living room archway when the phone rang.

"Call for Detective Fleming," sang out the technician.

Spinning on his heels, Fleming headed back to the kitchen. "Fleming," he spat as he jammed the phone against his ear. Static plagued the line. He glanced at the tech who was securing wires around screws in the connector box. "Hey, quit your diddling around," he barked. Then he spoke into the phone, "Say again?"

"Edwards here. Got orders to evac' the premises. Perp's vehicle's parked on the street, munitions onboard. Bomb squad's on the way. The 'hood's secured."

Fleming hung up and motioned to the tech. "Carry on." He adjusted the shoulder bag and tramped down the hall. As he stepped through the archway, a flash of lightning blinded him and on its heels came a crack of thunder so loud that instinct nearly drove him to dive for cover.

Rain sluiced down the balcony windows. Not about to kick anybody out into that kind of weather, Fleming scanned the scene of the crime. Pictures were being snapped. Male vic's got minor bumps and bruises. No open wounds—nothing even close to life threatening. Medics got a handle on it, though a lab technician's swabbing blood off the hook of the vet's prosthetic hand. Envisioning the gauze on the perp's face, Fleming smiled with a great deal of satisfaction. That one-handed vet held his own against a younger and stronger foe.

A couple of uniforms were in the process of up-righting a recliner. Two others had just pushed the television back into place. Several things got busted up. Blood splatters on the furniture and hardwood floor—easy to clean up, although the oriental carpeting should get tossed since it's saturated with blood. Costs too damn much to clean.

The butt of a female detective was sticking out from behind a Canadian rocker. Not bad for her age, thought Fleming. Works out more than me, that's for sure. What the heck's her name?

The female detective stood up, pencil in hand, and on the eraser end, a 9-mm semiautomatic Glock. She sniffed the barrel and said, "Hasn't been fired recently." She slipped it into a plastic bag that a lab tech held open. He sealed it up and labeled it while she logged the Glock onto a yellow evidence folder.

Things hadn't turned out nearly as bad as Fleming had anticipated on the way up in the elevator. He'd seen a hell of a lot worse, no doubt about it, though he was a bit antsy about not evacuating the building. He leaned against the living room archway and crossed his arms. Sure feels good to see the young lady in her husband's arms. He liked happy endings, though he knew the job here wasn't done quite yet. "Just a few minor details to clean up and then I'm outta here," he muttered under his breath.

Just then the woman detective stepped around Fleming. He bolted upright. She smiled at him. His face flushed. He nodded and probably would have tipped his hat if he was wearing one. "Good work," he stammered.

The lab tech followed her, but didn't make eye contact. Then the front door slammed. Except for Fleming, the condo was empty of law enforcement. He cleared his throat and asked, "So, what's that psycho looking for?" He already knew the answer, but procedure called for repeated questioning. Added clarity and all that rubbish.

"The clown," said Elizabeth.

"But it's disappeared," said Peter.

"It used to sit right over there," said Ken, pointing to the television.

Julie leapt to her feet, eyes bugging out. "I have it!" she exclaimed.

"You..." stammered Ken. "You've got the clown?"

"Yeah," she said, looking him square in the eye. "In my shoulder bag."

Ken railed. "For God's sakes, Julie."

She reached for the bag that ordinarily hung off her shoulder. Her jaw dropped. "My bag..." Numbness sheeted over her. "What happened to...?"

"This?" asked Fleming while swinging the bag off his shoulder. He held it at eye level.

Julie zeroed in on the bag and then gave Fleming a dumbfounded leer. She marched over, snatched it away, then dropped to her knees. Tearing through it, she fretted, "Where is it?" Frustration built until she dumped the contents onto the floor. "There it is." She held up the candy-colored clown, formless, a mere shadow of what it used to be. Only hands, feet, and head remained intact.

"What the heck happened to it?" asked Ken.

"Let's have a look at that," said Fleming. He caught it when she tossed it. His brows fused. "All this hubbub over this wretched thing?"

Julie stood up. "I went to see Curt and..."

"Hold it," interrupted Fleming. "Who's Curt?"

"A friend," said Ken. "He's also our family doctor."

"Doctor Curt Shirlington?" asked Fleming.

"Yeah," said Ken.

Fleming gave a hand signal to continue and eyeballed the clown's innards.

Julie looked at Ken and said, "I had this feeling that the clown had something to do with whatever's been bugging you and that Jake's after it, so I told Curt, and he seemed to think that drugs might be hidden inside, so he cut open the side seam with a scalpel, but only sand was in it." She fished a plastic bag of sand from the contents of her shoulder bag that littered the floor and handed it to Fleming. "Curt took some to have it analyzed, just in case. After that, I went over to Gretchen's. Jake had been there and beat up her and Leo, looking for the clown, but I had it, and he didn't know it, and..."

"Good heavens," gasped Elizabeth. "Are they all right?"

"Gretchen's banged up," said Julie. "I don't know about Leo. He's in awful bad shape."

"So what the heck is this Jake fella looking for?" demanded Fleming.

The passing storm rumpled the silence and then the telephone rang. "I'll get it," said Elizabeth. Moments later, she hollered, "It's for you, Detective."

Fleming trudged to the kitchen, eyeing the raggedy clown in his hand. Picking up the receiver, he said, "Yeah."

"Edwards. Got the all clear."

"Yes," spewed Fleming as his fist bunched up and jabbed at the air. No sooner did he hang up when telephone rang again. "Fleming."

"This is Doctor Shirlington."

"Just talking about you, Doc. How you cut open the clown and all."

"Is Jul...uhm...?" Curt swallowed hard. "Uhm...is everyone all right? Jake Waters just came into the ER, bloodied head to toe, face sliced up like chopped liver. Word is he's been in a scuffle over there."

"Everybody's okay, given the circumstances," said Fleming. "Not a bad idea if you were to hop on over here and have a look, just to be on the safe side."

"Be right over," said Curt, who wouldn't be satisfied until he saw with his own eyes that Julie was in one piece. He loved that girl more than he had a right to.

"Wait," exclaimed Julie and ripped the phone away from Fleming. "Curt!"

Curt's stomach flip-flopped.

"Jake *is* looking for the clown!" she exclaimed.

Ralph arched against her leg and clicked.

"He tore up Leo and Gretchen's place, looking for it. And hurt Leo real bad."

Curt winced. "Haven't seen them here… I'll check it out. Now I want you to calm down. See you soon."

"No, wait," she cried as Ralph stretched up to her thigh. His claws pricked her. "I don't understand. Why in the world did Jake go to Leo and Gretchen's to get the clown when he saw it here on top of the television?"

Curt felt like tracking down Jake and giving him a shot of something to put his miserable hide away permanently. Enough is enough!

"Curt," puffed Julie as she picked up Ralph. "Jake could've killed Mom and Dad. And Ken, too! Just like the day he took off with Regina and Katrina."

Ralph clicked.

"Why, Curt? They're supposed to be brothers!"

"Brothers," echoed Curt.

Meanwhile, back in the living room, Fleming was at a loss as to what to make of the mutilated clown. Learning that Jake had run off with Regina and Katrina, he was flabbergasted. "So Jake spilled the beans about your daughter being alive." His eyes leveled on Ken. "What about your wife…er, Regina?"

The thought of Regina still being his wife turned Ken's stomach, but it was shame, worse than any parent felt when a child wandered off accidentally, that made him hang his head. "All this time, I should've been looking for my little girl."

Fleming felt a tug in his gut. "Any idea where she might be?"

Ken filled his lungs with air and exhaled a nearly inaudible "No."

"Did Regina leave any kind of paperwork behind?"

Ken shook his head. "Everything burned in the fire. Clothes, furniture, business records…"

Peter rubbed his index finger back and forth across his upper lip. "Suppose there's anything in that metal safe?"

"Metal safe?" repeated Ken as his eyes shot to Peter.

"The one I dug out of the ashes the morning after the fire," said Peter. "I told you I found it back when you were in the hospital."

"Found what, Dad?" asked Julie as she came back into the living room, carrying Ralph.

"The safe I found in the ashes," said Peter.

She hitched her chin and sagged onto the arm of the couch. Ralph jumped down.

"Remember I told you guys about it in the hospital?"

"It skipped my mind," she said, brushing fur off her lap. "Ken was too far-gone at the time. I've had to fill him in on lots of things that happened before the fire and right after."

"Can I have a look at the safe?" asked Fleming.

Peter glanced at Ken and got a silent okay. "Give me a hand, Bethie?" he asked as he got to his feet.

"What's so important?" asked Julie.

Ken grabbed her hand and squeezed. His eyes teared with hope-riddled anxiety. "Katrina's alive!"

Julie gasped, "Alive?"

His head bobbed up and down. "My little Katrina's alive!"

"But how...? Where...?"

"I don't know," he wailed as his good hand covered his face. "I just don't know!"

Unable to comfort him or herself, Julie got up and went to the balcony door. Gnawing the inside of her lip, she stared out. The rain had stopped. The western horizon was clearing. And Katrina's alive. Geez, what about Regina?

Ralph rubbed against her leg and clicked.

She looked down and whispered, "What am I going to do if Regina comes back, Ralphie?"

The cat gave her an unconcerned eye.

Her mind raced as she opened the screen and followed the cat out onto the balcony. First, Ken freaked out over her being pregnant, then Jake and that silly clown, and now Regina. She raised the window. The breeze whistled in and cooled her face. How was she to stop Regina from coming back for Ken?

Fleming paced, pitching the flaccid candy-colored clown from one hand to the other. Then Elizabeth and Peter came back and placed the metal safe next to Ken. "I'll get the key," she said, taking off to get the extra set of keys that Julie left in the condo after locking herself out of the manse and car once too often.

Julie came in from the balcony and sat down next to Ken. She took hold of his hand. It was clammy. She looked at his face. Perspiration beaded above his lips. She knew how he felt, but for different reasons.

Elizabeth bumped into Fleming as she returned with the key. An awkward moment passed while both revisited that day in the hospital when they collided after Julie let go of his shirt. Fleming cleared his throat. "Sorry, Mrs. Blair. I'm so, so sorry."

As hopeful as everyone was, the safe revealed little—the deed to the manse, insurance policies, Julie and Ken's wills, savings bonds, a couple of pictures Ken had taken of Katrina, backup discs for the office computer. "Hmm, backup discs," mused Ken.

"Sure is a lot of them," said Peter.

"I never write over discs," said Ken.

"Maybe you should start," said Julie as she picked up a handful of discs and spread them like a deck of cards to read the handwritten dates. "Geez, these go way back."

"Good thing you had sense enough to keep important stuff in a fireproof safe," said Peter. "Keeps the IRS off your back."

Ken took one of the discs from Julie and read at the date. He jounced the disc up and down and then scratched his head with the corner of it. He squinted at the date again, which seemed to scream that it was just before the plane crash. So what, he pondered. He flipped it into the safe and rubbed his chest. Looking up, he found everyone staring at him. "Now what?" he asked.

"Good question," said Fleming. His jaw clenched. He paced, pitching the limp candy-colored clown from one hand to the other.

CANDY-COLORED CLOWN

The sun had come out beyond the balcony. Moisture steamed off the screen. The gray cat on the windowsill paused from licking claws that were devoid of fur and eyeballed the detective.

Fleming stopped pacing and raised the candy-colored clown to eye level. That cat didn't take its eyes off it. He pondered the clown and then the cat. "You know what this is all about," he muttered, "don't you, cat?"

Ralph clicked.

Fleming frowned. "When is science going to figure out a way of reading the minds of animals? Think of all the crimes that would be solved." His head jerked to one side as if a right hook had just caught his chin. "What if it's too late for that poor little girl, cat?"

Ralph meowed, eyes penetrating the detective.

A shiver raced through Fleming, one he tried to ignore as he turned to discover anxious faces looking to him to bring Katrina back. A hundred bucks says that Mrs. Regina Waters wasn't on the reception list. He sucked in a mouthful of air and leaned against the doorframe. His hand scraped across his five o'clock shadow that showed up a lot earlier this day than usual. "Trail's gone cold by now," he managed to say. "Judgment isn't good in cases like this."

Something stirred within Ken. *Judgment isn't good* rippled like water troubled by a skipping stone. He rubbed circles in the softness of his temple. "Judgment," escaped his lips.

"Did you say something?" asked Julie, stroking his forearm.

Ken grimaced. "Judgment...I just...can't..." He slapped his leg cast.

Julie fidgeted. Wasn't anybody going to bring up the possibility that Regina's alive?

Fleming, completely at a loss, said, "I better get a move on." He held up the candy-colored clown for all to see. "I'm taking this. Evidence." His hand dropped to his side, holding the formless clown by one hand much like a three-year-old holds a rag doll. "This, too," he said, picking up the bag of sand and stuffing it into the pocket of his brown tweed sport coat. "I'll nose around Jake's apartment and see what I can dig up." His fingers slithered into the breast pocket of his shirt and came out with two cards. "Here's my card. The other one's for somebody to call about cleaning up this mess." He handed the cards to Elizabeth. "Do yourself a favor—don't do it yourself. What happened here is going to get on your nerves enough. Pitch that carpet. Buy a new one. In the meantime, if you come up with anything, no matter how trivial, don't hesitate to track me down."

"If only we can find out what Jake wants with that clown," said Peter, "we might be able to figure out where Katrina is."

"That'd be nice," said Fleming then waved off Elizabeth who was starting for the door. "Don't bother, ma'am. I know the way out." He paused at the archway and turned. "I'll go anywhere, even East Oshkosh if that's what it takes to find your little girl."

Ken tapped his fingers on the leg cast and stared at a snapshot of Katrina. *Judgment. I'll go to East Oshkosh if I have to. East Oshkosh. Judgment. Know how much I love you, Daddy? Too much, my little Katrina, too much. There's no such thing as too much, Daddy.*

Fleming disappeared down the hall. The front door thumped.

Moments passed. Nobody spoke.

Ken ran his hand through his hair. *East Oshkosh. Judgment.* He stared at the open safe then the backup discs. Katrina's picture. A vision of Jake at the office computer formed in his mind. *Research, bro. Research.* The 9–mm semiautomatic pistol lay next to the keyboard. An empty vodka glass was on top of the monitor. *Back atcha, bro'.*

Know how much I love you, Daddy?

Too much, my little Katrina, too much.

There's no such thing as too much, Daddy.

The handwritten date. *East Oshkosh. Judgment.*

Backup discs. Mississippi.

Ken elbowed Julie. "Get Fleming back here!"

"What?" she cried.

"Go get Fleming," he bawled, giving her a shove. "I know where Katrina is!"

CHAPTER SEVENTEEN

"Don't you think you should call your mother and father?" asked Julie as she unlocked the wheelchair brakes.

Ken wagged his head while gesturing. "And say what? Hey, Mom, Dad, guess what? Jake tore up the Konstanze's place...and while he was at it, smacked 'em around. Yup, put good ol' Leopold right in the hospital, he did. Then he decides, hey, what the heck! Why not hop on over to Pete and Beth's and do the same over there? Oh, yah, did I mention that he knocked me out of the recliner and as I lay there on the floor like a limp weenie, he referred to Peter as crip' and old man? Not to worry, Pete's fake hand brought Jake down. Yup, sliced up pretty boy's face real good, too. Hey, get this! All over a stupid, stuffed—uhm, *gutted* clown. And by the way, Katrina's alive. Uh-huh. Jake squirreled her off to some God-forsaken place. She's been there all these years—can you imagine? Where, you ask? Somewhere in the backwoods of Mississippi. Place is called Judgment."

Ken rubbed his forehead.

Know how much I love you, Daddy?

"Judgment," he groaned. His entire body quaked. "Good God, what's become of my little girl?"

Julie leaned over and murmured in his ear, "I know this is hard, sweetheart, but please, you've got to keep it together...for Katrina's sake." She kissed his head and then maneuvered the wheelchair towards the bathroom.

"But Julie," he cried. "Mother and Dad aren't going believe one word of it! What the hell's wrong with Jake anyways?"

She twisted up her face and said, "All over a silly plaything." She pushed the wheelchair into the bathroom and up to the washbasin.

His eyes followed her every move in the mirror as she set the brake and then gathered up bath supplies. "And what about Katrina?" he asked. "My insides are all knotted up, hoping against hope that she's still alive. You know what Fleming said. It's been an awful long time. More than likely she's dea…" Choking on the words, he glanced at the ceiling. Anxiety overwhelmed him. "What am I going to do if I lose Katrina a second time?"

Julie dropped what she was doing and knelt in front of him. Cupping his face in her hands, she looked directly into his eyes and said, "I'm holding out that she's alive. I can't explain why, but she's alive, like you said, in Judgment, Mississippi. I feel it in my bones. Katrina's there. And she's alive."

Ken searched her face. Hope filled his eyes. His voice cracked, "You really think so?"

She nodded. "She's coming back to us, wait and see." A muted smile lifted her lips, but it was only a façade, for inside, she agonized, *if Katrina's alive, maybe Regina is, too. And if that woman comes back, what happens then? She knows all too well how to pull Ken's strings and make him dance. There won't be any contest. The loser will be me.*

Ken made eye contact with himself in the mirror. "All right," he said, "I'll make the call, but I'll only tell Mother and Dad that Jake's under arrest and we don't know any details." He got up on one leg. "I'll fill them in on Katrina when they get here."

"I think that's wise," said Julie with half a nod. "Then we can figure out how to handle the situation if they don't take it well. I'll go get you some fresh clothes."

On the way to the bedroom, her insides were mush. *What if Katrina is alive? Oh, God, what if she isn't? What will Ken do then?* She dropped on the edge of the bed, sick at heart.

"Julie?" called Ken.

She took a deep breath and got to her feet. After gathering up some clean clothes, she plodded back to the bathroom and placed the clothes near the basin. She took a step back, wringing her hands. If Regina's alive, what then? Her eyes narrowed. She'll rebuild the manse. I should tell Ken that Gretchen and Leo didn't buy it, tell him that Patty said Regina had money coming in from some unknown source— that's where the money came from to buy the manse, to buy fancy sports cars, clothes, more things than his income ever allowed. I should tell...

"You okay?" asked Ken, nudging her forearm.

She looked at his hand, the bloodstained tee shirt and shorts in it, and then into his eyes. Her lips trembled as she thought, if Regina's dead, will he ever let her memory rest? Will he ever love only me? She grabbed the soiled clothing and bolted out of the bathroom, blubbering, "Holler if you need anything else." She yanked the door shut and sagged against the back of it, sick at heart.

***

Ken drifted out of medicated sleep, his hand reaching out as his head turned. Julie wasn't there. He raised his head and squinted at the clock radio. 12:07. Must be in the bathroom, he thought. He listened. The bathroom fan's not running. No sound of washing hands. Maybe she's in the living room. After a day like today, it's only natural not to be able to sleep. "I should've faked swallowing that sleeping pill," he mumbled. "Should be holding her in my arms and telling her I love her, listening to her worries, the ones that drove her out of bed. Curt should've known better than to insist I take that sleeping pill. He must've known that she would need somebody." As medication took him away again, bad vibrations clung to him like bees from a ruptured hive.

At 12:31, he came out of it again. Julie still wasn't lying beside him. His eyes fixed on the back of the bedroom door and the empty hook. The shoulder bag's missing.

Panic got the better of Ken. Fighting off grogginess, he managed to get out of bed and into the wheelchair. Careful not to wake his in-laws, he wheeled open the door then manipulated the wheelchair into the hallway. He checked the bathroom then the living room. The kitchen, too. He squinted at the front door

215

and then his green plaid pajama top, tan boxer shorts and the casts on his arm and leg. "How am I supposed to drive like this? On top of that, Julie has the minivan." He rubbed his left shoulder wondering how he ever got in such a fix. Katrina had been calling to him—at least he thought so at the time.

Know how much I love you, Daddy?

Next, he was falling. And through it all, that stupid clown was there, egging him on.

No such thing as too much.

He scratched the side of his head. "What the hell does Jake want with that thing?" His fingers raked across his scruffy chin. Too bad the fall didn't do away with nightmares of that harpy.

Get out of my face, Regina!

Ken glanced over his shoulder. The hallway disappeared into dark silence. "I should wake up Pete."

As he scrutinized the front door, his fingernails dug into the leather armrest, leaving indentations unlikely to lift in the near future. "Open, you stinking door! Dammit, Julie, where are you? If only I could get out of this frigging wheelchair, I'd go out there and find you and never take another sleeping pill the rest of my life!"

His fingers ran through his hair. "I should call somebody." He manipulated the lever into reverse and backed the wheelchair to the kitchen. Zeroing in on the wall phone, he swallowed hard. "Who do I call? Curt? Cops? And tell them what? I've already had one wife run off on me." He swung the wheelchair around and headed down the hall. In the living room, the digital readout on the VCR, 1:07, illuminated the way as Ken steered to the balcony.

Ralph was huddled against the door. His perch was saturated by moisture blown in through the screen of the open window. Pupils glowed in the dim light, and fangs glistened as his mouth gaped open to release urgent clicks. The instant the door opened, Ralph scooted into the living room and then out into the hallway, seeking refuge on a friendly bed.

Ken piloted the wheelchair over the metal threshold and out onto the balcony. At the open window, he scanned the street below. Haloes surrounded street lamps and headlights of cars that moved along like ghosts through traffic lights that cycled red, yellow, and green. Tires whirred on wet pavement. A dog barked in the distance. On the Charles River, channel markers flickered in murky darkness. Dampness intensified the river's musty odor and that of the metal screen. Years ago, the river water smelled a heck of a lot worse. Much still had to be done to clean it up completely.

Just a year ago, the Charles had glistened on that sunny day when Ken had asked Julie to marry him. He was lying on his side, facing her, playing with a lock of her honey blond hair and gazing into her luscious brown eyes. He felt so happy, so at peace. The past was the past; bad times were over and done with. The future held nothing but the best. But then…then those words, "We're having a baby!"

A gust of wind whistled through the screen and peppered his face with moisture, cold against his skin, aggravating his nerves. A mouthful of single malt right about now would be easy to take.

"Booze isn't good for me," muttered Ken, rolling his eyes. "How well I know that. Neither is the memory of Regina." He ran his hand through his hair. "For crying out loud! I can't stand thinking about that harpy!" He willed himself to concentrate on Katrina and her infinite innocence.

Know how much I love you, Daddy?

"All these years my little girl has lived, hiding in my heart, refusing to be driven out. Oh my sweet Katrina, I should've known you were out there all the time."

Rain turned to drizzle as Ken sat in darkness—alone, so starkly alone. If only Julie was there. Her complicated simplicity would instantly make the world right. Her eyes gleaming in the filtered light always lit up the darkness of his cluttered mind. What if Julie doesn't come back? The thought paralyzed him. What if I've kissed her for the last time? And held her body

217

against mine for the last time? And told her for the last time that I love her more than life itself?

Visions of a car crash, flashing lights, and paramedics hauling a sheet-covered gurney towards a waiting ambulance terrorized Ken. And a small plane plummeted into a swamp. Mud splattered and a saw-tooth palm snagged a black dress. A tiny, white coffin.

"I can't take any more," he cried as his good hand pounded his forehead.

Night dragged on. Drizzle lightened into mist. Fog banked along the Charles. And Ken wallowed within oppressive shadows, eyelids heavy from medication, fighting off sleep, for sleep was not to be trusted. Cursed sleep had allowed Julie to slip away from him. "I'll never close my eyes again," he muttered. "I swear it." He lifted his face to the heavens and wept, "Oh, please, let Julie come back to me. Give me one more chance to make things right."

The arc of light that comes just before dawn on the eastern horizon was beginning to drive off the sodden night. Another hour or so, it would be light.

A noise rousted Ken. The front door! "Julie," he yelped, fumbling for the lever to turn the wheelchair around. He barreled through the living room and came around the archway, blubbering in a hoarse half-whisper-half-shout, "Julie!"

"Sh-sh-sh," she whispered while pressing an index finger against her lips. Her hair was wet, flat against her scalp as were her tee shirt and the stretched out white sweater that Ken didn't recognize. Blue gooseflesh riddled her legs below her cut off jeans. Her white sandals dangled from her hand.

"Where've you been?" he cried.

"I took a drive," she whispered while taking hold of the handgrips on the wheelchair.

He craned his neck to look up at her. "At four in the morning?" he bawled. "In the pouring rain?"

"Calm down," she whispered while turning the wheelchair around and pushing it down the hall. "You'll wake Mom and Dad. We'll talk in the bedroom."

"Where did you go, for crying out loud?" he demanded.

She closed the bedroom door and said, "Into bed with you."

Ken crossed his arms. "Not until you tell me what's going on."

Julie stopped short, crossed her arms, and stuck her nose in the air. "Not until you get into bed."

After moments of standoff, Ken huffed and got up on his good leg.

Julie stepped over to the bed and poked Ralph in the ribcage. "Out of the way, old man."

The cat snorted and got up to stretch, but found himself airborne when Julie yanked the top sheet and blanket out from under him. He landed a hare's breath away from Ken who was in the midst of hauling himself onto the edge of the bed.

"So where'd you go?" he demanded, while swinging his good leg onto the bed.

"Emma's," she said while lifting the leg cast onto the bed.

"Emma's?" he asked.

She brought the top sheet and blanket up over the cast and then to his armpits. "Where'd you expect me to go?" she asked.

"I don't know," he said. "Curt's?"

Their eyes met. "Don't be silly," she said.

"Who's sweater?"

"Emma's," she said. Seeing the confusion that masked his face, she bit the inside of her cheek. "I...I'm afraid I got her out of bed," she stammered. "I... This whole thing with Katrina... I mean... Well, I...I do want her back and all, but..."

His brows came together. Julie couldn't possibly think that he'd turn away his little Katrina. In a low, constrained voice, he asked, "But what?"

Julie rolled her eyes through a flood of tears, fighting off emotion. How could a sun-filled morning just a few days ago ever produce a tempest like the one that raged inside of her now? No imaginary windshield wipers could ever clear the deluge of troubles raining upon her miserable life. Emma's words echoed in her ear, *Life is never easy even in the sun. Remember, time has a way of working things out.*

"But what, Julie?" demanded Ken.

She swiped away tears that trickled down her face and gazed at him. Oh, God, I adore you so, she thought. But I'm going to lose you. No doubt about that exists in my mind. "Regina…" she choked. Her eyes rolled. "What if…what if she's out there too?"

The unimaginable swallowed up Ken. His brow furrowed. His mouth dropped open.

Terror raced through Julie, thinking that Ken was envisioning that possibility. Her fist shielded her lips.

His head whipped side-to-side as Ken blew out a mouthful of air. He opened his mouth to speak, but the idea of Regina walking back into his life after all this time soured his stomach and prevented speech.

"What if Regina comes back?" whimpered Julie.

In a slow, even declaration, Ken said, "Honestly, that never once crossed my mind."

"It hasn't?" she cried. "How can you even consider the possibility of Katrina being alive and not Regina, too?"

"I-I don't know," he stammered.

Julie turned and hid her fear against the wall. She looked like a little girl who had been sent to the corner for doing something wrong. She felt like one, too.

Ken gawked at her back. He could tell she was crying. "You can't possibly believe for one blessed moment that I'd ever go back to that woman?"

"Why can't you love me and our baby like you love them?" she sobbed.

"I never loved that woman," he spat. "Even in the beginning when she went through the motions of loving me. I knew she didn't love me. She didn't love Katrina either—her own flesh and blood!"

Ken wanted Julie in his arms but getting out of bed and going to her couldn't be accomplished fast enough, so he patted the bed, saying, "Come over here."

"But Regina's so beautiful, so elegant," moaned Julie. "I'm just a nothing, devoid of social graces, from the other side of the tracks—a nobody."

"Come over here," he demanded. When she shook her head, he snapped, "Do I have to get out of this bed and into that wheelchair again?"

Julie swiped away tears with the back of her hand, turned around, and gazed at him and then his outstretched hand. She took a tenuous step and then another. The second she was close enough, he latched onto a sleeve of the old white sweater and as he pulled her to him, it stretched over her hand.

"My life with Regina is over and done with," he said, looking deep into her eyes. "You're the one love of my life, not her. It's you and me, babe. Okay?" He coaxed a nod and then lifted the covers. "All right then, get into bed. You're an ice cube."

Julie slipped off her shoes and crawled under the covers, wet clothes and all. When he patted the right side of his chest, she huddled up close to him and rested her head on his chest. He felt so warm. She was so cold.

Ken pulled up the blanket. Cold knees and feet pressed up against him, but nothing ever felt so good. He kissed her head and said, "I've been such a jerk. The life I've been living's been all mixed up between what's passed and what is now, and I've gotten you mixed up in both. I'm so, so sorry. If you only knew what you mean to me."

"All I ask is that you remember I love you," she whispered. "I will till the end of time. No matter what."

Ken cleared his throat. "If only I can find some way to break free of the past. My sanity hangs by a thread at times; and you're the only one who understands. You don't know what it did to me thinking that I might've lost you."

Julie lifted her head and looked directly into his eyes. "You're never going to lose me." She turned away. "But I'm scared."

His hand cupped her chin and forced her to look into his eyes. "Scared of what?"

"I just don't know how to stop all the hurt that's bottled up inside of you," she said.

"Your father taught me a way," he said. "Know how?"

Julie wriggled her head no.

"Whenever Regina crosses my mind, I see your face, not hers," he said. "And I hear your voice, not hers." His arm tightened around her. "Dead or alive, that woman—or for that matter, anybody else—won't ever take you away from me."

Her spirits lifted, awakening to the possibility of happiness and eternal love. Regina was in for the fight of her life if she came waltzing back for Ken. A smile blossomed and her eyelashes fluttered like that day over a year ago when she and Ken rammed into each other at the hospital.

Passion raced through him. Even with rain-soaked hair, Julie thrilled him. "What would I ever do if I didn't have you?"

As though they were the only two people on earth, their eyes beheld the miracle of each other. Then they kissed, savoring the kind of love that survived incredible turmoil and deepened in the process. As her full weight pressed against him, the telephone rang. She rolled over and leered at the clock on the bureau. "It's 4:00 a.m."

Tossing off the covers, Julie swung her feet over the edge of the bed and started for the door. Halfway there, she stopped. The phone wasn't ringing anymore. She stepped over to the door and pressed her ear against it. She heard her father's voice but couldn't make out his words. She strained to hear.

"Holy mackerel," she heard her father exclaim.

She bolted back, away from the door. Eyes full of fear, she glanced at Ken.

Moments later, a tap came on the door. "Julie," whispered her father. "You awake, Pumkin?"

She gawked at the door and then cleared her throat. "Dad?"

"Detective Fleming just called. Jake is on the loose again."

Julie's fist rammed against her lips as she glanced over her shoulder. Ken's demeanor had turned hostile.

"Julie?" called her father.

Her eyes zeroed in on the door.

"You there, Pumkin?"

"Yeah, Dad."

"Everything's going to be okay."

"Uh-huh."

"Try 'n' get some rest." Getting no response, her father said, "Love you, Pumkin."

"Love you, too, Daddy."

Footsteps faded and then there was silence.

Julie glanced at Ken. His hand beckoned. She wobbled back to the bed. Snuggled up to him, she rubbed her forehead against his chin and heaved, "Oh, God."

CANDY-COLORED CLOWN

CHAPTER EIGHTEEN

"Gretchen, relax," said Julie while stepping over to the old woman. "This is the third time in less than five minutes that you peeked out of that window." As she drew back the curtains, sunshine spilled into the Konstanze living room. "Look! There's scads of cops out there. See?" She gestured and looked at the old woman. "Nobody's going to get through any of them without proving right down to his underwear that he's legit'."

Gretchen shook her head. "This no over. Nothing over for Jake."

Elizabeth cringed. "To think he's out there on the streets again."

"Mind-boggling to say the least," said Julie, letting the curtain drop. The shadows that took over the living room didn't help the uneasiness.

"Wonder how that poor guard's doing," said Elizabeth.

"Detective Fleming told Dad that he was easy prey for Jake," said Julie.

"Nobody understand evil that drive that devil," mumbled Gretchen.

Hush fell over the room as the three women visualized Jake overpowering the guard who had made a grievous mistake of assuming that the prisoner was too doped up after surgery to stitch up his mutilated face. During medication rounds, a nurse had discovered Jake missing from his bed and the guard lying on the bathroom floor, wearing only skivvies and handprints about his neck. Jake had wrested the service revolver away from the guard, pistol-whipped him, and then took off for parts unknown.

Now Jake's out there—somewhere—armed and dressed like a cop.

Julie studied Gretchen who looked so vulnerable, hunched over with worry and fatigue. The old woman had stayed by Leopold's side all night long and this morning, when the doctors reported that he was out of danger, telephoned Julie who managed to convince her to go home and get cleaned up. After that she was to come back to Elizabeth and Peter's condo and get some rest before returning to the hospital. It came as no surprise that Gretchen was too frightened to go home alone, so Julie volunteered to accompany her. That plan met with great resistance from Ken, Peter, and Elizabeth, all adamant that Julie was not going out on the streets of Brighton alone until Jake was securely behind bars. So it was decided that Elizabeth would go along for everybody's peace of mind.

Gretchen peered at Julie who gave a reassuring nod and said, "Hey, that jerk will find his butt in jail before he knows it."

A faint smile lightened the old woman's face. "Hope he shot dead," she grunted. "Jake he not let take alive. What hound of hell do next?" Once again, panic sent Gretchen to the window to peer out the curtain's outer edge.

"Oh no," gasped Elizabeth, hit by a raucous sneezing fit.

Gretchen squealed like a stuck pig and flattened her back against the wall beside the window. Fright zinged through Julie as she shot a look at her mother.

"God bless me," said Elizabeth when the sneezing fit ceased. She grinned sheepishly.

Julie shook off a shiver and said, "Come on," to Gretchen who was sniveling and nearing hyperventilation. Wrapping an arm around old, rounded shoulders, Julie guided Gretchen to a high back chair. "Here. Sit down." She understood how Gretchen felt. She was worn out, too, after a sleepless night of driving in the rain and agonizing over whether Regina was alive or dead. Even though Ken had given ample reassurances that Regina was out of his life, one way or the other, how was it all to play out? And don't forget about Katrina. If that poor child's dead, he's going to be devastated all over again—and he never got over her death the first time. If both Katrina and Regina are alive, an ugly tug-of-war between that woman and Ken was certain to take place. Katrina was Regina's tool to inflict pain. Then again, if only Katrina's alive, what kind of mother was Julie going be to an eight-year-old who in all probability had the most awful hang-ups from being torn from her family at the tender age of four? How much does one remember at that age? Julie couldn't recall ever being that age, but then nobody stole her from Mom either. Heaving a sigh, she said, "How about I make us all a nice cup of hot tea?"

Gretchen remained distracted, but Elizabeth nodded.

In the kitchen Julie grabbed the teapot off the stove and while holding it under the faucet, heard footsteps. She glanced over her shoulder. Her mother was wandering into the kitchen.

"Help me upright the sofa?" asked Elizabeth in a hushed voice as she leaned against the counter.

Julie checked the water level in the teapot. "Soon as I put the water on." Hearing no comment, she glanced at her mother. "Judging from the circles under you eyes, the night was a long one for you."

"What is it about that clown that's got Jake so riled up?" asked Elizabeth.

"You got me," huffed Julie. She shut off the faucet, brought the teapot to the stove and set it on a back burner. Squinting at the dials, she then turned one. Gas hissed, and a flame erupted under the teapot. She adjusted the dial to medium then backed away, brushing her hands together. "Okay, the sofa."

On the way to the living room, Julie and Elizabeth stepped aside to let Gretchen pass. Without acknowledging either of them, the old woman waddled into the bathroom and closed the door. Elizabeth got close to Julie and whispered, "None of this makes a lick of sense."

"Yeah," said Julie. "What's Jake got against Gretchen and Leo?" She glanced into the living room and scanned the devastation. "What a miserable thing to do."

"Sure got our hands full putting this place back in order," grunted Elizabeth as she went to the far side of the sofa.

"As if we needed it," said Julie while taking hold of the sofa and helping to right it. She straightened her back, hands on hips, and then stretched this way and that. Stopping abruptly, she said, "Geez, will you look at that?"

Elizabeth followed her daughter's gaze to the floor near the corner of the room. "Why, it's the portrait of Regina!"

A tremor rocked Julie to the core. With discoveries like that portrait, it's impossible to get that woman out of her mind. Turning away, she bit the inside of her cheek and wondered what was going to happen if Regina came back.

"This thing certainly gets around," said Elizabeth, stepping over and staring down at the portrait.

"Yeah," muttered Julie. "Just like that woman did."

Julie gathered up the sofa pillows and banged them together. I'm not thinking about her any more, and that's that, she thought. Should've given that silly clown to Jake in the first place. Then he'd've left us alone! We've had enough to contend with. Fire. Ken getting hurt. Katrina alive. And now that stupid picture shows up, again. Well, I'm not going to look at it!

Her insides wrenched. Her eyes bugged out. She dropped the pillows. "Mom?"

Elizabeth was on her knees, portrait in her hands, gawking at it. Slowly she looked up and asked, "You thinking what I'm thinking?"

Julie nodded. "Maybe there's something written on it."

Turning it this way and that, front to back then back again, Elizabeth murmured, "Nothing catches my eye." She fingered the hasps on the back. "I don't think I have the heart, or the right, to desecrate the only thing left of a dead person."

"Give it to me," said Julie, snatching the portrait. Her thumbnail pried the hasp. "Foolish thing won't budge." As her nail tore down to the quick, the teapot in the kitchen began to whistle.

"How about a butter knife?" suggested Elizabeth.

Julie grunted with her thumb in her mouth.

"Haven't seen you suck you thumb since you were two years old," needled Elizabeth.

As Julie started for the kitchen, she shot a look over her shoulder at her mother. Popping her thumb out of her mouth, she wagged her tongue.

Elizabeth covered her eyes and giggled.

Laughter surged from deep in Julie's belly. Popping her thumb back into her mouth, she turned back to where she was going and plowed head-on into Jake.

Dilated pupils bored into Julie. The business end of a service revolver jabbed her ribcage. Reflex hurtled her backwards and the portrait of Regina flew out of her hand.

Elizabeth uncovered her eyes. For a moment, she thought she was in the middle of a nightmare, because Julie was hurtling backwards and Jake, dressed in a blue uniform, a bandage swathing one side of his face, was standing spread-eagled in the doorway of the kitchen. A gun in his hand was aimed at Julie. A six-inch butcher knife gleamed in the other hand.

As the portrait of Regina whooshed overhead, Elizabeth ducked. It bounced off the corner of the coffee table and crashed against the wall. As glass rained down, she shielded her head.

Julie landed on the carpet in front of the credenza.

The teapot shrieked in the kitchen.

Elizabeth started for Julie.

"Freeze!" bellowed Jake.

Elizabeth stopped in her tracks. The hair on the back of her neck bristled as her eyes darted between him and Julie. Maternal instinct drove her to protect her offspring, to ignore Jake and save Julie. Her heart raced with indecision.

"Go for it, bimbo," lathered Jake. "Playing chicken is my favorite sport." The knife in his left hand beckoned while the gun in his right hand aimed between her eyes. His index finger tightened on the trigger. "Just about now, killin' the slut of that fucker crip' that hacked up my face sure's to make ol' Jakey feel a whole lot better."

"No, Mom," shouted Julie, shaking out her wrist. "Stay where you are! I'm okay. My hand caught my fall."

Jake's eyeballs rolled towards the kitchen and the wailing teapot. Muscles bunched on the side of his face. His head twitched at the incessant blare. He glared at Elizabeth and then Julie.

Elizabeth scowled, but then Peter's voice came into her head, reminding her of yesterday when he pretended to cave to Jake, but absorbed every move, anticipating the moment, a mistake, anything to get the edge on bringing down the fiend. She must do the same thing. When Jake decided to do something about that teapot, she'd make her move.

Reading her mother's thoughts, Julie cried, "Stay where you are, Mom!"

"Now there's good advice for ya, *Mom*, if ever I heard any," sneered Jake.

The teapot shrieked.

Elizabeth made a mental note of the layout of the Konstanze townhouse. Two bedrooms upstairs. Unfinished cellar. Main floor, living room, hallway, kitchen, and bathroom...*bathroom!* Gretchen's in the bathroom! Holy smoke! Jake's going to freak when she comes out of that bathroom! And the teapot's already got him bugged to no end! That's when I'll jump him! I'll bring that bastard down and get that gun. Nail his sorry ass to the wall. Her palms itched. Just give me one little excuse and I'll blow his friggin' head off.

Jake's eyes narrowed on Elizabeth. Wary of that hero vet's wife, he spat, "Don't trust you for one stinking second." His fingertips poked at the bandage, underneath, stitches tightened. "Damn pain killer's worn off. Feel like ripping these fuckin' stitches out! Any drugs around here?

"Aspirin," said Elizabeth. "In my pocketbook. But it's in the car."

His eyes shot to Julie.

She raised her empty palms and shook her head. She knew better than tell Jake that pregnant women shouldn't take anything without doctor's approval. Did he even know she was pregnant? Probably not. If he did, he'd figure out of turning her condition into more leverage to get what he wanted.

"I'll just have to score some coke when I'm outta here," he huffed and stepped over to Regina's portrait. "So, there's something written on this about where she put my stuff," he said. He eyed Elizabeth for a second and then keeping the pistol trained on her, loosened up on the trigger and squatted.

The teapot squealed.

Elizabeth set her legs to spring. When was Gretchen going to come out of that bathroom?

Jake ogled the portrait, a lecherous grin spreading across his face. He set down the butcher knife and picked up the portrait. "What a bitch this one was," he sneered above the din of the teapot. "One high-class whore." He scratched his head with the pistol barrel. "Sure knew how to please ol' Jakey. Tsk, tsk, tsk. Baggage—too much fucking baggage. Just couldn't back off the marriage crap." He snorted. "Ain't in the plans for this skirt chaser, uh-uh." He squinted at Elizabeth and then at Julie. "Damn teapot's driving me nuts!" He leered the portrait. "Shame, ain't it? How that the private bird she hopped out of Miami took a nosedive into the everglades and all? Gets kind of inconvenient, wouldn't you say? A leak mysteriously appearing in a fuel line?"

Any moment now, thought Elizabeth. Jake's completely wrapped up in getting away with murder. My chance to take him down is so close, and I've got the perfect angle to knock his legs out from under him.

"So you kept Katrina and murdered Regina," said Julie.

Elizabeth shot a look at her daughter. That's right. Distract the son-of-a-gun.

The teapot shrieked.

Jake leaned towards Julie and snickered, "People pay big money for blond, blue-eyed brats like that."

Julie didn't like him leaning towards her that way, but intimidation wasn't going to stop her from getting answers to questions that had been eating at her. "Give me a break," she huffed. "Regina didn't let you sell her child."

Jake chortled. "Oh-h-h, but yes." He tore apart the portrait. "She did, indeed, my little chickadee." He hurled a piece of the frame at Elizabeth who ducked. He laughed. "Didn't so much as bat an eyelash when I first brought up the subject. That dame didn't want that brat hangin' on her at all, but sure as hell she wasn't about to let that husband of hers have the kid."

"So she let you sell Katrina so you'd marry her," contended Julie.

"Well, yah," he jeered. "Like I told ya, pussy wanted to ball and chain my ass. She threatened to blow the lid off everything I've been working for plus hold out the goods until I made her an honest woman." He tossed his head back. "Honest woman. What a crock. She was the biggest slut this town..."

Gunshots crackled. Jake recoiled. White light exploded.

Elizabeth dove for Julie as successive shots spun Jake around and around and cut him to pieces.

Shielded against her mother's breast, Julie witnessed it all out of the corner of one eye.

Then the barrage of bullets ceased.

The teapot shrieked.

Elizabeth lifted her head. So did Julie.

Blood oozed from the mangled body, crooked in an unnatural position across the back of sofa. Right arm twisted up and over a half-missing skull—the other half blown to bits. His left arm jounced out to the side; a bullet had shattered the elbow. Skin was shredded like a flag ravaged by a level four hurricane. One foot faced one direction, the other in the opposite direction.

"Is he...?" whispered Julie.

"Dead," said Elizabeth.

Julie extracted herself from her mother's arms and asked, "But who...?" She turned. "Gretchen!"

The old woman stood in the doorway, both hands aiming an empty Glock 19 pistol at Jake's remains and index fingers continually squeezing the trigger—click, click, click. Her lips jerked with each squeeze.

Julie strained to make out the words.

"Morder! Morder!" repeated the old woman.

The front door burst open and cops swarmed in like enraged hornets. Several nailed Gretchen against the wall. Another cop yanked the empty gun from her hand.

Julie sagged against her mother and began to weep—not because Katrina's whereabouts remained a mystery. No, in her heart she knew that the child was bound to show up. She wept out of shame. Regina's dead—and Julie was glad.

The teapot whistle fizzled.

***

Ken didn't like the idea of Julie and her mother going off to the hospital to take Gretchen home—especially with Jake on the loose. He stewed about it while sitting in his wheelchair near the screen door that led to the balcony. His eyes ping ponged between the clock and the Charles River where usually he found solace from his troubles by watching day sailors. His eyes were blind to them, his mind reliving the horror of the last twenty-four hours. Sure, Julie claimed that nobody could get near Gretchen's place what with the posse outside and all, but Jake was Jake. Nothing stood in the way of whatever that bastard wanted. But Julie had begged and pleaded, "Gretchen needs somebody. She has nobody else but us."

Ken glared at his arm and leg casts. "I swear that once I get these damned things off, Julie and I are never going to be apart again. Not only that, I'm signing us up for self-defense lessons. Nobody's ever going to get the best of either of us again."

"Bethie and I'll join you," said Peter as his head popped around the archway. "Game of chess?"

"Nah," said Ken, his stomach churning. "Not right now." He glanced at the hands on the clock. "Foolish time is standing still."

Without Julie, Ken was like a river searching for the sea. He needed to see her now, wind blowing in her hair and leaning back on one elbow with eyes closed and listening to the tide roll in, children playing on the beach, seabirds. He didn't know which he liked better, her eyes opened or closed. Opened, the sunlight sparkled in them. Closed, her face took on such peacefulness. Either way, her eyelashes reflected the gold of the sun. Yet eyelids covered up the sparkle. Ah, what a vicious circle.

He loved how she sat with her legs tucked under her, feet leaving sand on the blanket as they ate cartons of clams and French fries gooped with mayonnaise, take out from that little clam shack that overlooked Scituate harbor. How Julie could eat so much was beyond Ken—and she never gained an ounce to boot! That clam shack had always been his favorite, but he had to drag Regina there, kicking and screaming. Finger-food and beach blankets were definitely not her forte.

"Although I share your concern," said Peter, "Bethie and Julie can take care of themselves. Look what your good ol' mother-in-law did to that Morton fella over there in Echo Lake when he hassled her. I guarantee you Julie's got her mother's genes. And Gretchen's no slouch either. After what that monster did to Leo, I don't think she... No wait, let me rephrase that. I don't think any one of those young ladies have it in their blood to take one more piece of crap from the likes of Jake."

Ken heaved levity. "Yeah. You got a point there."

Peter raised his prosthetic hand into the air and spouted, "Okay, then. I'm off to brew us up a fresh pot of coffee to go along with that fresh load of pastry the girls trucked in for us. Then, you and me, bud, well, we're gonna kick back and have a rip-roaring, down and dirty game of chess." As he disappeared down the hall, his voice became barely audible. "It's about time we get down to the business of finding out who's the champeen chess player in this humble abode."

Ken ran his hand through his hair. A weak smile lifted his face. "Well, I suppose..." He set about rearranging the chessboard, but the light mood ended with the ring of the telephone. Surely it had to do with Jake. "What has that lousy bum done now?" he grumbled. "And to whom?" His heart began to thump. "I never should have let Julie go. If only she and her Mom were here safe and sound. Damn this broken down body of mine. Puts the kibosh to everything!"

"It's for you," said Peter.

The hair on the back of Ken's neck spiked. It seemed to take him forever to manipulate the wheelchair out of the living room and into the kitchen. Dreading that call, he mumbled, "I swear Jake, if you hurt one little hair on Julie's head, I'll kill you. And you're never going to steal another child—or another man's wife again, for that matter. Damn you, Regina. Dead or alive, I don't care. You're out of my life. One thing's for damned sure, I'm never letting that woman get away with any more of the relentless cruelty that she put Katrina and me through. I swear to God that as long as I live no child of mine will ever go through anything even close to that." Heartbeats choked him as he raised the phone to his ear. "Yeah?"

"Mr. Waters? Detective Gage Fleming here."

"Uh-huh," was all Ken got out as his mind raced. Jake's got to Julie and she's... I knew he was going get to her! I knew it! I knew it!

"Your daughter's been located," said Fleming.

A cyclone of emotion whirled about Ken's head: worry for Julie, Elizabeth, and Gretchen, hatred for Jake and what Regina had done to him and his child, and trepidation for what might happen if that woman was still alive.

"Mr. Waters?" prodded Fleming. "Did you hear me?"

"Huh?"

"I said, we located your daughter, Katrina," said Fleming. "Mr. Waters?"

"Katrina?" Ken stammered, numb all the way to his toes. "Is she...?"

"Alive," yelped Fleming. "Yes, Mr. Waters, your daughter's alive, and as I understand it, in good health, too."

Lips moved, but words failed Ken. Tears flooded down his face.

"FBI got right on it," continued Fleming. "An anti-government faction had Katrina down there in Judgment, Mississippi. Just like you said, Mr. Waters, Judgment, Mississippi. Other kids were there, too, many missing and some presumed dead in accidents where the bodies were never recovered. Can you imagine? Training poor little souls for future terrorist acts? Right under our very noses? Right here in the USA?"

Ken looked skyward and cried, "Oh, thank You!"

"Your little girl will be back in your arms no later than tomorrow night. But listen to me, Mr. Waters. Your daughter's eight years old now. She's been through a lot, what with your first wife taking off and all. She's going to need lots of help, not only from you and new your wife and family, but also from professionals—and for a long time to come."

"Brainwashed?"

"You got it. Does anyone in his right mind believe otherwise?"

CHAPTER NINETEEN

"White hair snuffed a B and E in No Rugrat Zone," slurped the desk sergeant as he tossed an assignment sheet onto the desk.

"Like I told you, Mr. Waters," said Fleming, picking up the assignment sheet and using it to fan his face while talking on the phone. "Your daughter will be back in your arms no later than tomorrow night. Yes. Of course. I'll stay in touch."

Smiling with great satisfaction, Fleming hung up the phone. Nine out of ten times, this job sucks," he thought. Robberies, murders, sex crimes. Too much disgusting garbage these days. Whittles away at one's resolve, it does. On the other hand, handing good news to the parent of a missing kid, well, that makes it all worthwhile.

He glanced at the assignment sheet. His eyes snagged on the very first line. Satisfaction flew out the window.

"Konstanze?" He skimmed particulars. His voice intensified. "Jake Waters. DOA? Victims: Julie Waters?"

Fleming leapt to his feet and was out the door in a heartbeat. It never occurred to him when he broke the news to her husband about the kid being found that Julie wasn't there. The father-in-law—what's his name? No matter. He was there. He had answered the phone. Mom? Don't tell me she's at the scene, too?

Fleming screeched to a stop and scanned the assignment sheet. Elizabeth Blair. 'Crap. She is there."

He hit the parking lot at a dead run and leapt into his unmarked car. Fellow officers paused. They had never seen the detective move that fast.

Fleming grabbed the emergency beacon off the dashboard and jammed it on the roof. Slamming the door, he stomped the gas pedal to the floorboards. "That bastard always manages to slip through our fingers," he growled. "Well, shit-for-brains, the jig's up!"

The unmarked car fishtailed out of the parking lot and into the street, and it seemed to Fleming that China was closer than the community where the Konstanzes lived. "Should've been there to ward off that fiend. No excuse for such incompetence."

State cruisers, black and whites, and unmarked cars clogged the street where the Konstanzes lived, so Fleming drove up over the cement curb, across the sidewalk, and went the rest of the way, crossing patches of green and driveways. He did his best to ignore the Coroner's meat wagon when he got there; still, a chill skittered through him. He parked on the front lawn and barreled out of the car and into the condo.

A fellow detective by the name of Andrews glanced at the out-of-breath Fleming and said, "Nothing's here."

"No name? No date?" spluttered Fleming, his heart thundering from stress and exertion. He took the remnants of Regina Water's bridal portrait from Andrews and examined every last square inch of it.

"Nadah," said Andrews.

A female voice rose above the chaos, "So much violence and killing and still no explanation?"

Fleming spun around. That's Elizabeth what's-her-name—the vet's wife! He scanned the sea of humanity. Where is she? He braced his hands on his hips.

"Gretchen! You've got to tell us what this is all about!"

His heart skipped a beat as his hands dropped. "Julie Waters?"

"Over here."

Unable to draw a bead on her, Fleming weaved through the crowd and came upon her lying on the floor, a paramedic bent over her, running a fetal stethoscope across her bare belly and listening for heartbeats of the unborn child. Elizabeth Blair was toying with her daughter's hair. Both women were visibly shaken.

Angst robbed Fleming of breath he had just gotten back. He spun around and stomped his foot. "Always a day late and a dollar short."

"Detective Fleming," said Julie as a different paramedic pumped up a blood pressure armband. As air was released, it hissed.

Fleming turned to see her hand reaching out to him. He latched onto it without a second thought and crouched down.

"Jake," she gagged. "He's dead."

"Out of the picture, permanent-like," spat Fleming.

Julie tightened her grip on his hand and said, "Gretchen knows why!"

"Not good to get wound up like this, young lady," said Fleming. "Keep your wits about you."

"But Gretchen…" stammered Julie.

"I…I no know why…just…" Gretchen faltered.

Fleming patted Julie's hand and then withdrew his and stood up. Scanning the sea of law enforcement, he couldn't see the old woman, so he navigated through the tide in the direction of Gretchen's voice. He spotted her sitting on the floor, her back braced against the wall near the kitchen doorway. A younger woman in blue squatted next to her, speaking German. He stepped over and demanded, "Why, Mrs. Konstanze?"

The tone of his voice intimidated Gretchen, so she looked down at her hands.

He squatted and reiterated, "Why, Mrs. Konstanze?"

She focused on her wedding band. Her head tilted as a dreamlike voice emerged, out of place as far as Fleming was concerned, considering the gravity of the situation. "Very long ago, Leopold and me…" She sighed. "We young…"

"Yes, Mrs. Konstanze?" prodded Fleming. He was getting antsy. He wanted answers. Now.

The old woman didn't seem to hear.

"Go on, Mrs. Konstanze," he insisted.

In her own time, Gretchen began, "Oh, so much in love, Leopold and me." Her face darkened. "We hear rumors about wall divide Germany, east and west. Rumors come long time. Fear fill me and my Leopold. If door to freedom close, we never live way we choose, raise children in freedom. More and more rumors. Fear grow every day. So Leopold, he say to me, 'If we no leave soon, we trap…forever.'" Gretchen rotated her wedding band. "Day come Khrushchev, he talk on radio, say, last escape road close, and my Leopold say to me, 'Must leave right away or lose last bit freedom we have.'" Gretchen looked up at Fleming, her eyes chilled him. "But…how, I say?" Her head wavered side to side and then she looked down again. She drew in a deep breath and said, "Then miracle. Man, he wear Russian uniform, he come to me and Leopold in market place. He help escape homeland and we must decide now. No pay, man say, pay later, any way is ask. We no to question. Family leave behind die if we fail do way ask. They kill Leopold and me. They know where we live." Gretchen thought about that for a moment. Her eyes rolled and as she straightened herself, she spotted the frameless portrait of Regina in Fleming's hands. "So…Leopold and I come America, and wall go up. We can never return to East Germany." She took the portrait. "Years go and baby Regina she born to us." Arthritic fingers caressed the image. "*Arm, arm kind von mein.*"

Fleming squinted at the woman cop for translation.

"Ms. Konstanze said, 'Poor, poor child of mine.'"

He looked back at the old woman whose wrinkled hands pressed the portrait to a full bosom and faded blue eyes overflowed with sorrow. He felt sorry for her, despite all the nasty things he'd heard about her daughter. "Tell me about Regina," he said.

Gretchen looked into his eyes that demanded too many unholy answers. "Oh my little Regina," she whimpered. "She no to blame."

"She's not to blame for what?" pressed Fleming.

The woman cop gave him the hairy eyeball. Back off a bit.

"They take Regina," said Gretchen.

Fleming had the urge to ask, who's they and when and why did they take Regina? He glanced at the woman cop, who discretely shushed him.

Gretchen zeroed in on the front door, though her line of sight was cluttered with strangers. "Knock come on door," she whined. "They want Regina. Go camp, they say. No, no, she too young, I cry. Only five years! Man put hand under jacket. He have gun. Leopold and I no question." Old eyes filled with the kind of terror that only a mother could know. "They give Regina candy and she sleep. They carry her to black car and go." Gretchen's body shook violently as her hand reached towards the door. "Regina," she wailed. "We...we no know where find!"

The woman cop placed a hand on the old woman's shoulder and said, "Take it easy, Mrs. Konstanze."

Grief-stricken eyes fixed on the woman cop. "Leopold and I fear Regina no return. Cry and cry."

"But she did come back," said the woman cop.

Gretchen gave a sour nod. "Six week go by. Doorbell ring. I open." She pointed with one hand as the withered fingertips of the other hand fled to her bottom lip. "My eyes, they lie! Regina! I look. Nobody nowhere. Only Regina. She smile, skip in house like never go. Year and year, same, same."

"They drugged her and took her every year?" asked Fleming.

"Two year drugs. Then Regina go no drug," said Gretchen.

"How long did this go on?" he asked.

The old woman shrugged. "Stop maybe not. Regina no speak. Not for us know where she come and go, she say. We no

241

ask. We ask, she go away. Plane crash…Regina die…and Katrina."

Fleming stood up and rubbed his nose, thinking about telling the old woman that her granddaughter was alive.

"One day Jake, he come door," said Gretchen. "We know Jake, yes. He Ken brother. Jake push way in home. Say he and Regina comrades. He say Regina marry Ken."

"She married Ken because Jake told her to?" asked Julie.

Fleming turned. Julie Waters was standing just off his left shoulder. A concerned Elizabeth Blair hovered on the other side.

Gretchen shrugged. "Jake say Ken know computer inside out. Ken useful."

"Useful?" echoed Fleming.

"Useful for what?" demanded Julie.

"No know," said Gretchen. "Regina she mad, no can change Ken. Ken work all time and no care for things she care. She yell many, many time she marry Ken for nothing."

"So she carried on with Jake all along," said Julie.

"Regina say she and Jake run away and marry," said Gretchen.

"But she had to divorce Ken first," argued Julie.

"My Leopold say no divorce no marry Jake, but she laugh. She say Jake, he take care of Ken."

"Kill him?" belched Julie.

"Jake make Regina think Ken will die—that I think," said Gretchen. "But Jake, he worse than devil. He no die in plane crash. Jake trick Regina. She go plane. He no go plane—that I know. We try stop. Tell her no safe, anywhere go, but Regina say she live like want. Nobody stop her."

"So Jake comes back after the plane crash," said Fleming, "but waits until now to start wreaking your house and knocking you and your husband around."

"Jake say Regina hold out. He want what his. 'What, what?' Leopold ask, but Jake, he no say what. He destroy many, many treasured possessions. No matter because we move."

"He messed up your house before?" asked Fleming.

Gretchen gave a sad nod. "'I want it,' all Jake say. How can give if no know what he want?"

"You never reported anything to the authorities," said Fleming point blank.

Gretchen avoided his eyes.

"How many times did Jake do this?" asked Julie.

"Many," mumbled Gretchen. "Each time worse. We think move here. Many people make Jake afraid. No hit us. No destroy home. People mean nothing to Jake. Leopold, he buy gun."

"The Glock you shot Jake with," said Fleming.

Gretchen nodded. "Leopold hide it top shelf in bathroom. In towels. I hear Jake and I afraid. I get gun and I…I…" Her lips pursed and then she spat, "He say bad my Regina. I mad—mad! I kill devil!"

The room fell silent. Some stared at Gretchen; others at the dead man.

"Well, that's it then," said Julie. "We're back to the clown."

"Yah, yah, clown," said Gretchen. "Jake want clown."

"Wanted," corrected Fleming while eyeing one of the coroner's crew zipping up the body bag.

Julie glanced at Fleming. "Where is the clown?"

"FBI's got it," said Fleming as he stepped over to the body bag.

The coroner's assistant zipped it halfway down. Jake Waters was barely recognizable. "'Perp' was well armed," said the assistant. "Knives, guns, couple more things I never saw before. See this burn?"

"Yeah," said Fleming.

"Some sort of explosive device went off when a bullet hit it."

"Get back to me when the lab tags it."

The assistant nodded.

"Anything else?" asked Fleming.

The assistant shrugged. "Wasn't carrying ID."

"Why am I not surprised," said Fleming, taking one last gander at the corpse. Contempt bubbled in his gut. "Zip it," he growled and then turned his back on the dead. "At least we got these folks and little Katrina Waters out of this idiot's clutches."

Gasps echoed throughout the room. "Katrina's okay?" cried Julie, breaking from her mother's protective grasp and grabbing his arm. "Katrina's okay?"

He nodded, relief flowing from the depths of his soul.

Gretchen collapsed against the woman cop and began to wail.

"Not so much as a scratch," said Fleming, "so I'm told."

***

Shortly after getting the word that Katrina was alive, Peter was in the kitchen, giving Ken a lesson on the fine art of sculpting the ultimate pastrami sandwich—anything to keep their minds off their absent wives. The intercom buzzed. Chills shot through them. Julie and Elizabeth never buzz. Their eyes exchanged concern. Peter swiped his hands across his white butcher's apron and went to the intercom. Pressing the TALK button, he said, "Yes?"

"Hey, Pete. It's me. Curt."

Peter stared at the button that released the security door in the lobby. The last time he pressed it, a warlord invaded the premises. "Everything's cool, man," he told himself. "Cops are keeping a watchful eye on Bethie and Julie. Gretchen, too. Katrina's safe and sound and on her way home. And Curt's the best friend Ken ever had. Right about now, he's not the only one who needs to see a friendly face."

"Idiots like Jake win if we all hole up in fear," said Ken, peering around the kitchen doorframe.

"You're absolutely right," said Peter and jammed his finger on the release button. Then, like he had always done in the past, he opened the front door to the condo. Giving purposeful nods, he and Ken revisited the pastrami sandwiches.

The instant Ken laid his eyes upon his long-time friend, he hit him with the news about Katrina. Curt put out a closed fist and said, "Incredible, ol' chap."

Ken tapped his fist against Curt's. "Yup. She'll be here tomorrow night."

"Congratulations," said Curt. "M'lady home?"

Ken shook his head, although he knew Curt long enough to know that something else was eating at him. "What's up?"

Tension lifted off Curt. It was getting where he couldn't concentrate whenever Julie was around. He had to free himself of her. But how? Stepping over to the stove, he said, "This whole day's been incredible." He bent over and sniffed the pastrami frying in scads of butter. Straightening, he leered at the concoction and then Peter. "Not good for the arteries, mate."

Peter gave one of his world-famous silly grins.

Curt rolled his eyes. Like father, like daughter. Geez, everything comes back to Julie. He turned and watched Ken maneuver the wheelchair around the kitchen. He filled his lungs with air and exhaled, "Well, guess I don't have to tell you to sit down."

"Cut the baloney," spewed Ken.

"How about a beer," asked Peter who was spreading deli mustard on split Kaiser rolls lined up on a wooden cutting board.

"Sure," said Curt.

Peter set down the butter knife and swiped his hands across his apron. He took two cans of beer out of the refrigerator and tossed one to Curt. He held up the other, offering it to Ken who shook his head no while tapping his fingers on the arm of his wheelchair.

Curt popped open a can. So did Peter. Raising the cans, they saluted each other and gulped some down.

As Peter went back to building pastrami sandwiches, Curt belched, "Remember when I called you guys about Jake being in the hospital?" He pulled a chair from the table, spun it around, lifted one leg over the seat, and sat down.

Ken rubbed the palm of his good hand on the armrest of the wheelchair and drew out the word, "Yeah?"

"Julie got all flustered about Jake potentially killing you, his own brother," said Curt, hooking his arms over the back of the chair. "Well, I got this feeling in my gut—same one I got

245

from time to time ever since Jake popped on the scene eight years ago." He took a swig of beer and smacked his lips. "Bells and whistles went off in my head. Something didn't jibe. So I took it upon myself to check Jake's DNA, but you know what? Didn't have to. I looked up his blood type. It didn't match either Richard's or Patty's, which I happen to know because they've been my patients since I first hung out my shingle."

Dumbfounded, Ken stammered, "Jake…he's… he's not my brother?"

"Not even close, ol' chap," said Curt with a smug nod. "Now we know why he didn't follow Patty and Richard's lead when you asked him to use me as his primary physician when I started my practice."

"You double-checked?" asked Peter while doling out pastrami on the bottom halves of the Kaiser rolls.

"I wouldn't be here unless I was one hundred and fifty percent positive," said Curt.

"What the heck's going on?" demanded Ken.

Peter tossed slices of provolone on top of the pastrami and then jammed the top halves of the Kaiser rolls on top. "Mind boggling," he grunted.

"The guy busts up houses and marriages, steals kids, and wants a toy clown," said Ken. "Incredible."

Peter slid the sandwiches onto plates and brought them to the table. With the wave of a hand, he said, "Dig in, men."

Ken heaved frustration and wheeled up to the table. "So now what?" he asked.

Curt shrugged. "Beat's me." He got to his feet and turned his chair around. One hand towed the chair up to the table while the other slid a plate in front of him. As he sat down, he asked, "Got any pickles?"

All during lunch, Jake and the candy-colored clown played on Peter's mind. Afterwards, he kicked Curt and Ken out of the kitchen, saying, "Go watch the game. I'll be there shortly."

Peter rarely missed a Red Sox game, especially afternoon games; however, he had something else on his mind, a hunch, and it was bugging the heck out of him. He knew it wouldn't give him any peace until it got resolved.

After things were in order in the kitchen, Peter folded up the dishtowel and draped it across the counter. He untied his apron, took it off, and hooked it on the back of the pantry door. Then he put in a call to an old buddy by the name of Donny MacPhallon who had gone in country with him in the late 60s and again when he returned looking for MIAs that were still unaccounted for. MacPhallon now worked at the Federal Bureau of Investigation in Washington, D. C. Filled in on Jake, he said, "Lemme nose around a bit," and hung up. MacPhallon was never one to stand on ceremony, so when he didn't say goodbye, Peter thought nothing of it.

A short time later, MacPhallon called back. The news was grim, so Peter decided to wait until Elizabeth and Julie returned home. He didn't feel like going over the reason Jake wanted the candy-colored clown so bad more than once.

The ballgame was just about over when a frazzled Elizabeth entered the condo with Gretchen on her arm. The old woman looked a mess. Julie came next, her wrist bandaged. Detective Gage Fleming hovered over the women like a mother hen.

The second Ken saw Julie, his heart flip-flopped—so did Curt's. Ken got a loving kiss. Curt had to settle for a peck on the cheek. Leaving would make it so much easier, he thought. But his heart stood in the way.

The violence at the Konstanze home aggravated Ken, Peter, and Curt to no end. Not one was the least bit torn up about Gretchen shooting Jake dead. "I had the golden opportunity to kill that bastard myself," spewed Ken. "One handed with a candy dish. If I had, you girls wouldn't've gone through what you did today."

Curt gazed at the ceiling and scratched his Adam's apple. Lacing Jake old boy with strychnine would've been a better idea, he thought. Goes right to the gastrointestinal and respiratory tracts, it does. Violent convulsions would've tortured the bugger worse than the rack, say nothing of the muscular cramps in his neck and back, joint stiffness, muscle twitching, headache, severe blood-oxygen deficiency in body tissues, and cyanosis. Yup, that sorry excuse of humanity would've suffered dearly for his wicked ways. Gunshot's much too good for him. Ah, yes, strychnine a hard way to die indeed. Central nervous system toxicity, kidney failure, all would've added another dimension until respiratory arrest took him out. The picture was a gruesome one, and Curt took pleasure in it. Maybe he couldn't have Julie, but the thought of her in danger was unbearable. No question about it, death was just desserts for Jake, no matter how it happened.

Information that Peter got from Donny MacPhallon disturbed everybody even more than what had gone on at the Konstanze's. "Sarin gas?" exploded Curt. "In the hands and feet?"

Peter expelled a lungful of air. "Don't forget the clown's head," he said. His head bobbed up and down, lips pursed.

"But-but-but," stuttered Curt, shooting worried glances at the woman he secretly loved. "Julie and I... We... Holy mackerel! We played doctor on that thing!" He started to pace. "And all the while there were sarin gas vials in it?"

"Regina threw that damned thing at me," spewed Ken. Up to that moment, the incident had been locked in his mind. He ran his hand through his hair. "So many things come out of nowhere," he moaned. "How much more is there?"

Julie patted his hand.

"What the heck is sarin gas?" asked Elizabeth.

"A colorless, odorless gas first concocted by the Nazis," said Peter. "Enters the body by inhaling, ingesting, or getting in through the eyes or skin. Death comes within 1 to 10 minutes."

"Lethal dose for an adult is 0.5 milligrams," spat Curt. "Twenty-six times more deadly than cyanide gas."

Elizabeth covered her mouth with both hands, Julie gasped, and Gretchen sniveled something in German. Ken cleared his throat and muttered, "The whole world, gone to hell. Imagine. Katrina wouldn't be coming back to me tomorrow. I'd've gone to my grave never knowing she'd been kidnapped."

"Toast," said Curt, his head wavering side to side. "All of us toast."

Elizabeth ran her hands up and down her arms and asked, "What in the world was Jake doing with that stuff?"

"Regina, too," Julie added.

"Wasn't either of them afraid that his life was in jeopardy if one of those vials accidentally got broken?" asked Elizabeth.

"That thing was in the middle of Katrina's bed," bellowed Ken.

Gretchen began to wail.

"Hold it, people," said Peter, raising his hands. "Calm down. Everybody take a deep breath."

Ignoring him, Julie said, "Jake didn't know the vials were the clown."

"Regina know," sobbed Gretchen.

"But she's dead," said Julie. "That's why he went to you and Leo. You knew Regina the best, so more than likely you'd be able to figure out where the vials were."

"He must've had some idea or else why did he rig that plane to crash when he did?" asked Ken.

"But the vials weren't where he thought they were," said Julie.

"He didn't tell the Konstanzes what he was looking for," said Fleming, "because he didn't trust them not to go to the authorities; after all, as far as they were concerned, both Regina and Katrina were dead. They had nothing to lose if they squealed."

"I'll bet, at some point," said Ken, "that idiot would've used Katrina as leverage. If they knew she was alive, come hell or high water, they'd find those vials."

"I wouldn't put it past him," belched Curt.

"Jake, he worse than devil," sputtered Gretchen.

"My contact at the FBI believes that the vials were part of a carefully coordinated plan," said Peter.

"Plan?" asked Julie and Elizabeth simultaneously.

"Intelligence chatter indicates something's going down in the Middle East in a couple of years," said Peter. "To limit U.S.

involvement while one country—at this point it looks like Iraq—takes over Saudi Arabia and Israel, the four vials are—correction—were to be concurrently set off in four subways during afternoon rush hour in mid August in Boston, New York, Washington, D.C., and Chicago."

"Were to be set off?" asked Elizabeth. "Does that mean nothing's going to happen in the Middle East?"

"I wouldn't say that," said Peter.

"August heat and humidity," ranted Curt.

"Favors quicker evaporation," said Peter. "Means a higher casualty count."

Fleming scratched the back of his neck. "Time lag between release of sarin gas and its effects on the victims allows barely enough time for the perps to escape."

"Sarin gas," rambled Curt. "Armageddon in a cloud. Hovers close to the ground. Under wet or humid conditions, degrades swiftly. Temperature rises—lethal affects hang longer. Everything dies without damage to structures, paperwork, machinery, anything non-biological."

"Contamination is short-lived," said Fleming. "So perpetrators march right in. Control is immediate."

Ken grunted. "Even if only a quarter successful, a thing like that would wreck our economy."

"And," said Fleming, "the sheer terror of it all would freak people out so bad that chaos and rioting would overflow in the streets. A real nightmare for law enforcement."

"Law enforcement?" spouted Curt. "What about the medical end of things? People flooding hospitals by the thousands, all truly believing that they've been poisoned—purely psychosomatic ailments."

Julie shifted in her chair, skin crawling as if a thousand spiderlings were converging upon her. "But we're just innocent, run-of-the-mill smucks."

"Katrina's innocent, too," fumed Ken. "Little kids...being trained as terrorists...sheesh. Guess that makes terrorists like Jake feel like real men."

"Innocence means nothing with this form of aggressive, outward-reaching insanity," mused Gage Fleming.

Peter nodded. "Demands are so vague in this new type of evil that nobody understands them, let alone has any ability to satisfy them."

"Garden-variety madness having access to weapons of terror," remarked Curt.

"Terrorism," said Julie.

"We've never said it's terrorism," said Fleming.

"For crying out loud," blustered Ken. "What's it called if not terrorism?"

"Listen," said Fleming, dodging the question. "There's nothing to indicate terrorism at this point. What Jake was doing might very well fall into the category of a hate crime."

"Come on," said Peter. "Tell it like it is, man. You know very well that every day, unsavory elements come into the US to train and take advantage of American gun laws. Why, their firing ranges are state of the art. Lots of backing. Lots of money."

Unable to argue those points, Fleming tsked and said, "Right here under our noses."

"Is there any antidote to the sarin?" asked Julie.

"Atropine," said Curt. His eyes rolled. "But it must be administered within minutes."

"So by the time paramedics get to the scene, it's too late," said Julie.

Curt frowned and gave a reluctant nod.

"It frightens me to think how vulnerable we all are," said Elizabeth.

"How hard it was to build this country where we enjoy so many freedoms and move about in relative safety," said Peter. "How easy to bring it to its knees."

"Getting back to Jake," said Ken. "If he wasn't my brother…" His hand jounced in the air. "…then who the hell was he?"

Julie snagged his hand. Horror filled her eyes. "Not your brother?"

Gretchen wept uncontrollably.

251

Ken shook his head and drew Julie near, an effort to calm himself as well as her.

Fleming looked down at his shoes and shook his head. "Not related," he mumbled. How wrong he had been in thinking that this case was over the minute he walked into this place after the first Konstanze fiasco. Never in a million years could he have ever imagined the horrors that entangled this case.

"I took a look at the blood work," said Curt.

Julie shot a look at him.

"Ken and Jake are as far apart as elephants and roses," said Curt.

"So who was he?" asked Elizabeth.

"FBI isn't releasing any name," said Peter. "But his background is thought to be either Russian or Middle Eastern, although there is some question to that. So far, all that's known is he grew up in a military-like community somewhere in Russia. Family life didn't exist. No father. No mother. Never exposed to the opposite sex until after leaving."

"That explains a lot," said Ken dryly.

Peter's left eyebrow arched. "There are hints of him screwing up and suffering the disgrace of peers."

"Violence begets violence," muttered Elizabeth.

"But then the Soviet Union collapsed," said Peter, "and Middle Eastern terrorist factions stepped in, going out of their way to recruit kids who demonstrated a willingness to take risks not only with their lives but with peer respect and public opinion."

"Jake could care less about any of that," grunted Ken.

"That's why he was so antisocial," said Julie.

"To the point of being asocial," said Curt, "and communally autistic."

"It's difficult to head off guys like Jake," said Peter. "They keep their noses clean and work alone. Virtually no friends or close contacts."

"His apartment was a storehouse of chemical and biological weapons," said Fleming.

"Why didn't you tell us?" demanded Julie.

The detective bit the corner of his lip. Shouldn't've let that slip. Good thing I stopped before spilling the beans about those booby traps in his apartment. Sheer miracle that wire got spotted in time, otherwise, kaboom, no Roxbury. And how about those explosives in his sports car? Even in the framework!

"Well?" prodded Julie. "How come you didn't tell us?"

Fleming scratched his head and said, "I'm not at liberty to divulge such things."

Elizabeth eyed him. "Where'd Jake get all that stuff?" she asked.

When Fleming remained tight-lipped, Peter said, "Chemical agents are readily available commercially by theft from military or civilian stockpiles, which are less guarded than nuclear counterparts, or by receiving them from foreign state sponsors."

"Hey," said Curt. "I know of a company in Maryland where that stuff can be ordered at the drop of a hat."

"Yeah," groused Fleming. "Marijuana is more closely regulated in this country than access to and distribution of most deadly biological cultures."

"A note in Jake's apartment had provided clues to where a small amount of nerve agent VX is," said Peter, "which the U.S. government cannot account for."

Fleming's brows shot up to his hairline. "You found out about that?"

Peter gave him a sheepish grin and said, "His apartment's one of three units in a small building in Roxbury. He stockpiled protective equipment—gas masks, vaccines, antidotes, antibiotics, stuff like that. Theory is Regina put two and two together and managed to get a hold of the vials in Syria. Had them sewn into the clown not only to get past customs but also to throw Jake off the trail."

"Syria?" spouted Ken.

"She traveled there under an assumed name several weeks before the plane crash," said Peter.

"Wouldn't you think the person who sewed the vials into the clown would be a little suspicious?" asked Julie.

"Regina probably made up a story that the vials contained expensive perfume," said Curt. "A gift for somebody, and she didn't want to pay customs on such an expensive gift."

"The way people over there feel about America," said Peter, "it would've easily put an end to any question."

"Anything to tuck it to America," fumed Ken.

Fleming waved a hand and said, "Can't hide a thing from you folks."

"Geez," said Julie. "That idiot might've poisoned our water supply if he took it in his head to do so."

"That's less feasible," said Curt, "given the large quantities of agent that's required and the various filtering and purification measures already in place."

"Well," said Julie dubiously. "Guess that's comforting—a little anyways. What really worries me though..." She squeezed Ken's hand and looked into his eyes. "How many others are there like Jake running around out there?"

"Regina from me and Leopold," spoke up Gretchen. "Not Russia camp. She no same Jake."

"Oh, but she was the same as Jake," spat Ken. "A real terrorist—in a lot more ways than he ever was!"

Gretchen hid her face in her hands and sobbed.

"Ken stop," said Julie.

"Well," groused Ken, "I for one hope there's no more like either one of them infecting this world."

Fleming scanned the group and wondered how a small-time dick such as himself was supposed to protect good folks like these. What could he say to allay their fears? Tell them about the groups out there that are working to protect the nation—and the world for that matter? Then heap upon them that for obvious security reasons it is not a topic for general discussion? They won't accept that—not knowing what they know now. Nope. I'd rather keep my big, fat mouth shut.

CHAPTER TWENTY

"How was your flight, *Father?*" hissed Ken when his parents walked into the living room.

Julie hung back in the hallway, the telltale flush of embarrassment smarting her face. Geez, Ken isn't even trying to hide his feelings of betrayal. Her fingertips toyed with one another. This reunion is not going to be pretty.

"A bit bumpy over the Carolinas," said Richard, "but all in all…"

Julie stepped around the corner as Patty hurried to her son, blubbering, "My dear Kenny."

Ken had always kissed his mother warm hellos and goodbyes, but this time things were different. He turned away as his plaster arm cast fended her off.

Patty took a reflexive step backward and lamented, "Oh, my, look at your arm." Her hand shielded her heart. "And your leg! What on God's green earth were you doing out there on that cliff? And how did you manage to topple over it? And how did that horrible fire get started?"

Julie put herself between Patty and Ken and pretended to adjust his pillows. "Ken's doing as well as can be expected," she said.

Crooking his neck to look around Julie, Ken grunted in a voice caustic as battery acid, "Under the circumstances."

"I don't know about your mother," blustered Richard, his fingers combing his closely cropped mustache, "but I, for one, expected to see you in a whole lot worse shape." His hand gestured towards Elizabeth and Peter then semi-circled in Ken's direction. "No sooner we take off to Florida than a thing like this happens. Next thing we hear? Jake's been arrested."

"Dead," fired Ken.

Richard stiffened. His eyes bulged. "Wha…?"

"You heard me," spat Ken.

Patty reeled as color drained from her face. "J-Jake?" she hacked. "He's…He's…"

A shiver shot up Julie's spine. Things were going downhill real fast.

"That's right, *Mother*," sneered Ken. "Stone…cold…dead."

Julie felt like running for cover. Acrimony did that to her.

"What's the matter with you, Kenny?" whined Patty, her hand reaching out to him.

"Don't," he snapped and once again his plaster arm cast rebuffed her. His eyes impaled her like switchblades. "Don't you dare come near me."

Patty stopped in her tracks while Julie made for the safety of her mother and father.

"Perhaps we should leave," whispered Elizabeth as she and Peter shrunk away from the fray.

"No, Mom, stay," begged Julie.

"But, Pumkin," said Peter. "This is between Ken and his parents."

"Please," whined Julie, tears brimming her eyes. "I don't want you to go."

"Stick around," stormed Ken. "One way or the other, the whole world's gonna know."

"Gonna know what?" demanded Richard, grabbing hold of Patty's arm and tugging her out of the way. He stepped up to Ken and stared him down, fists opening and closing as he wrestled with anger. This couldn't be happening. After a lifetime of doing the best for his son, this was what it all came down to? Cutting, spiteful words wanted out, but in the end speech came tight and controlled. "Why do you speak to your Mother in such a manner?"

"Mother?" challenged Ken, red hot anger bloating his being. "Really. Is that who she is?" As he leaned towards Richard and looked him in the eye, the vein in the middle of his scarlet forehead throbbed. "And you. Who are you? My father? Or daddy *du jour*?"

Richard took a step back. His eyes widened. Confused and hurt, he looked at Patty, now huddled in the corner. His brows came together, and he looked back at Ken as though about to speak. Suddenly, he made for Patty, wanting to comfort her—wanting to take comfort from her.

"Ken," pleaded Julie as she left the safety of her parents. "You've got to calm down." She stroked his arm, but his icy stare remained on his parents. "Come on. This isn't helping."

As the room fell silent as the morgue that Jake's remains were lying in, Julie fidgeted then glanced at her mother. *Mom's thinking the same thing—this is one awful mess.* She cleared her throat and ventured, "Why don't we all sit down, uhm…and sort all this out?" She gestured to the loveseat and then to Patty and Richard. "Come. Sit over here."

Patty's eyes disclosed profound heartbreak. Richard remained transfixed, like an alabaster statue. Neither budged.

Julie twisted her fingers. She had no idea how to defuse this situation.

Then Richard took Patty's hand and in a watered down voice, said, "We will do as Julie suggests, Patricia." He led her to the loveseat and sat her down. Hiking his pants legs with modest decorum, he sat down beside her and draped his left arm across her shoulders while his right hand patted her knee.

Julie scratched the side of her neck while taking a sidelong glance at Ken. *Geez, he's so mad,* she thought. *I've never seen him that way—not even close to that mad.* She peered into his parents' bewildered eyes and swallowed hard. "We've learned…" she stammered, "that Jake is…is not…uhm…was not Ken's brother."

The terror that widened Patty's eyes sliced through Julie like white-hot spears. Unable to take it, she fled to the balcony doorway and pretended to look out at the Boston skyline. Weak and sick to her stomach, she hated herself for being so stupid, for being so incapable of fixing all the horrible stuff that constantly messed up in her life.

"Curt analyzed the blood," spat Ken. "Jake's blood type didn't match mine. Surprise! It didn't match either of yours, either!"

Julie turned around. All eyes were fixed upon Patty and Richard.

Patty looked down at Richard's hand that clutched hers like a drowning man going down for the third time. "There's no point in pretending any longer," she said. They exchanged uncertain glances. His hand released hers and came up to his bottom lip, rubbing back and forth. "He's dead. He can't hurt us any longer."

His hand dropped and his eyes locked on Ken as Richard said, "It's true. Jake was not our son. Not even adopted." His countenance seemed to say, there, it's out in the open at last. "Jake came to us, demanding retribution for being allowed to leave the Soviet Union long ago."

Julie shot an astonished glance at Elizabeth and said, "Gretchen told us a similar story about Regina!"

Ken's brows came together. "What are you talking about?"

"It appears as though Regina and Jake were pawns," said Peter, "made to look like they came from ordinary parents and homes, but in actuality they were programmed components of an underground network of international terrorism."

Ken turned to his parents and said, "So why did you go along with it?"

"Jake said he had ways of destroying our lives without killing us," whimpered Patty.

"We could handle that somehow," said Richard, "but then he said he'd fix it so you'd have an unfortunate accident. Or the police would find drugs or something awful in your car or apartment. You'd've ended up in jail. Losing your computer business."

"Why?" asked Ken.

"I don't know," said Richard.

"I swear to you, Kenny," sobbed Patty. Pausing, she scanned faces. "I swear to all of you that neither of us have any knowledge whatsoever of the reason Jake came to us when he did, where he came from, or what he was up to—nothing!"

Ken ran his hand through his hair and gripped the back of his neck. After a moment of thought, he asked, "What about me? Where did I come from?"

Richard looked at the tears trickling down Patty's ruddy cheeks. He lifted her chin and looked deep into her eyes. He smiled, and a timid grin wrinkled her lips. He kissed her cheek and then tightened his arm around her shoulder. "From us," he said and glanced at Ken. "You came from us. You are our son."

Patricia hid her face against his chest and in a muffled voice, said, "Our only baby."

Julie peered at Ken. He looked like a whipped puppy. She went to the wheelchair and brought it to him. He looked up at her and then at the wheelchair. His hand ran through his hair. Then without any assistance, he maneuvered into the wheelchair and worked the lever. The motor whirred and the wheelchair rolled to his parents. Taking his mother's hand, he placed it on his good knee then took his father's hand and put it on top of hers. Squeezing both, he said in a soft but emphatic voice, "I am so very, very, sorry. Forgive me?" He looked into Patty's eyes. "Mother?" He looked into Richard's eyes. "Dad?"

And Julie smiled that silly grin of hers.

***

Propped up against goose down pillows encased in yellow gingham, Ken lingered in bed and listened to the sounds of the condo coming alive. The entire household had been up since the crack of dawn, anticipating Katrina's return. Even though Katrina wasn't expected to arrive until late that afternoon or evening, there wasn't nearly enough time to get the many things done, cleaning, baking, whatever, to make the event absolutely perfect. Needless to say, nobody had gotten any sleep. He smiled. Lack of sleep was becoming somewhat of a habit around here.

Elizabeth and Peter had been rustling about the kitchen for an hour now, and the smell of sausage patties, cinnamon buns, and coffee was wafting into the bedroom. Shower water surged; so in addition to his daughter's return and hunger pains,

Ken was envisioning Julie stepping into a steamy cubical—without him. "Just ain't right," he huffed while running his hand through his hair and envisioning water beading up on her petal-soft skin. His stomach buzzed like a bee that happened upon the first nectar-filled blossom of spring.

Rubbing his scruffy chin, he conjured up honey-blond hair teasing his face and essence of honeysuckle delighting his nostrils. It had been a long time since he made love to her. Man, was he saving up for the day.

"Good heaven's, she's humming!" He swallowed hard.

Oh well, for the time being, he was going to have to be content to have her hand cradle his cheek and her soft warm lips kiss his. After everything that's happened, he's more than satisfied just hearing her tender voice say good morning. As Curt had said before leaving last night, "Count yourself one very lucky man, ol' chap. M'lady's still hanging out with you, standing by you every step of the way. I should be so lucky."

Ken shook his head. "How in the world could this brain of mine ever have jumbled the alive and vibrant Julie with sordid recollections of Regina?"

"Life is definitely going to get better from here on out, especially after Katrina gets here," Julie had told Ken last night after kissing him good night. With all his heart, he believed her, because everything that came in contact with her always blossomed and grew like a country garden in June. As sweet harmony flowed from the bathroom and through his being, he had no doubt that this was going to be the case. And then the baby. Whoa. Ken wriggled into a higher position on the bed pillows.

"Gosh, wonder what the baby's going to be," he murmured. His brows came together. "A boy would be nice, now that Katrina's on her way back. Hmm…" His head tilted slightly. "Another girl's okay, too—so long as she looks like Julie and not me." A silly look plastered his face. "Oh, what does it matter? Katrina's such a precious little cherub that another girl would surely fit the bill. Now wait a minute, a boy… Hey, think of the fun—baseball, hockey, sailing—geesh, the list is endless. Too bad we're not having twins. Yeah. A boy and a girl. Perfect! Imagine the five of us…"

"Are you ready to get out of those jammies, lazy bones?" spouted Julie, towel drying her hair as she came into the bedroom.

His face reddened. "You caught me daydreaming."

"I like that word, daydreaming," she said, planting a kiss on his forehead.

He tried to snag her arm, but missed. "You're a slippery one, Mrs. Waters."

She smiled that silly grin and fluttered her eyelashes.

He sighed and then said, "Daydreaming's better than nightmares."

"I'll say," she said at the bureau. She picked up a can of herbal mousse, shook it, and turned it upside down to shoot a glob of foam onto her fingertips. Fluffing the foam through her hair, she adjusted her stance to catch his reflection in the mirror.

"I'm going to make up for all the mean things I put you through," said Ken, swelling with love. "And Katrina and the baby too. I'm going to build a brand new home for all of you— per Mrs. Julie Waters' specifications, of course."

"Of course," she echoed casually and then started to hum a Rachmaninoff tune.

"Wherever you want," he said with a flip of the wrist. "You pick the design and the furniture—the best money can buy." He put his hand behind his head and stared up at the ceiling. "I can see us now, all decked out in brand new clothes, the four of us grabbing life by the teeth and exploring this big, beautiful country of ours, singing patriotic songs on the fourth of July. Yep, we'll watch fireworks explode over the Charles River as the Boston Pops pounds out the William Tell Overture."

A rap came on the wall outside the bedroom. Ken and Julie expected to see either Elizabeth or Peter entering, carrying in a tray of piping hot coffee and the morning's fare. That wasn't the case, for the vision that had roamed Ken's subconscious for the past four years raced through the door. Another dream, argued his senses. Yet, there's no mistaking the girl, all fleshed out. Older. Taller.

"Daddy! Daddy!" The voice sparkled like the one that lingered in his memory as the blue-eyed cherub with freckles that spanned the ridge of her nose and golden ringlets that swirled about her head rushed toward him.

His heart thundered, Katrina! Katrina! Moisture welled in his eyes, and for a moment there, he thought he might've even peed his pants.

Oh, God look at me, he fretted within. I look like something Ralph dragged in, in these dumb old pajamas with one arm and leg ripped with casts jutting out like broken down Roman pillars. I should've gotten up earlier, shaved. He ran his hand through his hair. Good heavens, my hair's all askew...

Since yesterday morning, Ken had known that Katrina was coming back. He intended to be ready, looking perfect, freshly showered, shaved, and wearing his best clothes—well, the best a guy could wear with casts on one arm and leg. He was going to splash on the just the right amount of aftershave, the kind he used to wear before she was stolen from him. Hopefully, she'd remember it.

During the night, his mind had poured over endless words, never settling on the right ones or the order in which to put them. All he could do at this moment was to open one good arm wide and the other molded in plaster as far as it could go. To his vast delight, there was no hesitation on her part to snuggle against him.

Ken and Julie gawked at each other. Clad in her mother's mint-colored Chenille robe that was much too big, she wrung her hands. Her hair was fluffed, out of control, still on the damp side. He winked and motioned with his head. She grinned nervously then went him. Fingers entwining, he whispered, "Think I need a couple more arms so I can hold my two girls and never let them go."

At the doorway, Detective Gage Fleming smiled with all-consuming satisfaction. Look at those big, beautiful, blue peepers on that kid. Looks no worse for the wear, although who knows what demons are floating about her little mind. And her old man—every moment of pain that's tormented his sorry soul has vanished like snowflakes in June. Even with those vile casts, he looks ten years younger.

Fleming turned to Elizabeth and Peter. "Sorry we got here so early," he said, "but Miss Waters wouldn't take no for an answer."

"We're kind of getting used to surprises around here," chuckled Elizabeth.

Peter squeezed her hand and added, "At all hours."

By the silly little grins the couple exchanged, Fleming had a good idea that there was a whole lot more to this family than what he was privileged to know. Yet he also had the feeling that it wasn't all bad.

"I just couldn't wait any longer, Daddy," said Katrina, her voice laced with southern drawl.

"And I'm glad you didn't," said Ken. He kissed the tip of her nose. "I was afraid that you might not even remember me."

She bolted upright. Taking her father's cheeks into her hands, she stared straight into his eyes. "I never forgot you, Daddy. I made up my mind not to. I made myself remember your face. Every night when I crawled into bed and tucked the covers under my chin just the way you always did, I made myself remember the sound of your voice and the way you always said, 'Night-night, my little cherub.' Remember? I made myself dream of you, that way I wouldn't cry." She winced. "If they caught me crying, they got real mad, and I got punished. I had to be a big girl...all the time..." She paused, and there was no doubt in anyone's mind that she was thinking about that wicked camp in Judgment, Mississippi. Her face scrunched up as her intense eyes looked at him. "I decided that I was going to run away when I got big enough." Her lips pursed and she nodded firmly. "No matter what, I was going to find you, even if it took forever and a day." She studied his face and then a smile grew on her face, big, toothy and brilliant as January snow on a sunny day. Her arms wrapped about his neck and she planted a kiss on his lips. "Know how much I love you?"

"Too much?" ventured Ken.

"There's no such thing as too much," she spouted with a decisive hitch of the chin.

Fleming sucked in a satisfied breath, turned, and extended his right hand. "This is what makes my job worthwhile," he said.

Elizabeth shook his hand, but Peter held back.

With a nod that indicated a great deal of respect and admiration for the disabled ex MIA and his family, Fleming took the prosthetic hand. Shaking it, he said, "I gotta go get this case wrapped up." His eyes rolled. "Funny, I thought I had a handle on things the day that nincompoop first invaded this place."

"Who could've possibly fathomed that things might turn out the way they have," said Peter.

Just then, gray streaked across Fleming's shoe. Instinctively he reached for his service revolver beneath his sport coat and shielded himself at the edge of the doorjamb. Then he spotted Ralph jumping up on the bed, head-butting Julie out of the way, and worming between Ken and Katrina.

"Ralph," squealed Katrina, clasping her hands over her heart.

Fleming winced and let go of the gun. His hand withdrew from his sport coat.

Katrina snatched up the cat and buried her face into the luxuriant gray fur. Loud purring filled the room. The tail that habitually jounced yellow and pink baby blankets in a doll carriage didn't move. "Never forgot you either, my little baby doll," she murmured and then held the cat out at arms length to gaze in his eyes "Know what they called me?"

Ralph clicked.

"Kitty," she spat. "Yup. Isn't that the most funniest thing you ever heard?

Ralph clicked.

"And you know what? That was okay with me," said Katrina. "My very own special secret. Every time they called me Kitty, I felt a whole lot better 'cause I remembered my Ralphie— and my Daddy."

EPILOGUE

"I want to live in Brighton," declared Julie while clearing breakfast dishes off the kitchen table. She was still in her nightclothes and slippers as was Katrina who was eating a raisin bagel slathered with cream cheese. Elizabeth and Peter hadn't stirred as yet. *Privilege of age* was how they put it.

Ken backed the wheelchair away from the table. "But Julie…"

She pretended not to hear, rinsing dishes in the sink and babbling, "Near the hospital and Mom and Dad. Emma. Geez, Brighton's near everybody—your parents, Gretchen and Leopold and…"

"Okay, okay!" he blustered. Clad in a white strappy tee shirt, boxer shorts, and no footwear, he hadn't shaved nor combed his hair—Katrina hadn't given him the chance, dragging him and Julie out of bed at the crack of dawn, bellyaching about being starved.

Although the eight-year-old had been back for only a couple days, everyone was accustomed to having her around, as if she had never been gone. Mom and Dad spoiled her rotten—a fair indicator of what's to come.

"But building lots in Brighton don't exist," argued Ken.

"Forget building," countered Julie. "Too many headaches."

"It's not all that bad," he said, watching her load dishes into the dishwasher.

"Look what Margi and Evan went through," she spouted.

"Great day in the morning!" he exclaimed. "Don't compare us to them! Margi's her own worst enemy; and Evan—God bless his soul—he goes along for the ride, singing a song, oblivious to it all. How he keeps his blood pressure under control is beyond me!"

Unable to argue the obvious, Julie dismissed it with the wave of a hand. "We'd be lucky to finish construction before the baby gets here," she said. "And I want to live in the house where our child is born forever."

"Correction," said Ken. "Chil*dren*."

Julie's eyes got big as golf balls. "Oh, my God..." she squeaked.

"What's the matter?" he yelped.

Katrina stopped chewing. One cheek bulged with food as her eyes filled with terror and shot to her stepmother.

"I felt the baby," whispered Julie.

Ken gawked at her. "You did?"

Julie turned to Ken, nodding. She looked down at her hand circling her growing belly. Her head tilted to one side, she glanced at him. "I finally felt the flutter of life," She gazed at her belly again and swallowed hard. "At least I think I did."

Mirth exploded within Ken. "At times, Mrs. Waters, you're such a child," he taunted. "More than Katrina."

"Hey," sputtered Katrina, casting her father an indignant air. Her lips puckered.

"Maybe it's indigestion," ventured Julie.

"No way," squawked Ken. "With all the stuff you put in your mouth and never once so much as burp?"

"I'm having lots of brothers and sisters, huh?" said Katrina. Popping the last bite of bagel into her mouth, she washed it down with orange juice. When a tiny bit dribbled out the corner of her mouth, she showed great concern and quickly set down the glass to snag a napkin and dab away the seepage.

Shades of the past, thought Ken, as he watched Katrina. He flashed back to the manse and four-year-old Katrina doing the very same thing to avoid Regina's wrath. Scraping invisible crumbs with the side of her hand, she then drove them to the edge of the table and dropped them into the napkin, which she immediately crushed in her hand.

Julie rammed her hands into her hips and breezed, "You two…"

"Whassamaddah?" blustered Ken. "We too much for you?" Father and daughter exchanged winks.

Julie zeroed in on the girl's blue eyes and sighed, "Wonder what color eyes the baby will have."

"Like mine," spewed Katrina.

"I don't think so," said Julie. "Your father and I have brown eyes. So does my Mom and Dad."

"You got your blue eyes from you mother's side of the family," said Ken.

"From Gammy Getchen and Gampy Leo," snapped Katrina. "Not Regina!" She adamantly referred to the woman who bore her as Regina.

Little by little, Katrina had been revealing her life in Judgment, Mississippi, which Ken and Julie found extremely difficult to hear. So Curt recommended a therapist who specialized in kidnap and brainwash victims.

"Forgetting the trauma is impossible," advised Dr. Edith Fitzgerald. "Best way to deal with it is to bring out as many details as possible, hash them over and crush the substance out of them."

Even at that, Katrina would never forget. "Daddy was on the floor," she said. "He wouldn't wake up. Jake kicked and punched him and yanked me away." She rubbed her wrist as if Jake were gripping it at that moment. "He squeezed real tight. I kicked and screamed like crazy. Regina slapped my face. She called me bad names. I got away and ran back to Daddy." Katrina drew in a cleansing breath and bravely puffed herself up. "I was four then, so I didn't understand how come Daddy didn't wake up; but I'm eight now. I know what Jake did, and it makes me very, very angry. I'm glad he's not my uncle! I'm glad he's dead!" She rubbed the back of her head. "He smacked my face so hard that I flew into the corner of the dresser. Regina didn't do one single thing to stop him or help me or make the hurt better. She didn't even look at me!"

"From that point on Jake Waters took charge of Katrina," wrote Doctor Fitzgerald in a report that the FBI requested. "The last Katrina recalls of mother, Regina Waters, is the back of her head above the front seat of Jake Waters' car and a gold earring dangling in and out of blond hair. Katrina was in the backseat.

"They were fighting," said Katrina, "because Regina wanted Jake to go somewhere with her, but he said no. He had to do something first. He told her to go someplace and wait for him. I fell asleep and when I woke up, she was gone. I cried, but not for her, because I hated her—and Jake too! I had to go pee, that's why I cried. He hollered, 'Shut up and hold it!' I tried to, but then I couldn't any more and had an accident and Jake got real mad and cussed and reached back and smacked my face and I got a bloody nose. I made an awful mess all over the back seat. I couldn't clean it up. He yelled I better stop crying or else and the car swerved all over the place, and I bounced all around that little back seat and banged my head first on one side and then the other. When he finally got the car going straight, he looked back at me. His eyes were very mean and big and black as black." A tremor wracked the eight-year-old frame. "All of a sudden, the car stopped and the tires made a lot of noise and I fell on the floor. He grabbed my hand and squeezed so tight my fingers squashed together. He yanked me out of the car. My legs hurt real bad and I couldn't stand up, so he lifted me off the ground by my wrist, and my arm twisted. Lots of dogs barked at us and charged at us, so Jake hollered bad words and kicked one in the head. It ran off kiyiking. That's when a big fat lady came out of a shack and hollered to stop kicking the dogs. He hollered he was going to shoot all of them and she hollered let go of me, but he wouldn't. She threw a stack of money at him, and it fell on the ground all over the place. He said more awful words and ran after the money, because the wind blew it away. The fat lady held my hand very tight, so I couldn't get away. Jake stomped to his car with money sticking out his hands and pockets and zoomed away. I didn't know what was going to happen to me, so I got really scared and wanted him to come back, but I know it was a good thing he didn't. The camp wasn't a very nice place, but it was better than him. Better than Regina, too."

Back in Elizabeth and Peter's condo, Katrina declared, "Don't nobody never say I got my eyes from Regina! I'm glad she's dead. I'm glad that stupid house on the cliff burnt down. I don't ever want to go there again!"

Julie put an arm around the eight-year-old and squeezed, taking comfort in the fact that Katrina bore little resemblance to Regina. Who needs Ken freaking out every time he looks at his daughter, she thought. Still, it's terrible that every time Regina's mentioned, Katrina pulls into herself like a turtle into its shell. "You deserve your own room, sweetie," said Julie, "but building a house takes a long time." She glanced at Ken and whined, "I want to have a nursery all fixed up before the baby comes and…"

"Now, before you go off half-cocked," he cut in, "It's only fair you to listen to my side. I put a fair amount of time and consideration into our future, you know."

One shoulder jounced as Julie said, "Go ahead."

"We should pick up an acre or two of land on the outskirts of a blue-collar neighborhood out in the Berkshires," he said. "Not many computers out there yet, which I might add is good for business." He squinted at the ceiling, stroking his chin. "Yup. We'll revel in the profundity of everyday life and ordinary working stiffs. Live in a quaint eight-room cottage we'll build with our own hands. And a barn, too! I'm sure we can pick up a broken-down Guernsey milk cow from some farmer. And a dozen or so Rhode Island reds."

Julie and Katrina exchanged sour gawks. "Cow?" they whined in unison.

Ken scratched his head, having all he could do to maintain a serious demeanor.

"But Ken," lamented Julie.

"Daddy," whined Katrina.

"Oh, all right," he said, a twinkle in his eye. "Where's that newspaper?"

"Yes," exclaimed Julie giving Katrina a high-five.

"If you two are quite finished," blustered Ken. He lifted his right arm and leg. "I'd go get the newspaper myself, but I'm a bit plastered."

"You silly," giggled Katrina, rushing over to plank a kiss on his cheek. Then she skipped out of the kitchen.

"You're too much to take all at once," said Julie. Grabbing his face in her hands, she kissed Ken square on the lips.

"Mmm, I like this," he said, groping for her. "Gimme more."

She jack-knifed out of the way and wagged a finger. "That's all you get, young man."

"But honey," he whimpered. "Please?"

She waved him off and gathered up the remaining breakfast dishes.

"Honeh?" he wailed plaintively. "Honeh?"

"Shush," she scolded. "You'll wake Mom and Dad. It's a miracle they're not up already, what with all the shenanigans going on around here this morning."

Ken studied Julie as she loaded dishes into the dishwasher. He wanted her so badly he could feel it in the pit of his stomach. "You're a fantastic woman," he ventured.

"Flirt," she said while twisting the dial on the dishwasher. As water surged, she turned around. Her hands gripped her hipbones. Her eyes bore into his.

"You're my best friend," he offered, his gaze swerving to the floor. "And lover?" He peeked out of the corner of one eye. Her face glowed with awkward delight—the same as that day when he ran her down in the hospital corridor. His heart fluttered. Looking straight into her eyes, he said, "And soon to be mother of the child that you and I made."

She picked up the dishtowel and threw it at him. "I feel like a mother already."

Ken plucked the towel off his forehead and wadded it into a ball. "I was so blown away yesterday when Katrina called you Mom," he said and hurled the towel. "She looks up to you as if you were her biological mother."

Catching the towel, Julie said, "I'm glad that she's taken to me." She tossed the towel onto the counter. "That worried me." She bit her lip, thinking how ecstatic she'd be if Ken would cast off Regina once and for all. Her eyes rolled. What are the chances?

In Ken's mind, Regina's memory was as dead as she was, and that was the best revenge for everything she had put him and Katrina through—and Julie, too. How could he have ever made it through the last few months without Julie? It was truly fortunate that she came along at when she did, just when he needed somebody the most. She made him feel alive, really alive, just like now.

"This one looks nice," said Katrina, trekking into the kitchen, newspaper open and concealing three quarters of her face. She spread the paper on the table and pointed at a classified ad.

Aware of four hopeful eyes, Ken skimmed the ad. His left eyebrow shot up his forehead. "Whoa," he blustered. "One hefty price!"

Katrina drew back. Her worried eyes searched his face and then Julie's.

"Let me see that," said Julie, yanking the paper away from Ken. She leaned on the table to read. The front of one ankle rubbed the back of the other. "Well, yah, but…" Her finger tapped on the newsprint. "This house is close to St. Anne's. Must be in that neighborhood just past Em's place." Her eyes were inches from his. "You know where I'm talking about…after her street." Her hand swerved to the left and pitched into the air. "The street that turns up the hill." When she looked down at the ad, Ken felt like a light had been switched off. "Oh yes," she said in a singsong voice. "It is. Look at this." Her finger underscored the lines as she read, "'Quiet established neighborhood. Panoramic view.'" She glanced up at him.

Hiding his amusement, he nodded thoughtfully while pursing his lips. He glanced at the ceiling, thumb and forefinger stroking his scruffy chin. "No other area in Brighton has that kind of elevation." He slid her a sidelong glance. Cocoa eyes bowled him over.

"Let's go look at it, Daddy," gushed Katrina.

This time, baby blues reined in Ken. His gaze bounced between the female connivers. A wry grin twisted his lips. "Holy smoke," he huffed. "I'm putty in your hands."

"So can we, Daddy?"

Julie had a hungry look about her.

Ken winced. "I suppose."

Julie and Katrina leapt to their feet, grabbed hands, and circled round and around, singing, "We're gonna buy a house, we're gonna buy a house."

"Hold on one blessed minute," he snapped.

They screeched to a stop and gave him the once over.

"What's the matter, Daddy?"

"Look at me, will you, please?" he squalled. "House hunting isn't possible."

Julie winked at Katrina and then at Ken. Arching her back, she poked her breastbone with her thumb, saying, "Stick with the kid an' me, babe. We are women! Watch us roar!"

"R-r-roar-r-r!" exploded Katrina as her arm crooked into the air, bicep flexing.

Noontime, an army of family, friends, and healthcare workers readied Ken for his first outing since the Cohasset fiasco. Whisked out of the condo, down the elevator, and into a conversion van that idled in the garage beneath the building, he went off to view the colonial homestead before he could say, "How much is the down payment?"

As the ramp of the van descended in front of a home that possessed the ageless beauty of a bygone era, a general sense of calm came over Ken. Rhododendrons, ablaze with pink and white blossoms, added to the rustic appeal. He didn't want to admit it, but the place did feel like home. Lifting his face to the July sun, he sucked in fresh, eighty-degree air, perfect for the green short sleeve shirt he had been thrown into by a thousand volunteer hands—well, it seemed like a thousand. His legs weren't the least bit cold in gray athletic shorts that those maniacs so nimbly stretched over the leg cast. He wore a sandal on his right foot while the toes of his left foot wiggled out of plaster.

"Daddy, I love this place!" exclaimed Katrina jumping out of the van. She ran to the gate of the picket fence that bordered the property, opened it, and glanced over her shoulder. She gave him a thumbs up. Wearing a blue gingham sundress and white socks and sneakers, Katrina skipped along the flagstone walk, looking like a blond Dorothy on the yellow brick road to the Emerald City.

Julie nudged the wheelchair off the ramp as Sandra, the exclusive realtor for the property got out of her Mercedes. Average in height, Sandra looked like she worked out regularly, shopped downtown, and got her medium length dark brown hair styled on Newbury Street. Her makeup was adequate on all scales. No doubt, she had a make-up consultant. The light blue summer suit she wore was impeccably tailored to her mid to late thirties figure. Julie felt self-conscious in a white peasant blouse, aqua stretch shorts, sandals, and no makeup.

"This turn-of-the-century lady is an example of the Second Empire style of architecture," said Sandra without referring the black leather folder she carried in the crook of her arm. "Few like it remain in this area. Convenient yet quiet, an easy walk to shops, dining, schools, parks, and the hospital. The library is three doors down on the left."

Julie stepped aside to let several burley individuals hoist Ken and the wheelchair up to the portico. "Your knowledge of the place is impressive," she said.

"I've been in the business long enough to know my houses," said Sandra, unlocking the door. "This home has been in the family since it was built. The heirs have decided to dispose of it." A hint of sadness tainted her voice. "This is the reception room. As you can see, this home was built with creature comforts in mind. I've seen pictures of it in its heyday, filled with mahogany furniture, popular during that period, and large family portraits, but it's all gone to auction."

Julie sighed. "Our pictures burned in the fire." Her hand cupped Ken's shoulder. "But friends and family are making copies of what they have. Lots more to come—right, sweetheart?"

Ken ran his hand across his freshly shaven chin.

In the study Sandra said, "I think this room fits your requirements for an office."

"There certainly is enough room for books," said Julie. "Ken and Katrina will have to start rummaging old books stores."

"Over here is a secret door that leads to a back hallway," said Sandra, pressing a button inside the bookcase. An entire section opened inward.

Julie poked her head through the secret portico and murmured, "Intriguing."

"That flying staircase is a rare find," boasted Sandra. She closed the portico then headed to the front living room that had bluish-purple walls and the original tiled fireplace. "Entertaining will be a pleasure in this gracious home. The foyer with its period woodwork, turned staircase, and French doors, gives a preview of the charm to be seen throughout this home."

The dining room was spacious with floor to ceiling bow windows. The kitchen had a butler's pantry and an atrium window over the sink. Julie envisioned jelly jars on the windowsill, brimming with dandelions, lily-of-the-valley, and yellow-eyed daisies—all picked by the littlest of family hands. "Imagine us living in a place like this?" said Julie.

Ken didn't respond.

Sandra gestured to a door inside the mudroom/laundry room. "Through there is a full bath. Over here is an additional room with private entry from a three-season porch."

"Ralph will love this," said Katrina while stepping out onto the porch.

"Oh, no," gasped Julie. Her fingertips shot to her bottom lip. "We never thought about Ralph! There are too many cars around here."

"We'll just have to keep Ralph inside," said Katrina.

Sandra tsked. "Hard thing to do once a cat gets a taste of the great outdoors."

Ken bit his tongue. Regina was the one who had exposed Ralph to the outdoors. Every time he turned around, she had thrown the poor furball out. He ran his hand through his hair. Maybe that's one good thing that the harpy did—that is, besides having Katrina. If Ralph hadn't been outside the day of the fire, he'd've been cooked. Hold on a minute, he was scratching at the French doors, acting strange…and I…was on my knees…

"The backyard is a bit of a jungle," said Sandra, trying to get a read on her clients. Mrs. Waters adores the place, but Mr. Waters… She slid a look at the reticent male in the wheelchair. He's kind of hardnosed.

"I like all that foliage arching over the winding wooded pathway like that," said Julie. "Sure would be easy to keep in touch with the seasons in a place like this."

"Century-old pine and oak shade most of the backyard and cushion the sounds of the city," said Sandra.

Katrina lifted her index finger to her mouth. "Shshsh. Listen to all the birds."

Julie pointed to a gravelly spot where a beam of sunlight filtered through the mantle of green. "We should put a picnic table right over there," she said, "and a bench under that oak. I love the ferns and hosta." She elbowed Katrina. "Hey, know what we'll do?"

Katrina squinted sideways. "What?"

"We'll have your father make a wooden footbridge over that brook."

Katrina rubbernecked. "What brook?"

Julie winked. "The one we're going to rig up right next to that boulder."

Ken gawked at the ancient hunk of rock with moss slithering about like wrinkled skin. Small seedlings had taken root in crevices, making the boulder look like a baldheaded old gent. Funny how the babbling brook, which didn't exist, filled his senses.

The tour advanced to the bottom of the turned stairway where a shiver raced through Ken as he looked up at the top landing. Julie put her index fingers in her mouth and blew a fragmented whistle. Several burly individuals came running and as they hoisted the wheelchair up to the second floor, Ken fought off memories of going up the stairs in the manse.

Sandra led the group through four bedrooms, two full baths and into the nursery. Julie bit the inside of her cheek, reluctant to follow, remembering the nursery in Cohasset. The crib. The comforter. Sheets and bumper. All with cavorting Teddy bears and butterflies. Was it bad luck to design another nursery the same way? The moment she laid eyes on the nursery, all thought of design vanished. It was one of the most whimsical rooms she had ever seen, the perfect blend of pale yellow and mint with a splattering of other happy colors. "What do you think, Ken?" she asked.

He heaved, "Needs a lot of TLC."

Julie exchanged surprise with Sandra, both thinking, this place doesn't need any TLC.

Sandra went to the window, clearing her throat. "There's plenty of storage," she said. "Don't forget the attached, oversized garage. Used to be a carriage house."

Julie leaned down to Ken's ear and whispered, "We have enough money from the insurance and sale of the land in Cohasset, don't we?"

"It's not the money," he muttered.

Sandra pretended not to hear. "I see your daughter in the backyard," she said. "Think I'll join her."

Julie looked down at wavy brown hair. Why didn't Ken say something? She stepped around to the front of the wheelchair.

He avoided her eyes.

"What is it?" she murmured.

He shrugged.

She got down on one knee and took his face in her hands. "I like this house pretty much like it is, but if you want, we'll hire somebody to fix it the way you want."

Ken ran his hand through his hair. He glanced at the ornate white metal ceiling. His stomach churned. He got so panicky he thought he was going to have a heart attack.

Julie stood up and wrung her hands. "This place is perfect for us. I'm sure of it as winds in March, showers in April, and flowers in May."

Ken looked at her as if she were some sort of freak.

Her stomach tightened into knots. She took off for the window and steadied herself on the ledge. The view was so different than Cohasset. Patty's voice ran through her head, *don't tell Kenny that Gretchen and Leo didn't buy the manse.* Julie faced Ken. Bracing a hand on her hip, she said, "This is about Regina, huh?"

"I let her fix up that hellhole and look what it got me. All I can think of is Re…" He choked on the name. "All I can think of…is…" He looked away.

Her hand dropped from her hip. "Is what?

Ken glanced at Julie. "Is that woman going to get inside my head again?" he asked. "I resent everything that she did to Katrina and me. And you, too! What I've put you through!" His hand ran through his hair. "How am I supposed to stop that woman from doing that again?"

Julie went to Ken, crouched down, and took his hand. "We'll work through all that, together, you, me, and Katrina. Doctor Edie is helping Katrina. She'll help you and me, too. It'll be like we've always been a family—just like I gave birth to Katrina myself, right here in our very own home."

Ken kissed her palm then rubbed it against his cheek. "That Curt," he said. "I can't understand why he puts up with me and all my problems."

"He's a good friend, that's why," said Julie. "Thanks to him and that silly candy-colored clown, things are different now. Katrina's back and things are out in the open. We know the enemy."

"And they're both dead," injected Ken.

Julie squinted at him. "Katrina never gave up on you. That's what got her through the last four years. So don't give up on her…or me. Like Emma says, time has a way of making good things happen. Give it a chance."

"What if I botch things up?" he whined.

"You won't," she said. "I won't let you." She clutched his hand and gently shook. "Throw away all that self-doubt and fear rumbling around in that head of yours."

Ken tried to turn away. Julie wouldn't let him. His eyes filled with grief. He looked into hers. "There's times when I feel like this, times when you're not around to make the madness go away." His voice quaked. "I can't stop feeling this way—I don't know how. All those changes you made to the main floor of the manse couldn't keep that woman at bay. I was trapped. All the memories…"

"You're not going to be trapped like that in this house," stormed Julie. "I won't let it happen! You and I are going to make new memories—good ones. And you better believe that even the not-so-good times will still turn out to be good ones. All we have to do is open our hearts and minds. And you know what? When Adrienne is born, Katrina will be her special guardian angel, wait and see."

His left eyebrow arced. "Adrienne?"

"You know, from 'Rocky'?" she said, swaying back and forth from heel to toe. "The movie?"

"Well, gee," said Ken. "What if it's a boy?"

Julie arched her back, made herself look big, and huffed, "Yo, Adriano!"

About K Spirito

    K Spirito holds a Bachelor of Science Degree from Franklin Pierce University, class of 1998 and an Associate in Arts for Interpreting for the Deaf from L. A. Pierce College in California, 1982. In the '60s, she built power supplies for the Lunar Excursion Module that now sit on the moon. She transcribed Five Little Firemen by Margaret Wise Brown and Edith Thacher Hurd into Braille for the L. A. Public Library. She was a licensed Cosmetologist and owned a hair salon.

    Born and raised in New England, K Spirito, always the history buff, loves to browse through microfilm of old newspapers. Noting articles of human-interest, she then weaves them into a variety of fiction—all set in New England.

    K Spirito and her husband of over forty years, Sal, raised four children and are now, blessed with three granddaughters and five grandsons. K and Sal Spirito enjoy traveling, in-line skating, sailing, kayaking, and Mexican Train dominoes—and most of all, volunteering for the Franklin Pierce Alumni Association.

    K and Sal Spirito are proud sponsors of Merrimack Youth Baseball. Among other organizations they support are the Franklin Pierce Alumni Association, the New Hampshire Association for the Blind, Concord TV, the Cape Cod Commercial Fisherman's Association, the Friends of Wrentham, the Granite Statesmen, Voices in Harmony, and the American Cancer Society. They are members of the New Hampshire Writers' Project (NHWP) and the Maine Writers and Publishers Alliance.

Other Books by K Spirito

FATHER SANDRO'S MONEY - *Historical Fiction*

The LaRosa family leaves Italy and lives through 30 years of real events spanning 1908 through 1930 in East Boston, MA, New England and the world.
- Available in print, on CD, Kindle & Nook

TIME HAS A WAY - *Inspirational Fiction*

Emma LaRosa loses her husband Seth after fifty-two years of marriage, and feels her life is over. She discovers Julie brutally beaten and life takes on new meaning. Mutual need creates a strong friendship and brighter futures for Emma and Julie.
- Available in print, on CD, Kindle & Nook

YESTERDAY, TOMMY GRAY DROWNED - *Mystery*

Death doesn't trouble kids. If it does, they get over it quick. That's what the big people of Echo Lake, Massachusetts professed back in 1959. So what in God's name is Elizabeth Blair doing thirty years later, wandering a cemetery, looking for the grave of a fourth-grade classmate? Echo Lake spawns too many secrets—secrets that folks—including Elizabeth Blair—might just as soon abandon to the murky abyss that time leaves behind.
- Available in print, on CD, Kindle & Nook

CANDY-COLORED CLOWN - *Thriller*
- Available in print, on CD, Kindle & Nook

Spiderling - Thriller

The White Mountains of New Hampshire is the setting for this Thriller. While attending Ecology Camp, Katrina Waters gets caught up in a terrorist sleeper cell. All she wants is her own identity and destiny—not the one her father wants for her and not the one terrorists intend for her.
- Available in print, on CD, Kindle & Nook

PISCATAGUA - *Adventure /Romance*

Seventeen-year-old Chas Riley who is no taller than the average five year old seeks the love of Katrina Waters. Chas struggles with self-esteem issues, a heart condition, and the aftereffects of terrorism. Will Katrina view Chas as a real man? Or will she pursue tall, bronze-toned Bert Moro, an FBI mole who is never around when she needs him? This sequel to *Spiderling* is set in the White Mountains of New Hampshire, Maine, and Massachusetts.
- Available in print, on CD, Kindle & Nook

Summer And August, A *Cape Cod Murder Mystery*

Yellow Umbrella Books is one of several Chatham locations featured in this great summer read. Eric Linder, Yellow Umbrella Books owner, plays himself in *Summer and August*; And Debra Lawless, reporter for The Cape Cod Chronicle, plays herself. There are twists and turns along the road to the end of this rainbow you will never expect!

"If you want to peek behind the idyllic setting of summer on Cape Cod to a place filled with secrets, deception, and a dead body or two, read *Summer and August*, a saga of genealogical consequence and intrigue."

-Debra Horan, Owner of Booklovers' Gourmet, Webster, MA
- Available in print, on CD, Kindle & Nook

Works in Progress

Kathleen - *Fiction—Historical Journal*

You meet Kathleen in **Father Sandro's Money**. Then you learn much more about Kathleen in **Summer And August**. And now you get to know the entire story of what happened after Armand was gunned down. Follow Kathleen and her two children on the path life leads them, through the intimacy of her journal.

www.ingramcontent.com/pod-product-compliance
Lightning Source LLC
Chambersburg PA
CBHW050353260626
47156CB00003B/715